As Conor McLeish's fortieth birthda... ...nre..... .... .lwa.s
dreamed of has finally taken shape. He has a steady day job, a debut no.e.,
and Will, his Buddhist boyfriend of nearly a decade. He should be happy.
The trouble is, Conor wouldn't know happy if it smiled, winked, and offered
to buy him a drink. With a hard-earned penchant for self-sabotage and an
unfortunate Jameson habit, Conor frequently finds a way to disappoint
himself and those he loves.

Solid Ground is a story of personal evolution—how we are each sculpted by
the past, carved out of childhood, shaped and molded by what we've done
and by what's been done to us. For better or worse, who we are is the
unavoidable sum of it all. But how we are, how we choose to love, and
whether we stand alone in the end, that—at least in part—is up to us.

SOLID GROUND

Jeff McKown

This is a work of fiction. All characters, places and events are from the author's imagination and should not be confused with fact. Any resemblance to persons, living or dead, events or places is purely coincidental.

Published by
NineStar Press
PO Box 91792
Albuquerque, New Mexico, 87199
www.ninestarpress.com

Warning: This book contains sexually explicit content, which is only suitable for mature readers, mentions of suicide, suicidal ideation, and religious homophobia.

Print ISBN #978-1-947139-06-0
Cover by Natasha Snow
Edited by Elizabeth Coldwell

To my grandmother, Gwendolyn June Humble

ONE

I WAS NEVER worth much. Growing up, I wasn't particularly clever or funny or handsome. I didn't sing like an angel or say the darnedest things, and I was never the adorable kid in the tiny plaid vest and bow tie. I played Little League for a while, but I was mostly tucked away in right field, which in retrospect didn't matter much since no one was there to watch me. My mother was too busy drying out my father to have time for shit like that.

Don't misunderstand, I wasn't a bad kid. I didn't light fires or torture cats. I just wasn't a kid anyone fought for. If it weren't for my grandmother, I might never have known there was anything decent in me. June was my one true believer, the only one who waved my flag, tattered piece of shit that it was. She was busy with her own life—sipping whiskey at blackjack tables and flirting with strangers—but she found time to pay attention to me, which in the end is all a kid really wants.

Some people learn from their childhood bullshit. They overcome nearly insurmountable obstacles and get invited to appear on *Oprah*, where they shine like beacons for the rest of the less fortunate. Others just grow up and make one awful mistake after another. I've always been somewhere in the middle, half fuck-up and half hidden-heart-of-gold, the kind of guy you love in spite of the horrible shit he's done.

I HEARD WILL through the screech of grinding metal parts and the clatter of a thousand porcelain dinner plates crashing to the floor. "You have to let it go, Conor."

"I can't." I glanced down at my phone.

"You can, but you won't."

"Who even taught her to text?" I took one hand off the wheel and mashed my reply into the small, flat keyboard.

"Pay attention to the road."

"I'm being careful."

"Jerking the steering wheel back after you swerve out of your lane isn't being careful."

"I'm using the little bumps in the road the way you're supposed to—to make corrections."

He shook his head and sighed. "If you have to keep texting, let me drive."

"Calm down. It's bumfuck I-10 on a Saturday morning." I checked the rearview mirror and turned my attention to an incoming text.

"Bitch," I whispered as I pounded another reply into the phone.

"Nice. She did give birth to you."

"It's not my mom. It's Aunt Doris." The phone beeped again and my eyes darted back to the screen.

He rested his hand on my thigh. "Try not to get so worked up. It's not good for your heart." I was barely middle-aged, but Will was ten years younger than me. It was a difference he liked to play up.

I smiled and rubbed the top of his hand. "You make me feel lucky."

"Show your gratitude by keeping me alive all the way to your mom's house." His voice was soft and earnest, as though by not sending him to his death in a fiery crash I was doing him a solid.

"Is it too late to turn around?"

"Just keep going."

Driving across Florida isn't all palm trees and pink flamingos. There's plenty of that shit down south, but up north there's plenty of rural nothing. My dad calls this lonely stretch of the Florida panhandle the "Eglin Desert." Other than the desert's namesake air force base, there's just mile after mile of pine tree-lined interstate, and a light sprinkling of highway exits, each of which leads nowhere and offers little more than a depressing, albeit useful, combination Exxon-Burger King-convenience store.

Beep.

I looked at Will, seeking his permission to check the phone. Two raised eyebrows implored me to stay focused on the road.

I checked the rearview mirror again, turned up the radio, adjusted the air conditioning vents, and then finally snatched at the cell phone in the console, knocking it to the floorboard in the process.

"Fuck." I fished around blindly on the floor mat.

"Let it go."

"Not a strength for me." I hunched low in the driver's seat, keeping one hand on the wheel as my other hand traced methodical rows across the faux carpet beneath me.

"Jesus Christ!" He thrust his hands onto the dashboard as we veered center and a twenty-ton Peterbilt rocketed toward us. I jammed the brakes and jerked the wheel, steering us out of the overgrown median and back into our lane. A rush of blood raced to my temples, blurring the outside world.

I took a long slow breath and eased the car to the shoulder. "Fine. You drive."

AFTER A HALF hour of silence and thirty more miles of pine trees, I needed a break. We stopped in Tallahassee, a mid-sized oasis in the midst of the panhandle's pine tree nothingness. Tallahassee is more town than city, but as home to two universities and the state government, it has some cosmopolitan luxuries. Like fast food restaurants and gas stations in separate buildings. We ordered diet sodas and six-inch meatball sandwiches and took a corner booth at Subway.

"Don't bite your nails," he said, as I chewed away at the tip of my finger.

It wasn't exactly a Valentine, but he was talking.

"Sorry. Habit."

"It's a nasty habit to watch while we're eating." He pretended to look away in disgust as he unwrapped his sub.

"These are the same fingers that hold my sandwich. And write books. And gently stroke your face."

"You've only written one book. But fine, eat your fingers. I'll sit quietly with my sandwich and soak in the ambience." He was cracking. He usually did.

"There's no gas station attached. That's what gives this place its charm. If they have a room for rent out back, we should skip Pensacola and spend the weekend here."

"It's two days with your family. You can handle it."

I sipped my drink and nodded my agreement.

"Are you ready?" he asked.

"For what?"

"For the book party."

"Of course I'm ready," I mumbled through a mouthful of meatballs.

"Good." He shook his head.

"Seriously, it'll be fine. It's just my family."

"No doubt. I know you can't wait to see Doris. All that important texting in the car."

I ignored the dig, keeping my eyes locked on my sandwich.

"I don't know why she makes you so jittery," he said.

"What was it you said a while ago? Oh right...let it go."

"I'm just saying, she makes you nervous."

"It's not nervous, it's angry. I thought you were gonna sit quietly and enjoy your sandwich."

"Mm-hmm." He flashed an open mouthful of half-chewed meatballs and whole wheat bread.

"Do I seem that uptight?" I asked.

"You're working those fingernails pretty hard."

"I always chew my nails. That's not necessarily a sign of anxiety for me." I examined my ruined cuticles.

"You're a little edgy. That's all I'm saying."

"I'm going home with my boyfriend to spend two pleasant days celebrating a personal accomplishment with my family. What's to worry about?"

"Right," he said.

"Right."

SOMETIME DURING OUR courtship, after we'd dated a few months, but before we moved in together, I told Will how fucked up my childhood was. I told him how my drunken father had nearly burned our house to the ground when I was five. How I'd been bounced around to a handful of reluctant and ill-prepared family members while my mom dried out my dad. I told him how Aunt Doris and Uncle Martin had finally decided to fulfill their obligation as Catholic godparents. How they took me in and cared for me, how for years they were closer to me than my own parents. I told him how puberty hit and how my unanticipated sexual deviance (Aunt Doris's words, not mine), along with her religious rebirth, drove a wedge between us. I stated it like facts, a timeline in a history textbook, like shit that happened to someone else. Growing up like I did, though, there was serious potential for awkward. But add the fuel of kid fears and insecurity to the mix, and the awkward burned and eventually exploded inside you. That was the part I never told.

IN THE LATE afternoon, we reached the two-and-a-half-mile concrete bridge that spanned Escambia Bay and marked the entrance to Pensacola. The setting sun cast a familiar coppery glow across the water as Bach cello suites carried us over the bay and across the last twelve miles to my parents' house. Driving, thinking, holding Will's hand, the world wasn't such an awful fucking place.

"Hello, hello, hello!" my mother yelled from the porch. She raced down the steps, her three-quarter-length Bea Arthur vest whipping in the wind, even as her stylish bob of gray hair hardly moved. "How was your trip? Need some help with your bags?" She always tried too hard, as if a broken egg could be put back in its shell.

"The drive was fine," I said. "And no, we've only got a couple of bags."

She kissed me on the cheek as I retrieved our matching black suitcases from the trunk. "Here, let me help you." She reached for one of the bags.

"Fine, Mom." I handed her the lighter of the suitcases.

"How have you been, Sylvia?" Will asked.

"Oh, things are good. Still finishing up the cleaning. Just ignore the clutter." My mother always implored her guests to forgive her messy house, despite the fact that any alleged untidiness was completely undetectable.

"The house looks nice, Mom. Smells clean too." I plucked an imaginary piece of lint from the carpet and held my pinched fingers up to the light as if to examine the invisible evidence. "Missed one."

"Smart aleck," she replied. "It's nice to have you home. Both of you." When Will and I first grew serious about each other, I couldn't tell whether my mother liked him as much as she appeared to, or if she was only pretending for my sake, or my father's. All these years later, I assumed she actually preferred Will over me.

She led us into the den, a room that she referred to as the study. My father's eyes blinked open when my mother announced our arrival. He pulled his wiry frame from the worn La-Z-Boy chair he had reclined in for most of my adult life. In the decades since he'd sobered up, my father had put in long work hours to make sure we had the money we needed and to keep himself out of trouble. He also slept hard and often, and retirement hadn't changed that.

"Fellas." He greeted Will first with a firm handshake and no eye contact. Then me—a quick but sincere hug, with accompanying man-pats on the back.

My mother provided an unnecessary review of our accommodations, including a tour of the closet and the bathroom we were intended to use. In our bedroom, she had positioned a crystal vase of bright purple irises on the bedside table.

"I'll give you a few minutes to settle in. The dinner table's set and the roast is warming in the oven, so we can eat whenever you're ready."

Always trying so hard to make up for lost time. *Good one, Mom.*

MY MOM AND dad weren't always so happy to welcome home their son and his boyfriend. Most parents wouldn't choose to have a gay kid, and mine sure as hell didn't, but they'd come a long way in the last decade.

Early on, they stuck their collective parental head in the sand and enforced a sort of familial "don't ask, don't tell." I had enough self-loathing to deal with, and I didn't push the issue until the first year I had a serious boyfriend at Christmastime. I insisted on bringing him home for the holidays, and my parents allowed it, though they made us sleep in separate rooms. At that point, they saw gayness as little more than body parts, just dicks and assholes rubbing together in ungodly ways. But hey, baby steps.

Will changed all that. My relationship with him, which was the same mixed bag of ecstasy and bullshit every couple goes through, forced my parents to think deeper. Looking through the powerful lens of my feelings for Will magnified things for them, and they finally saw it. What makes a person gay is not much more and nothing less than the gender of the person with whom they're compelled to fall in love.

Hundreds of miles lay between me and my family, but there were holidays and long, boring Catholic weddings and funerals to attend. I acquiesced and presented myself at these functions, but I refused to exclude Will. No one likes to suffer alone. I boldly dragged him to each drama-laden family fiasco, and there we were, the two of us sometimes blending in like pointillist lakeside loungers on a Seurat Sunday afternoon, but just as often, standing out like Botticelli's Venus, only with hair not long enough to cover our genitals.

I WOKE UP the next morning to the sound of digging. Shovel, scrape, shovel, hose. I lay still, visualizing the flowers my father must be pushing into the soft brown earth outside the bedroom window, but the quiet in my mind was short-lived as images of deep red begonias and bright yellow daisies morphed into the pastel pants suits of Aunt Doris.

I could fake it through a day or two with my parents, but keeping my shit together when Aunt Doris was around was a challenge. She wouldn't be outwardly hateful or show up at the book party with a carload of Bible-thumping zealots. That kind of overt disapproval would have been easy to overcome. Aunt Doris had a subtler style of shaming, a way of pursing her lips, clearing her throat, and casting a squinty-eyed glance that said, *I still remember what you did and maybe today's the day I put all our secrets on the table.* Even after more than two decades, that look made me want to hurl myself back inside the closet.

My mother and I spent the day dusting picture frames and knickknacks on glossy shelves that were already clean, and Will worked outside with my father. Since guzzling bottles of Jameson was no longer on Eamon McLeish's daily to-do list, tending the yard had become an obsession. A best-in-show lawn was my father's way of compensating; if you can't un-burn the house down, you can at least keep a nice yard.

They toiled most of the afternoon, and when the day's work was done, Will invited my mother and me to come outside and witness their handiwork. My father was too failed and damaged to boast, but his satisfaction showed. Standing on the front porch, hands on hips and a tight grin suppressed beneath his gaunt cheeks, he looked the way I imagined Monet might have the first time he unveiled *Bridge Over a Pond of Water Lilies.*

"Nice job," my mother said, having played this game a thousand times before. "Now, don't track up my floor with your dirty shoes when you come inside."

Before I could throw in my own half-hearted praise, a sleek black late-model Cadillac pulled up in front of the house. The car inched up the pavement, finally stopping at an awkward angle in the center of the double-wide driveway. A familiar shock of perfectly coiffed white hair stuck up behind the steering wheel.

"And you think I'm a shitty driver," I whispered to Will.

"At least she's not texting," he replied.

At eighty-five years old, my grandmother insisted on keeping her driver's license. She refused to depend on others for her transportation, and she lived alone in a modest townhouse she'd bought more than thirty years ago.

Growing up, my friends had frail elderly grannies who spent their evenings in vinyl recliners watching *Murder, She Wrote* and crocheting afghans for relatives they hadn't seen in years. These old-fashioned southern grandmothers woke at five a.m. every day and prepared big family breakfasts with biscuits made from scratch. They owned old wooden clapboard houses with white paint peeling off the sides and had big backyards with giant climbing trees. And, in most cases, right next to the kindly old grandmother, there was a wise and tender grandfather.

Like other grandmothers, June, as she had always insisted I call her, appreciated the love of a decent man. In fact, she liked a lot of decent men, which is why over the years she provided me with a wealth of different granddads, some of whom she even married.

Will leaned his broom against the front porch rail and bounded down the driveway to help my grandmother out of the car. June would have lectured anyone else on how she didn't need to have her hand held like a toddler, but she saw Will's kindness as chivalry, not eldercare. She smiled as he escorted her up the walk.

"Hi, Mom," my mother said. "Come inside and sit down. I still have work to do." Will, June, and I followed her into the kitchen where she finished prepping crocked weenies, meatballs, and other cholesterol-laden appetizers that passed for hors d'oeuvres in the South.

"Smells like heaven." June lifted lids and peeked into simmering pots. "But it looks like a goddamned heart attack."

"It's a party," Will said. "The food's supposed to be bad for you."

June continued poking around the kitchen, eventually tugging open the refrigerator door and finding several bottles of cheap champagne inside. "It's not a party yet. But if you crack open a couple of these, it's a start."

"Sounds good," I said.

"Isn't it a bit early—?" My mother attempted a cautious objection, but I'd uncorked the first bottle before she could finish.

"Who's ready for a drink?" Will asked, grabbing a handful of wine glasses from the cupboard.

"I'm always ready," June said.

"Me too," I added.

My mother dropped the slotted spoon she'd been stirring crocked weenies with, letting it clang into the shiny metal sink. "Conor, do you plan to drink all night?"

"No, Mom, I don't." Behind her back, I winked at June. "But you know things seldom go the way I plan."

"To Conor and his book." June raised her full glass of champagne to toast.

"To *Luck of the Irish*," Will said, nodding at the stack of books on the kitchen table.

I raised my glass, which, to my mother's horror, was already empty. "Hit me again."

TWO

WILL CARRIED A haul of assorted cheeses and heartburn-inducing sausage and meatball snacks to the dining room table, while my mother covered every available flat space in the living room with dishes of nuts and M&Ms. My father and I retrieved a padded card table from the garage, and at my mom's instruction, we flanked the table with fake ficus trees she'd adorned with tiny white lights. I stacked a few copies of my book on one corner of the table, opposite a photocopied page from my high school yearbook my mother had framed and insisted on displaying. In her mind, my junior year stint as assistant editor of the school newspaper was a critical stepping-stone to writing and publishing a novel. The entire setup looked like the reception table at a hillbilly class reunion. I took in the scene through the fog of a champagne buzz and appreciated the effort nonetheless.

For my mother, my work as a writer wasn't legit until she spied a few copies of my novel on a "Florida Authors" display at Books-A-Million. I had sent her an unfinished proof of the book, but until she saw it for sale, neither she nor my father believed anyone would spend money to read what I wrote. After she bought all four copies from the display, she called to ask if I would sign them so she could give them away as Christmas presents. Oh, and she had an epiphany.

"Wouldn't it be wonderful if I hosted a book release party? You know, just for close friends and family."

"I guess?" I said.

I wasn't comfortable with the idea of being the center of attention at such a gathering, but even less so, because some of the characters in my novel bore a reasonable, and not too flattering, resemblance to some of the likely attendees. I reluctantly agreed to the party and suggested she take a couple of days to read the book before finalizing the guest list.

"CONOR!" MY GRANDMOTHER yelled from the guest bedroom where she'd been readying herself for the party. "Come here for a second."

The room smelled like rich old lady, a potent mixture of floral perfume and money. My grandmother wore black slacks with a silky white top, unbuttoned at the neck enough to show off a string of shiny pearls. Her wiry white hair was teased and shaped to salon perfection. "You look amazing, June."

"Close the door. I have something for you."

I pushed the door shut behind me. "You didn't have to buy me anything. This isn't that kind of a party."

"Don't be silly. You've done something important." She sat on the bed, grabbed her purse from the nightstand, and began rifling through it.

"Lots of people write books. But thank you."

She patted the bedspread and invited me to sit beside her as she continued pawing through the bag. "I'm proud of you," she said, "but not because you wrote a book."

"Because my therapy finally paid off?" I asked. "Because I actually finished *something*?"

"Because you're a wiseass," she countered. "I'm trying to have a moment. Quit making it so hard."

"I'm sorry. Go ahead."

By now, she had located the object from her purse and secured it in her hand. "What you've done," she said, "is go your own way. You didn't let anyone else define you. That's braver and less common than you think, Conor."

My grandmother regularly dropped pearls of wisdom like that, not in a top-of-the-mountain way, but casually, in the middle of everyday conversation.

"That means a lot, especially coming from you." I leaned in for a hug, and she kissed me on the cheek.

"Here you go." She pressed the object into my palm.

I opened my hand and saw a heavy, half-dollar-sized, green-and-black checkered disc. On one side of the chip, "$500" was printed in gold-leaf lettering. The other side read, "Bellagio."

"Sorry," she said. "I didn't have time to shop."

"I'm not sure where you found such a unique gift, but it looks...expensive. Thank you." I hugged her neck.

"You're welcome. I hope it brings you luck." She placed her hand on my knee and pushed herself up from the bed, a signal that our bonding moment was over. "By the way," she added, "I read your book, and if any of that group of Irish rednecks cares enough to read it, you're going to need all the luck you can get."

UNCLE HENRY WAS the first to arrive, which took a little pressure off. He was one of my few relatives not caricatured in the story. It wasn't that *Luck of the Irish* told the story of any specific member of my family—it was more about all of them. Fictionally, of course. About none of them, actually. Not even fictionally. Composite characters, inspired by, not based on actual events, purely coincidental, blah blah blah.

Uncle Henry had married into the McLeish clan. He was the widower of my father's sister, whose death from breast cancer twenty years earlier broke his heart. Since Aunt Margaret died, Uncle Henry was the first to come and the first to leave from family functions. Maybe since he wasn't blood-related, he felt he didn't belong. More likely, he was just smart enough to make an appearance and then hustle a quick exit.

"Conor," he said as I opened the front door, "I guess you finally got to workin' at it. I thought you'd never finish that book." He smiled and tipped his Bass Pro ball cap, revealing a fringe of thinning white hair that hung like a halo over his creased and leathery face. He gave me the half-handshake, half-hug gesture of affection preferred by straight men everywhere.

"Don't *you* start on me." I was only half-joking.

"Nah, I knew you'd get serious, when you finally had enough life behind you to have something to say."

Uncle Henry wasn't a mentor or muse to me, but he had been supportive of my writing, and I appreciated that. Throughout my twenties, when I had most boldly proclaimed my desire to write but had actually written nothing, he asked each time we spoke, "You been working at it?" He wanted success for me, not because I was his favorite nephew or because he believed in my ability, but because, like June, he believed people ought to be encouraged to chase their dreams.

He had once chased his own simple but elegant ideal, marrying his high school sweetheart, securing a steady job with the city, and buying an old arts-and-crafts house on the east side of town. Idyllic isn't always all it's cracked up to be, though. Aunt Margaret came with a boatload of McLeish family baggage, the job became a hassle, and Daniel, their only child, got into early trouble with juvenile law enforcement. They disappeared off the family radar for a couple of years, and gossip circulated that Uncle Henry had lost interest and was looking for a way out. But, he never left. Aunt Margaret's breast cancer came out of nowhere and, shitty as it was, the illness brought them together for good, for as long as good lasted.

My uncle joined my father in a corner of the living room. They sat on folding metal chairs and sipped the unsatisfying non-alcoholic beers my mother handed them. Uncle Henry was a drinker, but in support of my father, or perhaps in capitulation to my mother, he didn't ask for anything stronger.

My extended family continued to trickle in. Eileen, one of my father's sisters, rambled in with her four teenage children, each of whom was named after an older or deader McLeish. Uncle Henry's son, Daniel, who it turns out did steal a ladder and vandalize an empty house—but was never a teenage hoodlum—arrived with his wife and their young son. The players from our family saga filled the house, and my stress rose in tandem with the noise. I switched from champagne to vodka, and with each knock at the door, I gulped my cocktail. Still, no sign of Aunt Doris.

My natural inclination at family functions was to gravitate toward June and Will, push them into a quiet corner, and set up shop. If we looked animated and lively, others would hover nearby, but ultimately be driven elsewhere by their own insecurities. Will was more sensitive to cocktail party dynamics, though. He wanted others to feel comfortable, and he was a skilled listener. Will's mingling talent approached the level of art form, which pissed me off to no end since it made him more challenging to hide behind.

The living room filled with aunts, uncles, and cousins, and I retreated to the kitchen for refuge. My mother came bustling in behind me, bumping my drinking arm and causing me to spill my refuge, which now took the form of vodka and grapefruit. I blotted the front of my new Ralph Lauren shirt, an adequately pretentious purchase by Pensacola standards.

"You know," my mother said, glancing at the spot on my shirt, "when you can't keep it in the cup, you don't need another one."

"It's your fault," I said. "You came barrel-ass-ing through the door like you're going to a fire."

"Relax. I didn't say I was cutting you off, although I probably should."

"Check me into Charter. I hear their residential treatment program is outstanding."

"Maybe I will," she said. "You can use the family discount."

I'M NOT SAYING all Irish families drink too much, I'm just saying mine did. It's in our blood, not because we originated from Dublin, but because of my grandfather. Seamus McLeish's greatest talent was guzzling Jameson with reckless abandon, and it was a gift he thoughtlessly handed down through the generations.

For my grandfather, a family gathering without whiskey was akin to a Thanksgiving table without turkey. Thirty years ago, when my father first climbed onto the wagon, my mother attempted to buck the trend. She invited the family for a backyard barbecue to celebrate my tenth birthday and served only lemonade and sodas as refreshments. Seamus played along for a while, hoisting me onto his bony lap, nuzzling my face with his gray stubbly beard, fishing a five-dollar bill from his pocket and presenting it to me as though it were a priceless family heirloom. It wasn't long, though, before he began to grouse about the absence of "one decent goddamn thing to drink." Soon after, he left the party, returning a short while later with two bottles of Jameson and a cooler full of beer.

My mother knew well that mixing alcohol and McLeishes was always waving the match a little too close to the powder keg. Over her objections, my grandfather pressured his sons into helping him dispatch his haul. My father, newly dry and vulnerable to temptation, quickly disappeared inside the house, leaving my mother alone to contend with his family. What followed was our family's most unfortunate drinking accident, if you can call a stab wound an accident.

Family recollections vary, but what wasn't in doubt was that Seamus had hit the whiskey with extreme diligence that day, and my father's youngest brother, Frank, did the same with the cooler of beer. When the burgers were gone and the ice cream and cake were eaten, the sober McLeishes wisely patted my head, wished me a happy birthday, and slipped away.

Aunt Margaret and my mother cleared dishes and cleaned up, suggesting all the while that the party was winding down. *What a lovely afternoon. So nice to see everyone.* But the hints fell on deaf ears and, thanks to Seamus, the afternoon of casual cookout drinking evolved into a night of loud-talking, drunken Irishmen. As darkness fell, my mother had finally had her fill. She announced it was time for everyone, including my grandfather, to go.

I still remember my grandfather's slurred voice, how his Irish accent grew thicker as the liquid level dropped in the greenish glass of his Jameson bottle. "Say, Sylvia, you're a bold little slapper when you get riled up. I bet Eamon wears you out every night."

My mother shoved the sliding glass door open and pushed me toward it. I stepped inside and stood with my face pressed against the glass.

"It's my son's birthday, you drunk son-of-a-bitch. Get outta here before I call the cops."

"Party's over, Daddy," said Aunt Margaret, who'd seen this all before.

"Come on, Seamus," said Uncle Henry.

"I'm not going anywhere. This is my son's house."

"Let's go, Daddy." Uncle Frank had sprung to his feet, sending his lawn chair toppling behind him. "You're acting like an asshole, and it's time to go." He apologized to my mother as he grabbed my grandfather's arm and pulled him to his feet.

"Get your hands off me, boy."

Seamus flailed and stumbled. Raised voices carried across the yard. In the mounting chaos, no one saw Uncle Frank pick up the barbecue fork and caress its long, wooden handle.

My grandfather stuck his finger in my mother's face. "This bitch ain't calling the police."

Six words, two drunk McLeishes, and one outdoor cooking utensil later, and Seamus McLeish was on his way to the West Florida Regional Medical Center. The two large, stainless steel prongs hadn't been driven deep into his upper arm, but they must have nicked a vein because the old man bled like the stuck Irish pig that he was.

Seamus was frail and old now, kept alive by little more than a pickled liver and the power of inappropriate lechery, but in his heyday, my grandfather was a professional-grade drinker and top-flight ruiner of lives. Which is exactly why Aunt Doris should have left him rotting in his nursing home bed.

THREE

WILL AND I sat on the love seat, our knees touching inconspicuously, like teenage sweethearts in a high school cafeteria. Around the living room, family factions made small talk, nibbling crudités from paper plates and sipping Korbel from plastic champagne glasses like redneck elite. My father, in an effort to disappear without leaving the room, had taken up residence in an oversized chair that swallowed his modest frame. Even after decades of sobriety, the smell of alcohol made him twitchy.

Most of the invited guests had arrived, and I knew the next tapping at the door would be Aunt Doris and Uncle Martin. It was odd, dreading interactions with people to whom I had once been so beloved. When I was a kid, Aunt Doris was a refuge for me, a safe haven. Since Patrick's death, though, or more accurately, since a few months before his untimely death, our conversations were mostly depressive, hand-wringing affairs. On occasion, there were raised voices and slammed doors, but more often than not, our encounters were low-key events riddled with snide innuendo and pitying glances. In the aftermath of Aunt Doris, I usually developed a powerful headache and a preternatural craving for vodka martinis. Quashing the truth and disconnecting from someone I love vexed me that way.

The knock finally came, and my mother bolted to the door. I wondered which Doris would arrive—the loving aunt who nurtured and cared for me as her own son, or the taut-faced Jesus freak who was mortified by the afterlife she feared I'd endure. I held my breath in a moment of hopeful anticipation, trying desperately to forget the previous day's angry text message exchange.

"Martin! Doris!" My mother's faux enthusiasm might have been believable, if not for the long pause and dip in tone that accompanied her next words. "I see you've brought Seamus."

My mother stepped aside as Aunt Doris brushed past, the furrowing of her brow barely visible beneath the frosted tips of her bangs. She was fit for a woman in her sixties. Her burgundy skirt and beige silk blouse clung tightly to her, highlighting her shape in a way that was both flattering and appropriately Christian. She strode across my parents' living room with the confidence of a woman doing the Lord's work. Uncle Martin walked in behind her, flashing an earnest smile in my direction as he ushered his elderly father to the nearest seat.

"Conor," Uncle Martin said, "me and your Aunt Doris just took your granddaddy to Sunday services at Holy Smyrna. We were going to drop him back at the rest home, and then we thought, I bet that old son-of-a-gun would love to see Conor and his new book."

"Wonderful." I stared at the floor. Uncle Martin wasn't the lying type. I assumed Aunt Doris had kept him in the dark and sprung the Seamus idea on him at the last minute.

My uncle sat beside my grandfather, leaning into the near-corpse to prop him up. Uncle Martin bore no resemblance to his withered and wrinkled father, a man whose decades-long commitment to Jameson had drained the life out of him, just as it had sucked every ounce of compassion from the family he'd abused. Uncle Martin, with his square jaw and thick head of brown hair parted on the side, reminded me of Patrick. Had he lived, my cousin would've been lucky to age as gracefully as his father.

Aunt Eileen, who had spent most of the evening snapping at her obnoxious adolescent offspring, sat on the sofa next to my grandfather, on the opposite side from my uncle. "Martin," she said, "did you say you took Daddy to a Baptist church?"

"Oh, Seamus loves it." Aunt Doris dragged the words out as though she were talking about a kitten who'd just discovered the addictive joys of catnip. "We've been taking him to Holy Smyrna for weeks."

"But he's Catholic." Aunt Eileen's voice cracked.

"Seamus just loves worshipping the Lord," Aunt Doris said. "And Reverend Lonnie has taken a real interest in Seamus."

Eileen cleared her throat. "I guess converting Martin wasn't enough."

"It's not like that," Uncle Martin said. "Come on, Eileen."

Will bobbed his head and whispered to me, "Classic eighties."

"Jesus fucking Christ." I was unamused by the attempt to keep me grounded.

"Conor!" my mother snapped. "There are children here."

"Daddy." Aunt Eileen's face was a deep shade of papal cloak red. "They don't even believe Mary was the mother of Jesus."

My grandfather, silent until now, shouted. "I don't mind!" He wasn't angry but hard of hearing. Volume control was no longer a relatable concept. "They got some fine goddamn women in that church."

I looked to my mother for help. She looked to my father, or rather to his empty chair.

"You know," Will said, "Conor hasn't signed any books yet."

I jumped up from my mother's early American, and contemporarily uncomfortable, sofa.

"Right. Let's get this show on the road."

"Not so fast there, sport," Aunt Doris said. "Martin...give Conor his present."

"It's not that kind of party," I said.

Uncle Martin handed me a small, plainly gift-wrapped box and a standard-issue Hallmark envelope. I wedged a finger in the top of the envelope and unsealed it, pretending for a moment to be more interested in the sentiment on the card than in the accompanying gift. *Something, something—Love Aunt Doris and Uncle Martin.* The real object of my curiosity lay within the contents of the tiny package. Judging from the size of the box, I guessed gift card, but maybe not. Too heavy. Perhaps, in celebration of my first book, Aunt Doris had given me a copy of her favorite book—a tiny, engraved New Testament? The "greatest story ever told" commemorating the publication of the most mediocre book ever sold?

I unwrapped the package and inside found a hinged velvet box containing an engraved pen set. The inscription on the sleek silver pen read, "Conor McLeish, Writer." A small handwritten note in Aunt Doris's scrawl read, "A good writer needs a good pen."

Even as I thanked them, the whispered voice of the ungrateful fuck inside me picked apart the engraved message. *Writer*? No, I was a bookstore manager with a thesaurus and a laptop. *Good*? Only because "mediocre" wouldn't fit on the side of the pen. I got a shit advance and a two-book deal with Mangrove Press, a mom-and-pop central Florida publishing house that likely warehoused their inventory in a two-car garage. My contract hardly constituted a ringing endorsement from the east coast literati. And who the hell writes with a pen anymore?

As my mind moved on to disrespecting the cheap gift-wrap job, Aunt Doris derailed my train of petty thoughts, wrapping me tightly in her wiry arms. "How about a hug for your favorite aunt?" she asked.

"Of course," I said, already trapped in her embrace. "I like the pen set." As she leaned in to kiss my cheek, the familiar scent of her perfume returned me to my childhood. Aunt Doris tucking me in, kissing my forehead, telling me she loved me as she turned out the light and left my room, a vapor trail of Estee Lauder in her wake. An honest hug and a whiff of cologne and I was eight years old again. Though she'd spent much of the last twenty years reassuring me that hellfire and damnation awaited me, I owed Aunt Doris something for the time before all that. She and Uncle Martin gave me a room of my own, enrolled me in T-ball, and bought my school clothes. I remember my first day of kindergarten. They drove me to school, held my hand, and ushered me up the front walk. When I reached the entrance, I looked back, tempted to run to them. I still remember how their faces beamed with satisfaction and pride. Before things went to shit, first because of Patrick and then because of Jesus, Aunt Doris had nurtured me. Now, she prayed for me, which I suppose for her, still feels like protecting me.

As we ended the unintentionally long embrace, Aunt Doris held my hand in hers just as she had when I was a boy. We stood together, like mother and son, until our hands finally separated and found their way awkwardly back to straightening our graying hair and fiddling in our grown-up pockets.

MY MOTHER INSISTED the family queue up for the book signing just as she'd seen it done when Books-a-Million hosted local celebrity Reverend Lonnie Casey—the same Reverend Lonnie, founder of Holy Smyrna, spiritual guru to Aunt Doris, and author of the regional bestseller *Believe and Receive*. I proceeded to sign books for my aunts, uncles, and cousins, an ironic exercise since, the Bible notwithstanding, most of them had never finished a book. With the exception of the heartfelt inscription I wrote in Uncle Henry's copy, I signed each book with no personalization. I scrawled my name on each title page and wondered which of my relatives would be the first to try to sell a copy on eBay. I imagined their disappointment at the lack of value my signature added.

When I worked my way to the end of the short line, I excused myself and dashed to the kitchen for another vodka and grapefruit. As I stirred my cocktail, the phone rang on the counter beside me.

"McLeish residence," I said.

"Hi. Is this Conor?"

"This is Conor. Who's this?" I'd heard the disembodied voice before, but I couldn't quite recognize it.

"Conor, it's John Morgan," he declared as if the name would trigger a synaptic frenzy.

"I'm sorry. I don't think I know you."

"John Morgan," he repeated. "You don't remember?"

John Morgan—Mister Morgan—my high school English teacher, the man whose relentless hammering on paragraph development and whose uncanny knack for finding biblical themes in great works of fiction nearly ruined literature for me. Why was the sultan of sentence structure calling my mother's house? Perhaps he wanted to deliver a graded copy of my book with sentence fragments circled and passive verbs underlined. I pictured him in a smoking jacket and slippers, curled up in a leather wing chair, the tip of his red pen catching fire as he raced through the pages of my book jotting gleeful criticisms in the margins.

"Conor, I've gotten myself lost. I'm on Davis Highway, but I'm not sure how to proceed."

"Come again?" I was more confused than ever.

"Your mom didn't tell you she invited me to the book signing?"

No, and if she had, I would have pummeled her. "She must have wanted to surprise me, Mr. Morgan."

"Please," he said, "call me John. I hope it's not too late to stop by."

"No, it's fine. It'll be nice to see you," I lied.

I gave him directions and, as I hung up the phone, realized he was only ten minutes away.

WHEN THE DOORBELL rang, my mother left her proud perch beside me and floated to the door. I'd forgotten how devastatingly handsome John Morgan was, how he'd ruined the twisted Nabokovian fantasies of more than a few high school girls when he wed a stunning brunette who substitute-taught regularly in the English department. He strutted into my parents' living room with the same confidence he had when he entered the classroom. His tanned face, thick sweep of graying hair, and pearly smile were instantly familiar. If he had aged at all, he had done it well. Morgan had doubled as the tennis coach at the high school for years, and the exercise and time outdoors had benefitted him. After some quick math, I realized he was probably in his late fifties now and might still be on the tennis courts each afternoon perfecting the half volleys and overhead smashes of overeager teens. In school, my friends on the tennis team told me John Morgan was as critical a son-of-a-bitch on the court as he was a know-it-all grammar hound in the classroom. I believed it. He was easy to dislike, an arrogant and demanding cock-of-the-walk guy. Still smoking hot, though.

"Hello, Conor. It's been too long," he said like we were long-separated college chums.

"How have you been, Mr. Morgan?"

He beamed his infomercial smile. "I've been terrific. Though not as well as you." He surveyed the room and added, "A loving family, a published book, and you still have your good looks."

I was unprepared for gushing. I ran through the comment like a fireman through a flaming doorway. "How's the Alma Mater holding up?"

"Chair of the English Department." He grinned. He had the aura of old money about him, a snotty yacht club demeanor, but I never knew if there was actually cash in his coffers. Regardless, John Morgan knew how to project the image. I offered him a drink, which, to my surprise, he accepted. Will fetched a Scotch on the rocks for the teacher while I signed the remaining books and carried on the embarrassing celebrity charade.

The rest of the clan had tired of the artificial festivities, and they used the arrival of a new guest as an opportunity to make their exit. June was the last of the family to leave. Lest anyone think she was too old to stay up late, she assured us she had an early appointment the next day.

With everyone gone except Mr. Morgan, my father went to bed, and my mother and Will shifted into clean-up mode. It was after 10:00 p.m., and I wondered what Mr. John Morgan was doing out so late on a school night. At the first sign of stalling conversation, I saw the opportunity for a wrap-up and pounced.

"So, you teaching tomorrow, Mr. Morgan?"

"Please Conor, call me John."

"Okay, John," I said.

His eyes were fixed on me as though I were a painting or a puzzle he was working to solve. I met his stare, but the intensity of his gaze unnerved me. Grasping for a sliver of common ground, I broached the obvious topic.

"Have you heard much about the book?" I still found it awkward and pretentious to refer to it as "my" book.

"Well..."

I instantly regretted the question. I chastised myself internally for not sticking to benign topics like humidity or the new Super Walmart.

"You were my star pupil, Conor. I pre-ordered the book as soon as I heard about it. In fact, I've already read it." He ratcheted his gaze from intense to full-on penetrating. "Very well put together, I might add." He flashed a glamor shot smile and, without so much as a blink, maintained the stare, which I was certain was now piercing my retinas and boring a hole through my skull.

"You liked it? I'm flattered."

"I loved it. Thought it was...inspired." He reached out his hand and placed it solidly on my thigh.

I glanced at the hand, which stayed put.

I had no recollection of John Morgan maintaining intense direct eye contact or flashing his brilliant smile unless a camera or a hot young coed was involved. Now, as we sat in my mother's living room more than twenty years after high school, the English teacher was nothing but eyes, teeth, and hand on thigh. John Morgan was flirting with me.

But he was married, for Christ's sake, or so I believed. He moved the hand down my thigh to my knee, which he squeezed and patted, before finally leaning away. *There*, I thought, *a total misread*. He was simply offering a coach's encouragement, a mentor's approval.

"So how's Mrs. Morgan?" I asked, looking for confirmation of his unremitting heterosexuality.

"Actually, she and I have been divorced for quite a while." Then, I swear, he winked at me. And not a friendly wink. A knowing wink, a power wink, a we-have-a-shared-secret wink. Like a dirty-minded old man winks at a flirtatious diner waitress who is forty years his junior. "We came to the conclusion," he added, "that after all these years, we really didn't know each other. I wanted things in life she just couldn't give me."

He stared into my eyes as if my pupils were the electronic eye chart at the Department of Motor Vehicles. I expected him to kiss me or call out the top row any second. I was about to stand and go check on something—

anything, actually—when his hand reappeared on my thigh. Upper thigh this time. Way upper thigh. Side of hand touching testicles upper thigh.

"So Conor, are you and Will seriously involved?" Touching my balls and asking about my love life was slightly out of the range of ordinary book signing chitchat. He must have sensed his window of opportunity was closing.

"Mr. Morgan," I replied, "your hand is touching my genitalia." I said the words without moving the older man's hand, which remained fixed on my upper thigh.

"Conor, things have been difficult for me the last few years, but I always felt like you and I connected. I knew there was something, but I didn't know exactly what it was. Now I think I do."

"I'm glad you've had an enlightenment, I really am. But I have an early day tomorrow." I glanced at his chest, which filled the short-sleeve turquoise pullover he wore impressively, and my eyes wandered involuntarily to his bulging biceps before I glanced up to see that I'd been caught looking. His hand still rested on my thigh. "You think we can get you a signed book and wrap this up?" I asked.

"I hope I'm not out of line, Conor. I've thought about you over the years, and I really do like your work."

I said nothing, and his hand finally moved away from my testicles.

He grabbed a copy of my book off the short stack on the table and pushed it toward me. "If you would just personalize this, that'd be great. Then, I suppose I should be going."

I opened the book to the title page and printed.

DEAR GRAMMAR NAZI,
BEST OF LUCK WITH THE GAY THING.
CONOR MCLEISH

I felt bold enough to leave such a love letter, but not brazen enough to have him read it in my presence. I closed the book and handed it back.

As he rose to leave, he placed his hand on my shoulder, and by the time we reached the front door, his well-muscled arm had worked its way down to where it encircled my waist.

"Wait one second." I returned to the card table to retrieve the pen Aunt Doris had given me. I took back his book, and, beneath the note I had written, I jotted my e-mail address.

I gave the book back to the English teacher, who hugged me good night and left with his signed *Luck of the Irish* tucked securely beneath his arm.

As I stood in the doorway and watched him leave, Will appeared and hugged me from behind. "That was a pleasant surprise."

"It was fine."

"He was nice enough," Will said. "And he's hot for an old guy."

"He's held up okay. And apparently, Mr. English Teacher has a thing for younger guys." I told Will the story—knee, thigh, genitals—all of it except the part where I scribbled my e-mail address in the signed book.

Some boyfriends would go apeshit about such an incident. Will boiled it down to loneliness, rationalizing the odd behavior, and feeling sorry for the old lech rather than disparaging him. Will always was the nice one.

FOUR

WILL AND I left Pensacola mid-morning on Monday after the roads emptied of school buses and commuters dragging themselves to their daily grind. One good thing about working a retail job was the flexible schedule, which allowed for midweek travel while others were busy at work. One shitty thing about retail was everything else. Bookstores were no exception.

Piles of abandoned books and magazines, long lines of toe-tapping customers, and asshole bosses, like Marshall, calling so often they are sometimes holding on not one, but two, phone lines. Most professions come with a degree of stress, which is why they're called jobs and involve a paycheck, but bookstore managers aren't putting out fires or cutting out cancer cells. We're just selling books. The secret our corporate bosses don't want us to know is that no lives will be lost in the process. In a public company, you're rolling the dice with someone else's money, so the overseers want you to think human civilization is teetering on the brink of collapse and the only hope for salvation is increasing the number of add-ons you sell. That's where I got into trouble with Marshall. I saw through the bullshit.

My cell phone rang as we made the turn onto I-75 and headed south toward Tampa. With a wag of his finger, Will reminded me of the texting incident with Aunt Doris.

"It's Marshall," I said, pointing at the screen and shrugging as I answered the phone. "Hello?"

"This one's gonna be tricky." Marshall started the conversation mid-thought. "I've never met her, but I hear she's a ball-buster. White glove tests and a ten-page checklist. We gotta nail this one, buddy."

"Hi, Marshall, I'm driving back to Tampa. What's up?"

"Visit." Other than jerking off the ungrateful public, the surprise executive drop-in was perhaps the great joy in retail.

"Do we know when they're coming?" I asked.

"Tomorrow. And there's no they—just her, the new VP of marketing. She's traveling alone, and I know jackshit about her. Vegetarian. That's what I know." A trivial fact to outsiders, but I understood the significance. Proper feeding of a traveling big wig was a critical component of executive visit success.

"It'll be fine," I said. "I'm sure she's just looking for a free trip to Florida."

"I'm picking her up at the airport at 8:47 a.m. In the morning." He added the clarifier, as though I might be unclear on the meaning of "a.m."

"Great."

"I'll make travel small talk, take her to the Starbucks on Howard, run through some numbers, and then we're headed your way." He reviewed the itinerary as though he were giving me instructions on defusing a live explosive.

"Marshall, I'm off tomorrow." I waited for a reaction but heard only heavy breathing.

"You mean you were supposed to be off tomorrow."

"I have one more personal day. You approved it."

"And now, I'm disapproving it." He was clever with language that way.

"You know how these things go," I said. "Thirty minutes of glad-handing, a quick sit-down where she tells us to do all the shit the last VP told us to stop doing, and a few minutes on e-mail before she disappears to a beach condo or a golf course."

"What time will you be in?" he asked.

"Come on, Marshall. I'm not even back in town yet. Tom opens tomorrow. He can handle it."

"Negator-y. I need the store spit-and-polished, and you and your people 110% visit-ready." An executive walk-through was anti-climactic and predictable, but for a scaly corporate climber like Marshall, it was enough to make him shit his pants.

"You know I would normally be up for this, but I can't do it tomorrow. I have an important personal thing I have to take care of." Messing with an employee's "personal thing" often leads to a cesspool of brewing human resource problems. In large corporations, any whiff of such an issue usually sends middle managers hightailing it like a puppy running from a vacuum cleaner.

After a pause and the pretense of thoughtful consideration, Marshall persisted. "Conor, it's best if you're there. At the store. Tomorrow morning. Seriously."

"Marshall..."

"I'm not asking," he said. "I've had some ugly visits this year, and I need all hands on deck. Are we clear?" This was a new level of stalemate, and "are we clear?" stung my ego.

"Marshall—tomorrow I'm driving to Sarasota and Bradenton to deliver copies of my book to a couple of indies, and I scheduled a signing in Clearwater tomorrow night. I can't cancel."

"I know you're a busy author with too much to do, but last time I checked, you're still getting a paycheck from us. If you can't handle running a store anymore, let me know now."

I was cornered, and before I could reply, he deftly plopped a cherry on top of the shit sundae he was feeding me. "Honestly, I knew this day was coming, but I thought you'd be able to handle it longer than this."

"Jesus Christ," I said.

Marshall stayed silent. The next move was still mine to make.

"I'll be there first thing in the morning. Wouldn't want you to make a bad impression."

"Good," he said.

"But I'm walking out at 11 o'clock whether you and your marketing girlfriend are finished or not."

"Don't forget to dust your displays. We'll be there by nine."

THE DOG-AND-pony show went off without a hitch, and the marketing VP, as predicted, was in and out in under two hours. I couldn't tell if she was headed for the beach or the golf course when she left, but I'd picked up a heavy lesbian vibe, so I had a pretty good idea.

I burned the candle at both ends for weeks after the visit. With the flood of incoming inventory, a dozen new seasonal employees, the influx of early holiday shoppers, and the need to hand-deliver copies of my own book to stores all over Central Florida, my emotional tank ran dry. Starting the holiday season dead on my ass was dangerous, but unavoidable.

After a particularly shitty Saturday, I arrived home from work feeling morose and empty. The late afternoon sun gleamed on the Hillsborough River just beyond the screened patio of our condo. I smirked in the general direction of the pastoral scene and trudged across the living room to the liquor cart. Will was in the kitchen, rolling out a pumpkin piecrust. I dropped my frustration on him like a pallet of cinder blocks.

"You're not even going to say hello?" he asked.

"I've had enough of this shit."

"You don't like pie?"

"I don't like people." I filled a glass with Maker's Mark.

"Yes, you do. It's just getting busy. You had a long week."

"The world is full of ungrateful assholes."

He raised an eyebrow and gestured at the piecrust on the kitchen counter.

"Present company excluded," I said.

"Thanks for that." He sipped from my glass and gave me a peck on the cheek.

"Something has to give. There's no way in hell I can do two more months of this."

"Yes, you can," he said. "Christmas always sucks in retail, and you always get through it."

"Not always." I'd had a traumatic holiday breakdown the year before I met Will, but I'd never shared the details. "It's not just work. It's spending every fucking day off driving from Gainesville to Fort Myers and begging busy bookstore managers to buy a few copies of my book."

"Some of them take you up on it."

"None of them want to. Believe me. I know how it feels, dealing with no-talent schlubs pestering you to carry their shitty first novels."

"Dreams don't come easy," he said. "If they did, everybody would chase 'em."

Will's brand of Successories poster wisdom hardly came in handy when I was dealing with asshole customers at the cash register every day. *Yes, ma'am, the lines are long. It's fucking Christmas.*

"I'm not sure it's worth it," I said.

"I guess that's a call you have to make."

I hated how right he was.

I DESPERATELY NEEDED one last weekend off before Thanksgiving. I made my case to Marshall, and after spouting an unnecessarily long list of preconditions, he gave me his blessing. I wanted distance, a couple of days and a few miles, between myself and my everyday existence, including Will.

Buddhist that he was, Will accepted that my plans for rejuvenation excluded him and included Ariel.

A few months had passed since Ariel and I had talked, but we never quibbled over trivialities like who last called whom. She was irreplaceable in my universe, and she knew it. During the tenure of our friendship, Ariel had served alternately as my psychiatrist, my sister, and my priest, inasmuch as I needed the occasional confession. She possessed the unique ability to dispense thoughtful advice while maintaining an impressive neutrality over my decisions. She could sit comfortably on the sidelines while I detonated entire chunks of my life because she knew the lessons hidden therein could be unearthed no other way. Ariel was a little younger than me but wise beyond her years, and mine.

Our friendship had taken deep root over the years, though, like many people who were important to me, a few common interests, mundane and superficial as they were, formed our initial bond. We shared an unhealthy appreciation for frozen adult beverages, we loved sunny afternoon walks, and we both had a weakness for attractive men in uniforms (or costumes), which made theme park people-watching a favorite natural pastime.

Ariel and her longtime boyfriend, David, lived in Orlando, the undisputed center of the theme park universe. I usually stayed with them during weekend trips to Disney, but this time I wanted Ariel to myself. I didn't want to be on my best behavior, or even on good behavior. I booked a room for us at the Peabody, an Orlando hotel that offered a comfortable escape from regular life, not to mention the odd but satisfying attraction of wild ducks freely walking the lobby and using hotel elevators.

FOR MANY NATIVE Floridians, theme parks were a white trash vacation spot, but for some of us, it was the only travel we could afford. Besides, theme parks were fertile hotbeds of blossoming love—at least, they were for me. I met my last two boyfriends at theme parks, including the one I'd managed to keep. Some people went to the mall, some people went to bars. I went to Disney World.

The Magic Kingdom lacked alcohol, the essential "magic" I needed most. Consequently, Ariel and I whiled away our first day at Epcot, the park that offered the widest variety of grown-up drinking options.

"Let's take a selfie," Ariel insisted. "I'm having an excellent hair day, and I have a new iPhone that takes marvelous pictures." I rolled my eyes and put my arm around her.

We centered ourselves in front of that giant silver golf ball, which I imagined has an official name, but anyone who'd ever visited Epcot would know the ball I was talking about. Then we discussed an emergency separation plan, a tradition that carried more weight in the days before cell phones.

"Is there anything you definitely want to see here?" I asked.

"*Oui*," she said. "I want to go to fake France to peruse fragrances. *Et vous?*"

"I want to see all of it, the whole world."

"Oooh, an adventurer."

I nodded, accepting the compliment, though I mostly just wanted to visit beer stands in each imitation country to learn about ales of assorted bitterness and drink them anyway.

We reached the edge of the lagoon that occupies the center of the Epcot universe and mapped out our path, which is to say we chose to walk in a counter-clockwise direction around the enormous circular park. I preferred it this way since it meant we would encounter Canada first. Always best to drink the lighter North American faux-beers before tackling the dark, warm European beers that looked like flat Coca-Cola. I'm Irish American, but already two generations off the boat. I needed to start slow and build up strength.

"You want a beer?" I asked Ariel, having encountered exactly one alcohol vendor.

She squinted and wrinkled her nose as if she were pondering the question.

"Do they have sparkling water?" she asked, a healthy hint of doubt in her voice.

"Sparkling water? These are the streets of fake Canada, not fake France."

She primped her bright auburn hair and glanced over the top of her Prada sunglasses. "Well, you don't get what you don't ask for." Ariel exuded the kind of charm that enabled her to complain without sounding like she was bitching.

"Would a nice bottled spring water do?"

"That'd be delightful," she said.

We trekked around the imitation world, browsing shops in nearly every country in search of that special something for our respective boyfriends. Will was easy to shop for as he'd harbored a Winnie the Pooh fetish since childhood, and Disney characters are nothing if not over-marketed. I passed on the Pooh pajamas, the Pooh umbrella, and French Pooh chef's hat before settling on a set of tasteful Pooh and Eeyore cast iron garden figures. Will was a landscaper by trade, after all.

At the checkout counter, Ariel reminded me of the bad judgment involved in making such a weighty purchase at a theme park, assuring me she could provide no logistical support in transporting my gift to our hotel.

"Get bent," I said. "I'll carry them myself." My relationship with Ariel encompassed everything from the embarrassing to the crushing to the mundane; conversations between us were pleasantry-optional.

With a unique blend of sophistication and sarcasm, Ariel possessed an air of diva that drew gay men to her in the way that, well, in the way that gay men are drawn to divas. For the first few years of our friendship, I wondered if there was any straight man who'd established enough self-esteem to appreciate Ariel's strength. And if there were such a man, how he'd wade through the congregation of gay men with whom Ariel perpetually held court. Enter David.

Ariel met David at a marriage equality fundraiser in 2006, back when the idea of gay couples tying the knot was less in vogue, and certainly less legal. I didn't know if it was love at first sight, but I was certain no other relationship candidate had warranted serious consideration since that night. David was the only straight man I'd met who appeared completely comfortable with Ariel, and watching them interact was a poignant reminder that stable couples are made up of secure individuals. If there was a breakfast cereal that celebrated successful couples instead of athletes, Ariel and David would be featured on the box.

WE PASSED THE afternoon ogling men from around the Epcot globe, judging them like pies in a county fair bake-off, parsing them into categories and awarding blue ribbons to the best of each variety. We took time to note which fake countries employed the park's most desirable employees as well. The French won, of course. Complete assholes, but always smoking hot.

By the time we reached pretend Mexico, the sun had dipped closer to the horizon and we were ready to put our feet up. Ariel scouted an empty iron patio table near the railing that ran along the edge of the giant man-made lagoon. She cleared the table of a half day's debris, and I entered the line at the cocktail bar. I stood behind three old women who, judging from the slurring, were not making their first trip through the line.

Ariel luxuriated at the cheap metal table, posing like a plus-sized model at a seaside resort. With her head tilted back, the setting sun catching her auburn hair on fire, she accepted the plastic cupful of frozen margarita I offered like a flute of Dom Perignon. "My angel of mercy," she said.

"I would have been quicker, but I got in line behind the Golden Girls." I nodded at the trio of gray-haired women settling at a nearby table.

"The tall one is a total Bea Arthur," she agreed. Ariel sipped the margarita, which showed in her rosy cheeks as quickly as it disappeared.

"Marshall's a total cunt."

"Right."

"And no one really cares about my book. Ten years I worked on that piece of shit."

"People care."

"Maybe, but I swear to God, it's not fucking worth it."

"It is," she said, unfazed by my sudden offloading of angst.

"I don't know." I sucked the last frosty lump of margarita through my straw.

She nodded while I bitched and moaned, and my stress eventually deflated like a week-old party balloon. As the gaps in conversation lengthened, our attention shifted to the nearby Golden Girls and their chatter about canasta, osteoporosis, and dead husbands. We listened intently as one of them shared a sordid account of Peter, her first husband, who left just two months after the birth of their daughter.

I looked at Ariel in disbelief. "Men are shit."

"Not all men," she replied, thinking, I imagined, of David and Will.

"Yes," I said. "All men, just not all the time."

We ushered in the imitation Mexican sunset with another round of margaritas and two deep-fried churros. Our conversation waned, and Ariel closed her eyes and breathed deep, as though in quiet contemplation of nothing at all. I was lost and uncomfortable in the silence.

"The trip home last month sucked," I said.

"Your mom's little party didn't work out?"

"Long story. But in a nutshell, Mom tried too hard, Dad was irrelevant, June gave me a poker chip, Doris bought me a pen, and my high school English teacher groped my balls."

Her eyes opened wide in disbelief. "What the fuck?"

"It wasn't that bad. He's a hottie for an old guy."

She laughed. "Where were all the partygoers while you were getting perved?"

"It was late. They were gone. Will and my mom were there, but they were cleaning up. I told Will about it afterward."

"Was he pissed?" she asked.

"Will? Please."

"Right." She reached across the table and touching my hand. "He doesn't get pissed. He's the level-headed one."

"So I've heard. Will is soooo balanced and soooo calm and soooo self-aware."

I must have been using my alcohol voice, as I now had the undivided attention of the nearby Golden Girls. "Will is strong like a lion," I said in a softer voice. "And poor Conor is a neurotic little kitten who hides behind the couch every time the doorbell rings."

"Don't be so defensive." She smiled. "But you do sound a bit stressed...and you can be a little fret-ty." Ariel sometimes invented her own language rather than hunting through her expansive vocabulary to find an actual word.

"I'm not fret-ty," I insisted.

"You can be intense...when you're under pressure."

"I might get extra focused...when things are spiraling out of control."

"Wow," she said, under her breath. "Spiraling? Is that a tiny bit exaggerated?"

"I traveled five hundred miles to spend a weekend with my fucked-up family, and I was groped by my high school teacher. I spend fifty or sixty hours a week jerking off the ungrateful public and kissing corporate ass, and in my spare time, I drive all over central Florida begging people to buy my shitty book."

"Spiraling?" she repeated, eyebrows arching up her forehead. "As if. Sounds like life to me." People like me need people like Ariel, mostly for unconditional love, but also to keep our bullshit in check.

Darkness settled on fake Mexico. After hours of tequila and the merciless stiffness of unpadded iron patio chairs, we packed it in and trudged to the Peabody's courtesy tram stop. The smoky glow of Disney's fireworks finale illuminated the skies overhead as we climbed aboard an empty bus and settled into the back row. I closed my eyes and tried to float away, but the cast iron Pooh and Eeyore I'd bought for Will weighed me down like anvils.

FIVE

I WOKE TO the sound of Ariel humming as she towel-dried her hair at the foot of my hotel bed. Having been less diligent in her pursuit of a hangover, she had gone for a swim, showered, and brewed two cups of in-room Starbucks while I clawed my way to consciousness.

I mustered the energy to crawl out of bed and dress myself for a second day of theme park carousing. "Where we headed?" I asked, pulling a neatly folded T-shirt from the dresser drawer.

"Look at you," she said. "Red Calvin Klein boxer briefs. Who you showing off for?"

"You." I tilted my head and winked disingenuously.

"The gentleman does know how to impress a lady." She sighed and placed the back of her hand against her forehead. "Alas, the skill is wasted on you."

"Don't be hurt."

"I'll survive the disappointment."

"That a girl." I pulled on a pair of shorts. "I was thinking Sea World today. That okay?"

She gave me a cheesy salute and a slap on the ass. "Aye, aye, Cap'n Sexy."

WE SPENT THE day drinking beer and meandering around the park before finally reaching the Key West Dolphin cove. Simulated stone walls rose out of the water and enclosed a shimmering blue-green pool that housed two dozen Atlantic bottlenose dolphins. Exotic plant life and lush St. Augustine grass lined the nearby walkways, and soft piano music drifted across the water, creating a pleasant but uninspired new age soundtrack for visitors.

The park's designers constructed the habitat so onlookers could stand at the water's edge and dangle their hands in the pool as dolphins swam by. The sleek gray creatures mostly passed just beyond reach, but if you were patient, a curious dolphin would eventually swim close enough to be touched. I leaned over the edge of the pool and traced my fingers along the surface of the cool salt water. Ariel stood next to me, face upturned, soaking in the sun.

"Doesn't this make you feel close to God?" She ran her fingers through a tangle of her luminous hair.

"As much as anything does," I said. "I feel a sense of nostalgia here."

"Isn't this the place you first met Will?"

I glanced around to get my bearings. "About twenty feet from here."

"I remember. You met David and me for dinner that night. We were surprised when you showed up with your new boy toy."

"He's not that much younger than me."

"He was barely twenty."

"And I was barely thirty."

"Don't be so sensitive." She chuckled. "It was a reeeeally good night."

Unable to contain my fondness for the memory, I smiled. "It was my birthday. I met him here, and we talked for an hour. Then we split up, and later on, we met you and David at Jungle Jim's. Two first dates on the same day."

"He gave you a special birthday present," she said. "A little bronze Buddha."

"And later that night, I gave him one too. A special present, I mean, not a Buddha."

"That's why you like it here."

"That's why I love it here." I leaned back from the rocky wall and took a slow, panoramic gaze at the peaceful, manicured setting. "I met the love of my life here. Well, one of the loves anyway."

Ariel and I had spilled an abundance of dark personal secrets during late-night drinking binges. She understood, but asked for clarification anyway. "Do you actually put Paul in the same category as Will?"

"I don't know. If anyone is prone to putting people into categories, it's me. That's a hard call to make, though. I love Will like no one else. But I miss Paul sometimes."

It was true that Will and I had our initial romantic encounter here, but he was not the first. In the long-ago time before Will, I wandered these same paths with his predecessor. I mentioned theme parks were a hot spot for me, right?

As Ariel and I had walked the bright, flower-lined paths, I thought of Will, but images of Paul had stretched themselves across my mind like a tight, colorful canvas, covering the muted mural of Will that was already painted there. Each time she and I strolled past an out-of-the-way corner where Paul and I had sneaked to steal a kiss, I said nothing, but the memories crept into my consciousness like dusk. Those deep, beautiful kisses had awakened me.

I don't know for certain whether what I experienced with Paul was love. Maybe it was a powerful breed of lust, where desire so thoroughly reinforces emotional bonds that it feels like love. What's the difference, anyway, between love and something that feels like love? In that moment, nothing.

"Missing Paul, missing Paul, missing Paul," she repeated in a monotone. "I swear to Jesus you don't learn. You've never known the difference between what's good for you and what your dick thinks is good for you."

I averted my eyes and crossed my arms, feigning pissed off. Somewhere between middle school and middle age, an abdication had occurred wherein my brain relinquished its authority to my penis. I was in my thirties before I recognized the bad decisions my penis had made over the course of my life, which still didn't empower my brain to retake command.

I defended myself despite her utter correctness. "I don't know what you're talking about. I just said I missed Paul. Don't blow it out of proportion."

Ariel leaned on the man-made rocks and returned her gaze to the water. "I heard what you said, Conor." She stood still and quiet for a minute, then took my hand and pulled me from the water's edge. "Just keep your cock in check. Will deserves that from you."

"As you wish."

"Let's move on. Shall we?" It wasn't a question.

THE TIMING OF my chirping cell phone couldn't have been better, or worse. I glanced at the screen and didn't recognize the number.

"Give me a second, will ya? Probably Marshall..." I moved a few feet away from the craggy embankment and answered the call.

"Hello, this is Conor," I said in an artificially professional voice.

"Conor! I hope I haven't caught you at an inconvenient time?" Not Marshall.

"Oh...hi there." I put another few feet between Ariel and myself.

"Remember how I said I couldn't swing the trip to Orlando?"

"Yes. I remember your e-mail." I spoke in a hushed tone, though I could see that Ariel was distracted by the stingray petting zoo.

"I was able to work it out after all," the voice said. "If it's not too late, I'd still love to connect for a drink or something."

"You know," I stammered, "unfortunately, I've made other plans. I'm glad you called, though. I'd hate for you to make the drive to Orlando for nothing."

"Nonsense." His voice dripped charisma. "I'm already here."

I took a panicky look around.

"Here? At Sea World?" My voice cracked like a thirteen-year-old boy. A mixture of disbelief and fear competed with a surge of testosterone for control of my next words.

"Here in Orlando," he confirmed. "Checked in at the Peabody, just like you said."

I HUNG UP and joined Ariel, who was up to her forearm in salt water and stingrays.

"You okay?" she asked. "You look like someone punched you in the stomach."

"I'm fine," I said. "It was Marshall. I told him I didn't need his permission to take a shit on my day off."

"Awww, did your boss put you in a foul mood?" She turned her attention to a passing stingray who had stopped to investigate her outstretched hand.

"I'm okay," I insisted. "He was following up on some work stuff I'd already taken care of."

"Good." She stood up and shook the water from her wrists. "You want to touch a stingray? They don't have their barb thingies, and they're not rough like you'd think. Kind of slippery."

"Ariel, I'm sorry, but my stomach is starting to churn. I think today's beer might be rumbling with last night's margaritas. Can we head back to the Peabody?"

"Suit yourself." She sounded disappointed that I'd passed on the petting tank. "I thought that combination of slimy and velvety-smooth was pretty interesting."

Certain people in your life gain a vivid, almost psychic, comprehension of the things that motivate and sometimes haunt you. Ariel possessed that clarity about me, and it sometimes made me feel transparent. Having someone in my life who saw through my bullshit exposed an Achilles heel in a way that was both a blessing and a curse. With Ariel's unflinching willingness to rank out my weaknesses and beat them up, there was no point in hunkering down. My only hope was to outrun her or to try to distract her and throw her off the path.

I LAY ON the hotel bed and watched Ariel transfer the contents of her theme park purse to her evening purse. "Is your stomach feeling more settled?" she asked.

"A little," I said. "But not much. I don't want to spoil your evening, though."

"Don't worry about it." She grabbed a lipstick from her bag and applied it. "I know how it is. Some people can't handle their liquor as they get older."

"Don't make me jump off this bed and come after you." I sat upright and clutched my stomach, then added a soft moan for effect.

"Doesn't sound like you're going anywhere."

"No. I'm not moving. I totally understand if you want to cut our weekend short and head home."

"No way! What kind of friend would I be if I just left you here to suffer alone? And, what kind of girlfriend would I be if I surprised David by coming home a day early and ruining his bachelor weekend?"

"You're too thoughtful."

"It's true," she said. "But I'm also hungry, so I'm going to go find dinner. I'll be back in a bit. Do you want something?"

"No, thanks. If I start feeling better, I'll head down to the restaurant and find something mild to munch on."

She left the room, and before she and the Peabody ducks had likely completed the elevator ride down to the lobby, I leaped from the bed and jumped in the shower.

I MET MR. Morgan, John, in the bar downstairs twenty minutes later. I had slipped on pressed khaki pants and a Tommy Bahama button-down, and John wore a pair of form-fitting navy blue slacks and bright yellow Polo shirt. As they had at my book party, his biceps refused to be corralled by his short, tight sleeves. The cut of his thick, graying hair looked expensive and salon fresh, parted ever so gently on one side and sweeping back across his forehead. He looked like he'd just stepped off Ralph Lauren's sailboat.

I sat on the barstool next to him. He scooted his seat closer, the way you do when you need elbow room in a crowded pub, only there was no one seated within ten feet of us. He pressed his thigh hard against mine.

"He'll have a vodka and grapefruit," he said, catching the bartender's attention.

"You remember," I said. "How attentive."

"I remember a lot about you, Conor. And not just from your little family get-together."

"Do tell." I felt smug and desirable.

"Things from your high school days. The clothes you wore, your hair, your smile. How you sometimes snuck a glance at my ass when you thought no one was looking."

"It's nice to see you again...John." I used his first name with emphasis, partly to put us on even ground. No more student-teacher bullshit.

"I have to say I was a bit surprised when I received your e-mail, Conor."

I guzzled my drink, mildly uncomfortable but forging ahead. "Surprised? You're not that hard to track down."

"I assumed you preferred younger men, that's all."

"Will is the exception," I said. "I usually prefer more mature men."

"Good to know. How long have you been with young Will?"

"About nine years."

"What's he up to anyhow? Did you bring him along? The more the merrier, right?"

No doubt, he intended the last bit to sound more tantalizing than disturbing. Mission, not accomplished.

"No, Mr. Morgan. John, sorry. Will, who's thirty by the way, is home in Tampa. I'm here on my own."

"Just as well." He spied my nearly empty glass and motioned to the bartender. "Another scotch for me," he said, "and another vodka for my friend. And bring the check."

Two drinks and the check? Things were moving fast, and thanks to Captain Anxious Pants, I had not only thought of Will but had spoken his name aloud.

Our next round of drinks showed up, and I committed to nursing the cocktail, resisting the overwhelming urge I had to down it in one swallow.

"So, where were we?" I asked.

"I remember right where we were." He growled under his breath, and in a flash, the hand was there. Like a replay of my mother's living room— thigh, upper thigh, way upper thigh touching testicles. It was the same movie, only with time-lapsed photography. "What do you say?" he asked. "Shall we?"

He placed his room key on the bar in front of me and slapped a fifty-dollar bill on top of the tab.

"Could you excuse me a moment?" I asked. "Just a quick second?" I needed a moment to gather my thoughts and headed for the restroom in the hotel lobby. As I passed the elevator, the doors slid open. With a glance over my shoulder to make sure I was unseen, I bolted inside and nearly trampled half a dozen flabbergasted mallards.

I collapsed against the back of the elevator, catching my breath and heaving a momentary sigh of relief on the ride to my room. Having escaped for the moment a grotesque carnal trap of my own design, I still needed to figure out how to hide from Mr. Morgan (no more "John" for me), who, upon realizing I had disappeared, needed only walk to the front desk and have the clerk ring my room. I opened the hotel room door and found a pissed-off Ariel waiting inside.

"Hi. You made it back quick," I said as if stating the obvious was somehow helpful.

"I ordered takeout because I wanted to get back and check on you. I guess your gastro problems healed miraculously?" she asked.

"Actually, they didn't. In fact, I think I might throw up right now." I was finally telling the truth.

"If you didn't want to spend time with me, you could've just said so." She looked suddenly unfamiliar, un-Ariel, her face drooping and soft.

"I just needed some fresh air. Really. I'm glad you're here." Another instance of truth. If John Morgan showed up at the door, Ariel's presence could provide much-needed protection for my genitals.

"It's not my business to ask where you were, but we've been friends for a long time. You can tell me what's going on."

I said nothing, surprised at how readily my "fresh air" defense had been shot down.

"Don't make it worse, Conor. I already know where you were."

"Where?" I asked, challenging her for no good reason.

"You were at the bar having drinks." The role of busybody investigator didn't fit with Ariel's style, but if her intent was to rake me over the coals, I'd play along.

"Yep, you got me. Guilty as charged."

"I saw you there with your whore."

"My whore?" I held my breath.

"Your little cocktail."

I puffed a loud awkward sigh of relief. "Right. I love vodka more than anything."

"You do. And I got the evidence on film, or whatever these things use nowadays." She removed her iPhone from her purse and showed me a photograph she'd taken from the doorway of the lounge. A picture of me, my drink, and my English teacher.

"When the hell did you take that?" I asked.

"After I grabbed my takeout. I was walking through the lobby, and I saw you in the bar." She grinned. "That's when I got the idea to pretend I was mad."

"Not funny," I said.

She crossed the room and stood toe-to-toe with me, staring squarely into my eyes before cracking a smile. "Calm down. So you snuck a drink while Momma went to get dinner. Who cares!" She hugged me and patted my back.

"Jesus." Relief exploded from deep inside me, manifesting itself in a fit of hysterical laughter. "You had me going. I really thought you were pissed."

"Nope. I just wanted to pay you back for having a drink without me."

"Well, you definitely got me."

"That was priceless," she said. "Wait until Will hears how you reacted." She tossed her head back and laughed like a Disney villainess.

"What's that?" The question sounded more grave than I'd intended.

"I can't wait to tell Will the rest of the story. I thought you were going to pee your pants."

"I'm confused." I was barely able to mask my swelling panic.

"No offense, honey, but sometimes we make fun of how uptight you are." She wiped tiny laugh-tears from her eyes.

"Ariel," I said, pretending to giggle. "What do you mean 'tell Will the rest of the story'?"

"Don't be mad. I knew he'd appreciate the joke, so I called and told him about it."

"You dirty trickster." Playing it cool was getting easier. She clearly suspected nothing more than that I'd slipped away for a drink.

"Poor baby, you looked sooo guilty."

"Well, yeah. I thought I really hurt your feelings."

"No way, honey." She mussed my hair.

"Did Will think it was funny?"

"He laughed when I called...but he hasn't texted back since I sent the picture."

SIX

I STEERED CLEAR of total emotional collapse on the way home by driving ninety and focusing my attention on staying alive. I forced myself to take an optimist's view of the situation. *Maybe the photo hadn't gone through?* Reception can be spotty and big image files can be troublesome. *Maybe Will's phone was dead?* He often forgets to charge his phone on weekends. *Maybe Will received the photo, but failed to recognize John Morgan in the picture?* It was a dim hotel bar and Will never got that great a look at the English teacher at the book party. An infinite universe of variables might work in my favor. Or... *Maybe Will saw the photo, recognized John Morgan, and already threw all my shit out on the lawn?*

Manufactured optimism only lasts so long before it fades and instinct returns.

THE SIGHT OF Will's car parked in front of our condo flooded me with a simultaneous rush of relief and anxiety. He hadn't run, which meant I couldn't, either. I had raced home to face him, to explain it to him, but I was unprepared to confront the truth. So, I didn't.

I loved Will and didn't want to hurt him. If I embellished, or rather just omitted a fact or two, no one had to get hurt. Yes, I went to Orlando to spend time with Ariel. Yes, we visited theme parks. Yes, Ariel and I lodged at the Peabody where, *as it happens*, John Morgan was also staying. We had a drink and nothing else.

Simple, and with the exception of three meaningless words, completely true.

Will hadn't been rampaging through the house breaking my things, nor had he tearfully packed my bags. He had been calmly tending to houseplants, reflecting and remembering.

"If this was the first time we ever had this conversation, we wouldn't be...having this conversation."

"That's why I came home," I said. "As soon as Ariel told me she sent you the picture, I freaked the fuck out. I knew you'd think the worst."

"And you were right. I hate that it works that way, but it does." He circulated around the living room, watering pothos and orchids and crotons.

It wasn't Will's nature to be petty or jealous, but I had given him reason. Early in our relationship, I got bored, confused maybe. Not because of anything he did or didn't do; I don't know why. I started flirting with a guy at the bookstore, an attractive older guy I'd hired whose day-trading strategy was slumping. One thing led to another, and Will eventually caught me in a lie. He didn't find me in bed, thank God, but he found a few e-mails. We talked it out, and I'd mostly behaved since then. Still, once the seed of doubt is planted, it's always there beneath the soil, even if it never sprouts.

"I can't make you believe John Morgan being at the hotel was a coincidence. But I can tell you this, nothing happened. I swear."

He plucked a dying yellow leaf from an ivy plant. "I want to believe you."

"Then, believe me. Nothing happened. For God's sake, he's an arrogant dick who, by the way, is a little old and creepy. Why would I risk losing you over a piece of crap like that?"

He put down the plastic watering can and looked at me. "Maybe that's your thing."

"You're my thing," I said.

"My dad was an asshole, and my mother tolerated it for years. I'm not gonna be like that."

"So, that's what this is about? I remind you of your trailer-trash daddy? Jesus Christ," I muttered.

"I didn't say that. I'm still here because you're not that. But I'm putting you on notice, Conor. Don't do this to me."

The words were a gut punch. Ariel was right—Will deserved better *from* me, and maybe better *than* me. Still, I wasn't ready to give up on us. I couldn't. Not over a couple of stupid drinks I'd shared with a dirty old English teacher.

"I'm sorry," I said. "I can't promise I'll be able to avoid every unlucky coincidence for the rest of my life, but I can promise to be honest."

"How honest?" he asked. "There are degrees of truth, you know?" I did know. I was treading all over them.

"Totally honest."

"I want to believe you, Conor."

"Totally honest," I repeated. "If I even think about another guy, I'll tell you."

"I don't want to hear about every restaurant waiter who catches your eye. I don't have that kind of time." He didn't smile or laugh, but the joke was a hopeful sign.

"Totally honest," I reiterated. "Not waiters or delivery guys, but if I'm genuinely tempted, you'll know. I swear. At least that gives us a chance to deal with it before something happens."

Will asked for a night to weigh his options, which, under the circumstances, seemed more than fair and a better outcome than I had expected. My bag was still packed in the car, so I drove to a nearby La Quinta. I spent the evening immersed in anxiety and a pint of Maker's Mark. After a couple of hours of sulking, I called Ariel and confessed the reason for my rapid departure. She listened quietly and then delivered another stirring reprisal of the "stop-thinking-with-your-dick" speech. It was a genuine pearl of wisdom, but it had done little to change my behavior in the past. Some of us learn more from a two-by-four than a lecture.

I lay awake most of the night, flopping on the lumpy hotel bed like a fish suffocating on a dock. When I closed my eyes, I saw John Morgan, graying and handsome, sitting alone at the hotel bar waiting for me. I saw him lean into me, felt the grip of his thick, strong hand on my thigh. For that, a good haircut and a pair of impressive but aging biceps, I'd risked losing Will. I climbed out of bed before sunrise. Still in yesterday's clothes, I tipped the empty whiskey bottle to my lips and drained the last drops. I drove home and snuck into bed beside Will, afraid it might be the last time I'd ever enjoy the warmth of him.

Without turning to face me, he spoke. "I don't know if I believe your coincidence."

"Okay. I can't make you believe it—"

"Let me finish. I don't know if I believe you, but I'm not ready to end it, so I'm giving you the benefit of the doubt."

"Trust me," I said into the darkness, "I don't want to lose you. Nothing happened with John Morgan." That part's all true, every word.

"Total honesty from here on out."

"Total honesty. I swear it."

SETTING TRAPS AND then falling into them is a repeatable feat of stupidity I mastered early in life. I'd ruined perfectly good relationships with predictable regularity. Committing colossal blunders around milestones like birthdays and anniversaries had proven to be my special talent, and the holidays, of course, had been a particularly powerful shit magnet for me.

By the time I started long-overdue therapy in my late twenties, I'd come to believe that being a fuck-up was in my DNA. The preponderance of evidence supported my theory. Howard Clausen and a few bottles of Prozac did their best to convince me otherwise, but their work was in vain. Howard was a customer at the first bookstore I managed in Tampa. After witnessing one of the most epic holiday meltdowns in modern retail history, he also became my therapist.

When Howard first diagnosed me with major depression, I insisted that lots of people got sad around the holidays. He reminded me that all those people hadn't snapped on the job, and shouted, sobbed, and sworn at a mean-spirited old lady. Though I now admit to being mental, I still maintain she brought the whole thing on herself. In the midst of a particularly long and hectic December rush, she heckled my staff for fifteen solid minutes while waiting in line, calling us "misfits" and "shit-for-brains," and insisting "Mongoloid four-year-olds" could ring the registers faster. In my defense, I did ask her politely to calm down before eventually calling her an "impatient old cunt" who needed to have "her loud fucking mouth washed out with soap."

The incident, once reported to my bosses by the aforementioned elderly cunt, resulted in a serious ass-chewing and a short suspension, but Howard's firsthand account and subsequent clinical diagnosis kept me employed. That, and the leniency of a regional HR rep who actually had a child with Down syndrome.

Sessions with Howard were fine, but their impact was limited, probably because therapy was the company's idea, not mine. I saw him every Wednesday for a few months until I maxed out my free visits under the company's Employee Assistance Program. When the company money ran out, so did my commitment. Not helping myself escape from the traps I fell into was another talent I possessed.

Years had passed, but when I called, Howard fit me in. Scheduling an appointment lifted me, and I hoped things would be different. This time, getting help was my idea. This time, I could feel the darkness coming.

His office had a diminutive, unattended waiting room furnished with two upholstered wingback chairs and a small, round table, which looked more like they came from an estate sale than a furniture store. Inside the softly lit therapy office, there were more comfortable touches: dark cherry bookcases, a bona fide leather couch, and a large and colorful saltwater fish tank along one wall that emitted a constant hum and gurgle. I was certain that Howard, whose curly gray hair, thick goatee, and plastic-framed Tootsie glasses made him look like a shrink, had hired someone else to decorate.

"Conor," he said. "It's nice to see you again."

"Thanks for seeing me." I paced in front of the saltwater aquarium, ogling starfish and neon-colored wrasses until Howard gently steered the conversation in the direction of my emotional well-being.

"Have a seat and tell me how you've been."

"I'm great," I said. "Well, obviously not that good or I wouldn't be here."

He smiled. "What brings you to my neck of the woods?"

"You mean, what have I fucked up?"

"Okay. If you prefer a more direct approach."

"I don't think I should be here," I said. "I'm not ready for this."

"It's natural to feel afraid when we confront our challenges. But you're here, so we may as well make the most of it."

"I saw Aunt Doris a few weeks ago."

"How was that?"

"No big deal." I shrugged. "She was at my book release party."

"Book release?"

"Yeah. Finally finished and even got published."

"Congratulations," he said. "That's quite an accomplishment."

I nodded. "If you say so."

"What's your book about?"

"Growing up Irish. You know, big family, lots of drinkers, stuff like that."

"So, it's a memoir?" he asked.

"Fiction."

"I'm sorry. I didn't mean for that to sound—"

"It's fine. Considering all the shit I've told you, it's an honest mistake."

"So, you were saying you saw Doris?" Way to keep us on task.

"We didn't talk about Patrick," I said. "If that's where you're going."

"I wasn't going anywhere, but if you'd like to talk about your cousin, that's fine."

"It was a party, Howard. I try not to bring up cousin-fucking at family gatherings."

"You're starting to sound angry."

"I'm not angry."

"I sense that you are."

"Well, aren't you keen?"

He paused long enough for the sarcastic cloud between us to dissipate. "You were just a boy, Conor. It's okay to be angry."

"I wasn't molested," I said. "We were fucking around like kids do."

"Kids explore their bodies, that's true. And yes, you were just a kid."

I wasn't aware of the tears until I felt them running down my cheek.

"You didn't do anything wrong, Conor."

"I don't know why I'm here. I need to get going."

He glanced at the hourglass of sand on the glass coffee table. "We still have a few minutes."

I wiped at my cheeks and stood to leave. "Could you prescribe something for me? Xanax maybe?"

"Let's talk about that next time." He grabbed a small, spiral-bound calendar and flipped through the pages. "Next week's Thanksgiving—"

"Jesus Christ," I muttered. "Thanksgiving."

"I think you have your holidays mixed up."

"Funny, but don't quit your day job. Will and I are hosting my grandmother and a few other people for Thanksgiving. I need to get my shit together."

The last drops of sand slipped to the bottom of the hourglass. "I can see you the Tuesday after Thanksgiving," he said.

"And then you'll prescribe something for me?"

"We'll see."

I looked down at my fingertips, at the shreds of cuticles where my fingernails were supposed to be.

"So, can I put you down for the Tuesday after Thanksgiving?"

"I'll get back to you on that."

SEVEN

A FEW YEARS back, Will and I began a tradition of hosting orphans on Thanksgiving. Not sad, abandoned children, but the alienated, grown-up variety. Some of our orphans were far from home, some were gay men and women whose loved ones no longer welcomed them, and others, like June, just preferred the company of a diverse, albeit manufactured, family to their own blood relatives.

Having nearly destroyed my relationship with Will, I was ready to cancel Thanksgiving. Better yet, why not skip the whole overrated holiday season and just get on with a new year? Will thought we needed to stick to our traditions, though, and I was in no position to argue what was best for us. If nothing else, cooking and cleaning and having June around might distract us long enough for the dust to settle from the shit storm I'd caused.

June called the day before her arrival to share her flight information.

"I'll take a cab from the airport," she said.

"That's ridiculous. I can see the airport from the parking lot at work. I'll take off a little early and pick you up curbside."

The next day at work, I was trampled by a predictable crush of holiday shoppers, and June's flight was likely at the gate by the time I remembered to pick her up. I hauled ass to Tampa International and arrived just in time to be trapped behind a lengthy backup at passenger pickup. But not in time for June. As I neared the Delta curbside, my cell phone rang.

"June's here." Will threw in a loud sigh to show his disgust.

"What? I'm at the airport. I'm like twenty minutes late."

"You're forty-five minutes late."

"Did she call you to pick her up?" I asked.

"No. I just got home from work. She was on the porch waiting for one of us to get home."

"Goddammit," I said. "Was she pissed?"

"Not at all. She was sitting on her suitcase talking to Harlan."

"That's a conversation I'd love to have on tape."

WE SHARED THE front sidewalk to our condo with our next-door neighbors, a single mother and her sixteen-year-old son. Rose and Harlan moved to Tampa from Starke, a backwater shithole in central Florida that consists almost entirely of a sad stretch of highway, a Tastee Freez, and a handful of mostly abandoned strip centers. If that's not depressing enough, it's just a ten-minute jaunt from Starke to the state prison, where Florida houses its death row inmates.

I fiddled with my house key and tried not to notice Harlan, who sat on an upright cement block on his front porch. Bringing the country into the city was just part of Harlan's charm.

"Dude," he said, "your granny's here." The thin, ruddy-faced kid took a long pull on a cigarette.

"So I heard. She say anything to you?"

"She said you didn't pick her up." It didn't appear his tall frizz of wiry hair had seen a comb in recent weeks, nor had his jeans visited a washing machine.

"Did she look pissed?" I asked.

"She looked old."

"Thanks for the update, Harlan."

"Anytime, man. Anytime."

JUNE SAT AT the table in our breakfast nook, looking out at the Hillsborough River.

"Hi." I leaned down to kiss my grandmother. "How was your flight?"

"Short, thank God. I hate the little Wright Brothers' airplanes you have to fly out of Pensacola. Even when I go to Vegas, they stick me on one those puddle jumpers."

"I'm really sorry I was late. I got tied up at work."

"I'll forgive you," she said, "if you open a bottle of wine for us."

"How did you get here?" I asked, picking out a Cabernet from a countertop wine rack.

"I met a nice Air Force lieutenant on the plane. He gave me a ride."

"That sounds safe."

"He was a handsome kid with an honest face. Besides, my grandson forgot me. I had to improvise."

"Ouch. I'm really sorry, but I'm glad you figured something out."

"I'm old," she said, "not stupid. The day I can't navigate my way out of an airport and across town is the day I settle into an old folks' home and wait to die with the rest of the zombies."

We sipped our wine, and before the second glass I was pouring out the pathetic details of my mounting stress. Marshall, the holidays, struggling to establish myself as a writer. I told her about my attempt at rejuvenation with Ariel, though I selectively edited out the John Morgan element of the story and the dramatic conclusion to the weekend. I needed compassion from June, and telling her about my aborted hookup with the English teacher wasn't likely to yield a sympathetic ear. She was prone to digging through layers of bullshit and quickly unearthing the unmitigated truth about such things.

I excused myself to change out of my work clothes. When I returned, Coltrane played on the stereo, and Will and my grandmother had moved the tiny party to the patio. Through the sliding glass doors, I watched them, the two people I loved most, sitting at an ordinary table, sipping ordinary wine from ordinary glasses, and talking, I imagined, about nothing in particular. The setting sun turned everything a shimmering copper. The Hillsborough River some fifty yards away, the wooden bench along the riverbank, the tops of the trees, the air itself; everything radiated a soft golden glow. In that vacuum of time, I was thankful for the life I had built. I wish I knew how to sustain that feeling, but I never lived long in those moments. I wanted to. I yearned to embrace the joy of being present, but even with Will as a role model, I couldn't get it right. At thirty-nine, I was still busy trying to wrangle life, to control it. I let go at times but, more often, I squandered my energy, lamenting fuck-ups gone by and fretting over crises, both real and imagined, that loomed on the horizon.

I settled into the patio chair closest to Will. Under the table, I let my barefoot rest on top of his—like holding hands, only more secret, more intimate. He slid his foot away and tucked it behind his chair leg safely out of my reach, a purposeful signal or an instinctual reaction that showed his lingering disappointment.

Will shared colorful cell phone pictures of a huge flower project he'd just finished at Busch Gardens. June recounted gambling stories from a recent Lake Tahoe vacation. They were easy together.

"I'm a shitty gambler," I said. "A poor loser."

"I don't mind losing," Will said. "As long as it's not slots. I like games where strategy makes a difference."

"High stakes chess!" June slapped the table with her palm. Our second bottle of wine was beginning to show in her voice.

Will laughed. "Easy there. I don't even know how to play."

"Even better," she chuckled. "Get out your cash and bring on the chess set."

"Sorry to disappoint you," he said. "We don't have a chess set."

"You should buy one. I'll give you lessons and we'll play for money."

"Sounds...unfair?" he said. "But I have always wanted to learn to play."

"I'm a good teacher. You'll see."

The conversation hit a natural lull, and we shared a still moment, staring out at the slow, black river. Unaware of how to find comfort in comfortable silences, I spoke up. "June, you know you're the only one from the McLeish clan I ever invite to Thanksgiving?"

She reflected before answering. "Wrong. On two counts."

"No other McLeish has ever been here for Thanksgiving," I said. "How am I wrong?"

"It was William, not you, who invited me to Thanksgiving. But I won't pick nits. More importantly, I have never been part of the McLeish clan. I don't come from prize stock, but it'll be a cold lonely day in hell before anyone lumps me in with Seamus and that band of idiots."

IN THE NEXT few days, I tapped a reservoir of energy I didn't know I had left in me. Fuck Howard, I could pull this off without therapy or Xanax. I was knee deep in customers and pre-Christmas corporate freak-out at work, but in my "spare" time, I still managed to arrange three book signings for December and spend time with June prepping for Thanksgiving. June was a low-maintenance houseguest, but she wasn't a high contributor in the kitchen. Will, to the contrary, had strong culinary skills, but he was still licking his emotional wounds and required careful handling.

Two days before Thanksgiving, Will and I reviewed the dinner menu and guest list.

"Some of the usual orphans got adopted," I said. "So other than you, me, and June, we have five people for dinner."

"Emily and Alex," he said.

"And Aaron," I added. "Did I tell you he confirmed?"

"You mentioned it, but I have no idea who he is."

Emily was an older lesbian friend of Will's with whom we'd shared Thanksgiving for years. Alex was a landscaper Will worked with at Busch Gardens who had recently moved to Tampa. Aaron was one of mine.

"He's the college kid I hired at the bookstore. His family's in North Carolina, and this is his first Thanksgiving away from home."

"Touching. Anyway, that's only three people."

Perplexed for a moment, I realized I had omitted two of our regulars. "Oh, Ariel and David."

"Did you ask her to leave her iPhone at home?" he asked.

"What?" I flinched, annoyed by the untimely callback. Will hadn't spoken to Ariel since the John Morgan photo. The mention of her name brought the afternoon back into sharp focus.

"We don't want Ariel snapping any candid pictures." He spoke without a hint of jest, and to make sure his sarcasm penetrated the target he threw an even sharper dart. "You know, in case you decide to blow the college kid after dessert."

"You're fucking hilarious," I said.

"Eh. The joke's on me."

I had wishfully interpreted our recent string of low-drama days as evidence of healing, but any progress was apparently superficial. That's how some wounds heal, I suppose. Scars forming on the outside long before the real damage is repaired on the inside.

WILL PASSED OUT mimosas to each Thanksgiving guest on arrival and the pre-dinner conversation was lively. June mingled, seeming to especially enjoy Emily, whom she chatted up as though they spent regular weekends hanging out at Provincetown lesbian bars.

My grandmother was eminently capable in conversation. With anyone. She knew how to draw people out, asking questions about things that mattered to them and quickly discovering their core. She was also remarkably short on inhibition, an endearing old lady trait that often carried high entertainment value.

Before we dove into the turkey and trimmings, we took turns giving thanks. Our collective gratitude list hit the usual highlights—friends and loved ones, food and shelter, a beautiful day and time together. Aaron, the college kid, was the last to speak up. Throughout the afternoon he'd been mostly quiet. We knew little about him, aside from the insights we gleaned from his glazed look, longish hair, and oversized Che sweatshirt. He had a website and fancied himself a writer, which made sense. The kid did have a way with words.

"First off," he said, "I'm grateful ya'll invited me here today. Conor, you guys throw an incredibly tame party for thirtysomething gay dudes, but this still beats the shit out of eating pizza for Thanksgiving." He grinned and paused, waiting for the murmur of chuckles to die down. "Second, I'm grateful ya'll let me drink mimosas all day. Bet you didn't know I'm only twenty!" We laughed at the admission and held up our glasses to toast him. "Hold up. I'm still going. I love the way the warm sun feels, and I'm thankful for coffee and for having a car that starts every time I crank it." He patted the front pocket of his sweatshirt as though he were six months pregnant. "And thank God for good weed. Amen."

"Amen," we responded in unison, and we gorged ourselves and drank to inebriation, in the gluttonous way that only Americans can. The weed comment, Will and June discovered later in the evening, wasn't a casual throwaway line.

As night settled in, I lit the candles I had scattered atop the tables in the living room and around the ledge of the screened patio. We sipped cups of coffee and ate pumpkin pie with homemade whipped cream. Aaron and Will enjoyed seconds, and thirds.

The shrill ring of the telephone pierced the moment, and before I reached the handset, I knew it was Aunt Doris. Since the third grade, when I moved from her house back home with my parents, Aunt Doris hadn't missed a single Thanksgiving, Easter, or Christmas Day.

—*Orphan's Thanksgiving?*
Yes, there were eight of us this year.
—*June?*
Yes, she's here.
—*The turkey?*
Juicy and delicious. Mm-hmmm, we had all the fixings.

—Work tomorrow?
Of course I do. It's Black Friday hell. I'll be there at 5:00 a.m.

She ran through the litany of questions and superficial commentary that I imagine comprise most family holiday calls. She also failed, as usual, to mention Will. I didn't expect her to ask about his job or his hobbies, or even his health, but a passing reference or perfunctory inquiry would be nice. Normally, I let the purposeful omission slide, and I probably should have done so again, but with a full day's drinking getting the best of me, I picked a fight.

"Aunt Doris, why is it you never ask about Will?"

"Do what?" she asked, her Southern roots showing.

"You call every holiday to say hello and see how I'm doing, but you never ask about Will?"

"Now, Conor, you know I'm not going to do that." Though our conversations seldom included more than a vague allusion to my gayness, she spoke as though we'd covered this ground a thousand times before.

"You aren't going to do that?" I was rolling. "Don't I ask about Uncle Martin? It's basic fucking courtesy."

"Conor, I don't think we want to go here tonight." Avoidance was her version of kindness, but I'd opened this can of worms and if I had to eat it, so be it.

"Just tell me why asking a simple question—'how is Will?'—violates your religious values?"

"Conor, we can talk about this in person. You know I harbor no ill feelings for your friend." She sounded more concerned than exasperated. "It's just your...lifestyle."

"I've heard that load of horseshit before."

"Well," she said, ignoring my inflammatory swearing, "I hate the idea of your soul burning in the flames of eternal hell because of your sin. I cannot in good conscience do anything to encourage that sin."

"Jesus Christ." It was an ironically poor choice of exclamations on my part. "Do you understand that what you are saying hurts me?"

Aunt Doris, for perhaps the first time ever, said nothing. We had engaged in lightweight versions of this conversation in years past, but this level of emotional honesty was new.

"Aunt Doris," I continued, "you're nice enough to Will when you see him or when you call and he answers the phone." It was a declaration, but a plaintive, whiny one, probably the same tone I used thirty-five years earlier when she'd put me in pajamas and sent me to bed before I was ready.

"Of course I'm nice to him. I don't want to be unkind." She paused before going on. "Honestly, Conor." *Here it comes.* "I just can't encourage your relationship. I'm afraid that's what will land you in hell."

"So you don't ask about Will," I summarized, "because you reject our love. And you reject our love because you care about my soul."

"Bingo!" she exclaimed. "That's it in a nutshell, honey." She radiated with satisfaction at having conveyed her point of view. "But just so we're clear," she said with utter sincerity, "it's hate the sin, not the sinner. I love you, Conor. I always have."

"I love you too, Aunt Doris." And I did, even the Southern Baptist parts of her.

EIGHT

MY ALARM CLOCK shrieked at 4:00 a.m., an ungodly hour at which no human should have to leave the comfort of a warm bed. This holds particularly true if the reason for leaving the bed is work, and your work is at a store in a mall, and the day you're working at a store in a mall is the day after Thanksgiving. The idea of suffering through another high-anxiety Christmas was a black belt kick in the groin. I showered and dressed, then shuffled down the hallway in pitch blackness, keeping the house dark as though somehow the awful weeks ahead wouldn't begin until I turned on a light.

At the kitchen table, I stared into nothingness, vaguely aware of the bowl of Honey Nut Cheerios and the prescription pill bottles illuminated by the nearby stovetop light. In the dim light, I made out the clock on the wall: 4:27 a.m. Thirty-three minutes of peace left in the next six weeks. I gathered my strength and lifted the spoon from the bowl to my mouth. Bowl to mouth, bowl to mouth, bowl to mouth. I could do this.

A sense of overwhelming despair at Christmastime wasn't new for me. Things had bottomed out the year the old bitch sent me over the edge at work, but even that Christmas had its upside. Howard, and drugs. He prescribed Prozac and Xanax to stabilize my mood and fend off any further panic attacks. I took the drugs for a year until Will entered the picture and everything changed. Life looked suddenly shiny and new and being with someone who managed his own stress somehow helped me manage mine. I tapered my meds down and eventually stopped taking the pills altogether.

That was nearly a decade ago, though, and Will and I no longer lived in the starry-eyed bliss of new lovers. My reoccurring tendency for self-sabotage had ensured that. Faced with the consequences of my non-sexual sexual escapade in Orlando, along with six-day work weeks, Marshall, and book signings in my off-hours, I needed a helping hand. When no one else stepped up, the unfinished prescriptions in the back of the bathroom cabinet volunteered.

Nausea, restlessness, irritability—according to the label on the bottle, these were some of the delightful by-products of mental health I'd forgotten. Cranky mornings and stomach cramps would hardly improve my long workdays, but I needed a preemptive strike against the looming hopelessness. I started with Prozac, surreptitiously washing the pills down with my first cup of coffee each morning, and once the insomnia kicked in, I added a nightly dose of Xanax to my regimen. If I was going to vomit and be pissed off all day, I could at least be well-rested.

I SCHEDULED MY first signing for *Luck of the Irish* on the last Wednesday night in November at Haslam's Bookshop in St. Petersburg. True to form, Marshall popped in that day for a surprise store inspection, and it was late in the afternoon before I convinced him we were ready for the busy weeks ahead. I bolted out of work and literally ran to my car in hopes of finding time to shower and change clothes before the signing.

At home, Will and June had prepared an early dinner of fajitas. I attacked my plate like a stray dog and washed the meal down with a homemade margarita. After a terse and uncomfortable conversation, wherein I begged them to skip the book signing, I jumped in my car and raced across the Howard Frankland Bridge. I pulled into Haslam's at 6:30, giving myself just enough time to jot down a handful of notes about the book. Let me say for the record, that the events that followed were not the fault of the bookstore. They promoted my "appearance" on their website, they ordered and displayed copies of the book, and they set up the signing space exactly as expected.

As a bookstore manager, I should have known that these activities, in the absence of other press or promotion by a heretofore unknown author, would yield a crowd of approximately four attendees, including an empathetic off-duty store clerk who sat in the audience out of obligation or pity. I should also have remembered that bringing one's boyfriend and grandmother to a book signing is always a welcome audience builder.

Haslam's had set up a lectern in front of thirty neatly arranged seats. In an attempt to salvage my dignity, I stood at the podium long enough to introduce myself, and then suggested the five of us pull our folding metal chairs into a cozy circle. In addition to me and the off-duty employee, our intimate group consisted of a mentally ill Haslam's patron who dutifully attended each of the store's events, a sports fan who'd heard the overhead announcement and mistakenly thought *Luck of the Irish* was about Notre Dame football, and a middle-aged woman who had read about the signing in Haslam's newsletter and actually thought the book sounded interesting. The small group pretended to sit in rapt attention as I shared not-too-distressing stories of how my own childhood inspired much of the book. As I talked, my mouth grew dry. I sipped the bottle of water I'd been given. It made no difference. Desert dry. My saliva disappeared as though I'd stuffed my cheeks with sponges and cotton balls. My tongue went numb. I rambled on as a drenching sweat formed beneath my arms and around my collar. I guzzled the bottled water.

"So," I said, "while my grandfather Seamus isn't directly mentioned in the book, his colorful life is more than represented."

"When did you play football for Notre Dame?" the sports fan asked.

"I didn't go to Notre Dame. There's no football in the book."

"Do you think rainbows are pretty?" asked the mentally ill woman.

"Yes. My people are quite fond of rainbows."

"You mean, Irish people?" asked the store clerk.

"Yes," I said. "Leprechauns and all that."

"Your family sounds very interesting," said the middle-aged woman who'd read the synopsis of *Luck of the Irish* in the newsletter. "Will you sign a book for me?"

"Of course." I opened her copy to the title page and ignored the chill of cold sweat that ran down my back, and then, thanks to the ill-considered decision to load steak fajitas and a frozen margarita on top of Prozac, I puked.

FRIDAY WAS MY eighth straight day at work, and I'd staffed up so I could leave early to enjoy one last lunch with June before her flight home to Pensacola. I picked her up at noon, and we headed across the bridge to St. Pete again. This time we visited The Moon Under Water, a British colonial pub I liked that overlooked a grassy expanse of Vinoy Park and had a distant view of Tampa Bay.

We both ordered Indian curry and pints of Guinness. For a trim elderly woman, June held her liquor well. As I sipped the room temperature beer, it occurred to me that I should avoid mixing alcohol with Prozac again, but "shoulds" seldom carried much weight with me.

"Wasn't your signing in St. Petersburg the other night?" she asked.

"Yeah," I said. "But not near here." The Moon Under Water was across town from the grisly scene at Haslam's, which now ranked as the most horrific book signing experience I'd had. Granted, there had only been two, but at least during my mother's book release party, I'd remained vomit-free throughout the evening.

"Sounds like it was pretty awful," she said, correctly qualifying the event without specifically calling out the poor attendance or upchucking.

"I screwed up, which is nothing new." Such a fine line between self-deprecation and self-pity.

"So, you puked. Don't let it ruin your life." She swigged deep from her Guinness, leaving the outline of a frothy beer mustache on her top lip.

I crumpled my napkin and dabbed away the foam.

"Thank you," she said. "Your Aunt Doris wears her facial hair attractively, but it's never been a good look for me."

"You do know how to make a boy smile."

She nodded. "I've had practice."

I laughed. "There's so much crap going on. Not just work and puking."

"Do tell." She leaned back to make room as our food was delivered. "I assume you're talking about the English teacher?"

"Two more beers," I said to the departing waitress. I searched my grandmother's face for signs of disgust and saw none. "Will told you?"

"Don't be mad at him," she commanded. "You're not the only one who needs support."

"I'm not mad, I'm embarrassed. What I did was awful. The way it turned out was even worse." She quietly mixed the rice and curried chicken, leaving the floor open for me to lay it all out. "Will thinks the meet-up with John Morgan was coincidence, but it wasn't."

"I'm not sure he thinks that," she said between bites. "But he wants to believe you."

I sipped my beer and pushed my plate away. Telling the truth was a relief, and now that I'd committed to it, the curry could wait. "Do you remember him from the book party?"

"Sure I do. He was handsome."

"Well, I sent him an e-mail to thank him for coming that night. We had a flirty little exchange and, somehow, I manipulated that into a hookup at the Peabody."

"Sounds seedy." She didn't look up from her meal.

"It does, but it seemed innocent enough at first."

"It wasn't," she said. My food cooled as she worked unimpeded on the Indian dish. "Can you pass the naan?"

I handed her the bread and rushed to the story's ending, imagining her empathy would kick in when she heard about the awkward touching and the teacher's creepy threesome reference. "The guy was an asshole. Really awful," I reiterated. "I left after fifteen minutes."

"So, everything turned out for the best," she said.

"I'm sorry?"

"It turned out for the best." She paused and looked up from her plate. "Because fucking him would have been worse."

The waitress checked in, and June declined another beer but complimented her on the rich flavor of the curry. I asked for another Guinness and a to-go box. I'd done most of the talking, and June had done what she does best. She'd listened without judgment and then told the truth with no malice and no mercy.

We had a few minutes to kill before heading to the airport, so we crossed the street to Vinoy Park and sat on a bench overlooking the bay. June put her arm through mine and rested it there, which surprised me since she was usually averse to public displays of grandmotherly affection.

"Sitting here staring at the bay reminds me of my years in Monterey," she said. I'd heard stories of June's wild days in California. She'd worked in a posh boutique hotel in an artist community, where she managed to meet several writers and famous people.

"The good old days?" I asked.

"Some of them."

"Did you really meet Steinbeck?"

"I did. And Henry Miller. Met them both. They were hotel regulars."

"Incredible. Like being part of history."

"When I started at the hotel, it was 1952. The same year I divorced Jerry." To ensure a clear distinction between Jerry and the countless other men she'd dated or married, she added, "He was your mother's father."

"Right."

"I was young...in transition. Jerry was fourteen years older than me. I only married him to get off the farm, but within a few months, I got pregnant. It all happened so fast, you know?"

Before I could answer, a hungry seagull landed nearby and hopped in our direction. "Goddamned rats with wings," she said, scooting toward me on the bench.

"I thought that was pigeons."

"All the same to me."

"Anyway..." I wanted to hear the rest of the story.

"Anyway, I married Jerry because he offered me an escape from my parents' farm. We grew artichokes. Big thrills, right? But Jerry was in the Navy, so I thought, maybe there's some adventure with this guy. Only, after I married him, I discovered he was past that part of his life. Jerry wanted stability and kids, and a wife on his arm at Navy functions."

"And that wasn't for you. You were no one's wife."

"For a while," she said with a laugh, "I was everyone's wife."

The curious seagull inched closer, and I didn't want him to bring a premature end to the conversation. I stood and stomped my feet in the direction of the bird, sending it fluttering away.

"You were saying," I said.

"What was I saying?" she asked. "Oh, the years in Monterey, after my first divorce. I had some crazy times and a lot of fun, but I have some regrets."

"What kind of regrets?"

"After Jerry, I was wild for a time. I had a few boyfriends, and your mother was very young. A guy would hang around, your mother would get used to him, and then he'd piss me off, and I'd move on."

"That's your big regret? You had a few boyfriends and you think that somehow fucked up Mom?"

"Your mother's not messed up," she said. "If anything, seeing the revolving door of men in my life may be the reason she's stuck it out with your father so long. He should thank me."

"He should." I kissed her cheek and then threaded our arms together again.

"It's not about your mother, though. My big regret is for myself. For me and Jerry."

It was my turn to stay quiet and let my grandmother lay it all out.

"I left him for the wrong reasons," she said. "Jerry was a good husband and father, but something inside me was unfulfilled, and I wasn't mature enough to deal with it. I wasted years trying to find answers in men before I figured out what I needed had nothing to do with them."

Her tone turned solemn. I regretted having encouraged her to relive such a painful period. "You said it yourself, June. You married Jerry to get away from home, you got pregnant, you got divorced, and you lived on the wild side for a while. All that before you were even thirty years old."

It hurt to think my grandmother's past still haunted her. I offered a final consolation. "We all make bad decisions when we're young."

"It's true." She smiled and touched my face. "But we're older now, aren't we?"

NINE

OTHER THAN DRUGS, the one thing I took from my year of sessions with Howard was the ability to recognize when I was falling and my parachute wasn't opening. He dissected my psyche like a corpse on an autopsy table. Rampant growths of doubt and despair had grown from the damaged cells of my messy boyhood. They spread like cancer, expanding silently inside me and lying dormant but deadly until triggered by some outside force. Everyone gets sad, he'd said, but for some people, the down cycles of life sometimes spin out of control. The trick was to recognize the inevitable oncoming downward spiral. Thinking about my sadness like that, like science, helped for a while. But downward spirals have two truly problematic properties: (1) Downward spiraling objects gain momentum as they fall, and moderately applied opposing forces don't always reverse an object's course. (2) Downward spiraling objects travel fast, and it may not take long for an object to hit bottom.

I WAS NOT a practicing Christian, or even an out-of-practice Christian, actually. I was a recovering Catholic turned atheist, and Will was a Buddhist, which I think made him technically an atheist too. Still, Will always liked Christmas. He'd always believed it was important to take time out for meaningful reflection, reverential moments of gratitude, and shit like that. Though I complained about this time of year, I was grateful for a few things about the holidays too. Like how, with all the celebration and revelry, you could be drunk a lot and not draw so much attention.

Decembers always exhausted me, but this year's demands of working, promoting my book, and generally trying not to fuck up really wore me down. I turned down invitations to parties. I disappeared when it was time to decorate the tree Will brought home. And I sure as hell didn't feel like shopping. I called my mom and told her I was too empty, both financially and emotionally, to buy any gifts. I wanted to ask Will if we could skip the present exchange, but waking up Christmas morning with nothing under the tree seemed too Scrooge-like, even for me. I worked in a mall, after all. It's not like I had to travel far to pick up a few trinkets to remind Will I was worth keeping.

Will and I set aside a Friday evening to accomplish our individual shopping, divvying up malls and department stores to ensure we didn't run into each other mid-purchase. I called dibs on Westshore, the mall where I worked, and nearby International Plaza. Will had the rest of the town.

I didn't need to shower Will with expensive gifts. He wouldn't like that anyway. I planned to buy a few stocking stuffers and, in light of what I'd put him through in recent months, one truly thoughtful gift that conveyed the depth of my love.

There are few exercises in the complete catalog of human undertakings that are less enjoyable than shopping for the "perfect gift," particularly when you've had your head up your ass the entire time you should have been thinking about your options. Rather than set about wandering forlorn and empty-headed among the bustling crowds, I stopped to think—at the one place in our mall that offered a full bar. I sat at a high-top table in the upscale Italian restaurant and ordered an appetizer and a vodka martini, a drink which made it hard for even the most miserly bartender to screw you on alcohol content.

I jotted down a few gift ideas. An iTunes gift card was a dependable, if predictable, gift-giving staple. Will collected old movies, but with the exception of the latest "high-octane thrill ride," DVDs were getting harder to find. He wasn't a clothes whore, and he never wore cologne or jewelry. Will was a simple, earthy boyfriend, like an old gay farmer. Too bad I'd already given him the Winnie the Pooh and Eeyore garden figures I'd bought at Disney. He deserved something unique and personal this Christmas. Maybe a piece of artwork he'd connect with, an antique Buddha—or, better yet, a framed piece of poetry, something I wrote, an original just for him.

My food arrived, and I finished half the appetizer and a second martini. I stared at the scrawl of uninspired gift ideas as I sipped my third cocktail, and by the time I downed a fourth drink, I'd sworn off list-making. I would trust the divinity of the universe to provide any other guidance I needed (which is the exact sentiment that makes "perfect gift" shopping feel like the burning pit of hell).

I don't say this often, but I should have had another drink, maybe even two more. Another half an hour in that bar and I would not have failed myself and devastated Will.

THE MARTINIS BUZZED in my brain. I drifted in and out of random stores, waiting in vain for the flash of inspiration that never hit. I eventually found myself inside FAO Schwartz staring at a ten-foot tall giraffe and wondering who would pay $1200 for a stuffed animal. More importantly, I wondered what a kid would do with this monstrosity in a year when she moved on to nail polish and boy bands.

That's when I saw him.

Through the window of the toy store into the mall, peering through the outstretched arms of a $900 gorilla that hung from the ceiling, I saw him. He faced away from me at a coffee kiosk in the middle of the mall, and though years had passed, I knew from his hair, from the shape of his body, from the swagger, it was him. I made a decision in an instant, which, in retrospect, scarcely felt like a choice at all. He walked away from the coffee stand. Alone, I noted. I bolted from the store, nearly taking out a tall wooden display of stuffed cackling birds in my hasty exit. Funny, in the second that I made or didn't make a decision, I never noticed the meteoric acceleration of the downward spiral.

When we first broke up, I'd kept a fire burning for Paul longer than I should have and he was more than happy to stoke the flame. After enough heart-wrenching bouts of makeup sex, though, I wised up and finally recognized that each encounter only left me more broken than the last. Since then, I had done everything in my power to ensure we never met. But even cities as large as Tampa, even miles of piled-up interstate traffic and acres of sprawling suburbs and strip malls, can't deter the spiteful hand of fate.

Paul and Will were different, so *not* two peas in a pod. My attraction to Will began with his charm and boyish handsomeness. His disarming smile and authenticity. His realness. With Will, what you see is what you get.

With Paul, the first thing I noticed was his shoulders, how broad and stout they were, how sturdy he was. His square jaw and the clean lines of his body. His kind brown eyes drew me in further. With Paul, something bubbled below the surface, something primal.

Will smiled, Paul grinned. Will warmed, Paul smoldered. I felt good when *I was with Will, I felt good* because *I was with Paul.*

I followed him from a distance, admiring a fashion sense he had that neither Will nor I possessed. Though his naked body was immaculate, Paul looked just as sexy with clothes on as he did without them. Tonight, he had dressed things up, sporting tight jeans, a gray V-neck, and a dark blazer with sleeves pushed up as though he was ready to get down to business. He wore his sandy brown hair parted on the side and swept at an angle across his forehead, in a way that left you perpetually expecting a wink and a coy smile.

I caught up to him when he stopped to glance in the display window at Things Remembered; a coincidence, I swear. I leaned over his shoulder and whispered hello. When he turned to face me, his eyes opened wide, and he wrapped me in a long and powerful hug. As he held me, I couldn't help but envision the bulging biceps beneath the jacket.

We each stepped back and took stock of the other. I smiled and shook my head in disbelief at how little he'd changed. I told him so, and he replied in kind. We made small talk for a few minutes, which I suspected felt more casual to him than it did to me.

I soon realized our position at the entrance to the store was hindering scores of nine-year-olds from picking up their engraved "World's Best Dad" key chains.

"If you have time for a drink," I said, "the Italian place here in the mall makes a mean martini."

"Cool." Then he flashed the grin that had first slain me so many years ago.

TIME STOOD STILL as we downed cocktails and caught up on the details, intimate and otherwise, of each other's lives. I told him about Will, the comfortable riverfront condo we'd bought, and my book. He told me about the boyfriends he'd had after we broke up, none of whom lasted longer than a year. He was dating no one now, a significant change for someone who sucked at being alone. Though he was a few years older than me, Paul had needed to mature, and he did. He'd even bought a house.

His striking appearance and fit body made it easy for Paul to find lovers, but he depended on the presence of others to make him feel whole. He knew he looked good, and he used that to his advantage, but he also needed to be loved. As confident and alluring as Paul was on the outside, he was insecure on the inside, as so many beautiful people are.

"You should see the house," he said.

"I'm happy for you, Patrick." I smiled and raised my glass to toast his accomplishment.

"Who?"

Jesus Christ. "Sorry. I had a couple of drinks before I ran into you tonight. Patrick was my cousin."

"Why don't you come over?" he asked, brushing off the slip-up. "Seriously, I've shopped my ass off, and I'm done for the day." Even through the dense vodka fog, I saw the danger surrounding the idea; an unnecessary risk at best.

"Sounds good." I ignored the chorus of inner voices that begged me to decline.

We left the mall in my car, so engaged in conversation, which is to say so turned on, that we couldn't stand the thought of driving separately and losing our momentum. After a quick beer stop, we pulled into the driveway of a modest South Tampa house. The furniture and decor were simple but elegant, not the odd mix of contemporary gay life and man-cave I expected, and he'd accessorized the living room with little more than a couple of bonsai plants and an unframed Asian watercolor. I was drawn to a two-shelf bookcase I spied, and I stooped and scanned each title, an urge book lovers find irresistible when entering someone's home for the first time. Windows to the soul, and all that. Paul had filled the shelves with celebrity and sports biographies, some self-help titles, and a handful of literary classics, which I assumed were as much for decoration as anything else. At the end of the bottom shelf was *Luck of the Irish*.

"You have a copy of my book."

"Of course I do."

"You played dumb when I mentioned it at the restaurant."

"Because you seemed so excited to tell me about it," he said. "I like that."

"I was just rambling."

"Well, you're cute when you ramble."

The palpable attraction between us had been forcibly submerged years ago, but held under water did not mean drowned. That's why I stayed away. With Paul in sight, though, his body within my reach, my desire rocketed to the surface. Later, I could blame the encounter on vodka or fate or nature. Will, quite rightly, would blame it on me.

He lit candles and put on the Cowboy Junkies before settling on the couch next to me. I looked at him with longing, he looked at me for approval—that much hadn't changed.

"Your place is beautiful."

"Yeah." He beamed. "I needed to do this, to live on my own a while. It's been good."

"I hate to say I told ya so..." I smiled.

"But you will. I know you will," he replied with a grin.

A quiet moment passed before he kissed me. As our lips parted, he pulled back and stared into my eyes, wondering, maybe, if I felt it too. We exchanged no words but slid closer, letting our lips meet again, this time for a longer, slower kiss. Tongues entwined. He caressed my cheek with his fingertips. I touched his face with my hands and then let them slide down the familiar path to his neck and shoulders and chest. The feel of Paul's body ignited a fire inside me that lit my way like a beacon, irresistible flames that torched the anguish inside me to cinders.

Our bodies responded. Our embrace became frantic, our movements instinctual. Heartbeats and friction, hands wandering places they shouldn't go. We said little, though our eyes and hands spoke volumes.

"This feels so familiar, so natural." His words carried a sincerity I hadn't heard from him before. My gaze fixed on his waist and moved up his body to his powerful chest, his thick neck, his soft eyes.

"I wish I could freeze this moment." I leaned in this time, my lips seeking his. "I want this so badly," I whispered, before pulling away and falling back on the couch with a thud.

"What's the matter?" he asked.

"This can't work for me the way it works for you." I rubbed my face, as though waking from a dream. "I'm a fucking idiot."

In his eyes, I saw that he understood my dilemma, empathized even, but he made no move to alter or end the intimacy. His silence urged me onward.

"I can't stop thinking of Will," I said. "And not because I feel guilty. I do, but it's more than that." Caressing Paul's thigh, I whispered, "He's right for me, and this is wrong."

Paul stiffened with the rejection. I couldn't know where his imagination had led him, if he saw this unexpected reunion as a fated chance to close the circle. He had done the right thing, learned to live alone and to love himself so that he could better love someone else. Paul, who had always been a pretty face, had become so much more, while I had become so much less.

"I still love you," he said. "The way we ended was fucked up, but I never stopped loving you." He took my hands in his, kissed my fingers one at a time. I closed my eyes and tilted my head back as the memories flooded my body and mind. He climbed on my lap, straddling me, interlocking our fingers and kissing my neck.

If it was only a question of control, I might have avoided the incident that would cost me the trust of the man I loved more than anything. But things are never that simple. It was not just desire, the lust Aunt Doris sees in the hearts of men, but a lifetime of unworthiness in need of repair.

He unbuttoned my shirt and kissed down my body to my nipples and stomach. What I once thought was love for Paul, I recognized all over. I was consumed by fondness, driven by a powerful engine of desire. He took off his shirt, and I touched his smooth, flat stomach. His toned pecs and biceps heightened my excitement. We stood and embraced for a long moment, our bare chests pressing together.

He took my hand and led me to the bedroom, where we cast off our remaining clothes like they were on fire. He lay me down on top of the covers and crawled onto the bed, taking my erect dick into his mouth. My mind exploded in a spastic flurry, and my head fell back into the soft pillow as I let go.

AN HOUR LATER, we lay naked in Paul's bed. With everything said and all the deeds done, I cried. Paul did the right things to comfort me, kissing my tears and stroking my hair, holding my hand and telling me everything would be okay. I wanted it to be true, even as regrets mounted around me like a fortress. I kissed his mouth and looked into his eyes, my mind empty of all thoughts but one—Will was right for me, even if I was wrong for him.

The burden of guilt I carried was immediate and heavy, but it was fear that hit me like a fist in the mouth. Fear of life without Will. For a moment, I imagined Paul and me together in a parallel universe where Will didn't exist, and as quickly as the idea surfaced, I banished it. There was no world without Will, not one I wanted to live in.

We shared a few awkward moments before the intimate cuddling that follows sex gave way to my burning need to get the hell out of there. I drove him back to the parking garage at Westshore, and for the first time since we met, when we kissed, it felt like good-bye. As his tail lights disappeared around a corner, I closed my eyes and saw not Paul, but Will, his sad, boyish face a reflection of the painful collision of hope and doubt. My breathing grew shallow as he mouthed two words in slow motion. *Total honesty.*

TEN

I PULLED OUT of the empty parking structure, but couldn't turn the steering wheel in the direction of home. I drove behind the mall to a remote corner of the parking lot that overlooked the north runway of nearby Tampa International, where I'd said good-bye to my grandmother a few days before. Planes came and went as I sat in silence, searching for courage and a few deep breaths. A Delta 737 floated softly onto the runaway in the distance, and I counted the windows on the plane. Thirty windows, each representing one row, each row containing six seats. A full flight of one hundred and eighty passengers, each of whom had likely done less than me to make his own life miserable.

I drove home. Once inside, I crept quietly through the house to the hall bathroom, where I'd stashed the expired meds behind a stack of guest towels. I grabbed two Xanax and swallowed them with a splash of water from the sink.

Since Will hadn't taken time out from his Christmas shopping to have sex with an old boyfriend, he'd been home long before me. It was after midnight, but in the era of twenty-four-hour Target stores, he gave me the benefit of the doubt and didn't ask where I'd been. He was propped up in bed reading Thich Nhat Hahn's *Peace Is Every Step*. Maybe not every step.

I wanted to tell him the truth, all of it. How innocently the night had started, how well-intentioned I'd been. How I'd wandered stores and looked for gifts, minding my own business and browsing displays, until I glimpsed Paul through a toy store window. How we'd made casual conversation at the entrance to Things Remembered, and then shared a few drinks. How I'd talked all about my life with Will and how right we were together, and how that had somehow turned into betrayal.

I crawled under the covers beside him and played out the ludicrous conversation in my head.

"You bought me a new leather journal for Christmas? How ironic. I was going to write you a poem, but I got distracted and sucked my ex-boyfriend's dick instead."

A seedy gay *Gift of the Magi.*

Total honesty. But all that would come from admitting everything to Will was my relief at his expense. I had committed to telling him the truth, the whole truth, but total honesty didn't have to mean immediate honesty. There would be consequences.

He set the book on the nightstand and took off the nerdy black-framed glasses he wore for reading. He was adorable. "How was your night?"

"Mediocre," I said. "Didn't think you'd still be awake."

"I probably shouldn't be," he said, "but it's not a school night."

"Right, weekend. I can't keep up anymore."

"Tomorrow's Saturday," he said. "Comes after Friday each week."

"Fuck you."

"Wow, testy. Did a mean old lady snatch the last Oster rechargeable wine opener before you could buy it for me?"

"Sorry, long day. Thanks for the subtle hint, though."

"I'm helpful that way." He curled up next to me, resting his head on the edge of my pillow. "Did you finish your shopping?"

"Not even close." I kissed his forehead and rolled over to face the wall, hoping to put enough distance between us to hide the stench of my lust and guilt.

"What's left? Want me to pick stuff up this weekend?"

"Nah," I said. "This is all shit I have to do myself."

THE PHYSICAL SIDE EFFECTS of my daily pill regimen had mostly subsided, so I upped my dosage of both Xanax and Prozac in hopes of dulling myself enough to make it through Christmas. If Prozac had improved my mood, it wasn't apparent to me, and since no one else knew I was taking outdated anti-depressants, second opinions weren't available. It's hard to distinguish between subtle shifts in emotional stability and the quiet bubbling beneath the surface of an impending meltdown.

The bookstore was swamped with truckloads of merchandise and swarming masses of anxious holiday shoppers, and the twenty temps I'd hired to deal with the melee weren't enough. First day no-shows and second-week resignations left us shorthanded, and a mid-December dropout significantly amped up my stress levels. Every year, at least one shithead swore in the interview he'd be there until the doors are locked on

Christmas Eve, and then, when he'd made enough money to finish his Christmas shopping, he suddenly had an ailing out-of-state grandparent to visit.

"Sorry, but I have to spend one more Christmas with PeePaw before he dies."

"Of course, you do. Merry Christmas." Dick.

I liked Aaron, the nouveau-hippie college kid who'd come over on Thanksgiving, which is one of the reasons firing him sucked. College students are a good fit for bookstores, as long as they're reasonably committed to their schedules. That's where Aaron screwed up. I had painstakingly sewed together a delicate patchwork of schedules, and Aaron shit all over my pretty little quilt.

If I hadn't been in the middle of a stretch of thirteen-hour workdays and didn't have thirty-six copies of *Luck of the Irish* to deliver to three local stores that day, Aaron's monkey wrench might not have ground my gears so badly. If I hadn't also nearly fucked my high school English teacher and actually fucked an ex-boyfriend, I might have been in a better place to hear the news. If I hadn't vomited in the trash can next to my desk two minutes earlier, I probably wouldn't have been a pale, sweaty mess when he entered my office.

"Seriously, Conor. I'm so sorry." He sounded sincere, but I didn't care. "If I knew my parents were going to send me a plane ticket home, if I knew that, dude, I would have told you. For real. Totally would have told you if I knew."

"If, if, if," I said. "If *ifs* and *buts* were candy and nuts, we'd all have a Merry Christmas, right?" He wrinkled his brow, the outdated reference sailing past him. "Never mind."

"I can see you're not in a good place." He glanced at a puked-on paper wad in the trash. "But hey, they sent me a ticket, so I gotta go. I'll totally be here today and tomorrow, though, and I'll be back right after New Year's."

"Oh, you will?" I swigged from a Mountain Dew bottle to wash the acid taste from my mouth. "Dude." I spat the word. "Dude, you made a commitment, and now you're breaking it and fucking me in the ass at the worst possible time. Why would I want you back?"

"Hey, I said I was sorry. And I do appreciate what you've done for me, so there's no reason to get like that." He was right, it wasn't personal. A rational person could surmise that and move ahead, but reasonable Conor had left the building.

"I expect some asshole to disappear every December right when I need them most, but I never thought it would be the same kid I was kind enough to invite to my house for Thanksgiving." I couldn't change things, but applying a dose of guilt satisfied me.

"Thanksgiving was cool, Conor. Never expected to chill at my boss's house, smoking weed with his granny and his boyfriend." He hadn't sounded threatening, but the notion of blackmail was now on the table.

"Clean out your locker and get the fuck out of here."

"You're seriously firing me?"

"You bet your ass I am." I picked up a pen and shuffled papers around my desk, as though something more important had come up.

"You're a bigger asshole than I ever knew," he said, backing out of the tiny office and giving me the finger.

"And you're a more ungrateful prick than I ever knew," I yelled after him. "Merry Christmas, you fucking fuck."

Even effective swearing disappears once you've stepped off the ledge.

I LEFT WORK early, communicating nothing to my staff about Aaron beyond the need to replace him on the schedule. I wanted to curl up with a fistful of tranquilizers and a bottle of vodka, but I still had copies of *Luck of the Irish* to deliver. I managed quick stops at two bookshops and made a promise to a third store to drop off books before the weekend.

Being home alone in the middle of a work day was oddly exhilarating. Like I was in tenth grade again, ditching chemistry to sneak a drink under the bleachers with my friends. I shed my work clothes and put on shorts and a ratty Smiths T-shirt that had once been Will's. I popped a couple of Xanax and grabbed a bottle of Grey Goose from the freezer. By the time Will came home from work, I had put a sizable dent in it. He stepped out onto the patio and surveyed the table, noting my glass and the half-empty bottle. "You're home early."

"Another banner day," I said. "Wanna drink?"

"I'm good. Are you?"

The simplest questions often elicit the most profound responses. This was not one of those times.

"I'm good too," I assured him. "Why wouldn't I be?"

"Home from work early, daytime drinking, not much to say? Two of those things aren't like you." He smiled, hoping his charm might wear me down.

The fire in my veins died down a little, but I stayed silent, gripping my rage like the proverbial hot Buddhist coal.

"I'm hopping in the shower," he said. "Try not to finish that bottle before I get out." After years together, Will knew how hard to push and when to let up.

He emerged from the bedroom showered and clean-shaven, something neither his landscaping job nor his boyish face usually required. He wore worn jeans, a tight, white T-shirt, and bare feet, the iconic anti-fashion look that sends gay men everywhere swooning. Our sex life had evaporated since John Morgan, and I wondered if he was sending a subtle message about the evening ahead. Or maybe he was simply hoping to cheer me up. I appreciated the effort either way, though it sparked a fresh wave of guilt.

He picked up the bottle of Grey Goose and eyed it to gauge my progress. "Have you thought about dinner?" he asked.

"No." I sipped the icy vodka from one of the oversized highball glasses Ariel had given me. From the patio, I watched through the open sliding glass door as Will rifled through the pantry and refrigerator looking for dinner options.

"You look sexy," I said, the vodka asserting its influence.

"Thanks. You look...intoxicated?"

"I'm not drunk. Come here."

He stepped out to the patio and sat across from me, leaning his elbows on the clear glass tabletop. "Chicken for dinner."

"I fired Aaron today."

"Wow," he said, pushing himself back from the table as though it had cut him. "Where did that come from?"

I shrugged.

"The kid from Thanksgiving?" he asked. "That Aaron?"

I nodded.

"That's awful. What did he do?"

"He pissed me off."

"Obviously. Did he steal or come to work high or something?"

"Nothing like that." My eyes grew wet. I gripped the highball glass, as though I were over a cliff and it was the end of my rope.

"What the hell happened?" He stood, moved behind me, and rested his hands on my shoulders. I had fired employees in the past, but none had affected me like this.

The glass shook in my hands, and my voice quavered as I told him about the confrontation with Aaron. The tiny hole in the dam soon gave way to tears and then to heaving, convulsive sobs. I buried my head in my arms and wailed like an animal. I cried for my weakness, my wrongness, my fucked-up-ness, and for the devastating mistakes that had begun to define me. I wept because I hadn't been true and because the cost of broken promises is high. A cold sweat set in and an ocean of acid churned in my stomach, foreshadowing the retching I feared would come next.

Will brought me a box of tissues and a glass of ice water. "You can be an asshole sometimes, and that kid definitely had a butt-kicking coming, but there's something else. I haven't seen you like this in years."

I blew my nose and gulped the cold water. "Shit builds up, you know?"

"What shit?"

"*My* shit. The job, Christmas, the stupid fucking book. I puked at my own book signing, for fuck's sake." I paused long enough to see that Will was listening, and waiting. "And John Morgan."

"Okay," he said. "Do you have something else to add to that story?"

Confused at first, I quickly realized his concern. "No, no. You know everything there is to know about that." Though not everything about the one before that, or the one after. I could have unloaded all of it, but neither of us was ready.

"So all this shit has been weighing you down?" he asked.

"Did you know Patrick killed himself in December?"

"You've mentioned it before, but I'd forgotten."

"A week before Christmas." And a few months after the shit hit the fan. Howard says I was just a kid.

"Jesus Christ."

"The reason for the season, right?"

He leaned down and encircled my neck in his arms. "You know you can talk to me."

"I went to see Howard," I said. "The shrink."

"Good. You need to get out of your own head."

"It sucked. Nothing but bad memories. I went once, but I'm not going back."

"Maybe you should see a different therapist."

"Oh, I have been. I see Dr. Prozac every day and Nurse Xanax every night."

"Seriously?" He didn't raise his voice, but the gravity in his tone betrayed his annoyance.

"It's nothing. I started back on my meds a couple of weeks ago."

"When Howard prescribed these drugs, did he mention you might not want to mix them with alcohol?"

"Howard didn't prescribe these. Well, he did, but it was years ago. These are leftovers from the first go around."

"You're taking outdated anti-depressants and drinking like this?" He backed away from me.

"Yep." I needed to rebuild the walls he'd scaled before he stumbled on my cache of secrets. "I started feeling *dee*-pressed, so I took an anti-*dee*-pressant."

Will refused to be drawn into battle. He took a deep breath and stared at the stucco ceiling as though he might find answers written there. "There is a reason why pharmaceutical commercials say consult your physician if you think these drugs might be right for you."

"I did consult a doctor—in 2003."

"I can't tell you what to do, but I can connect a few dots for you." He spoke with clinical precision, angry, but in total control of it. "You've had a rough couple of months, and you've made some mistakes. You felt yourself slipping, and, in desperation, you turned to some old medications. I don't blame you for that." He paused and took a sip from my water glass.

"Please, continue," I said, as though he were proposing a new hypothesis on string theory.

"You've been edgy as fuck for weeks, and you barf at the drop of a hat."

I stared at him, hands folded in my lap, emotionless and disengaged.

"I care about you, Conor. I want you to stop taking the fucking pills and see a professional who can help you do this right."

"Okay." I looked away, not agreeing to any specific course of action.

"If you won't stop taking them, at least stop drinking. That's all I'm saying."

"That's all?"

"No," he said. "There's one more thing. Total honesty...is there someone else?"

I looked into his eyes. "Total honesty," I repeated. "No."

AFTER A NEAR silent dinner, Will cleaned the kitchen and went to bed early. I returned to the patio with only my overburdened conscience and trusty Grey Goose to keep me company. I stuck with the same recipe I'd used all day—pour a two-shot jigger over ice, seek solace, repeat. Around midnight, I held the bottle upside down and shook out the last few drops.

I stood and staggered across the patio, only instead of going inside to crawl in bed beside Will, I stumbled out the patio gate toward the river. There was no path across the lawn that lay between me and the river, but the terrain was flat and grassy, and my trek was unobstructed.

Alligators lived close to residential areas all over Florida, and Will and I had seen them swimming in the Hillsborough several times. Once we'd even seen a seven- or eight-footer sunning itself on the bank. Gators are impressive and daunting creatures, but they only cause trouble when they're hungry. Of course, it's hard to predict when that might be, so it's generally best not to let small children and Yorkies wander too near a body of fresh water in Florida.

As I approached the river's edge, my bloodshot eyes struggled to adjust to the brilliant light of a nearly full moon reflecting off the smooth surface of the water. I didn't know how cold the Hillsborough ran in Florida in December, but as the day had been warm and the night air was still comfortable, I imagined it couldn't be too intolerable. I kicked off my shoes and then pulled off my jeans and shirt and tossed them on to the dewy grass. Clad in only my boxers, I inched down the embankment to the water's edge and dipped my toes.

Near our part of the Hillsborough, the riverbed is gently sloped, without steep declines or sharp drop-offs, or so I told myself as I waded into the river. I had never been in the river, and I expected the bottom to be rocky. Instead, I felt thick, soft mud ooze beneath my feet and fill the spaces between my toes. A few steps further, and I sank up to my knees in the muck. The dark, cold river water rose up my legs and nipped at the bottom of my boxers. As I attempted another step, my feet refused to cooperate. Drunk and delirious, I chuckled at this curious and unexpected development. I strained to pick up one foot, and then the other, but the suction of the squishy riverbed refused to let me go. Lifting straight up with all my might, I pulled at my right leg, and then at my left, but each forceful tug only cemented my position.

Despite the Xanax and vodka coursing through my bloodstream, the chilly black water lapping at my testicles sobered me a little, and the absurd humor of the situation faded with my buzz. I took a panoramic survey of my surroundings and saw darkness in the houses across the river, only a few lights in the distant condos behind me. Not that I would have yelled for help, but it would have been nice to know someone was listening if I did.

With the moonlight illuminating the river around me, it occurred to me for the first time to look for the telltale break at the surface of the water that was made by both the long snout and powerful tail of alligators in motion. I saw nothing, but the idea of seeing something ratcheted my anxiety up significantly. I scanned the riverbanks as far as I could see, looking for large, dark masses or signs of movement. A lawn care company maintained the riverbanks, keeping them clear of tall grass, branches, and other debris. Thankfully, as far as I could tell, they were also clear of carnivorous reptiles.

Having drunk all afternoon and evening, it was an inconvenience, though not a surprise, when I realized I had to pee. I was mid-stream, no pun intended, with penis in hand and boxers pulled slightly down, when I heard the splash. I can't say for sure it was the sound of a gator entering the river, but it wasn't likely an unseen fat kid doing cannonballs off a boat dock in the middle of the night. If I had been wearing pants and hadn't already been urinating, I would have pissed myself.

My inclination was to wave my hands and scream for help, but I feared the neighbors wouldn't be the first to heed my flailing and splashing. With as little noise or disturbance as possible, I tried again to lift my legs, pulling straight up with every bit of force I had. First one leg, then the other, but I made no progress. As I reevaluated my options, I scanned the surface of the water once more for any sign of movement. There were no waves, no ripples, no wakes, which in my mind meant a stealthy underwater attack was imminent.

Fearful and desperate, I attempted a new tactic—I bent at the knees and leaped as hard as I could, hoping to somehow free both feet at the same time. The jump took me nowhere, though it did cause me to lose my balance and plummet headfirst into the water. To my drunken delight, the forward motion from my near-fall also loosened the mud's hold on me. If falling forward worked, falling backward might help too. I heaved and lurched, forward and backward, and as I felt the mud give, I leaned harder and faster in every direction, bobbing on the water like a windblown buoy.

I pulled myself out of the murky river, and, still unsure of the origin of the splash I'd heard, I grabbed my clothes and scrambled up the grassy bank. I was halfway across the lawn when I tripped on a sprinkler head and took a header into the grass. Short of breath but out of danger, if there ever was any, I rolled onto my back. My heart pounded in my chest as I envisioned the grisly fate I could have brought on myself. With wet boxers clinging to my otherwise naked body, and my clothes and shoes scattered around me on the lawn, I lay there and wept.

I never wanted to be a bad person, I really didn't. But having lied, almost cheated, lied more, puked in public, self-medicated, actually cheated, puked some more, fired a nice kid, and lied again, all in the span of two months, I had to admit the evidence pointed in that direction.

I wasn't making excuses, and I knew there's always bullshit in families, but I'd been through more than my fair share. My father wasn't as bad as Seamus. He didn't beat me, but he was a stupid, drunk son-of-a-bitch for the first few years of my life. My mother was sane and sober, which makes it all the worse that she chose my alcoholic father over me. She pushed me off on Aunt Doris and Uncle Martin like an unwanted Christmas fruitcake. Knowing your parents gave you up stings, I couldn't lie about that (although, clearly, I could lie about plenty of other things), but Aunt Doris loved me like I was her own son—until she stopped loving us both. But hey, kids get fucked over all the time, right? Shipped back and forth between incompetent adults? *Grow up and quit your bitching, Conor, it happens.*

It does happen, and it fucks kids up. And fucked-up kids grow up to be fucked-up adults.

That's when it hit me. As I stretched out in the thick, wet grass looking up at Orion's Belt, the Dippers, and some other starry shit I could barely make out, June's words came rushing back.

"We're older now, aren't we...?"

I ran dripping wet across the lawn, wiping my muddy feet on the grass before I reached our patio gate. I raced to the kitchen, grabbed a block of notepaper and a pen, and scribbled my epiphany on the small, blank page.

I am older now, no longer a damaged child.

Everything is on the line, and I must deliver.
I will get my shit together and make amends.
I will stop taking pills and I will control my cock,
I will face my demons and stop sabotaging my life.

I read and reread the words, relishing the clarity of my sacred new mantra, the outline of a life-affirming strategy, boiled down to a Post-it note.

I showered and slid into bed beside Will, my head still spinning as it hit the pillow. I closed my eyes and saw a huge drive-in movie screen. A staticky speaker crackled in my ear as my words scrolled across the screen in an endless loop. The charter was hopeful, aspirational even, but I couldn't escape the nagging feeling that something was missing. I rolled onto my side and, as I put my arm around Will, the glaring omission crystallized at the bottom of the screen—*I will tell Will that I had sex with Paul.*

ELEVEN

I WAS HUNGOVER the next morning at work, but energized by the idea of finding a way out of the deep hole I'd spent my life digging. I closed my office door and took the crinkled slip of paper from my pocket. I scanned the nearly illegible scribbles, mouthing the words silently as I read them. Leaving my childhood bullshit behind, righting my wrongs, moving ahead with life. It all made sense. I typed each line into my computer, scrunching the font and squeezing the words into one corner of the page, and then I printed and laminated my manifesto. I admired my handiwork and even smiled a little, relieved by the notion that this durable pocket-sized reminder of one night in a river might actually change me. I tucked the plastic card into my pocket and stashed the handwritten notes in my wallet, for reference, or framing, or I don't fucking know what.

I wanted to be a more decent man. I'd pissed and moaned enough about my shitty childhood. All parents make mistakes, and kids get fucked over all the time. My parents passed me around like herpes, and that's nothing compared to the shit Patrick had to deal with. But I'm a grown man now, and Patrick's dead.

Becoming a worthwhile human isn't as easy as it should be, though, and as I began to act on the steps in my miniature manifesto, some parts of the plan proved more difficult than others. Since puking was the only change in my behavior I could tie directly to Prozac, giving up the antidepressant was cake. Cutting out Xanax was a bigger ask. In the absence of other ways to douse the neurons that crackled through my brain like fireworks, I continued to sneak a couple of pills each night so I could sleep.

I wanted to talk to Aaron, but the kid was gone to North Carolina for Christmas so making things right with him would have to wait. Apologizing for being a dick and re-hiring him wasn't just the right thing to do, it was the prudent thing. Aaron didn't seem like the type to run to Human Resources, but he was an underage college student I'd served alcohol to, while he smoked pot with my boyfriend and grandmother. Probably best to get back on his good side.

Selling *Luck of the Irish* got easier too, though that probably had more to do with the proximity of Christmas than with my fledgling efforts at self-improvement. I had book signings at two busy Barnes & Noble stores that were next to crowded shopping malls, and the stream of desperate shoppers proved to be easy marks. I sold half the stock the publisher had fronted me, and, more importantly, I puked on no one.

The item I hadn't officially added to my to-do list, confessing to Will that I'd had sex with Paul, proved to be as daunting a task as I feared it would be. Telling someone you love about the soul-crushing thing you did, the thing you most wish you hadn't done, warranted significant extra care and consideration. I truly wanted to keep my honesty promise, but a truth of that magnitude could exact a price I wasn't sure I could pay.

I strung together a couple of good days, and one evening I made it home from work in time for a sit-down dinner. Will was quiet but in a good mood, and I was calm, my thoughts crisp and clear. I felt ready. After dinner, we cleaned the kitchen and put on our favorite kids' holiday movie. We didn't snuggle but sat close and comfortable, as Christmas approached in the quaint riverside Muppet world of Frogtown Hollow.

I cleared my throat, unsure of where to begin. "Will?"

He didn't answer but placed his hand in mine. I laced my fingers with his and squeezed our hands together. In Frogtown Hollow, a boy laments his dead father and worries he'll have no money to buy a Christmas present for his mother. The boy and his mother begin to croon tenderly.

"*When the River Meets the Sea*," Will said with a soft, sweet smile. "That one always gets me."

"Yeah." I wiped a tear from the corner of my eye. "I know what you mean."

Emmett Otter's Jug Band Christmas hardly made things perfect, but a quiet evening together pushed the drama of the past few weeks a little further into the rearview mirror. The idea of a spending a quiet Christmas alone with Will should have held great appeal, and it would have, had I been able to forget that I was naked with Paul just a few days before.

I MADE PANCAKES on my day off, smiled more often, and bought Will an iPad for Christmas, which I wrapped and stashed beneath the tree with a dozen other presents I'd picked up. Through a cynic's eyes, my kind deeds and lavish gifts might appear vile and deceitful, but I wasn't trying to trick Will. I was rebuilding his confidence in us, in me, while I figured out the right thing to do.

While my conscious brain waffled on the choices that lay before me, my subconscious had a field day. I held on to powerful images of Paul and populated my dreams with them. Some were tantalizing, straightforward dreams—Paul's lithe and sinewy body reclined naked on cool marble steps as I crawled between his legs and ravished his long, hard cock. Others were more perplexing—the same marble steps scenario, only when I glanced up mid-blow job, I saw not the square jaw and tousled sandy hair of Paul, but the coal-black top hat and Amish-bearded face of Abraham Lincoln.

If my supposition was true, that the confessions of adulterers mostly served to relieve the guilty and punish the innocent, why did I wake up each morning with an overpowering desire to confess everything? Because I needed to clear my guilt-laden conscience? Because I'm a selfish prick whose weaknesses brought suffering to others? Because life isn't fair? All true, but not a complete explanation for why I decided to tell Will.

I chose to tell Will the truth because I loved him. Because the news of my unfaithfulness might lead to ruin, but the secret of my unfaithfulness ensured it. Because for much of my life I hid from the truth, or sidestepped it, but I was old enough to know by now that the only way out is through. If I wanted to start on a fresh path with Will, being truthful was the only gateway.

THE REVELATION OF my sexual liaison with Paul fell like an unseen sledgehammer. When I began the story of my chance encounter, my patient and tolerant Buddhist boyfriend did not sit quietly and wait for the narration to unfold. He erupted, shooting a blinding spray of disappointment and a deafening explosion of painful debris into the air between us. He never heard my clever musings about the callous hand of fate, nor did he see the magic of my post-coital epiphany—that moment of pristine clarity where I saw how empty my life would be without him.

To say I overestimated Will's capacity for maintaining perspective is a tragic and grotesque understatement. The Will I knew, the one I expected, usually maintained calm about *everything*. But the usual *everything* was not a supernova that vaporized his universe and left the cold, dark nothing of a black hole in its place. The usual *everything* was never really everything.

"Why are you telling me this?" he screamed.

"Because I swore I'd be honest."

"You also swore you'd stop sucking other people's dicks."

"That's not fair."

"What's not fair?" he asked, vomiting the words.

"You can't make me promise total honesty and then hate me for telling the truth," I said.

"You think I'm not being fair? Fuck you." The thin line between his pain and anger was no longer visible. "Total honesty is not the same as total amnesty. There is no amnesty."

I wanted so much to take away his pain by helping him see how the events of my life, the circumstances of our lives, led us to this place, though I was only just beginning to see it myself. If I was lucky, there would be time to hash that out later, but not now.

"I understand there's no amnesty," I said. "Only consequences."

"You're goddamn right. Tell me something, did you have sex with John Morgan too? Was that whole fucking thing a sham?"

I had not had sex with John Morgan, but I also had not told the entirety of the truth. Whether this was a cleansing by fire or a burning at the stake, I had to throw everything on the pyre. "Nothing happened with the English teacher. But since I'm being totally honest, I will tell you that meeting him at the Peabody wasn't a coincidence. I arranged it, but I realized the whole thing was wrong and nothing happened."

"So you lied when you said he just happened to be in Orlando for a fucking teacher conference?" He was not fact checking, but rubbing salt in the wound.

"Yes." There was no excuse, so I offered none.

"What else is there to tell?" he asked. "Might as well hang all your disgusting laundry on the line."

"That's it," I said.

His stare was piercing. Behind his eyes, I saw a fire that burned so hot and bright, it could only be fueled by hate, or by love.

"That's all," I assured him.

"Whatever."

"You never defined the consequences," I said, holding it together better than expected.

"What do you think the consequences should be?" The threat level in his voice had escalated beyond "danger" and now crested "imminent doom."

"I don't know, Will. That's up to you. I don't know why I did what I did, but I know this—it won't happen again. If we stay together, we won't need a stupid fucking honesty pact, because I will have nothing to hide. Ever."

"That sounds reassuring. And familiar." Sarcasm replaced disdain as his anger slipped below the boiling point.

"I was wrong," I said, "but I had to be honest. If I didn't tell you, I couldn't live with myself."

"And since you did tell me, you can't live with me." I wasn't being tossed out yet, but he was putting the option on the table.

Nothing productive would come from more conversation, but ending the argument was his call. "I love you, Will, and I'll do anything to convince you of that. I don't want our relationship to end. But, I'm fucked up." For the first time in the conversation, my voice cracked. "Something inside me is broken. I don't know what it is, but I'm figuring it out, and I'm going to fix it."

"Conor had a shitty childhood, and now he's all broken." He repeated it as though he were interpreting my sentiments for a classroom of kindergartners. "I'm glad you finally figured out what the rest of us already knew." He spoke as though I bored him, as though he'd heard it all before, because he had.

"You stuck around a long time, and you're not stupid," I said. "There must be something about me you think is worthwhile."

He rolled his eyes and exhaled loudly. "I'm sure there *was* something."

I felt the intended prick of the past tense and said nothing.

"I need space, Conor. Are we done here?"

"I don't remember if I told you already but I'm sorry."

Tears filled his eyes. "Me too."

WILL HAD MADE it clear that a life-altering decision was imminent. For the next few days, he worked things out his way, and I did the same, only from the unfamiliar comfort of our guest bedroom where my bottle of Xanax now lived openly on the bedside table. After work, I hid out in the guest room to shield myself from Will's apathetic glances and to drink away the tension from hectic days at work. I tried to reason my way through the fallout of my personal catastrophes, but honest contemplation of my failings didn't come naturally to me. After one lengthy evening of laying on the bed alternating between crying jags and juicy rationalizations, I surmised this about my infidelity: fucking Paul was a curious irony—an event that cemented my feelings for Will but shook the foundation of his feelings for me. Not much of a self-realization, but an interesting truth.

When Will announced one afternoon he was ready to talk, I suggested we drive to Clearwater Beach. Growing up in Pensacola, the beach figured into several key moments in my life. Coming out to friends, breaking up with lovers, even losing my virginity—all events where the vastness of the ocean and the infinity of the dark night sky gave me perspective. On this night, I hoped the squish of soft sand beneath my feet and the kiss of a cool evening breeze on my skin might comfort me if I needed consolation.

Will stayed quiet as we drove across the Courtney Campbell Causeway. He gave me no clues about what swirled in his head, beyond his choice of the more despondent moments from Annie Lennox's *Diva* as our soundtrack. As we headed west across the bay, the choppy water reflecting the sinking sun like a billion tiny scraps of foil, I wondered how I had let this happen, why I had risked everything that meant anything for something as common as lips and abs and blow jobs.

The beachside parking lot was empty except for an old VW bus in the far corner. I hoped we would have the beach completely to ourselves, just me, my love, and the Great Wall of China I had erected between us, but this would do. I turned off the engine but left the Annie Lennox playing.

We sat in stillness in our bucket seats as evening settled hard on the world outside. Though darkness blanketed the ocean that lay just beyond our windshield, the stars had yet to climb into the night sky. Quiet and fidgeting, we tried to figure out what to do with our hands, which for so many years had clasped without a thought. I reached my hand down to cover his, but he withdrew, shifting his body away and folding his arms, as Annie Lennox crooned on about how our trouble's only just begun.

The evening air was mild, even in December, and I needed to breathe it in, out of the car and away from the suffocating melancholy. "Do you want to get out and walk?"

"We drove all the way out here." His tone didn't bode well for an evening of listening and understanding. Adulterers were clearly more receptive to the elucidating benefits of "emotional distance" than adulterees.

We crossed the boardwalk that bridged the dunes and began a silent walk along the shore. The horizon glowed pink and purple. A steady slap of modest low-tide waves lapped at the shore a few feet away.

After a hundred yards of cold shoulder, I spoke up. "There's no point in being here if you aren't going to talk to me."

He stopped and cocked his head. "Sorry. I wasn't sure how to get started. Let's see..." His voice trailed off and then he launched on me. "How is Paul? Has he changed in the last ten years? What's he doing for work these days?" Before I could open my mouth to speak, his rant continued. "How about that dick of his? Still tasty as ever?"

"Fuck you."

"Love to, if there's any left for me."

I turned and walked a few feet away, unable to imagine anything worthwhile coming from such an auspicious beginning.

With nothing to add to his sarcastic monologue, he stared out across the black Gulf of Mexico. I kicked over the remains of a half-built sand castle. As I skimmed my bare foot through the cold, wet sand at the water's edge, an alien green glow ignited in the tiny bioluminescent creatures in the surf. A heartlight, I imagined, if they had hearts at all. I scanned the shallow, foamy water in search of answers I could give Will, but no serendipitous message in a bottle drifted to the shore.

Will inched closer and I tried again, though I was unsure how to transition from my last poignant comment. What was a reasonable follow-up to "fuck you"?

"There's a lot of those glowy things in the water tonight," I said.

I felt him next to me, staring at me, and I returned his gaze.

"You know one thing I don't like about you," he said. "Anytime there's quiet for even one second longer than you're comfortable with, you say something ridiculous to fill the space."

"Nice. Maybe if we go straight for the jugular tonight we can make some progress." He offered no reply, which I interpreted as encouragement. "Thanks for making this a personal attack."

He moved toward me until his face was inches from mine. "Did it cross your mind that your lies and adulterous cock-sucking might be a personal attack?" He spun and headed up the beach, leaving me reeling from the whipcrack of his words.

I followed him to the car and climbed into the driver's seat. "Why did we come here? Just so you could dump on me some more?"

"I thought I was finished being angry and petty," he said. "Apparently, I'm not."

"I hope you feel better." I started the car and flicked the volume knob down on the stereo.

"I do feel better, actually. A little."

I deserved whatever punishment he wanted to dole out, but the flogging was taking its toll. "What's it going to be, Will?"

"I don't know." He was serious, focused, less cavalier. "I thought I knew, but I don't. I need more time."

"Fine." I struggled to harness my frustration. "If you're going to keep raking my ass over the coals..." I stopped, realizing there was no ultimatum available for me to dish out. "Just stop, please."

I don't know if Will had intended to finish the job that night, to drag our life together into the chilly waist-high salt water and drown it, but if that had been his plan, he hadn't done it. I guess that was something.

TWELVE

FOR THE NEXT few days, I gave Will space, and like an obedient toddler, I spoke only when spoken to. When he chose to engage me, I stuck strictly to the topics he introduced. I picked up extra chores around the house and tried to be thoughtful in ways I usually wasn't. His favorite Spanish wine was back in stock at the liquor store, so I picked up two bottles and left them on the counter with a casual note. *The Marques was on sale.* It was not-so-subtle ass kissing, and he noticed the gestures, but I'd fucked up too big to buy my way out. I kept it up anyway. Even if these random acts of kindness got me nowhere, they felt like baby steps toward penance.

When he could no longer hold it inside, Will broached the subject of my infidelity, mostly in the form of earnest questions laced with bitterness. His fixation on the gory details revealed an insecurity I hadn't seen before.

"Did you plan to meet Paul that night?"

No.

"Have you cheated with Paul before?"

Never.

"Did you tell him you love him?"

I did not.

Obsessive struggling to order a chaotic world was my territory, and watching Will traverse that desperate landscape was difficult. Still, I answered each question directly and honestly. I doubt he found comfort in my replies.

He put the small puzzle pieces together, but the larger mystery remained. Why did I do it? Neither of us grew any closer to understanding what makes humans go astray, what compels us to do the awful things we know will hurt the ones we love. No one knows those answers. Or maybe they do, but the reality is just too difficult to admit. Maybe we cheat because when we peel back the layers of complex emotion and cognition, and strip away our hopes and dreams, when we are boiled down to our base and only our rotten core remains, we are nothing more than stray dogs, acting on instinct, humping as nature intended with no regard for consequences.

I CAME HOME late from a closing shift one night and found Harlan sitting on his front porch smoking a cigarette and listening to *Sweet Home Alabama* on an outdated boom box. He nodded and watched as I fiddled with my key chain in search of the house key. Before I put the key in the lock, I stopped and looked at him.

"Harlan, you know that shit is bad for you. It's bad for all of us."

"I been told, man. Cigarettes are killers."

"I was talking about Lynyrd Skynyrd."

"Ha, that's funny." He lowered the volume and took a long drag on the cigarette. "What's shakin', Mr. Conor? Been out prowlin'?"

"I'm too old for prowling," I said.

"True," he replied, noticing my khaki pants and sensible retail shoes. "Plus those ain't exactly stud clothes."

I looked the kid's outfit up and down. "Maybe Santa will bring me a confederate flag T-shirt with the sleeves cut out and a pair of camouflage cargo shorts."

"If you're lucky."

"Merry Christmas, Harlan."

"Same to you," he said, "and your old man."

IN THE DARK living room, an empty wine bottle and Will's puffy eyes told me I had missed something significant. I hoped it was something that worked in my favor.

"You okay?"

His eyes were vacant. "I'm fine."

"You look like someone just ran over your puppy."

"Don't," he said.

I tossed a throw pillow aside and sat next to him on the sofa, an intrusion into his space I hadn't allowed myself in days. "Don't talk about your puppy?"

"I'm fine," he repeated, disregarding the half-hearted attempt to make him smile. "I just got off the phone with June."

Not the direction I expected the conversation to go. "So, June's puppy died?"

He ignored the lame and awkward follow-up. "I called her to discuss our situation."

Will told June about my hookup with John Morgan even before I did, so I shouldn't have been surprised that he sought her counsel again. Still, she was *my* fucking grandmother.

"It's bad enough that my grandmother has to accept my preference for dicks. It'd be nice if you didn't call her every time I sucked one."

"Calm down. She doesn't judge you."

"Still, she's *my* grandmother."

"She's not just your grandmother. She's also my friend."

"Jesus Christ," I said. "You don't have any other friends to confide in?"

"You know I have other friends, asshole, but they don't know you like she does."

He had my attention. I was more than mildly curious about their counseling session.

"So, what did she say?"

"Some things are private."

"Forgive me for prying into a discussion of my personal life."

"Not everything is intended for public consumption."

"It's my life too."

He moved the throw pillow back into the space between us. "Fine. She said leopards don't usually change their spots."

"What the fuck does that mean?" Will disclosing my transgressions with June annoyed me, but the idea of them bonding in unity against me was crushing.

"She told me a story that didn't mean anything." He tried to put the bullet back in the gun, but the shot had already been fired.

I closed my eyes and visualized something soothing—a lemon drop martini and a half dozen Xanax. I reached into my pocket and felt the laminated card I'd carried for weeks. *I will face my demons and I will stop sabotaging my life.*

"What story did she tell?" I asked.

"She told me about her first husband."

"What about him?"

"Conor, she didn't tell me if I should stay or go. She knows that's not her place."

I fingered the manifesto in my pocket but said nothing.

"She said it didn't work out with her husband because she thought they wanted different things, but she was wrong. She should have stayed."

"She told me that story too." I breathed a sigh of relief and sent June a telepathic thank-you note.

"Don't read anything into it," he said. "And don't think I want to keep talking about this shit."

I HADN'T BEEN allowed back in our bed since the day of my confession, but on Christmas Eve, a late-night viewing of *A Christmas Story* and a bottle of Marques weakened Will. I was headed to the guest bed when he said it would be okay if I slept in our room.

"Cool." I tried to keep things breezy in the way desperate lovers do.

We crawled into bed, bodies not touching. Will fell asleep almost instantly, while I lay awake for hours with just eighteen inches and one colossal mistake in the space between us. In the last seconds before I drifted off, I slid closer. I wondered if touching Will, holding him and feeling the ebb and flow of his breath, would get me banished to the guest room. I rested my hand flat against his chest and felt his slow, steady heartbeat. I lay still as a statue, fearing the slightest movement would end my waking dream.

We woke up spooning on Christmas morning, my chest against his back, my arm draped over him. I needed a low-key Christmas, and in the hopes of finding a sense of normalcy, I suggested we attempt our usual holiday routines. We put on Christmas music and ate a quiet breakfast of pancakes and mimosas. Our interactions were hollow and mechanical at best, and our gift exchange was even worse.

"What a perfect gift!" said no one.

"What a perfect gift...if one of us hadn't sucked someone else's dick," thought everyone.

Christmas Day phone calls with loved ones, though less surreal than the gift swapping, were uncomfortable and disingenuous. Only June knew we were in trouble. With everyone else, Will and I agreed it was premature to share the news of our demise until we—or rather, Will—determined whether there would be a demise to report. After a morning of pretending, I lacked the strength to pick up the phone when Aunt Doris called just after lunch. I let the call go to voice mail.

"Merry Christmas, Conor, can't imagine where you could have gotten off to, probably not church. Hehe. I didn't forget your Christmas gift. I had to order it so it'll be late. Everyone misses you in Pensacola. Uncle Martin says hello. We love you."

A predictable omission of any reference to Will. Ironic—it was the one call I could have answered all day without having to lie.

We'd had flashes of normalcy in the morning, but the boring regularity of the afternoon beamed a spotlight into the chasm between us. There was no lighthearted afternoon wine drinking, no late in the day stroll to combat the turkey-induced narcolepsy, no lazy evening cuddle on the sofa. We were civil and pleasant, but the unfaithful elephant in the room refused to be ignored. We wandered the house like ghosts until darkness eventually crept in unnoticed.

When the sluggish day ground to an end and no invitation to share a bed arrived, I sulked to the guest room. I washed two Xanax down with a glass of brandy and grabbed a Jonathan Tropper novel from the bedside table. Before I cracked the book, I looked up to see Will standing in the doorway.

"What're you reading?" he asked.

I glanced at the jacket and noticed the title of the book. *This Is Where I Leave You.* "Novel," I said. "Something funny, not too heavy."

"Can we talk?" he asked.

I slid over and made room for him on the bed. My mouth grew dry and my heart began to pound. I was moments away from discovering the full extent of the damage my betrayal had caused and, soon enough, the day would become the best or worst Christmas ever.

"Something June said stuck with me," he said. "Leopards don't change their spots."

"Leopards don't *usually* change their spots," I corrected. He'd left out only one word, but it was a critical omission.

"Right. Cheating on someone makes them feel inadequate. Like they're lacking." He swallowed hard. "It makes me feel like who I am isn't enough for you."

"You're exactly enough for me." I was ready to throw myself on the mercy of the court.

"I'm talking about how you make me feel. Not how you see it, or how you feel."

"Okay," I conceded. He was gentle, composed. He'd gotten his head around the events of the last few weeks and was simply sharing his conclusions.

"When you cheat or almost cheat or want to cheat, I feel like I'm less."

"But you aren't," I assured him. "I'm the one who's small and pathetic."

"I'm still talking about how you made me feel, Conor. I'm not talking about you."

I nodded.

"I know your cheating isn't *really* about me," he said, "but it makes me feel so goddamn disrespected." He breathed deep and gathered himself. "Those are my feelings, so that's my problem."

"I won't do anything ever again to make you deal with those feelings. I swear to God, Will. I won't." I sounded like a broken record, but I said it because I believed it.

"No," he said. "Just no." Tears streamed down his cheeks now.

"I'm so sorry, Will."

"I'm sorry too." He held his head high.

I took his hand in mine. "It doesn't have to end this way. I'm different now."

"I don't think either one of us knows whether anything is different for you," he said. "But for what it's worth, I believe you want to change."

"I do. I really do." Guilty as charged, but I've seen the error of my ways.

"We can't drag this out." The foreman stood, ready to pronounce sentence. "I love you, but until you fix what's broken inside, you'll just keep hurting me."

"What does that mean?"

"It means I'm moving out."

I grabbed the glass of brandy from the nightstand as his words sunk in.

"You'll be okay," he said.

"I won't." I was unable to look at him.

"I'm sorry this had to happen tonight."

I glanced out the window at the patch of dewy grass where I'd lain drunk a few nights before. I tilted the glass to my lips and drained the last drop.

Thirteen

WHEN THE EXECUTIONER'S blade has been hanging over your head for weeks, the severing blow is as much about relief as it is about death. Still, it hurt like fuck. Will and I had no kids to tell or attorneys to haggle with, but the emotional untangling was complex. Untying the physical and financial knots that bound us would be less painful, but not without complication. In addition to bath towels and spatulas and the black Ikea swivel chair with the padded footrest, we owned the condo together.

Will wanted a "clean break" and he began looking for a new place right away. By the first of February, he expected to be out of our home and, I presumed, out of my life.

"You can keep the condo," he said. "I don't care how much it's appreciated since we bought it. Just give me back my half of the down payment." It was matter-of-fact, like he was giving me a list of things to pick up at Target.

"That's generous," I said, "but I don't have that kind of money."

"What about your 401K? You can buy me out with that, right?"

I was still struggling to come to grips with the concept of living without Will, and he had already had the time and wherewithal to think through the logistics. I brought this on myself, but it was hard not to take his readiness personally.

I USUALLY DESPISED the workdays between Christmas and New Year's, but the flood of annoying customers returning unwanted gifts and swooping in like vultures for post-Christmas clearance items was a welcome distraction. Some days, I was nearly as overrun and impotent as I had been in mid-December, but I refused to fall apart. I reached into my pocket and patted my tiny, laminated life plan. Next in line, please.

My gloom subsided at work, but my emotions at home churned near the surface. I dreaded the day Will would tape together that first cardboard box and begin dividing our possessions, just as he now built walls to partition our emotions. His job demanded more of his time, and he had a never-ending stream of errands to run after work. We no longer coordinated meals, and Will often ate alone in his room where he had long, private phone calls behind a closed door. We lived together, alone, which I guess is how breaking up is supposed to be.

I returned to writing, an act that had been cathartic for me in the days before I began trying to turn words into money. Despite a contractual obligation to produce a second novel, I had little inclination to write fiction, but in the empty space of my life, the space that Will once filled, I had plenty to say. For hours, I scribbled my conflicted and disjointed notions of love and lust, of honesty and commitment, all topics that neither my mind nor body comprehended beyond a fifth grade level. It wasn't my style to bleed poetry onto the page or to shape my feelings into tortured song lyrics. I didn't pen a ream of sappy letters to Will, begging forgiveness and professing my love, though I was sorry and I did love him. I wrote stream of consciousness, an unregulated outpouring of brain and heart, of demons and saints alike. No beginning or ending, no organizing principles, just words spilled on the page with an unmitigated randomness that would make John Morgan cringe. The self-examination sometimes made me feel worse, but it beat the shit out of eavesdropping on Will's phone calls and wondering who he was talking to.

I spent days exploring the jagged internal terrain of my lonely new planet. I pretended to find my bearings and grow comfortable in my solitude, but when Will finally reached out to me, it was clear that I hadn't. I could say my heart didn't skip a beat when Tom turned to me at work and said, "Phone. It's Will." I could say I didn't see the call as a sign that he missed me, that breaking up was harder for him than he had let on. I could say Will's invitation to an evening of takeout Thai and Hitchcock films didn't make me want to leap across the checkout counter and kiss strangers on the mouth. I could say all that, but I'd be lying.

We had once attended a matinee double-header of *North By Northwest* and *Vertigo* at a historic art deco movie house in downtown Tampa. Will raved about both afterward, so last Christmas I'd surprised him with a Hitchcock DVD boxed set. We made a New Year's resolution to see each film in the collection, and with a couple of days left in December, we were only two movies short.

We dumped pad thai noodles and panang curry onto the Mikasa plates Ariel had given us a few anniversaries ago. Will always insisted on eating meals at home using regular dinnerware, even if the food had been delivered in cardboard containers. He maintained that food eaten from disposable foam containers felt artificial and less nourishing than the same food eaten from dinner plates using regular silverware. I maintained that he never did dishes, but in truth, I agreed.

"After *Rope*, what movies do we have left?" I mixed steamed rice into the curry dish I had spooned onto my plate.

"Just *Rear Window*."

"I'm off until Wednesday," I said. "Let's do both tonight. I can pull a late-nighter if you're up for it." Too eager, I thought. Better to dial back the enthusiasm. Keep it light, breezy—there's the lesson rejected lovers never learn during failed comeback attempts.

"I'm glad you're getting a few days off," he said, formal and polite, as though we were in-laws. "I don't know about the slumber party, though. We'll see."

I was a kid once. I know what "we'll see" means. As suspected, I'd pushed too hard. "I put in six days again last week," I said, sticking to the safety of benign work chat.

"Things finally slowing down though?"

"Yeah." I rested my fork on the edge of my plate and watched him eat. He focused on his food, alternating bites of pad thai and panang, unaware or unbothered by the fact that our conversation had regressed to the level of coworker breakroom banter.

"I did some writing this week," I said.

"Starting another great American novel?" I was certain he didn't intend it as an insult, but his comment still mocked the minuscule success of *Luck of the Irish*.

"Just a brain dump. I filled the journal you gave me for Christmas."

"Less fiction and more Ralph Waldo." He smiled, invoking one of my favorites as an apology for his previous comment. "You writing about us?"

I had his attention after all. "Not exactly about us, more about what we've been through."

"What we've been through?"

"Yeah. What we went through with Paul."

"*We* didn't go through anything with Paul. In fact, I don't even know him. It was more like *you* who went through something with Paul."

So many open wounds. I should have stayed with the fluff. I tried to bandage the sore, but botched that too. "I didn't write about you and me and Paul. It was more philosophical, about infidelity. Where it comes from, what it does to people, how we move past it."

Will finished chewing and swallowed hard. He scowled, tossing his fork to the edge of his plate and propping his elbows on the table with a thud. Glaring at me over his clasped hands and interlocked fingers, he looked like an irate—no, disappointed—father. Probably his own.

"You figured it all out? You an authority now on how cheating ruins everything?" He paused to make sure I felt the full sting of the sarcasm. "Oh wait, you really are an expert at that."

The evening was quickly jumping the rails and I slammed the brakes, hoping to salvage our first meaningful interaction since the break-up. "It's just random thoughts and feelings. It's not a big deal. Honestly, I just wrote it for myself."

"Then why mention it?"

"You're right," I said. "I was stupid to bring it up."

"I didn't want tonight to be like this."

"Me neither. I'm sorry I upset you." I wasn't sure how many more times he wanted me to fall on my sword, but I was ready to oblige. Everything was on the line, and I had to deliver.

"It's fine." He picked up his fork and pushed rice and chicken around his plate. Will seldom raised his voice or slammed a door, and even now, as he fingered the fresh open wounds of adultery, a few harsh words and a sarcastic tone had been the extent of his anger.

"Okay," I said. "Still up for watching a couple of scary movies?"

"Hitchcock isn't scary. He's suspenseful."

"Right. The master of suspense." Whatever it takes, Conor.

We only watched one movie, *Rope*, which it turns out, was brilliant. Two friends strangle a college classmate on the day they're hosting a dinner party, and they stuff the dead body in a large chest they end up using as a table throughout the evening. As partygoers mingle, the killers notice a hunk of rope, the very weapon they used to strangle their classmate, hanging out of the top of the chest. Hitchcock creates knife-edged tension for the movie watcher by simply cutting in shots of the rope at various points throughout the movie. The killers become paranoid and agitated as they struggle to maintain a cheerful facade. As their fear of discovery escalates, tempers flare and the anxiety becomes paralyzing. I can relate.

We finished the film and a bottle of wine, but we didn't make out, snuggle beneath a warm blanket, share a tearful moment of forgiveness, or sleep in the same bed at the end of the night. In my deepest place, though, I believed Will and I could survive. There's a weird but understandable swallowing of pride that accompanies staying with a spouse who cheats. In modern society, we say we value love and family above all else, but when someone fucks around and the spouse stays with them, even for all the right reasons, we judge without mercy. Must be a marriage of convenience, we say. No self-respect. A leopard doesn't change its spots. It's all so hypocritical. Climb any mountain, swim any river, fight any battle—make it work and never give up. Oh, but if he cheats, boot his ass out and throw it all away.

NEW YEAR'S EVE has always been a good night for couples. Midnight kisses, whispered promises, stolen moments of quiet gratitude. The chance to take at least a small step in the direction of reconciliation was obvious, but I'd have to play my hand with uncharacteristic subtlety and patience. On this most introspective night of the year, emotions lay just beneath the surface. I had to be sure not to dig up the wrong ones.

Will and I both recognized the need to break from our norm, and after a little brainstorming, we chose to make a rare appearance at a downtown Tampa gay bar. A frivolous night out might serve us well. We spent twenty minutes searching for parking and another half hour pushing our way through a throng of overdressed and heavily cologned bodies. When we finally hit the wall of pulse-pounding bass, we remembered why our visits to dance bars were infrequent. The Masquerade was not our scene, not even on a night defined by carousing and reveling.

We left the bar before eleven and walked to Bayshore Boulevard to join the mass of people lining the street for the waterfront fireworks show. After a quarter mile or so, the crowd thinned. We discovered an empty knoll beneath a cluster of palm trees that partially obstructed our sight lines, and we settled there, sacrificing view for an ounce of privacy. As the fireworks painted the sky, the crowd erupted.

"We picked a pretty shitty spot to see the fireworks," I said.

"Doesn't matter," he said. "Fireworks were fun when I was twelve."

"But we're older now."

"Happy New Year." His voice was soft and weak, defeated. My supposition that New Year's Eve would raise the level of emotion had been right on, but I hadn't expected sadness to be the sentiment that surfaced.

"Don't sound so cheerful."

"Sorry. It's been a long day. And a long year."

"You want to get out of here when the show is over?"

"Why wait?" he said.

Neither of us stood to leave. Our outstretched legs touched and I closed my eyes. Images of the day we met flashed in my mind, those sacred moments at an artificial dolphin cove so many years before. The honesty of his smile, his laugh, the first touch of his hand.

In the midst of this bustling drunken crowd and with the sky full of fire, the world around us welcomed an unknown future. I couldn't have been less aware of it all. I was here, in this moment, under a palm tree on a tiny patch of grass, with Will. If only he would stay.

DOWNTOWN TRAFFIC WAS heavy, and after forty-five minutes, we'd made little progress. In the midst of the snarl, we chugged to a stop in front of Krispy Kreme. "Hot Doughnuts Now," I said. "The neon sign says so."

"Might as well. We aren't moving anyway."

With a dozen melt-in-your-mouth glazed to occupy us, we rejoined the bottleneck waiting to enter the freeway. We munched on doughnuts and joked about our melancholy New Year's Eve, mocking ourselves by seeing who could share the most depressing song from his iPod. My run through various Smiths songs was an admirable effort, but Will's campy singalong to Dolly Parton's *I Will Always Love You* was the clear winner.

"Good call," I said, "going with Dolly over Whitney."

"More intimate."

"Crushing," I added. We both laughed.

"You want to finish our New Year's resolution when we get home?"

"Too late," I said. "It's after midnight. That's last year's resolution now."

"Yeah, but we haven't gone to bed yet, so it's still yesterday. If we watch *Rear Window* before we fall asleep, I think we're good."

"Sounds reasonable." We pulled into the parking space in front of our condo. "You get the movie, I'll get the wine."

Will queued up the movie and turned out the lights, and I threw a couple of bed pillows and a blanket on the couch. His sudden desire for togetherness confused me, but I was afraid to ask questions. Better to ride the wave while it lasted.

"What's this one about?" I set a glass of wine in front of him and plopped at the opposite end of the couch.

"Just watch," he said, pressing play and stretching out with his bare feet in my lap.

We emptied our wine glasses by the end of the opening credits. I quickly refilled them. Will slid further toward me on the sofa and extended his legs across my body. His whole body was now within my reach. On the television, Jimmy Stewart played a photographer who is housebound for weeks with a severely broken leg. In his boredom, he spends hours staring out his window and into the apartments and secret lives of people in nearby buildings. It's harmless fun, until he witnesses suspicious behavior on the part of a neighboring salesman, who Stewart deduces has murdered and dismembered his ailing wife. I draped my arm across Will's torso, as Stewart told his day nurse and girlfriend what he thinks he has seen. They're doubtful at first, but they take turns observing the salesman, and soon they too are convinced of foul play. My fingers traced gentle circles on Will's stomach through his shirt, as Jimmy Stewart alerted a detective friend to the suspected murder, only to have his claim again met with skepticism.

My usual modus operandi, particularly after a lengthy coital drought, would have had me kissing his nipples before the opening credits had finished rolling, but tonight was different. I focused on the movie, while my hands slowly and gently remembered Will's body. I massaged his legs one at a time, foot to calf to thigh and back down. I let my hand move under his shirt, and I rubbed his firm stomach, his chest and biceps.

He moved to one side, making room for me to recline my body next to him. I traced the length of his neck, and let the back of my hand brush softly against the line of his jaw. With the tips of my fingers, I touched his face, his ears. I felt the softness of his hair. I ran my fingers lightly down his forearms and wrists, and let our fingers lace together. I knew this feeling. It was coming home.

On the television, mayhem ensued, the girlfriend risked her life to get evidence, and in the end, Stewart was vindicated. The salesman had murdered his wife. As the closing credits rolled, my touch had relaxed Will and he had fallen asleep. I let my hands roam again, only this time not limiting my touch. Leaning down, I kissed his cheek, and then his mouth. His eyes stayed closed, but with a gentle movement of his lips, he returned my kiss.

"Baby..." I said. He opened his soft brown eyes as though it were a question and then put his finger to my lips, quieting me.

He reached his hand to the back of my neck, rubbing it softly as he pulled me down to kiss him again. Our bodies writhed, and we both grew hard as our grinding became frenetic and wild. We stood and undressed each other, still kissing and exploring with our hands. He led me to our bedroom, where we made love and fell asleep.

FOURTEEN

I AWOKE ALONE.

I dragged myself out of bed and into the living room, where Will sat curled up in a blanket on the couch. I stood behind him and ran my fingers through his thick brown hair. As I leaned down to kiss him, he offered me his cheek.

I glanced at the television. "What you watching?"

"The end of the Rose Parade," he said.

"How was it?"

"Sucked. All those beautiful roses stapled together to make rolling billboards. They should stick to giant cartoon balloons."

I noted his half-empty coffee cup with envy. "I need caffeine. Want a refill?"

"I've had too much already."

"How long you been up?"

"Too long."

"Sorry." I gave him another peck on the cheek.

I filled a bowl with Cheerios and returned to the living room with the bowl in one hand and a mug in the other.

"Want some?" I said, offering a heaping spoonful of cereal.

"Nah. Cheerios has to be the most boring breakfast cereal."

It wasn't uncommon for me to wake up in an undefined funk, but Will was a rise-n-shiner.

Seeds of doubt about our night together sprouted in my brain, and I began to wonder if more than just my breakfast choice was being rejected. I patted my thigh, instinctively searching for the manifesto, my new laminated security blanket, but I'd left it on the bedside table.

I squelched my instinct to make a joke about the previous night's sexual escapade and played it safe instead. "Feel like a day of lounging?"

"Ariel called this morning." He hadn't spoken to or even mentioned my best friend since Thanksgiving.

"I didn't hear the phone ring. How is she?"

"She invited us over. David's cooking some kind of Southern New Year's meal."

"Sounds okay." I tried to sound interested but noncommittal. One careless step and I could hit a land mine.

Will sipped the last of his coffee.

"David's from Boston," I added, "but he likes to experiment in the kitchen." Safe.

"Mm-hmm," he said.

Jesus, this was like pulling teeth. Ariel's involvement in my John Morgan screw-up had been strictly incidental. Surely, Will believed that. Regardless, I couldn't imagine they'd discussed any of that on the phone. Still, something had changed in the hours that elapsed between my orgasm and my Cheerios.

I swallowed the last bite of cereal and tipped the bowl up to finish the milk. "What do you think? You in the mood for a Southern fried New Year's?"

"I'm going to stick around here. Maybe you should go visit Ariel, though."

Alarm bells rang in my head, but I was unable to stop myself from racing headlong into danger. "Will?"

"Conor?"

"What the fuck?"

He had something to say, but he seemed to have run into a wall of confusion.

"I was hoping to spend the day with you," I said, retracing my steps and backing slowly out of the minefield.

He kneaded the fabric on the arm of the sofa like he was making a loaf of bread but said nothing.

"Help me out here."

"I'm not trying to be an asshole," he said. "I don't mean to jerk you around."

"Okay." I waited for the other shoe to drop or hit me in the face.

"I owe you an apology."

Don't. Don't say it. Don't say you're sorry for last night. I'm not sorry.

"I don't regret last night," he said. "It felt good to be with you."

I held the empty cereal bowl, frozen.

"But I'm worried that having sex sent the wrong message."

I set the bowl on the table and faced him on the sofa. "Well, the message I got was there's still love between us. Was that a miscommunication?"

"No. There's still love."

"Then why are you apologizing?" I asked.

"Because I'm worried..." He was thoughtful and sincere, no longer angry. "I'm worried you might take it a step further and think there's still hope."

If my pajama bottoms had been designed with pockets, I'd have grabbed the laminated manifesto in the sweaty palm of my hand and that timely reminder of my new commandments might have trapped the next words in my brain before they escaped my mouth.

"Nooo," I said. "I'd never make that mistake. What idiot couldn't see that last night was just a pathetic pity fuck?"

"I knew this was a mistake."

"I thought you just said it wasn't a mistake?" I was pissed and trampling through the minefield now.

"I said, I didn't *regret* it. But to be honest, I'm changing my mind on that pretty quick."

The *Rear Window* DVD case sat on the coffee table between us. Jimmy Stewart had spied on his neighbor, and though he had no proof, what he saw led him to believe something was true. And in the end, it was true. Things worked like that for Jimmy Stewart, but they didn't work that way for me. The renewed connection I thought I'd felt on New Year's Eve was a pleasant night of Krispy Kreme, Hitchcock, and orgasms, but nothing more.

"You're right," I said. "I'll go see Ariel."

For a second, I wondered how Paul was celebrating New Year's Day. Wondered if maybe he'd want to ride to Orlando. I really needed some new pajamas. With pockets.

IT OCCURRED TO me on the drive to Orlando that Ariel could have invited other friends to this shindig, and I was in no mood to socialize. I called to check the guest list which, to my relief, included no one else. I told Ariel Will wouldn't be joining us. He would have enjoyed spending time with David and learning to make grits and hog jowls or whatever delicacies Southerners ate on New Year's Day. If Will had come along, though, clouds of awkward silence would have floated above our heads and cast polluted shadows across the day. I also needed time alone with Ariel to spill my messy guts.

Visiting Ariel and David's house was like spending an afternoon on pages 44-52 of the summer Pottery Barn catalog. They had a perfect Florida balcony replete with white wooden furniture and bright striped cushions. Their view overlooked one of Orlando's hundreds of man-made lakes. It was here, while David slaved in the kitchen, that I told Ariel about Prozac. And Haslam's and puking, and Aaron and puking, and Paul.

At first, she mothered me—hugs and reassurance, drying of tears, "you poor, poor dear"—and then, Ariel reamed me. She was generally less of a hard-ass than June, but she had known and loved Will as long as I had, and she hated to see him hurt as much as she hated to see us apart.

"I told you to stop thinking with your dick."

"I know," I said. "And you were mostly right."

"Mostly?"

"No, I mean, completely right. I can't let my dick make decisions. But I also need to figure out why that happens in the first place."

"Okaaay." She grabbed a cord by the balcony rail and tugged it, lowering a screen that sheltered us from the afternoon sun. She refilled our wine glasses and tucked her feet beneath her in the chair.

"After Thanksgiving, I fucked up one big thing after another. I just...melted down." The image of my mostly naked and nearly eaten body swaying in the current of the Hillsborough River flashed through my mind. I didn't share the story.

"Did you talk to Will? Tell him how deep you were sinking?" It was like she read my mind.

"At first, I told him all of it...except the Paul thing." The generic reference to my infidelity was mild and ridiculous, as though the "thing" had been Paul and I arguing over a restaurant choice. "He knows I had sex with Paul."

She leaned in and took my hand and adopted an exaggerated Southern accent. "Honey, you made yourself a big, dirty bed. You best get ready to lay in it."

THE AFTERNOON'S WINE buzz slowed after dinner, and David served coffee with chicory, pushing me further in the direction of sober. I left for home late in the evening, winding my way through the streets of suburban

Orlando before hitting the unusually open road of I-4. I plugged in my iPod and scrolled down to Simon and Garfunkel. With the cruise control set at seventy mph, I cranked up "The Boxer" and sang at peak volume, certain that my vocals added a rich third layer no one had ever noticed was missing.

As I exited the freeway ninety minutes later, I caught sight of my puffy, red-rimmed eyes in the rearview mirror. Loving Will, losing him, and having him love me again, if only for a few short hours. Opening my veins and bleeding the last bleak month onto Ariel's balcony. I was lost, so absorbed in the acoustic melancholy, I hadn't noticed the tears.

I drove past the unmanned guard shack and through the gates of the condo complex, as Simon, Garfunkel, and I tenderly closed out our set. I pulled into a parking space and noticed two new messages waiting on my cell phone. The first call, missed an hour ago, was from my mother. *"Conor, it's your mother. Call me as soon as you get the message."* No "Happy New Year," no "love, Mom." She sounded unusually subdued. Not her usual.

The second call, this one from my father, had come twenty minutes later. My father wasn't a fan of the brave new world of telecommunications. He seldom initiated phone calls, had never checked a voice mailbox, and saw no need for toys like cell phones. Like the voice mail from my mother, my father's message gave little information, beyond a plea for a returned call and a disturbing subtext exposed by the quaver in his voice.

It was past my parents' bedtime but, given the circumstances, I returned the call. I expected to hear my mother's groggy voice, but the answering machine picked up.

"Hey. It's Conor. Got your messages. They spooked me a little. How 'bout you give me a call when you get this."

I called my mother's cell phone next, and when she didn't answer, left the same message.

On my way up the sidewalk, I passed Harlan, who meandered in front of our building, maintaining his usual late-night vigil. I nodded, hoping to keep the interaction to nonverbal cues.

"What's up, brother man?"

"Brother man?" I asked.

"Term of affection," the teenager said with a wink.

I shook my head and continued walking. "Happy New Year, brother man."

Inside the condo, the muted glow of a table lamp provided the only light. I crossed the room to turn off the lamp and saw Will's note on the table.

Your parents called. Didn't answer. Left message saying they'd try your cell. Have to work early tomorrow. Let's talk after. Will

I considered checking to see if he was still awake, but he had made a point of saying he had to be up early. I left him alone.

I changed into my pajamas and turned on the television, hoping for the distraction of a West Coast college bowl. Settling into the same place on the couch where, twenty-four hours earlier, I mistakenly thought I'd been reborn, I pulled my legs close to me. I buried my face in the blanket I'd brought out for last night's movie and inhaled deeply, but detected no traces of Will.

I bit my fingernails and stared through bloodshot eyes in the general direction of ESPN. My thoughts were scattered as my mind rifled through a hundred tragic scenarios, one of which surely loomed ahead. I thought of waking Will again, if only for the comfort of his company, but it wasn't like that now and I had given him enough sleepless nights.

I wanted to call my parents again, or maybe June or Uncle Henry, or even Aunt Doris. If something had happened, one of them would know. I picked up the handset, and, like a bottle of Jameson to the side of the head, it hit me. New Year's Day, my mother sounding forlorn and my father calling to explain. After three decades of recovery meetings and near-beer, my father's demons had won. He was drinking.

The phone rang in my hand. "Conor?" my father asked.

"Hi, Dad."

"It's June."

"What's going on?"

"It's June," he repeated.

"I heard you, Dad. What about her?"

"Stroke."

FIFTEEN

WILL FOUND ME bundled up and dozing on the sofa. He touched my shoulder and rocked me awake. "What are you doing out here?"

Lethargy had anchored itself into every cell of my body. "June had a stroke."

"Jesus Christ." He sat down beside me and weighed his next words. "Is she alive?"

"She's alive, but it's not good."

"When did it happen?"

"Late last night. She was staying overnight in Alabama for New Year's Eve."

"What?"

"Atmore," I said, as though that clarified anything.

"What the hell was she doing in Atmore, Alabama?"

"Indian casino."

He rolled his eyes. "Where is she now?"

"Sacred Heart in Pensacola. Mom and Dad are with her." I had been in his place a few hours before, gathering facts and piecing together events, looking for a sense of order.

"Fuck," he said.

"I'm going to Pensacola." Before my brain could weigh-in on the fairness of my next words, my heart blurted them out. "Please, come with me."

"Okay." His voice cracked. I had wept overnight, and now it was Will's turn. He broke into sobs, and I pulled him close. I squeezed tight to calm the tremors that shuddered through him, tidal waves of emotion not only for June, but for the wretched alcoholic father he buried in high school and his trailer-trash mother who died a few years later. Will's parents had been even bigger fuck-ups than mine, and he had had no Aunt Doris, blessing and curse that she was, to lift him out of the chaos. He buried his head in my chest and rested it there until he collected himself with a few deep breaths.

"Jesus, Conor," he muttered in disbelief.

I loosened my grip. "Jesus?" I asked. "I hope you're not having a religious epiphany. I haven't fared that well with the other Christians in my family."

He raised his eyebrows. "Not funny, Conor. Not now."

"Sorry." Turning up a bottle of Grey Goose would have been frowned upon so early in the morning. Humor was my only other defense against the army of invading emotions.

"Let's go see your grandma," he said.

"Grandma? If she heard that cutesy shit, she'd pop out of her hospital bed and slap you."

"I'd say it to her face if I thought that was true."

I PACKED A small black toiletry case to the brim, wedging my bottle of Xanax and, in case of emergency, my Prozac safely into the mound of hair gels, Q-tips, and lip balms.

Will eyed the half-empty medicine chest. "Did you just sweep your hand across the shelves and shove everything in there?"

"Mind your own business," I said, zipping the bulging bag.

"Are you ready?" he asked.

"Let's go." I tossed the toiletries into my suitcase and hefted the bag from the bed.

"Conor." He sounded serious. "Before we get on the road, there's something I need to say."

"Okay." I put the suitcase down and steeled myself. No one ever takes that tone to tell you things are great.

"Don't get freaked out. But after our...misunderstanding, the other night, I want to be sure you know that nothing's changed."

"Why are you saying this?"

"Because we're about to do a thing that couples do."

"I'm confused. Are we about to have sex?"

"Rushing off to take care of a family emergency. It's a couples' thing. But it doesn't mean we're together."

I groped the cold plastic manifesto in my pocket. I fingered the card and remembered the words I'd written. I felt the black muddy river bottom, gripping me, sucking me down, trapping me, while I waited to meet my grisly demise. "I get it."

"I'm not trying to be an asshole," he said.

"I understand. We're not a couple." I reiterated the sentiment without bitterness or anger. "I still need you to come with me."

"And I still want to. For you and for June."

As he said her name, I imagined my grandmother, lying broken and afraid. Dying.

"One thing, Will. We can't tell her."

"She knows everything anyway." *Leopards and spots, I remember.*

"She knows I slept with Paul, but she doesn't know you and I broke up."

"No," he said, "she doesn't know that. I haven't talked to her since…Christmas." Christmas, an unfortunate euphemism for our break-up day.

"We can't tell her we split." Dishonesty was my forte, not Will's. He was unconvinced. "Please," I implored. "She needs every ounce of strength she has right now."

"It's a lie."

"If she lives, we'll tell her in a few weeks. If she dies, she'll go to her grave believing we made it. Is that so wrong?"

He considered the proposal. "Okay. We won't tell her. Not yet."

It was a compromise I could live with. Almost. "Not my parents either, Will. They'll screw it up and say something in front of her."

"Fine. Our secret, for now."

I HAVE THE road bladder of a seven-year-old girl with a lemonade habit, and we were less than two hours into the trip when I asked Will to stop at a rest area.

"I thought you were going to sleep the whole way."

"Nature calls when it calls," I said as we pulled into the lot. "I'll hurry."

When I returned to the car, a small box sat on the passenger seat. "What's this? My prize for being a good boy and washing my hands?"

"No. It's your prize for being quick and not stopping to suck off any strangers."

"What the fuck?"

He rested his forehead on the steering wheel. "I'm sorry. I don't know why I said that." Leaning back in the driver's seat, he rubbed his face. His fingers pulled down the bottoms of his eyes and stretched them unnaturally wide.

"That's an attractive look, Lurch."

"I guess I'm not the only sarcastic asshole in the car," he said, with a hint of a smile.

"Guess not." I shook the small box he'd placed on the seat for me. "What's this?"

"Look at the address." He backed the car out of the space.

It was a UPS package addressed to me from Aunt Doris. "Where'd you get this?"

"It was delivered yesterday while you were at Ariel's. I left it on the kitchen table, but I guess you missed it."

"Must be something good if she paid for New Year's Day delivery."

"Martin works for UPS. I'm sure he gets a discount."

He eased the car onto the highway. I rattled the toaster-sized box and detected a slight rustling inside.

"No idea," I said.

"Probably a *Queer as Folk* boxed set."

"Wow," I chuckled, surprised and delighted by his show of sarcasm.

"I'm sure it's a thoughtful gift, in her mind anyway." Will's mean streaks never lasted long.

I unsealed the box, which contained a card and a flat, gift-wrapped item that my trained bookstore eye immediately recognized as an oversized paperback. I opened the card and shared the handwritten sentiment out loud.

Conor—Sorry this gift is belated, but it's never really too late, is it? Merry Christmas and Happy New Year! Love, Aunt Doris and Uncle Martin

I tore off the wrapping paper and sat in stunned silence.

"What is it?" Will's eyes were fixed on the interstate.

"A book."

"What kind of book?"

I turned the book over in my hands but didn't answer.

"You're awful quiet over there. Is it a Bible?" He laughed as he said it.

"Worse." There was no amusement in my tone. I rested the book on the dashboard between us so he could read the title.

"Holy shit," he said, as *A Christian's Guide To Ex-Gay Living* slid off the dashboard and onto my lap.

"Fuck her." Angry tears filled my eyes, and I brushed them away with my fingertips.

"I'm sure it doesn't help, but you know she means well."

In a twisted and painful way, she did. On the back cover, the book promised four rewarding outcomes to those who followed its simple program. I'm sure Aunt Doris wanted nothing in the world more than she wanted those things for me. I read the list aloud to Will.

Learn how your homosexuality hurts you and others.
Leave the empty shell of your gay existence behind.
Be proud of the new man you become.
Spend eternity basking in the love of God.

"That's fucking horrible," he said.

"It's a total rejection of me. I don't understand how anyone could give this fucking poison to someone they love. Someone they practically raised."

"I'm sorry. It's brutal."

I needed no more provocation, but Aunt Doris provided it nonetheless. On the back of the title page, she'd written a note calling my attention to the list of ex-gay ministries in the book's appendix. She added that Pastor Lonnie, her divine spiritual leader at Holy Smyrna Baptist, was a "close personal friend" of the book's author and had made himself available for any guidance I might need. She closed the inscription with a reminder that, no matter what, both she and Jesus would always love me.

I gripped and twisted the book tightly in my hands as though I could choke the stupidity from it. I lowered the passenger window and, as the rush of wind dried the last tears on my cheeks, I hurled that piece of shit as far as I could into the murky Florida swamp.

I'D LEFT A voice mail for Marshall letting him know I'd be out for a few days because of a family emergency. He called back a few minutes after I sent my Christmas present from Aunt Doris to its watery grave along Interstate 75.

"You know appraisals and performance plans are due by the end of the month, right?"

"Seriously, Marshall, is it necessary to cover all this right now?"

"You haven't exactly been on your game in the last few months, Conor. I'm trying to help you stay on track."

"I appreciate your...help," I said. "When I get back to work, I'll be more focused." Will glanced at me, as I shook my head and jerked off a giant invisible penis.

"Conor, we've had this conversation before, and it hasn't been that long ago."

"This has nothing to do with my book. This isn't the 'outside distractions' conversation we had a few weeks ago. I have a legit family emergency."

"Sometimes circumstances work against us, Conor. When that happens, we have to decide if we are going to be victors or victims."

I despised his plural inclusive pronouns and canned management speak. I played along though, hoping to speed the end of the call. "I'm a victor here, Marshall. Definitely a victor. Taking the bull by the horns and all that." I looked at Will and amped up my nonverbal mockery for comedic relief, masturbating the imaginary penis with frenzied near-orgasmic gusto.

Will shrugged and raised his eyebrows. I replied with more faux wanking and added a tongue-in-cheek blow job gesture.

"We need to talk about next steps, Conor. Commitments we can make to each other going forward." It was as though he was reading random phrases from a beginning leadership book.

"Marshall, listen," I said, "I'm kind of in the middle of a crisis here. My grandmother had a stroke, and right now, we don't know if she's going to live. You think you could hold off on any more helpful coaching until she's off the respirator, maybe?"

"I wish the world stopped revolving every time one beloved old lady has a stroke, but that's not the way it works, buddy."

A few weeks before, that kind of asshole remark would've sent me over the edge, but my mind was clear now. I had bigger concerns. Marshall had poked me long enough, though.

"Losing my signal here in the sticks," I lied. "Call Tom if you need anything." *Click.*

SIXTEEN

AS WE CROSSED the bay bridge and reached Pensacola, I imagined my first glimpse of June's stroke-mangled body. I saw her silent and broken, propped up in sterile white bedsheets like a department store mannequin, only with a tangle of tubes and cables coming out of her. I pictured a half dozen beeping and hissing machines stationed around her bed, each of which was designed to either prolong her life or measure how little of it remained.

We pulled into the parking lot of Sacred Heart and careened around row after row of occupied spaces. "You'd think a place where sick people come to die would be designed with a little more compassion," I said.

Will was aware of my preexisting disdain for hospitals. He recognized the oncoming rant and stayed out of the way, letting it run its course like a fever.

"Sitting for hours in tiny, overcrowded waiting rooms they keep at meat locker temperatures, with blaring televisions and shitty, outdated *Field & Stream* magazines."

"Mm-hmm," Will said as he scouted for parking.

"These little hellholes are designed to break your spirit, so by the time you finally hear the bad news all you want to do is get the hell out."

"I need some gum," he said, finally pulling into a space. "Let's find a gift shop." His utter disregard of my tirade poked a precision pinhole in the tension I'd worked so hard to create.

In the elevator on the way to Intensive Care, I leaned against the wall and closed my eyes.

"Are you ready for this?" he asked.

"It doesn't matter. It's not like we have a choice."

A friend's father had suffered a massive stroke when I was in college. I had seen firsthand the devastating consequences of that kind of brain damage. An investment banker transformed overnight into a mute idiot child. Nothing could prepare me to see June like that.

The elevator chimed as we reached the fourth floor, and Will put his arm around my shoulder. "I hope she's alert, but be ready."

"I love you," I said as the doors slid open.

He smiled.

My contempt for hospitals wasn't limited to parking lots and waiting rooms. I hated everything about these prison-esque fortresses of disease. I hated the long, identical corridors lined with closed, heavy wooden doors, most of which were accompanied by sturdy plastic sign plates identifying the rooms beyond as *Radiology* or *Administration*, or, if you're lucky, *Restroom*. I hated emergency rooms full of old people shoved into corners, slumped in wheelchairs, throwing up in pastel-colored, kidney-shaped buckets. I hated stifling hot and bitter cold lounge areas with reinforced glass walls and cheap Home Interiors paintings. I hated sitting in total discomfort, shifting from one ass cheek to the other, and watching *The Price is Right* at earsplitting volume, while I worried more about the misbehaving children of strangers than they did. I hated wandering the antiseptic hallways, bewildered by a maze of directional signs that either sent me in circles or to remote places I didn't need to go. Most of all, though, I hated the waiting, the standing in doorways in the middle of the night, the napping upright in uncomfortable chairs, the whispering in hushed tones, as if anyone in the whole goddamn place got a decent night's sleep anyway.

MY MOTHER STOOD beside my grandmother's hospital bed, but my gaze locked on June. On the twisted, asymmetric scrunching of the muscles in her face. On her glazed eyes, which were open but saw nothing. On the contorted mess that was neither her smirk nor her smile.

Uncertain of June's lucidity, I directed my attention to my mother.

"How is she?"

My mother hugged me long and hard. "She's had better days."

"What are the doctors telling you?" Will asked.

"We don't know much yet," my mother said, finally loosening her grip on me. "We know it's not good, but we don't know exactly how bad it is."

Will stepped forward and embraced my mother. They both tried unsuccessfully to fight back tears. Funny, but seeing my lover, or ex-lover, and my mother so distraught gave me courage. It somehow made it easier for me to suppress my own powerful urge to weep. I moved toward them, suddenly the supportive one, the one who muttered clichéd words of comfort and solace. *Everything will be fine. She's a strong woman.*

People never know what to say in times like this, and so we use all the generic reassurances we've heard a hundred times before. But in a case like June's, it didn't matter. All the affirmations and optimism in the world were useless against the damage caused by the prolonged interruption of blood and oxygen to the brain.

Her eyes were open much of the time, but I knew by the rhythmic slapping of the bedside respirator she was not breathing on her own. She was "non-responsive to external stimulus," or so I read on her chart. It didn't take a medical professional to reach that conclusion. I'd surmised as much when her only reaction to my kiss on the cheek and whispered reassurance was a vacant stare.

Will sat in the chair nearest the bed and squeezed my grandmother's hand. He trailed a finger down her arm and wrist, careful to avoid the tender spot where the IV tube was inserted. Swirls, waves, circles, unnoticed and unfelt. He touched her forehead, primping her bangs and then pushing her graying hair back behind her ears. All the while, her empty eyes acknowledged nothing. He grazed her neck with the back of his hand and gave her shoulder a soft, reassuring caress. Will tried in vain to connect with her, but even the drip of his tears onto the back of June's hand went unnoticed.

"You'll do anything to be the star of the show, won't you?" he whispered. "You'd never admit it, but you like a little attention from time to time."

No answer.

"It's hard to relax with all the prodding and poking, I'm sure. You know Conor hates hospitals, but I don't mind them so much."

Nothing.

"We'll be here to help out until you're feeling better. Or until you feel well enough to tell us to go the hell home."

Still nothing.

He stopped speaking and sat with his head in his hands. I knelt on the floor in front of him, next to my dying grandmother. I yearned to subvert this bitter reality, to make the ugliness go away for Will and my mother, for June. A bottle of vodka and a half dozen Xanax might do the trick for me but, for once, I didn't allow myself that escape. I wanted to stop this nonsense, or at least to understand it. But I could do none of this. All I could do was be there, and while that was something, it still felt like nothing.

AS THE SUN was setting, or so I imagined from June's windowless cell, I realized that my entire extended family had been absent from the hospital. This struck me as odd since McLeishes usually dominated waiting rooms and hospital cafeterias for even the most mundane medical events. We liked to pretend our strong hospital attendance was born out of an abiding sense of family commitment, but I suspected it was more the need for meaningful distraction from our shitty everyday lives. A medical hurricane party. Access to the ICU was tightly regulated, though, and too many visitors only complicated matters. My mother had asked that no one come to the hospital. I suspected she was also sheltering June from the unnecessary aggravation of visits from my father's family, most of whom my grandmother regarded with pity, if not disdain.

With support from my father and Will, my mother and I ran around-the-clock vigils for the next couple of days. We alternated shifts in the ICU so if June awoke she'd find a familiar face. I was weary but stable, which I credited to my rock-bottom river epiphany and the absence of Prozac. I'd grown stronger in the last few weeks, and melting down now was not an option.

On the third morning after the stroke, Dad and Will arrived in the ICU waiting room with freshly shaved faces and slightly smaller bags under their eyes than they'd had the day before. Knowing we'd eaten nothing since the previous night's dinner, my father brought breakfast. He presented an overstuffed McDonald's bag like a huntsman sporting his kill...of McMuffins.

Because it was early, or maybe because there was a lull in the death and dying business, we had the waiting room to ourselves. My mother and I sat exhausted, while Will fashioned a budget dining room out of a Formica-topped coffee table and a handful of McNapkins. My father retrieved a filter pack from the nurse's station and brewed a fresh pot of hot coffee. As we quietly ate our cold fast-food breakfast in the tiny, uncomfortable waiting room, strange and unfamiliar feelings warmed me. Closeness. Security. Unconditional love. The kind of love that, in some families, only rears its head when tragedy renders the usual conditions irrelevant. There is always bullshit in families, but that's not all there is. Sometimes, there's love and kindness. Not perfection, but comfort. I unwrapped my breakfast, sipped the watery coffee, and savored the fleeting moment.

For days, we alternated shifts in teams of two at the hospital, with the occasional respite at home. Late one evening, showered and rested, my mother and I returned to Sacred Heart, arriving in tandem with the hospital's overnight shift. As we joined the scattered trails of nurses and doctors winding their way across the parking lot, I wondered if any of them had provided care for my grandmother. Had one of them diagnosed her? Administered her IV? Connected her to that respirator? What was it like, I wondered, to know that what you do may save a life? I reflected on my job for a moment and remembered the call with Marshall, who I decided could shove his performance appraisals and backroom checklist up his ass.

We established rituals and adapted to our circumstances in the way that humans do. From bad marriages to prison camps, during decades of famine or moments of calamity, human beings find ways to normalize. We took the same seats in the same waiting room, watched the same shit on the same loud television, and walked to the same cafeteria to eat the same bland meals every day. Exhaustion and routine anesthetized us, and through it all, June made no progress.

In the midst of tragedy, I searched for order, for the ordinary. I tried to picture a time in the distant future when the trauma would have passed, but I was too far in it to imagine a time beyond it. Still, imposing logical order helped me survive. I relaxed into the patterns and habits we created amidst the chaos, without ever realizing this new world order was temporary.

JUNE'S DOCTOR WAS a short Filipino man of nebulous age and impeccable grooming. He wore tailored pants and pressed shirts, and his white lab coats were crisp and clean. I imagined he was on a first name basis with his dry cleaner. Dr. Gonzalez made early morning rounds, and throughout his examination of June each day, he discussed her prognosis with clear and precise language. As he outlined her progress, or the lack thereof, he was matter-of-fact but never brutal.

On the sixth morning after the stroke, my mother and I were alone at June's bedside in the ICU. It was almost 7:30 a.m. when our world was rattled, not by an event, but by a simple question.

"Good morning," Dr. Gonzalez said, speaking as much to June as he was to my mother and me.

"Morning, Doc," I replied.

"I didn't see you in the waiting room. I was hoping I'd find you here." He began his survey of June, gliding around the bed from side to side, reviewing charts, watching monitors, bending and moving parts of my grandmother. Without looking up, he asked, "Are you all getting some rest?"

"We're doing okay," I said. "But June doesn't seem to be making any progress."

"Unfortunately," he replied, "you're right about that." He raised each of her eyelids and shined his pen light into her eyes.

He walked to the nurses' station in the center of the ICU, scribbling on clipboards and charts, and then returned to June's bedside. "Let's step out for a moment." His tone sounded more like a gentlemen's invitation to dance than a precursor to a medical consultation.

In an empty conference room, he motioned for us to sit and then positioned himself on the edge of the table, half-sitting, half-standing.

"I'm afraid June is showing no signs of improvement, and I want to talk with you honestly about our options." Our options. He was one of us.

"Okay," my mother said as we moved in unison to the edge of our seats.

"Do you know if June has a living will?" The words landed like a fifty-pound sack of flour on the table. I had anticipated this conversation, but there was no adequate way to prepare for it. "Do you know what a living will is?" he asked.

"We know," my mother said. "We know damn well what a living will is, and we understand its purpose." She leaned back in the chair and drew sharp, shallow breaths.

"Mrs. McLeish, I'm not trying to put you on the spot or imply that you should make decisions at this point. But I need to be sure we have the relevant information."

"She's my mother." Her tone softened, and her eyes grew moist.

"Mom," I said, putting my arm around her shoulders, "I don't think Dr. Gonzalez means anything by the question. I think he..."

"He's asking if she should be unplugged. That's what he wants to know."

Shades of red flashed on her cheeks. "He's letting us know it's time."

"Mrs. McLeish, I appreciate how hard these situations are. But I hope you understand we need to have conversations of this nature."

"You want to know if my mother had the goddamned forethought to make this easy on us?" She began to sob as her rage boiled away and left the bitter residue of grief in its place.

Dr. Gonzalez excused himself and returned with a box of tissues and two bottles of water. "Thanks for talking with us," I said. "Can we pick this up a little later, maybe?"

"Of course. We can talk in a day or two." As he rose to leave, he patted my mother's shoulder and shook my hand.

We sat alone, holding each other awkwardly in the small sterile room. If this space had been built for the purpose of delivering life-shattering news to families of patients, it was a shit design. No art on the walls, a faux-wood corporate conference table, and built into the door, a rectangular window, about three feet long and offset to one side, that gave passersby a glimpse inside. Everything was semi-private in hospitals, even the most sorrowful, gut-wrenching moments of your life. Add that to the list of things I hate about these places.

I held my mother's hand. "We don't have to decide anything now."

She wiped her tears with a tissue she'd stowed in the cuff of her sleeve. "We don't have to decide ever."

"Not until we're sure we understand the facts completely."

"There's nothing to decide. She wrote a living will." She spat out the words like hot coffee.

"Okay." I had never seen such a document, but I understood the concept. "What does it say?"

"She never showed it to me."

"Then maybe there is no living will," I concluded. In retrospect, I don't know why I would have hoped the document didn't exist.

"It doesn't matter," my mother said. "We talked about it, and I know how she felt about being kept alive this way."

"What did she say?" I asked though I knew the answer.

"She told me if I ever left her on a respirator...that when she eventually died, she'd make sure her ghost haunted me every day for the rest of my life."

MY FATHER AND Will stood beside June's bed when my mother and I returned to the ICU. "Will," I said. "Can we take a walk?"

I led Will to the same conference room where we'd just met with Dr. Gonzalez, and I recounted the scene. After a week of uncertainty, we had each begun to grapple with the inevitable reality that June would soon be gone from our lives forever.

"Can your mom handle this?"

"She didn't do too well this morning."

"What about you?" he asked.

"I can't stop thinking about it. June being unplugged...wheezing...sucking in that last breath...unable to tell us she changed her mind. Then she suffocates and a fucking stranger pulls a sheet up over her head."

"Jesus Christ, Conor. Maybe not so graphic?"

"That's how I visualize it. Saying it out loud doesn't make it any more or less likely to happen that way."

"You have to see the other side too. Keeping her plugged in—she lays there forever and suffers." When I didn't respond, he spelled out his conclusion. "If she needs to let go, we have to let go too."

"Because that's my specialty, right? I'm the king of letting go."

We returned to the waiting room where I expected to find my parents having a similar conversation, but they were not talking about June.

"Henry called," my father said. "He's thinking about you, and June of course. And Mildred Guzman from the Altar Society at the church called. They want to drop some casseroles by when we get home."

"That's sweet," my mother said. "Tell them to hold off. Maybe they can bring something by after the funeral."

"Goddamn, Mom," I scolded.

"Relax, please," Will said, more an order than a request.

My father continued, not derailed by the exchange. "And Doris called. She said she loves us and to remember that God works in mysterious ways. She told her pastor about June, and he asked for God's mercy during their church service."

"Which one?" I asked. "Sunday morning, Sunday afternoon, or Sunday night? Or was it Wednesday? She goes to church twice on Wednesdays too, right?" I hadn't told my parents about the hurtful Christmas gift Aunt Doris had sent me, but they knew how I felt about Pastor Lonnie and Holy Smyrna.

"Don't be bitter, son," my father said. "Of all people, you shouldn't judge things you don't understand." Using phrases like "of all people" was as close as he ever came to discussing my gayness.

"I'm not bitter, Dad. I'm hateful." Will shot me a sideways look, a silent warning to get a grip.

My mother, who looked nearly as catatonic as June, spoke up. "Just remind your family June is still in the ICU and can't have visitors."

"They didn't say they were coming here," my father said, turning and heading for the door. "I just wanted you to know we got some goddamned calls."

My mother ignored the outburst and smoothed June's bedsheets. "I'm not in the mood to entertain his family," she muttered. "That goddamned circus can find another town."

SEVENTEEN

DAY SLEEPING LEAVES you disoriented and confused, but a few hours of rest in actual beds had done us both good. My mother stood hunched over the kitchen counter, and from behind, I couldn't see the dark circles beneath the tired slits of her narrow brown eyes. She managed a smile as she slid a turkey sandwich across the counter to me.

"Lunch," she said.

"Or dinner?" I glanced at the clock on the kitchen wall.

She laughed. "Just eat it."

The brief respite from the eternal hell of the waiting room had blunted the sharp edges created by the living will question, and by the time we returned to Sacred Heart, we were nearly human again.

We wound our way through the parking deck before finally wedging the Honda into a tiny space on the top floor. The word "Compact" was painted on the curb, which I assumed was hospital-speak for "near fucking impossible." We navigated the hospital hallway maze, passing the now familiar faces of other friends and family of the dead and dying.

"Mom," I said, "I need to duck into the bathroom. You want to wait?"

"No. You catch up. I do enough waiting as it is."

When I entered the ICU, my parents stood on one side of June's bed. Aunt Doris stood on the opposite side next to a tall, well-proportioned man in a gray pinstripe suit. I vaguely recognized his face from the back of his book jacket.

I approached my parents and forced a smile. My mother, her face flush and eyes bulging, wrung her hands as if she hoped to squeeze her hostility out through the tips of her fingers.

"Where's Will?" I asked.

"Downstairs in the cafeteria," my father said.

"I guess we just missed him." Aunt Doris shrugged. "That's too bad." I offered no reply, harnessing all of my energy to hold the fake smile.

"How rude of me," Doris said. "Conor, this is the Reverend Lonnie Casey. He's our pastor and a dear, dear friend of mine and Uncle Martin's." I half expected an exchange of knowing winks and nudges with the introduction—*he's the homosexual one.*

We shook hands across the bed, our arms outstretched over the unresponsive body of my grandmother. The heat built in my face. Doris was clad in standard holier-than-thou wear: a white silk blouse, frilly near the top, and a navy blue polyester skirt that clung a little too tight to her body, highlighting her round and apparently still firm buttocks. Her light brown Miss Clairol hair curled just above her shoulders, and she gripped a black zippered Bible in her hands. She was well put-together, attractive but proper, the perfect sidekick to the righteous reverend.

"I wasn't expecting to see you here, Aunt Doris. I thought everyone knew they discourage visitation in the ICU." She made no effort to defend the surprise visit so I continued. "I didn't think they'd even let this many people in at one time."

"Anything is possible when you bring a revered man of God with you," she said.

"Right," I said. "This is real loaves and fishes shit."

She smoothed the pleats on the front of her skirt. "I kept thinking about your grandmother laying up here fighting for her life, struggling on her own without the clear and present support of the Holy Spirit. I just had to do something to help."

I'd seen the kind of help she provided. In fact, I'd thrown her help out the window of a moving car just last week. She wasn't exactly beaming, which in this situation would have been crass even for her, but Aunt Doris's bright eyes and tight smile betrayed her zeal.

"I wanted to make a difference, but I felt so useless," she continued. "I explained our situation to Pastor Lonnie and told him how desperate we were. He had the most generous idea." Her voice was eager, excited, like a toddler in training pants, beaming with pride and pointing at a turd in her potty chair. *Look what I did, Mommy.*

I interrupted her enthusiastic recitation. "Don't take this the wrong way," I said, knowing there was no right way, "but I don't think you really fit into 'our situation.' It's nice that you care, but you don't have a place here."

We hadn't spoken since I'd opened the mortifying Christmas gift, and I was ready to mount my soapbox and let it fly. My voice jumped an octave as I rolled on. "Do you know how fragile June's condition is? She cannot have non-family, non-essential visitors...at all." I eyeballed the man in the tailored suit. "Not even *revered* members of the clergy."

"Conor, if you no longer want to call me family, that's your choice. But I won't allow you to demean Pastor Lonnie. He's a respected member of the community and a healer."

"Doris," my mother said with an exhausted sigh, "Conor is right. We appreciate the thought, but it's best you leave. Mother needs rest."

Pastor Lonnie cleared his throat. "Mrs. McLeish, we don't mean to intrude. Doris simply wanted to help, and so she called me." Then, as if none of the previous discussion had occurred, he went on. "Now, I understand your mother was not a particularly Christian woman."

My mother was confused, fatigued, and drained, and my father stood idly by, a spectator. Any fighting spirit he'd ever had died thirty years ago in the blaze that nearly killed his family.

"She was baptized as a child," my mother responded. "She was—she is a Christian."

Pastor Lonnie interpreted my mother's acquiescence as consent. "Does she accept Jesus Christ as her Lord and Savior?"

"Mother," I interjected before she could answer. "Can we talk for a second?" I led her past the thick glass walls of the main ICU room and into the adjacent hallway.

"What the hell are they doing here? Did you invite them?" It was more accusation than question.

"Calm down, Conor," she said.

"It's a simple question, Mom. Did you invite them?" I paced in frantic circles with my head down and arms crossed, resembling, I imagined from Pastor Lonnie's viewpoint, an angry gay Al Pacino.

"No, honey. I didn't invite Aunt Doris and her friend to come here. You know I didn't want visitors."

"I know that's what you said, so why the fuck doesn't she know that?"

"Conor," my mother said in a forceful but whispered tone, "lower your voice or you are going to get us kicked out of here."

"*We* will not be kicked out of here," I boomed. "But that self-righteous bitch will be." I glared at my aunt through the giant sheet of glass. "I'm going to tell her one time to get the hell away from us, and if she's smart, she'll listen."

"Honey, calm down. Her intentions are good. She only wants to help."

"Mother, June wouldn't want this kind of help."

"You may be right. But Doris was only thinking about what's best."

"Stop it, Mom. She doesn't know what's best."

"Conor, God isn't dead for all of us."

I wouldn't let her make this about me. "June despises that holier-than-thou brand of Christianity. If she had four words left in her right now, they would be 'Go to hell, Doris.'"

My mother stood in the center of the hallway, flabbergasted, shocked by the depth of my rage and clueless as to how to respond to it.

"I don't know why, but I know you and Doris no longer get along. That doesn't mean..."

"That's crap."

"She loves you, Conor."

"She doesn't love me. She loves the idea of me. She's done nothing but traumatize me since the day she figured out I was a little 'prettier' than other boys."

"Conor," my mother said, "this is not about you and Doris."

"You brought it up, Mom. I'm just saying we need to get her and her boyfriend out of here now." Aunt Doris had "discreetly" shared with the entire family the news of Uncle Martin's performance problems in recent years, a fact which I attributed to her increasingly frigid vagina. She talked about Pastor Lonnie like he was the captain of the high school football team. I suspected her pathetic "celebrity" crush was picking up Uncle Martin's slack in the bedroom.

"Conor, don't—"

"If you think June will haunt you for leaving her on a respirator, imagine what she'll do for this." I took a deep breath, fingered the laminated card in my pocket, and headed back to the ICU.

Things might have unfolded differently if Will had not tired of hospital food and walked across the street to the food court in Cordova Mall. If he'd been willing to eat the vegetable platter in Sacred Heart's cafeteria for a fourth consecutive day, he might have been back at the ICU, and his presence there might have mitigated my meltdown. For the record, I haven't always mistreated people—fired or fucked or puked on them, when the going got rough. I've mostly just found quiet ways to make things worse for myself. This wasn't about me, though. This was about June.

It hadn't been my intention to punch a man of God that day. I wasn't a believer in Christian faith, but I didn't believe that gave me the right to assault those who profess it, at least not without serious provocation. No one was allowed to lay hands on my grandmother, though. No one, that is, save for a uniformed medical professional or a gentlemanly tax accountant who bought her drinks and made clever conversation in the bar at The Venetian.

Pastor Lonnie's left hand cupped June's forehead, while his right hand rested, open palm, on the sheet that covered her chest. In retrospect, his hand was somewhere in the vicinity of June's heart, which, when seen from a healing perspective, makes good sense. In retrospect, I realize that my mother and father, though having not objected strongly enough to the reverend's presence, were nonetheless in the room next to June's bed. In retrospect, the setting is vivid and clear, an intensive care unit full of doctors and nurses, swinging their clipboards and stethoscopes, circling and prodding the ailing and infirm. But, we don't live in retrospect.

Pastor Lonnie was an unwelcome stranger who, in the heat of the moment, appeared to stand over my unconscious elderly grandmother with his hands resting on or about her comatose breast. The reverend whispered prayers or spoke in tongues. Whatever it was, he ceased the mumbling when I bounded into him and my fist glanced off his chin. It really wasn't a punch, so much as a lunge and a shove. If I happened to do some of the lunging with my fist, and his face happened to be the part of his body that I shoved, well, that's unfortunate. It was definitely more shove than punch, though. That's how I remember it, and in the unlikely event that there really are harps and angels and pearly gates, that was my story, and I was sticking to it.

My father helped Pastor Lonnie off the floor, while Aunt Doris, who likely feared her own salvation might be jeopardized by association, gushed apologies and insisted that God have mercy not only on my grandmother, but on the whole heathen lot of us. My mother nudged me into a corner and held my hands firmly, whether for support or restraint, I didn't know. Intensive care nurses rushed across the room, and a couple of doctors who'd witnessed the debacle through the glass walls of the ICU stormed in behind them.

"I called security," said one of the nurses. "We need *all* of you out now." The entire assembled medical staff escorted us out and then emptied the ICU of all the other patients' families and friends, some of whom leered at me and the bloody-lipped pastor as they passed us in the waiting room.

Aunt Doris continued her sniveling suck-up. "Pastor Lonnie, I'm so very, very sorry. Believe me, if I had had any idea that such violence could erupt, I—"

"Doris, we should be going." He straightened his expensive silk tie and dusted off the sleeves of his tailored suit coat. "Our work here is done." Pastor Lonnie dabbed at his lip with a handkerchief, offered God's grace and blessings to us all, and hurried away down the corridor. Aunt Doris, desperate to follow in the reverend's dramatically exiting footsteps, turned on her heel and scampered away in his wake.

"Conor!" my mother snapped but then fell silent when Aunt Doris reappeared in the doorway of the waiting room.

"I seem to have lost my Bible in that regrettable fracas," she said, passing through the waiting room and returning to the interior of the ICU. She emerged a moment later, clutching the zippered black book in her hand, and addressed my shamed and embarrassed parents. "I know you don't take your commitment to the Lord as seriously as I do, but God can work miracles for the righteous."

"Doris," my mother said, "we believe."

Aunt Doris straightened her clothes and primped her hair, looking up and down, but into no one's eyes. "You're good people, more or less." With a sweep of her hand in the general direction of me or June or both, she added, "It's not your fault that God cursed your family with all this."

My face flushed with anger as she hurried out to catch Pastor Lonnie, nearly blindsiding a security guard who had appeared in the doorway.

"Sir," the guard said to me, "may I speak to you privately?"

"It's okay now." My father finally broke his silence.

"I need to speak with you out here in the hallway," the guard repeated.

"It's fine," I said. The mix of disappointment and anger in my parents' faces saddened me. "Everything is fine."

But it was not fine. Nothing was fine. Things would never be fine again.

The security guard agreed to spare me from permanent expulsion, under the conditions that I leave the ICU for the rest of the night. I told my parents I'd be going home for the evening and followed my escort downstairs.

The elevator doors opened in the lobby, and there was Will. He followed me to the sliding doors at the hospital entrance.

"What's going on?"

"Take me home. Please."

We reached the car and he opened the passenger door for me. I crawled inside and succumbed to sleep before we had even wound our way out of the godforsaken parking lot.

SOME DREAMS PROVIDE a keyhole glimpse into our subconscious, a peek into the shadowy corners where we hide our secrets and lies. Most dreams just function as the brain's garbage disposal, though, chewing up the day's scraps and sending them down the drain. There's one type of dream that's different. One kind of dream that always holds a kernel of significance. Recurring dreams, the leftovers that back up in the sink. They clog up the pipes and refuse to be flushed away with the rest of the day's detritus. Recurring dreams tell us something's left undone.

In my early twenties, I had a recurring dream in which I was wrestling a large alligator, or a crocodile maybe. In my dream, I lost no limbs and shed no blood. The monstrous gator never bit me, but I never conquered the animal either. The dream always ended with me exhausted and nearly bitten but still wrestling. If I had dreamed it only once or twice, I would have let it go, but the alligator kept coming back. After a few weeks and a dozen or so appearances of the dream, I did some research which, it turns out, was hardly necessary. I grabbed a dream dictionary off the shelf at the bookstore and leafed through the various images and symbols. Finally, I found it...*Alligators*.

Alligators, being eaten by—you are sensing danger

Alligators, surrounding you—you are sensing danger

Alligators, wrestling with—you are sensing danger

I looked up *Crocodiles*.

Crocodiles—see *Alligators*

According to the book, it didn't matter if you were being chased, maimed, or eaten. If the subject of your dream was a giant reptile, you were sensing danger. I was unimpressed with the dimwitted insights, and I remain unconvinced about the interpretation of the contents of dreams as enigmatic symbols. In light of recent midnight river swims, though, who knows?

My dream was vivid and real that night in the guest room at my mother's house, just a few miles from the hospital bed where my grandmother lay dying. There was a boy standing on a gray beach. He wore long wool pants and a heavy black coat. The boy was alone. He held a string that was tied to a shiny white balloon that floated high above, in a dark, ominous sky. The balloon, too far aloft, whipped and thrashed in the wind. It was ill equipped for such use; it was not a kite. The boy gripped the string as tight as he could. He yanked and pulled, but the currents were powerful. The balloon bobbed and jerked and lurched. It had drifted too far from the quiet of the earth, but not far enough for the tranquility of space. The boy wept for the tortured balloon. He heaved and tugged, but the string only frayed. He cried, he prayed for help, but none came. The boy was powerless to pull the balloon down from where it fluttered in the far away distance—suffering, cold, alone. He cried and cried, and his tears flowed with such volume and ferocity that they puddled at his feet. The puddle of his tears formed a river, and the river flowed into the ocean. At last, the boy did the only thing he could to end the vicious torment of his precious balloon. He collapsed on the sand, and he let go. The balloon shot up, racing rapidly at first, and then drifting slower, higher, further into the abyss until his beautiful white balloon was little more than a speck, floating gently away, into the atmosphere, out of sight and into space.

EIGHTEEN

I COULDN'T SEE him in the pitch blackness, but I felt the weight and warmth of his body. I rolled onto my side, and in my mind, I slid closer and embraced him. I wanted more than anything to let my body follow suit, but the notion of Will recoiling at my touch kept me in check.

I lay still, listening to the soft rhythm of his breath. For the first time in days, I became aware of my own choppy and shallow panting. Meditation was in Will's bag of tricks, not mine, though I had given it a shot once at his urging. I tried hard to think of nothing, to feel nothing, to let my thoughts float by like clouds. I ambled inside my head, walking without purpose through peaks and valleys, seeing from a distant hilltop the labyrinth of trails I had darted around in prior days. But my relaxed stroll was short-lived. As the paths came into sharper focus, so too did my compulsion to choose one way over the other. Shortcuts and wrong directions. Wandering replaced by searching. In no time, I was lost again, no longer above the maze but in it.

I kept my eyes closed and watched the events of the day before like a movie—the hurtful words, the punch, the awful fucking hiss of the respirator. It was a short journey back in time from the ICU to the other dramas I'd inflicted on myself in recent months, a Chutes and Ladders downward slide into the rest of my reality. The English teacher, a wasted weekend. The bookstore, wasted effort. My novel, a wasted dream. Paul...I won't say wasted, but careless. A careless encounter that ruined everything. A man who cares for someone wouldn't risk so much for such little reward. Care-less. Thought-less. Worth-less.

I slipped out of bed and tiptoed across the dark room to my suitcase. I laid the bag gently on the floor and slowly tugged the zipper around the perimeter, until I could slide my hand inside. My fingers fished around the pockets, but didn't find the prescription bottle I was certain I'd stashed there. I rummaged through flaps and pouches, finding only a flash drive I'd lost months before and a small unopened hotel soap. My frustration mounted as I peered into the black interior of the suitcase. It felt like months since I'd packed in Tampa, but I was certain I'd tossed the pill bottle in the bag. I grabbed the toiletry bag and snatched at the zipper.

Will stirred on the bed behind me as I rifled through the bag.

"It's not in there," he said, groggy but serious.

"What?"

"Your pills are gone." In the pale morning light, I made out the image of Will leaning up on one elbow and watching me.

"I want a clean shave," I lied. "Where are my fucking razor blades?"

"You bought disposable razors. Cut the bullshit."

Dishonesty quickly proved to be an inadequate defense. "I can't believe you went through my things," I said, hoping righteous indignation would serve me better.

"I threw your prescription in the trash. In a dumpster, actually. At the hospital."

"Those weren't your pills to throw away. Fucking busybody." It wasn't like my last round of self-medication had produced positive results, but I had few lifelines left and Prozac was one of them.

"I'm sorry if that pisses you off. But I'm not sorry I found them and threw them away." He sat upright in bed and put on a T-shirt.

"You broke up with me. Why are you still playing the concerned boyfriend?"

"Because I *care*."

"How sweet," I replied. "I didn't know you still worried about me."

"I didn't say I cared about *you*."

"Fuck you."

"You need to get your shit under control. You lost it yesterday. This isn't the time for you to fall apart." He was out of bed, pulling on pants now.

"No shit," I said. "That's why I want to get back on the meds."

"So you can lay awake all night, puke all day, and flip out on people?" he asked. It was like a "best of" retrospective for December.

"So I can get my balance. Prozac worked for me before. Is that so hard to understand?"

He threaded his belt through the loops in his pants and dug through his suitcase for clean socks. "You punched a fucking pastor in an Intensive Care Unit. Do you think that made things better?"

"It made things better for me."

"And it's all about you, right?"

"I get that Jesus crap shoved down my throat, but I'm the asshole?"

"Exactly. And you're an asshole with or without Prozac." He slipped on his shoes.

"You going somewhere?"

"Yes," he said, "anywhere."

I SHOWERED AND dressed. As I slid my keys and cash into my pants pockets, I came across the laminated card on the dresser. Fourth line down. *I will stop taking pills.* There's no guarantee I would've gone back to the pills, but Will was right to toss them. Still, he didn't have to be such a smug asshole about it.

I was at the kitchen table eating a bowl of my father's Bran Flakes when the front door opened.

"You're back," I said, hoping to spark conversation.

"I'm back," he replied, offering none.

"Breakfast?"

He tossed the *Pensacola News Journal* from my parents' driveway onto the table. "What'd you find to eat?"

"Bran Flakes without raisins. I don't know why anyone would choose to eat this."

"Helps them shit." He poured a bowl for himself. "It's better than the sugar-coated garbage you eat." He sat opposite me and grabbed a random section of the newspaper.

"First you trash my pills, and now you're bad-mouthing my breakfast choices?"

He shoved his chair back, eliciting a screech from my mother's freshly waxed floor. "Never mind," he said. "I'll eat in the living room."

"Calm down. I was joking." He shoveled a spoonful of cereal into his mouth. "Too soon?"

"Not for me. You're the one who got all bent out of shape."

"Starting another round of Prozac might not have been the best thing," I conceded. "But it would've been nice if we talked about it before you dumpstered my pills."

"You can't talk about things." He took another bite of Bran Flakes. "You yell or shut down or punch people, remember?"

"I'm trying to call a cease-fire here."

"Because you're the peacemaker," he said, maintaining his focus on the cereal.

"Fuck this." I stood and jolted the table, sending coffee sloshing out of both our cups.

"I'll clean it up," he said. "I always do."

I SAT ALONE in the dim morning light of my parents' living room, where my mother's signed copy of *Luck of the Irish* was centered on the coffee table like a trophy. I appreciated the prominent placement, but taking time to read the book would have been a more moving gesture.

My parents' house was littered with souvenirs and reminders of the closeted half man, half boy I used to be. The Hummel figurines I bought my mother each year for her birthday—not my style, but who was I to judge if she had a thing for rosy-cheeked German kids with umbrellas? My framed senior portrait, me sporting a rented burgundy tux, a white ruffled shirt, and thick, side-parted game show hair. The reclining chair my father snoozed in for hours each day, not the same piece of furniture, but the same style of upholstered armchair he passed out in thirty-five years before, the night he nearly set our house on fire.

Ever since that near-disastrous fire, my mother couldn't have enough family pictures. Framed photo collages adorned every inch of space. I flipped on a table lamp as I examined the wall of pictures in the living room, and for the first time, I noticed Will's face in a grouping of more recent images. I wondered if he'd stuck around long enough to earn a permanent spot, or if my mother would take the picture out when she learned about the breakup. A different cluster of photographs was an homage to the dead—my father's mother, Uncle Henry's beloved wife, and a few McLeish elders I couldn't name. A diamond-shaped arrangement featured pictures of June and me. Black-and-white prints of her cradling me as a baby, a grainy image of us hunting for sand dollars in the surf, and a casual shot of June and thirteen-year-old me playing Scrabble at the kitchen table, a Chek cola in front of me, a lime-garnished gin and tonic next to her.

Wandering through the images took me back in time, which I suppose is what family pictures are meant to do. The journey is always incomplete, though. Photographs preserve the good times and the smiles, the wedding days, the Christmas mornings and first-ever bike rides, but they never tell the whole story. No one snaps a photo of a dazed and frightened toddler, the day his parents pawn him off like a mangy stray on a series of relatives who don't really want him but don't have the heart to put him down. There are no pictures of the paralyzing fear on the face of a confused and closeted gay kid when he's asked for the thousandth time about the absence of girls in his life. And decades later, when his secret lover comforts him as he weeps for his sins, no one captures that special moment on film. Those photographs don't exist, and if they did, they'd never get out of the shoebox.

I had nearly completed my trip through the brighter days in McLeish family history, when one last frozen moment caught my attention. The three by five print from my teen years was hidden in plain sight, tucked in the corner of a bronze frame that held a dozen photos of assorted shapes and sizes. I took the collage off the wall and sat on my parent's sofa, holding my breath as I stared at the washed-out image of me, Aunt Doris, Uncle Martin, and Patrick.

Will came in from the kitchen. He stood silently, processing how the sizable picture frame in my lap fit neatly into the empty white space on the adjacent wall.

"Truce," he said.

I nodded in lieu of formulating an actual response, as the photograph dredged images from twenty-five years earlier to the surface of my consciousness.

"Let's move on from Prozac," he said.

"That's fine." I glanced at Will, but my mind was somewhere else—a muggy Georgia afternoon in the summer after my freshman year of high school.

"What are you looking at?"

"A picture," I said.

"I see that." He ran his fingertips over each image in the collage. "Which one?"

"The one with me, Aunt Doris, and Uncle Martin. And Patrick. It's Six Flags over Georgia."

"You guys are soaked," he said, observing our drenched clothing and matted hair. "But you're all smiles."

"I was fourteen."

"I thought you lived back home with your folks by then."

"I did, but Aunt Doris and Uncle Martin still took me on road trips and summer vacations."

"Good times."

You think you know everything... I thought the words but didn't say them. He was trying to move beyond our tumultuous morning, and I didn't want to fuck it up.

"This was right after we got off the log ride. Aunt Doris looks like a wet terrier."

"Patrick looks like your Uncle Martin with those big brown eyes and that grin. How old was he?"

I touched my cousin's face in the photo. "Seventeen. He died that same year, about six months after this picture was taken."

Will cleaned the dusty edge of the frame with his fingertip but said nothing.

"I haven't thought about that afternoon in forever," I said.

"Looks like a fun day."

"It was. It's just hard to remember the good times when the shitty memories are so strong."

"He looks happy." There was an element of confusion in Will's voice.

"Things hadn't gone to shit yet."

"It's crazy how someone goes from being a smiling ordinary kid to suicide in just a few months."

"Did you ever disappoint your mom?" I asked. "Really disappoint her? Like, crush her?"

He raised his eyebrows. I had his full attention.

"We were visiting Aunt Doris's mother. She lived south of Atlanta. Near Macon, I think." The memory was like a jigsaw puzzle, and each sentence I spoke aloud filled in a missing piece. "We went there after Aunt Doris's dad died, to paint the house and help her mom sort through some old shit she wanted to throw out."

"How'd you end up soaking wet on the log ride?" he asked.

"It was hotter than hell. We took a break after a few days. Went to Six Flags and then went back to Aunt Doris's mom's to finish cleaning and painting."

"I didn't know you ever met Doris's mom."

"Frances Meeks." The name surfaced with surprising ease. "But Tom Meeks would have been the one to meet. Aunt Doris's dad was a Southern Baptist preacher and a total son-of-a-bitch."

"She's mentioned that—the preacher part, I mean."

"She tells you what she wants you to know."

He sat rapt as I shared the rest of the story. Patrick and I, up and down ladders with Uncle Martin, putting a fresh coat of white paint on the clapboard siding of the house. Afternoons with Aunt Doris in the steaming attic, weeding through musty trunks of old clothes and Christmas cards. Old-fashioned Southern fried dinners, and one sweltering hot night.

The Meeks house was an old, two-story colonial with four, or maybe five, bedrooms. There were plenty of beds to go around, but on the hottest night in Georgia that July, ceiling fans were a premium. Three of the bedrooms had working fans, including the one Patrick had been sleeping in, which is why Aunt Doris moved me in there. That innocent decision is one we'll both regret for the rest of our lives.

At fourteen, I didn't understand much about what it meant to be gay. It started out innocently enough, and as far as I'm concerned, it ended that way. We slept in a double bed, adequately spacious for a scrawny kid and his only slightly larger cousin. It was hot, and we crawled under the light cotton sheet wearing only our underwear. When Patrick leaned up and turned on the lamp on the bedside table, I saw the clean line of his body, the tight bronze skin of his back, the smooth nape of his neck. I didn't understand much about what it meant to be gay, but even at fourteen, I was aware of the male form and I knew it made me feel different.

I didn't know before that night that Patrick was gay, and in retrospect, I imagine he was only just figuring it out himself. He was seventeen, but he'd been conditioned to believe that sex was an activity a man explored only after falling in love with a respectable woman and marrying her. Add to that, the 1980s was the decade of Reagan, and if that wasn't enough repression, the birth of AIDS hadn't exactly laid out a welcome mat to gay culture.

Patrick and I were virtually identical in our shared lack of sexual awareness, but there was a three-year difference in our bodies. It was that difference that my cousin and I were curiously investigating, underwear on the floor and erections in hand, when Aunt Doris walked in. Her scream penetrated the night, but apparently not the walls of the old house. No one came running in behind her.

She trembled with rage as she assailed us with the horrible and harmful words you'd expect. "Nasty little bastards. Where on earth did you learn this filth!"

I pulled the covers over my naked pubescent body and sat stunned.

"I'm sorry, Mom." Patrick wept and begged forgiveness.

"Sorry? What you've done is pure sin. It's evil, and all you can say is 'I'm sorry'?"

He slid from the bed, holding the sheet in front of his shameful nakedness, and grabbed his underwear from the floor. "I'm sorry and I'm ashamed."

Her eyes filled with tears as she approached the bed. "I didn't give birth to a deviant."

"I'm sorry, Momma."

She grabbed her son by the shoulders and stared directly into his eyes. "You disgust me."

We didn't speak of that night again, but Patrick was never the same. He was withdrawn and disconnected. I innately understood his desolation, the hopeless uncertainty of how to interact in a world that required him to be something, someone, he wasn't. Still, inner turmoil was a challenge he might have conquered, if that had been his only foe. The torment I imagined Aunt Doris put him through after that hot summer night—shaming him, embarrassing and threatening him, hating him—that was something worse. Patrick's quiet nightmare went on for months, until that chilly December night when Uncle Martin found his son's lifeless body hanging in the garage.

I have often envied Patrick.

Though I was undamaged by the boyhood curiosity I shared with my cousin, the toxic fallout from that night of innocent exploration rained poison on my life.

I finished the story and returned the photo collage to its space on the wall.

"Jesus Christ," Will said.

"Yeah, he's in the story somewhere."

The shrill ring of my parents' telephone jolted us back to the present. I jumped to answer it. My father's voice was that of a man twenty years older than the one I knew the day before. "She's having trouble. It's been a rough night."

"Why didn't you call and wake us up?" I was more confused than angry.

"There's nothing you could do. And you needed to rest. You can't lose it like you did yesterday."

"I'm fine," I said. "I promise."

"All right." He sounded less than convinced.

"We'll be there shortly, Dad."

"Henry's here too."

"Mom didn't want anyone there."

"We called him," my father said. "It's time..."

I knew the words he'd left unspoken—*to say good-bye.*

NINETEEN

WE RACED THROUGH the maze of glossy hallways and finally reached the ICU waiting room, where my mother and father sat quietly in the corner. I kissed them both on the forehead.

"Henry wanted a minute," my mother said.

"We'll wait in the hall."

Will opened one of two large, wooden doors and we walked together down yet another polished corridor. We stopped at the thick glass wall that separated the dozen or so beds of the intensive care unit from the real world. A pulsing bundle of raw emotions swirled and twisted inside me, prodding and pushing at the walls of my chest. I wanted to lash out, to rage, but my anger sparked and sputtered. There was nothing left to burn. Will placed his hand on my shoulder, but I took comfort from nothing except the feel of the cool glass against my forehead.

Through the glass, I saw Uncle Henry sitting alone at June's bedside holding her hand. He wore wrinkled khakis, a pit-stained T-shirt, and bedroom slippers. He'd dressed in a hurry. Uncle Henry was in good shape for a man approaching seventy, but his skin betrayed his age. Decades of saltwater fishing under the sweltering Florida sun had left his face leathery and lined with creases. The gray stubble he wore added a few more years to his appearance.

We milled around the hallway until he finished his one-sided good-bye and called us in with a wave and a smile.

"Mornin' fellas. I was just reminiscing with your grandmother about old times."

"Not too conversational these days, is she?" The question prompted a sideways glance from Will.

Uncle Henry squeezed June's gnarled hand. "I don't know about that," he said. "Maybe she's just in the mood to listen more than talk."

"Wouldn't it be nice," I said, "if this was all as simple as June being in a shitty mood?"

"Yeah," he chuckled. "We'd cheer her right up with a martini and a couple of wisecracks about your pain-in-the-ass Aunt Doris."

"You heard? About the reverend?" I tried to sound apologetic, hoping Will might appreciate the humility.

He shook his head. "Nah. Didn't hear a thing." Uncle Henry wasn't one to shout from rooftops. He conveyed himself in subtle ways, which somehow made his show of support all the more fortifying.

Will leaned closer to June and touched her face. "Did they say what time...they expect to see the doctor?" He preferred the wrong question over the painful truth.

Uncle Henry placed a hand on Will's shoulder. "They have some paperwork to sort out, and then they'll go ahead with it. Sounds like she'll be out of this mess by noon."

I moved to the far side of June's bed, so she was now flanked by Will and me. "Well," Uncle Henry said, "I'll let you boys have a few minutes with your grandmother."

"Okay."

"Oh, Conor, how's your book sellin'?"

"Slow and not so steady," I said.

"Keep at it." He winked and patted my arm. "You keep at it."

He dabbed at his twinkly eyes and kissed June's forehead. "Good-bye, sweetheart." He turned and, without a backward glance, walked away.

Will stroked the back of June's hand and combed his fingers gently through her coarse gray hair. "I guess this thing is winding down."

I moved a few feet away and took a seat in a molded plastic chair near the ICU entrance. I held my face in my hands, partly to hide my anguish, but mostly to shelter myself from Will's.

"When I lost Mom and Dad, I didn't have a chance to say good-bye." He paused and looked at the ceiling. "Lost, what a fucking euphemism. I'm pretty sure this trumps getting lost."

I smiled and wondered if June would have laughed at the observation—or told him to get the fuck on with it.

"I'm babbling," he said. "And I don't even know if you can hear me." He smiled and wiped a tear from his cheek. "Anyway, Conor and I are here to..." His mouth was open, but no words came out.

"Will..." I stood and moved toward him, but he waved me away.

"I feel lucky," he said. "So lucky to have had you as my friend. You listened and you told me the truth, whether I liked it or not." His words reminded me that June would leave this world believing my relationship with Will was intact. For that, I was grateful.

He cupped her twisted hand in his and continued. "One thing I like about you, you never take the easy way out."

He straightened the bedsheets and adjusted June's hospital gown. He was stalling for time, trying to stave off the inevitable. Finally, he leaned in, gave her a soft peck on the cheek, and whispered his last words to her.

"I'll miss you, June."

He laid my grandmother's hands across her stomach, mimicking a natural pose she could no longer make on her own. I saw my mother and father a few feet away, frozen in grief like marble statues with red, puffy eyes.

My father broke the silence. "Conor, have you...said good-bye?"

"No."

He put his arm around my mother. "We don't have much longer. They want to take care of things this morning."

Take care of things? His choice of words annoyed me, but I let it go.

As I approached June's bedside and held her hand, my chest ached with the memory of all that she was. I hoped she hadn't been too disappointed by all that I was not. June was self-made. Strong, honest, brave, sometimes reckless, always ready to roll the dice. She fought like hell and usually won, though she was never bitter in defeat. She loved with ferocity and without fear. June saw the beauty of growing up and the ugly reality of growing old. She accepted the world around her but refused to be defined by it.

She would have despised the pomp and circumstance of this moment. I closed my eyes and imagined her words. "Everyone has to die, but no one wants to lay here like this. Now be a good grandson and unplug that goddamn machine." The voice was imaginary, but the sentiment was real, and she had filed the Living Will to prove it.

I asked for a moment alone with June, or at least a moment alone amongst the various strangers who were busy visiting, working, or dying in the ICU.

"You look a little rough," I whispered to her. "You wouldn't like it." I smoothed and patted her hair. "I don't know what to say, except thank you for making me feel like I was worth a shit. I know you believed it, but I still don't know if I am. I've fucked up. A lot."

Her eyes, which had been open at times since her stroke, were closed now. I moved to the foot of her bed and placed my hand on the blanket that covered her feet.

"I have a going away present for you," I said. "Do you know *Desiderata*? I memorized it back in tenth grade, and I've held onto it for all these years. Now I know why." I took a heaving deep breath and cleared my throat.

You are a child of the universe
No less than the trees and stars
You have a right to be here.
And whether or not it is clear to you,
No doubt, the universe is unfolding as it should.
So be at peace with God
Whatever you conceive him to be.
And whatever your labors and aspirations
In the noisy confusion of life
Keep peace with your soul.
With all its sham, drudgery, and broken dreams,
It's still a beautiful world.

I kissed her on the forehead, and though the word wasn't audible, I said it. *Good-bye.*

THE MEDICAL STAFF met with my mother to review the details of "the disconnection," which sounded like we were having our cable shut off. They sent in a social worker who told us we could be present when the respirator was removed. Will and my parents accepted. I left them in the small consultation room, where they waited to be called into the ICU to hold my grandmother's hands while she gulped her last breaths of air.

I wandered the halls, slouching past room after room of the sick, diseased, and dying, trying to convince myself that it was still a "beautiful world." Hospitals must heal someone. Kidneys were transplanted, tumors removed, broken limbs put together again. Somewhere in this maze, adoring families gawked at beautiful, healthy babies. Maybe there was beauty here, but people like me seldom found it.

I eventually found myself standing outside another nondescript wooden door, behind which I might discover rows of filing cabinets, dying children, or a janitor's mop and bucket. It seemed as good a doorway as any to duck into as I tried in vain to hide from the truth.

Hospital chapels are fucked-up little closets of worship. There's no grandeur or ornate decor, which is unsettling for those of us who grew up attending Catholic churches, but the kind of solace sought in hospitals is best rendered in more intimate settings anyway. A few pews, some mood lighting, Christ on the cross, a little velvet here and there. Just enough religious staging for a spiritual encounter. While I was no longer a Christian, I didn't mind seeking comfort in the presence of a crucifix. Catholics get used to icons and symbols, and their familiar presence comforted me like a favorite pillow on an out-of-town trip.

There was no one else in the chapel, but I still sat in the last pew. I was a non-believer, a second-class zealot, and I knew my place at the back of the religious bus. I knelt down with my back straight and my elbows resting on the pew in front of me. I interlocked my fingers in obedient altar boy fashion, closed my eyes, and I prayed. Though the effort seemed futile, I prayed to God above, and on the side, and in both front and back, and within. "Dear God," I prayed, "what the hell are you thinking?"

I yearned for the great epiphany. I was desperate to believe that my Father, who art in Heaven, hallowed be His name, was looking down on me, watching events unfold, and preparing to alter the future on a moment's notice, to deliver me from every evil.

That's not how things happen for me, though. If God exists at all, he is blind to my world. It's not supposed to be like this. I leaned back in the pew, and I broke. My tears came hard and I surrendered myself, but no spirit came to comfort me. No reassuring strength, no guiding hand, no transcendent connection to a higher power. I sent my signals into outer space, longed to get a reply, prayed for anything, a single sign, and got nothing.

Funny how after a good cry, a total breakdown, your first reaction is to feel you may have overreacted. Over the course of a few hours, my psychotic pendulum had swung from excessive drama to eerie calm to an almost unsettling perspective. *Why all the fuss? Aren't we all a part of a bigger tapestry anyway? Everyone dies eventually, especially older people.*

Besides, she's better off now that she's moved on and left you behind. And so is Will, since we're on that subject.

True, but not like this. June should have never had to lie in this whitewashed prison, waiting to die. And no one should ever have to decide to end someone else's life, even for the sake of mercy, whatever that is. She should have died with more dignity, in her sleep, peaceful and quiet, at home in bed like fucking grandmothers do.

I SAT IN the tiny makeshift house of God tucked away on the second floor of Sacred Heart Hospital, my mind barren and my body numb. Time didn't move, and without prompt or provocation, neither did I. I'm not sure how long I'd been gone before Will texted to ask where I was.

Chapel, I replied. *No, not kidding.*

Minutes later, the door opened behind me. He sat and put his arm around my shoulder. "Conor," he said, "it's not over."

TWENTY

THE RESPIRATOR THAT had churned at her side for days was wheeled into the corner, its dark screen and coiled hoses serving as stark reminders that June was on her own now, unplugged, sentenced to die. As I might have anticipated, she refused to go quietly or quickly, but what might have been a prizefight felt more like a slow execution. Death by plodding suffocation, not the absence of breath, but the reduction of it, with each labored breath shallower than the one before, until there was nothing. I watched as her chest heaved and sputtered in search of oxygen. The noise, the sound of air gulping and gurgling as she forced it through her broken body, was different from the rhythmic slap of the respirator, but no less unnerving.

We passed the days after June was disconnected in much the same way as we had passed the days before. We sat on our achy asses for hours and waited for her to die, while she lay flat on her back in the ICU, not dying. She clung to her mortality, but it was a hopeless treading of water destined to end in drowning.

We abandoned the overnight hospital vigils, but we still stayed in the ICU late each night, rotating shifts in pairs and making sure one of us was nearby in case something changed. We spent countless hours trying to spark some life in June, talking to her, taking turns manipulating her arms and legs the way the nurses had shown us. During long, tedious stretches, we passed the time reading and watching TV, and talking to strangers in the waiting room about their god-awful misfortunes. There were plenty.

The waiting was exhausting.

When my mother fell asleep one night in the waiting room, I left her napping and went to the ICU alone to say goodnight to June. As I approached the bed, I heard the change in her breathing before I saw the spastic rise and fall of her chest. Her puffing and panting sounded distressed and erratic. I rushed to the duty station and described June's deteriorated breathing to the nurse behind the counter.

The nurse was an attractive, slightly overweight, black woman, whose full head of graying hair and regular mention of grandchildren in Tampa told me she was older than the fifty years she looked. The kind-hearted woman I would come to know as Ms. Henrietta Broussard reminded me that labored and difficult breathing was not an unexpected turn of events.

"We're doing everything we can to keep her comfortable," she said.

"She looks pretty goddamned uncomfortable now." I glanced at the nurse's crucifix lapel pin and immediately regretted my choice of words. "I'm sorry. Can you just take a look at her?"

"Of course." She went to June's bedside and performed a cursory inspection, which I imagined was mostly to pacify me. She flipped a switch, turning on a machine that was connected to a tiny hose she maneuvered around my grandmother's mouth and throat to suction mucus.

"That's a horrible sound," I said.

Ms. Broussard nodded as she finished and turned off the machine. She gently shifted the dead weight of my grandmother's body and adjusted her head on the pillow. "There you go, sweetheart. All better."

"Thank you," I said.

The nurse smiled. "I was talking to your grandmother. But you're welcome."

I followed her to the nurse's station and thanked her again for her kindness.

"I can only imagine how terrible this is for you," she said.

"I've had better days."

"Letting go is hard. But none of us knows when the Lord is going to call us home."

"I just wish this was over. For all of us."

June's living will didn't expressly prohibit the continuation of a feeding tube, and though she was off the respirator, she still received intravenous nourishment. I wondered if this was a technical oversight on her part, or if she had simply been okay with the idea of suffocating, but not with starvation. Either way, she was stuck in the shit now.

Before I woke my mother to say goodnight to June, I completed the comforting set of nightly rituals I had developed. I pulled June's bedsheets taut and straightened her gown. I fluffed and primped her hair, and positioned her balled-up fists on her stomach. As I leaned down to kiss her good-bye, I whispered the verse from *Desiderata* into her ear, the same one I had recited to her after she was unplugged, the day she should have died.

I finished the poem, and as I pushed myself upright from the bed, I nudged the pillow, causing June's head to loll to one side. I slid my hand beneath her shoulder and leaned her forward. As I tugged the sterile white pillow back into place, her eyelids fluttered and opened.

When she'd first opened her eyes after the stroke, the ICU nurses told us it was an involuntary reflex. I reluctantly accepted the explanation, and each time it happened afterward, I kept my reaction in check. This time, though, the timing of her vacant gray-blue eyes popping open chilled me.

She registered no awareness of my presence, but I still wondered if there was meaning behind the gesture. I remembered my mother's words when we first debated June's end-of-life decision. "She told me once, if I leave her on a respirator she'll come back to haunt me."

The living will made June's wishes clear. We'd carried out her instructions to the letter. We removed the hissing monstrosity that had forced air into her lungs and kept her artificially alive. In a way, though, yanking the respirator felt like a pathetic half-measure. As she lay helpless and silent, trapped inside her damaged shell, maybe she expected more from me.

There was a direct line of sight from the nurse's station to June's bed, but for the moment, the desk was unoccupied. I cradled her head in one hand and kept the other on her pillow as she gasped and gulped, her eyes bulging like a fish on a beach. I looked for confirmation, a signal, any vague reassurance that what I was about to do was intended to end her misery, not mine. I leaned close, my ear just inches from her lips, and listened intently, imagining her last whispered wish: *Do it, Conor. Put that fucking pillow on my face.*

My grip tightened. I knotted the pillowcase in my fingers. *Give me a sign*, I prayed, *a gesture, a word, anything.* But none came.

I ASKED MARSHALL for an indefinite leave of absence, which he acquiesced to after a lengthy lecture on personal responsibility. Will, who didn't have a stroke-addled grandmother, at least not as far as the Busch Gardens Human Resource department was concerned, had to go back to work. My mother insisted she and my father could keep watch at the hospital, so that

Will and I could have quality time together before his return to Tampa. I'm not sure what activities she assumed we'd fill our "quality" time with, but since we were no longer a couple, I knew what activities we weren't going to do.

A fancy restaurant meal felt too celebratory, so Will and I decided on a simple Sunday brunch on his last day. As a Bible Belt northwest Florida city, Pensacola had a disproportionate church to brunch restaurant ratio. The wait was lengthy. We were eventually seated, and soon after, served mediocre pancake breakfasts with matching sides of limp, greasy bacon.

"What else is there to do around here on a Sunday?" he asked.

"Bookstore?" I suggested.

After brunch, we drove to Barnes & Noble, where we went our separate ways as soon as we were inside. "I need more caffeine," he said. "You want something from the cafe?"

"Nope. I'm heading to Fiction."

"I'll find you in a while." He walked away but turned back. "If you don't find the author you're looking for in Fiction, you might check Local Interest."

"Ha." I was unamused. "What's wrong with checking to see if my book is on the shelves of my hometown bookstore?"

"Nothing. It's just amusing to see you act like a celebrity. Check the inventory and then identify yourself at the counter and make witty chitchat with the help."

"Enjoy your coffee," I said. "Try not to burn your tongue."

I cased the bookshelves for half an hour before engaging in the shameless self-promotion Will had accurately predicted. The store was busy, so I kept my schmoozing brief and left the store manager to tend to his customers.

I walked the perimeter of the store until I spotted Will browsing the Puzzles and Games section. "Guess what? They received four copies of my book initially and sold out before Christmas."

"Is that a good thing?"

"It would have been better if they'd ordered more, but yeah, it's a good thing."

"Unless they sold them all to your mom." It was unlike Will to knock the wind out of my sails, but in our new alternate universe, nothing made sense. Once upon a time, he had been supportive and enthusiastic when we talked about my writing career, but the English teacher, ex-boyfriend, Prozac, and stroke changed all that.

"Anyway, I convinced the manager to order four more copies."

He raised his eyebrows and nodded, singularly unimpressed.

"Thinking about buying something?" I asked.

"Something for June." He grabbed a Sesame Street-themed children's chess set from the shelf. "Big Bird is the king and Cookie Monster is the queen."

I looked closer at the image pictured on the front of the box. "With Bert and Ernie bishops and Oscar the Grouch rooks."

"It's stupid. But it made me think of her."

"High stakes chess. I remember."

"This is the last one. It's been opened, but I want to get it."

"Okay," I said. "I'm no chess master, but I can teach you the basics since June can't."

"I'm buying a book on chess rules too. But, thanks."

Though my parents had ICU duty for the day, Will was eager to present his gift to June. When we arrived at the hospital, a small crowd had gathered on the sidewalk directly in our path to the main entrance. I recognized my father's face in the midst of the group. To my dismay, Aunt Doris was also there, and, to my horror, the right Reverend Lonnie Casey stood next to her. I quickly surmised that this much polyester could only mean the rest of the throng were congregants from Holy Smyrna Baptist.

I stopped at the edge of the gathering. Will whispered to me. "Don't cause a scene. No one needs the stress."

My blood had already reached an instantaneous boil. "What the hell is this?"

"We're just concluding our prayer service for your grandmother, Conor," answered Aunt Doris. "Would you care to join us for our closing invocation?"

"Un-fucking-believable." Will placed his hand on my shoulder, putting himself in quick restraint position, if needed. "It's okay. I'm not going to punch anyone."

"Conor," Doris said, "I wish you could see we're only here to help."

"We offer only the miraculous healing light of God's love," chimed Reverend Lonnie.

"Was the message not clear enough from your last visit?" I glanced at the reverend, who appeared to have healed since my unfortunate slip and fall into his face. "You're not welcome here, and if you don't respect June enough to see that, you can at least respect my mother's wishes."

"We are respecting your mother's wishes," Aunt Doris replied. Her use of the royal "we," I imagined, represented her, the reverend, and the tiny gold Christ on her lapel.

My father, usually a bystander, spoke up. "Conor, we called Doris. We know you don't believe like we do, but we think your grandmother being unplugged and not dying is a sign."

The dozen or so congregants from my aunt's church encircled us on the sidewalk, and my father and I faced off like contenders in the Holy Spirit fight club. In my father's corner, stood Aunt Doris, the reverend, and the army of almighty God, each of whom clutched a leather Bible like a baseball bat. Behind me, there was Will, who wielded a venti non-fat latte and a Sesame Street chess set.

"Dad, what sign is God sending? I'm a little slow so help me out here." I wouldn't resort to violence again, but sarcasm was in my wheelhouse.

"There's a bigger plan unfolding than we can understand. Something special is happening." I was stunned as my father continued. "God's at work here, Conor, and we need to show our faith and beg for his mercy."

The most complex sentence I remembered my father speaking before today was, "Hey, Conor, toss me the remote." As I processed his religious pronouncement and accepted that he was capable of at least a modicum of eloquence, the realization stung me—my parents had staged my morning with Will so they could pull off Aunt Doris's little prayer circle without my knowledge.

"We knew you wouldn't understand," he said, "but believe me, something special is happening here." His originality clearly still had limits. "I'm sorry, son. We're just asking for God's mercy. It's all for the best. It's for June."

I stared into his pleading eyes. "Jesus Christ, Dad. She's been working on Uncle Martin for years, and she's finally brainwashed you too."

He met my gaze and shook his head, smirking in pity at my lack of understanding. "It's not like that. That's not how it is."

"I'll tell you how it is," I said. "There is no God, and there's no fucking mercy. It's that simple." I turned on my heel and headed up the sidewalk, my relieved ex-boyfriend and his children's chess set trailing behind me.

JUNE'S PROLONGED ABILITY to breathe on her own necessitated her relocation to a step-down unit, where care was critical, but apparently not so "intensive." We received directions to her pseudo-private, semi-monitored, quasi-critical care room and walked the maze until we found it. My mother sat in a recliner next to the bed, holding June's hand, and staring at the television mounted absurdly high up on the wall.

As the potential for life-threatening medical crises lessens, hospitals give more consideration to the comfort of both the patient and their visitors. In addition to the BarcaLounger and cable television, there was a dresser opposite June's bed. A cheaply framed generic print of a vase full of sunflowers hung on the wall above it.

"Hi, June." Will brushed the hair back from my grandmother's forehead and kissed her there. "I see all your complaining about the service upstairs finally paid off."

"You're so silly," my mother said with a smile.

I kissed June's cheek and held her hand. Standing opposite my mother, I wanted to interrogate her about the prayer service. I wanted to scream, to ask why she allowed, or worse, invited, a gang of self-righteous hypocrites into the space where my grandmother grappled with death, knowing that June had little use for Doris and her fundamentalist friends.

I yearned to say all those things, but during our trek to June's room, Will reminded me this was not the time or place for a showdown. June was, after all, my mother's mother, and no matter how complicated the situation, watching the last ounces of life seep out of a parent earned some measure of leeway.

"Conor," my mother said, "I didn't expect to see you here today, but something wonderful has happened."

"Mom, stop," I said. "We've been over this a hundred times with the doctors. June's breathing means nothing. Her motor skills were less damaged than we thought, but that only means she dies a little slower."

"Conor," Will admonished me with a headshake. We had no way of knowing what June was or wasn't comprehending.

"She squeezed my hand." The tears in my mother's eyes overflowed their banks.

"Fine. But it doesn't mean anything."

"She squeezed my hand." She said it slower this time, as though I were new to the English language.

"Goddammit, don't do this."

This roller coaster was harrowing enough without my mother adding vertical drops and hairpin curves. I let go of June's hand and turned away, folding my arms like a pouty eight-year-old. There was no safe place to turn my gaze.

It was then that I noticed the weighty black Bible on the bedside table. I picked it up and turned it over in my hands, browsing the back cover as if I might find laudatory blurbs from admiring authors.

I wondered if the Bible was a gift from the hospital, which was, after all, Sacred Heart, a Catholic institution. Gold lettering on the spine indicated this was a King James Bible, though, and as an accomplished bookseller, not to mention a graduate of Saint Mary's Saturday morning catechism, I knew Catholics used a different version. I flipped open the cover and saw the inscription.

Discover the healing word of God and you shall live forever.

Love, Doris

I looked up to see my mother staring at me, her eyes wide with anticipation, maybe even fear. "Did you let her bring that fucking charlatan in here?"

She didn't answer.

"Did you let Aunt Doris and the Reverend back in here to see June?" I asked, louder this time.

"Conor. Mother squeezed my hand. She's trying to communicate with me."

Will moved closer, though it was unclear if he intended to provide comfort or restraint.

"She has involuntary reactions," I said. "It was just a spasm or something."

"Conor, listen to me." Her words were slow and deliberate. "After Doris and Reverend Casey prayed over her, I asked her to give me a sign if she heard us. She squeezed my hand. I didn't believe it. So I asked her to do it again, only to squeeze twice. And she squeezed again. Twice."

An ache had been building behind my eyes, and it pounded now. "Will," I said. "Help." But he sat still and quiet, confused or eager for my mother to continue.

"She's going to be okay." My mother's voice was hopeful now. "I know you can't accept that, but it's true. God moves in mysterious ways, Conor. If you trust him, turn things over to him, he will provide."

"Talk to her, for Christ's sake," I said, but Will paced the room in silence, wading through his own turmoil, rubbing his face as if to erase the dream and restore reality. "Mom, I'm sorry you wasted your time with this shit. And I am even sorrier that you disrespected June by letting those lunatics in here. If June squeezed your hand, it was only because she wished it was your neck. If she had one ounce of energy left, she'd use it to choke the life out of you."

Will cleared his throat. "Let's take a break, Conor. You're saying things you don't mean." He pulled my sleeve and ushered me toward the hallway.

I offered no resistance but stopped in the doorway to take a last shot. I stared at the Bible, inert and harmless on the nightstand. "I'm glad you *'discovered the healing word,'* Mother, but do me a favor, and keep that bullshit to yourself."

"You'll see, Conor." She was less angry than hopeful.

"I won't."

"You'll see," she said through a thick veil of tears, "and you'll be glad when you do."

I GRABBED A wad of napkins to wipe off a dirty table while Will ordered coffee at the counter. He smiled at the cashier while he waited in line and made small talk with another customer. Will could maintain perspective under any circumstance, with the notable exception of the cheating spouse scenario. I could mimic his capacity for calm for short periods, but fear or rage or disappointment always won out in the end. He tried twice to teach me how to meditate, but I was the world's worst Buddhist and I had the bubbling rage and rampant insecurity to prove it.

He took the hard, plastic seat beside me and propped his elbows on the damp tabletop.

"Will, I panicked."

"It's okay," he said. "Everybody's tense."

"I panicked, because she squeezed my hand too."

"What?"

"When I leaned down to kiss her, before Mom said any of that shit, June squeezed my hand. Twice."

"Okay." He took a deep breath and leaned back so far, the molded plastic chair nearly snapped.

"What if it's true? What if she's alive inside? I don't want to get my hopes up, but what are we supposed to fucking do?"

"We aren't supposed to do anything." He spoke in a near whisper. "We don't control this. It's out of our hands."

"Oh Jesus." I said, a bit too loud. "You too? You think we're in fucking loaves-and-fishes territory?"

"Don't be an asshole. All I am saying is nothing is for sure. We don't know why she's responding, or if she even is."

I sipped the lukewarm hospital coffee and wished it was Starbucks. There's something worth praying for.

"One thing, Conor...you can't explode every time things get complicated." He paused, allowing time for rebuttal, but I offered none. "We have to wait it out together."

"I understand that. I just don't see this turning around."

I pushed the foam cup around the tabletop, nearly toppling it and spilling the dregs, before putting the coffee to my lips and downing it as though comfort could be gulped. It held my calm on the outside, but my temples throbbed and my stomach filled with acid. If June continued to breathe on her own, what miserable existence could she look forward to? A half-life of eating through tubes and having her ass wiped by strangers, or worse, by loved ones? Why didn't I suffocate this nightmare with a pillow when I had the chance? I wanted to ask the questions, to argue them, but there was no point. There were no good answers anyway.

TWENTY-ONE

AFTER WILL WENT back to Tampa, there were more long days at the hospital, sitting in spine-busting chairs in claustrophobic rooms that were never intended for long-term occupancy. Most nights, I was in no mood for small talk, so I'd leave my parents behind and drive to Pensacola Beach, where I rediscovered the bars I hung out in when I was in my twenties. I was particularly fond of a dark, rickety hovel called Bali. The bar wasn't on the waterfront and there was nothing South Pacific about it, but the bartenders had a heavy pour, the crowds were sparse, and I could usually find a quiet corner to sulk and piss and moan, if only to myself.

I drifted far from shore each night, unanchored, bobbing and floating in a sea of anger and vodka highballs. I resented June's illness for interrupting her existence and mine, which is not to say that my poisoned relationship, shit job, and stillborn writing career constituted the good life. When June's stroke turned my life upside down, it hadn't derailed a grand plan, but an ill-fated salvage effort. Each time I eyed June's pillow and considered snuffing out this torture, that sad truth only heightened my guilt.

THINGS HAVE A way of not fucking going how you planned, and more often than not, runs of good fortune turn to murky puddles of shit. But sometimes, when you least expect it, the broken pieces of life, the fucked-up dead ends and no-win dilemmas, bring warm, sunny days and fuzzy puppies. That's my only explanation for June's recovery. Whether through the marvel of modern science or the strange and mysterious workings of the Lord, or maybe just because life is a complicated and fucked up wonder, June showed modest signs of improving sensory awareness. There were no more demonstrations of miraculous on-demand hand squeezing, but during stimulus testing, the name they gave to pricking June's hands and feet with pointy objects, doctors noted encouraging responses. Still, each ounce of optimism was tempered with a pound of caution.

For two months, her facial expressions conveyed only primitive awareness, the unspoken vocabulary of a trapped animal. *Pain, fear, help, no, ughh*. But on a chilly morning in late February, her face lit up with something different, a faint glimmer of recognition.

I arrived at her room as I did each morning, with a backpack that held my laptop, a couple of books, and a few snacks. I set the bag on the floor below the window ledge that now served as home to the Sesame Street chess set, and I fished out a snapshot Will had sent to June. In the picture, he looked as if he'd stepped out of the shower, dressed, and done little more than run his hands through his short brown hair. He wore khaki shorts and a powder-blue T-shirt, and he sat at our patio table, his bare feet propped on a chair. He smiled and held a copy of *Chess Made Easy* in one hand, a glass of red wine in the other. On the back, he'd written, *June, Wish you were here. Love, Will*. I positioned the photograph on the game board between the Big Bird king and the Cookie Monster queen, at an angle where June could see it.

I set out on my daily half-mile trek to the cafeteria, stopping by the duty station to take drink orders from the nurses. They were thoughtful and caring professionals, but it never hurt to suck up a little. A couple of lattes was a small price to pay for priority bedsheet changes. No one manned the desk, but I'd seen Nurse Henrietta Broussard scurrying from room to room on my way in. I bought a hot chocolate for her, which I left at the nurse's station with a scribbled note that read, *Thank you, Ms. Broussard. Love, June*.

When I returned to June's room, her head was tilted awkwardly to one side, and a slim string of spittle hung from her lip. I grabbed a tissue and dabbed the corner of her mouth, then propped her head on the pillow. I fussed with her hair and adjusted the sheets, just as I did every day. That's when I saw *it*. I can't say exactly what *it* was, eye contact maybe, or the first crinkle of a smile—a distinct sign of comprehension, that if I had to name, looked like gratitude.

Afraid of seeming like the drunken idiot I sometimes was, I hesitated to tell Ms. Broussard what I'd seen when she stopped in on mid-morning rounds. My astonishment quickly outweighed my paranoia, though.

"She looked at me," I said.

"She did?" The question was affirming, but not enthusiastic.

"She actually looked at me."

"Might have," said Ms. Broussard. "Surely might have."

"There was something there, in her eyes. Like she was aware."

The nurse's fingertips grazed the crucifix lapel pin she wore. "Stranger things have happened."

WITHIN A FEW days, there were other subtle indicators of June's improving consciousness, sparking a flurry of activity. Nurses and specialists buzzed in and out, assessing, evaluating, and guiding her rudimentary steps toward rehabilitation. The frequency and vigor of physical therapy increased, and skilled technicians stopped by daily to bend and manipulate June's arms and legs. It was a bizarre puppet show with my grandmother taking center stage as a life-sized but, ironically, lifeless marionette. Nonetheless, if the process increased the flow of blood through her body and slowed her deterioration, I was a fan.

Though words, even with drunken and slurred delivery, hadn't returned for June, a speech pathologist was assigned to her. She spoke to my grandmother like a toddler, showing her where to place her tongue and how to shape her lips to generate noises that might someday be strung together to form words.

June inched her way out of the fog, and my numbness began to subside. The lessons from the night of my chilly December river swim resurfaced in my mind. I once again stuffed the laminated card in my pocket each day. I still visited Bali, and on more than one drunken night, I thought about calling the English teacher. We were in the same town and I was technically single, but I could see now that John Morgan offered nothing but a cheap thrill and a chance to chip away at my fragile self-esteem. After a few vodkas, images of Paul also seeped out of my subconscious. The lure hadn't vanished, but with a few months and a few hundred miles between us, Paul was a silhouette, a faint shadow that lacked the vitality of the original.

Last fall, my life had capsized in a sea of chaos and turmoil of my own making. June's stroke had plucked me from the battering swells of that sorry drama and thrust me into the turbulence of a new and unfamiliar ocean. I was starting to tread water again, though, and while that wasn't swimming, it wasn't drowning either.

BY THE THIRD month of June's recovery, I witnessed marvels I never imagined on that day when we disconnected her oxygen supply and said good-bye. Gasps became breaths and grunts formed into sounds. There was life in her eyes. According to her doctors, most stroke recovery that was going to happen would occur in the first six months, as swelling in the brain was reduced and circulation increased. Science can't explain the totality of the internal processes involved, though. Neurological reorganization is, in part, a medical mystery—or, as Aunt Doris might phrase it, Jesus magic.

My mother and I arrived at June's bedside, as Ms. Broussard spoon-fed my grandmother's lunch to her like an infant. Though she had relearned to chew and swallow, June was incapable of transporting food from her plate to her mouth. What was left of her stroke survivor blue plate special looked like strained peaches and cottage cheese.

"Hello, ladies." I greeted my grandmother and her nurse.

My mother said nothing but kissed June on the cheek and immediately busied herself, straightening cards and flowers, wiping dust off the chess set in the window sill, and inventorying the personal items in June's dresser drawer, something she did each day.

"Good morning," said Ms. Broussard with a wide smile. "How are you folks doing today, Conor?" She cleverly included us both in the question but addressed it to me.

"Doing well, Ms. Broussard. Is June mistreating you today or is she behaving herself?"

"We've been chatting and having a fine time, haven't we, sweetheart?" She worked small teaspoons of the mushy peaches and lumpy cottage cheese into June's mouth, occasionally wiping her face with a washcloth. As we talked, the nurse grinned in my direction but maintained her focus on my grandmother.

"She likes these peaches okay, but I'm not too sure she cares much for cottage cheese." June uttered an audible but incoherent burble. "She almost gave me a word or two this morning."

"Really? The speech therapist said she's improving, but we're probably a long way from words." I grabbed June's hand and squeezed. "You still have work to do, old lady."

"Conor," my mother said, "don't disrespect your grandmother."

I rolled my eyes.

"I'm going to get some coffee." She grabbed her purse. "You need to let Ms. Broussard do her job."

The nurse continued her patient spoon-feeding, and I marveled at her tender touch. In some ways, it's easier to be gentle with a complete stranger than a loved one.

"Come on now, sweetheart," she said. "You need this cottage cheese to build your strength." She pronounced it "strinth", reminding me that Pensacola is as much a part of southern Alabama as it is northern Florida. "Let's go, Miss June. You're going to need some energy when that physical therapist shows up." She worked the spoon in swirls like an artist's paintbrush, scooping stray cottage cheese bits from my grandmother's chin and working them into her mouth as quickly as June could spit them out.

Another slurred mumble from June.

"She has a lot to say when you're around."

"Is that right?" I asked. "Are you trying to tell me something?"

More incomprehensible murmurs.

"She'll be talking again in no time," Ms. Broussard said.

"And she'll have a lot to say about all this."

June hummed and burbled, a steady stream of spit and cottage cheese running down her chin, as Ms. Broussard wiped her face clean and prepared the next spoonful.

"Kaahhn," June said. It wasn't much, a single syllable drawn out and slurred, but it was clear.

Dumbfounded, I looked back and forth from the nurse to my grandmother. "I'm here, June. I'm right here."

Ms. Broussard gaped wide-eyed at my grandmother. She filled the spoon and rushed it to June's mouth, as if somehow cottage cheese could fuel speech. "Okay, lady, eat up."

June spit out the curds. "Kahhn. Kaaaahhn." She sounded panicked, drawing the start of my name out longer.

"It's okay," I said. "We're right here. Everything's okay." I leaned toward her, unsure of whether her eyes processed my image, hoping to reassure her if they did.

"No!" she snapped, like a defiant kindergartner refusing a spoonful of Robitussin.

Ms. Broussard put the cottage cheese on the rolling cart beside the bed and regained her composure. She smiled. "Like I said, she'll be talking in no time."

"I think something's wrong."

"Well," Ms. Broussard said, "we can't know for sure what she—"

And then another sharp burst, "Kaaahhn." Captain Kirk in the second *Star Trek* movie. Then again, this time with a casual tone and no hint of distress. "Kaahhn, Kaahn, Kahn." Shorter and crisper each time.

I locked eyes with Ms. Broussard and we laughed.

"Nothing to worry about," she said. "She's just getting her voice back." Ms. Broussard returned her attention to the task at hand. First, a spoonful of peaches, then cottage cheese.

June bellowed again, angry this time. "Kaahhn!"

"What? What is it?" I stared into her eyes, hoping to read the answer she couldn't verbalize. "What's the matter?"

She cast her eyes left, shooting a sideways glance at the spoonful of cottage cheese that Henrietta Broussard held frozen in place a few inches from June's mouth. Then, for the first time since the stroke, my grandmother stared into my eyes.

"What is it?" I asked, leaning closer.

She raised her eyebrows, a plea for understanding, before her eyelids fluttered and shut.

"Come on, June. Talk to me."

She reopened her eyes, glanced at me, and then shifted her gaze back to the waiting spoonful of cottage cheese.

"Kaahhn...offfff." Pause. "Offffah." Pause. And then, with crystal clarity, my grandmother finished the first fully formed original thought she'd had in months. "Offhul shiiit."

Ms. Broussard, a devout Christian woman, stood motionless, save for the dropping of her jaw.

"I have to get Mom," I said, though I made no move to leave. For months, I'd struggled to accept that June, a woman whose independence and intellect defined her, could no longer interpret her surroundings beyond the level of a two year-old. And now, by virtue of a pointed two-word sentence, I had to erase and redraw my understanding of reality again. To begin a sentient conversation with June had seemed ridiculous, and now, not to do so seemed cruel.

"You heard that right?" I asked Ms. Broussard. "You heard 'awful shit,' didn't you?"

"I did. That's what she said."

"What do we do?"

"I guess the first thing we do is scratch cottage cheese off the lunch menu." She chuckled.

"She made that clear." I wiped moisture from my eyes.

"I hope you aren't upset about that," Ms. Broussard said, her tone suddenly serious. "About how that came out, I mean."

"What do you mean?"

"Suffering a stroke sometimes changes a person," she explained. "When a patient starts to regain their faculties, they often aren't exactly the same as before."

"Okay." I was unsure of the point.

"Their personalities can change. They can be short with you, harsh or mean. That may be why your grandmother was so...direct."

Tears of relief ran down my cheeks. "Ms. Broussard, I understand what you're saying, but believe me, that's standard behavior for June. She has always been...direct."

"Well, okay." She looked down at the floor. "Okay, then."

"June isn't one to keep quiet about things she finds distasteful. But I didn't know cottage cheese was so high on that list."

"All I'm saying," Ms. Broussard said, "is don't be surprised if she is cranky and a little ornery."

"I'd be more surprised if she wasn't." I kissed June's forehead, seeing her differently now, knowing that some wheels turned behind her hazel eyes. "I'm going to find Mom," I said to June. "Be nice to Ms. Broussard while I'm gone. She's been good to you."

TWENTY-TWO

BEFORE WE LEFT the hospital late one afternoon, my parents were called to Dr. Gonzalez's office for a consultation. They returned a half hour later. My mother trudged into June's room like a B-movie zombie.

"What was that about?"

"We'll talk about it later," she said.

"Fine." If the nature of the conversation was potentially upsetting to June, it could wait until the ride home.

"So then," my father said, "let's get going."

I climbed into the backseat and waited patiently while my mother gathered herself. She stiffened and looked out the passenger window in an attempt to appear resilient, but the facade was difficult to maintain. Strength through defiance works for a while, but sooner or later, it leaves you worse for wear.

"We met with Dr. Gonzalez and a woman from social services. It was good news, I guess. They never expected Mother to breathe on her own, much less start talking again."

"None of us thought she'd get this far," I said.

She stared out the side window, making no effort to face me in the back seat. My father listened and drove us in silence.

"Dr. Gonzalez thinks her mental capacity is severely limited." She swallowed. "And he's certain she won't regain much mobility."

"That's not good news," I said. "But it's nothing new."

"We also discussed...." She inhaled and then let out a long breath. "We also talked about our options at this point."

"Options?" The hair stood up on the back of my neck. I thought we'd already made all the shitty decisions we'd have to make.

"She's stable, and she doesn't need constant medical attention. What she needs now is long-term care."

"Okay..." I waited for the other white, cushy-soled nursing shoe to drop.

Her back stiffened. She continued to stare blankly out the window. "We talked about possible next steps, and none of them are worth a shit."

"None of this has been worth a shit," I said.

My father provided an ambiguous mélange of silent support and disengagement as he motored us past Pensacola's standard offering of rundown strip centers and repurposed gas stations.

"We have two choices," my mother said. "One that's...challenging, and one that's heartbreaking."

"I'd go with challenging."

Her unsteady voice betrayed the tears she suppressed. "We can put her in a facility...a nursing home. Or your father and I become full-time caretakers for as long as we can handle it."

"Are you shitting me?" I asked. "There are places that specialize in rehab for stroke victims."

"Space is limited in those places, and Mother would have to be further down the road than she is now."

"That's fucking great."

"Dr. Gonzalez believes she won't make much more progress, so she's caught in between—too well to stay in the hospital, but too damaged for rehab."

"That's just fucking great," I repeated, because such brilliance needs reiteration. "Too fucked up to live, and not fucked up enough to die."

As her own frustration mounted, tears cascaded down her cheeks. "There's only so much science can do. The rest is in God's hands." As she spoke the words, she no doubt wished she could gobble them up.

"Yeah. He's doing a bang-up job so far."

"Looking at the money," she said, ignoring the blasphemy, "and thinking about Mother and how she is, I don't think a nursing home is a good idea."

"What about the other option? What about her moving in with you and Dad?"

My father, a man of no opinion until now, chimed in. "It's not out of the question, but we ain't getting any younger. We have, uh..." He struggled to finish the thought, which he eventually did with a single, uncomfortable word. "Limitations."

I sat still and quiet.

"Limitations. Things we can't do on our own. You know?" He sought validation, and yes, maybe I did know, but I said nothing. "This is an around-the-clock deal. Bathing and feeding and lifting her in and out of bed." I could see he and my mother had hashed this out already. "Nursing homes are nicer these days. They got television and Internet."

I didn't respond, because I didn't know how. I was shell-shocked by the image of my infantile grandmother, slumped in a wheelchair as spineless as a jellyfish and parked in front of an old Dell, where her clenched fists would twitch their way randomly across the keyboard. *Are you sure you want to delete this file?*

"We have to do what we have to do," he said. And then, to throw in an element of finality, "That's all there is to it."

How had we reached this point? I closed my eyes and touched the crisp hospital linens. *The soft, cool fabric of the pillow gathered between my fingers as I mashed down with all my might and held it over her face. Best to leverage the full weight of my body; make sure I get it right the first time.*

My mother gathered herself enough to reinforce my father's hollow rationale. "We have to do what we have to do. That's all there is to it." It was as though they had rehearsed the lines.

I gazed out the car window at laundromats and baseball, as my mind echoed the phrase. *That's all there is to it, that's all there is to it.*

My mother jolted me back to reality. "Well?"

"Well," I said. "I guess...that's all there is to it."

HENRIETTA BROUSSARD SAT at the nurses' station, filling out forms and doing whatever cover-your-ass paperwork hospitals make doctors and nurses do. It was difficult to pin down what I liked about the plump, older nurse. She was gentle with my grandmother, but there was something more. As I approached the desk, I studied her face—the softness of her cheeks, the smooth skin around her eyes. Her smile was natural and easy, but she was all business when she needed to be.

"Good morning, Ms. Broussard."

"Hello," she said, glancing over her reading glasses.

"Save any lives today?"

"A few." In her hands, she held a handwritten letter, not the clipboard I expected. "I was actually just reading a note from my son."

"He's in Tampa, right?" We'd had this geography conversation before, but I didn't mind revisiting it. There was little other common ground between a white, middle-aged gay man and an aging African-American nurse with a Jesus fetish.

"Cedric is still in Tampa. Stationed at MacDill, remember?"

"Right." I leaned on the counter. "You been down for a visit recently?"

"No, but I'm due for one. I miss my grandkids."

"I'm ready to get back too. No place like home."

"I'm sure you miss your life there," she said. "And your friend."

It wasn't clear if she'd said "friends" plural, or "friend" singular, as in "special friend." The shiny crucifix pin she wore day in and day out had kept me from referring to Will as anything other than "my friend," but I wondered if she had intuited the true nature of my relationship with him—or what it used to be, anyway.

"I do miss my life," I said. "I'm worried if I don't get back soon there won't be anything to go back to."

"I'm sure the people and things that matter most will be there waiting for you."

"Yeah." I nodded longer and more vigorously than needed, as though wishing could make it so. "Everything under control here?"

"We're doing fine. Your grandma and I held down the fort while you were gone."

"I better get in there and check in before she comes looking for me."

"Wouldn't that be a wonderful surprise," she said.

"It would. Nice talking with you, Ms. Broussard." She placed her hand on my shoulder and gave it a squeeze.

As I turned to leave, she called out to me. "Conor?"

"Yes, ma'am?"

"There's one thing I forgot to mention."

"Okay."

"June already had a visitor this morning."

A tight knot formed in my stomach. My parents were still at home, and Uncle Henry always checked in with us before dropping by. "Ms. Broussard, I'd prefer June not have visitors when my parents and I aren't here."

"I'm aware of that. That's why I'm bringing it up."

I attempted a smile to mask my frustration. "If you knew she wasn't supposed to have visitors, why'd you let someone in to see her?"

"Oh, no one got in to see her."

"You said she had a visitor?"

She took off her reading glasses and wiped at the corner of one eye with her fingertip. "We aren't in the business of policing visitors to each individual patient's room. We stay busy, and on top of that, it's bad policy for a nurse to put herself in the middle of family squabbles."

"Who was it?" I asked.

She spoke in a low hushed tone. "A nice lady, early sixties, I'd say, stopped by with a handsome man in a suit." My eyes grew wide as she continued. "They had Bibles and they wanted to pray with your grandmother."

"And?"

"And I explained that your grandmother had just had a messy bowel movement that needed taking care of." The nurse smiled as her hand came up and touched the crucifix pin.

"So they left?"

"No, they wanted to wait so I sent them to the lounge down the hall. Said I'd come and get them after I cleaned her up and changed the bedsheets."

"And then they left?"

"Oh no, they waited quite a while. I guess I owe them an apology. When I checked in on June, she was clean as a whistle. I must have mixed her up with someone else. But then her physical therapist showed up, and I totally forgot the nice lady with the Bible."

"So they're still down there waiting?"

"Nooo. I think they left eventually." She picked up a clipboard and her reading glasses. "I get so scattered sometimes," she said under her breath. "Lord, help me."

JUNE WAS ASLEEP, so I settled into the reclining chair between her bed and the window ledge, where the photograph of Will leaned against a Sesame Street lamppost pawn. I rested there with the early spring sun filtering through the window, toasting my chest and shoulders. I picked up the picture and let my fingers touch his face.

During the early years with Will, in the time before my wandering eyes and meandering cock ruined everything, he restored me. Inasmuch as someone who doubts the existence of God can, I felt blessed when I first loved Will and he loved me back. It wasn't a feeling I was used to. The notion of being *blessed,* even the word itself, never suited me. Ariel and I had a long philosophical discussion about it one night, the kind of debate you only have when it's well after midnight and empty Merlot bottles litter the coffee table.

"There oughta be another word," I'd said. "Something that means to the atheist what blessed means to the believer."

"You don't have to believe in God to enjoy blessings," she'd said.

"Yes, you goddamn do."

"Blessed can just be a sort of spiritual luck."

"Bullshit. A blessing is a sacred gift, and for me, there are no sacred gifts because there is no sacred giver."

Of course, there was a word, and I found it years later in *Oprah* reruns. Gratitude. For an atheist, gratitude is the closest you get to divine wonder— a luminescent-blue butterfly floating before your eyes, just as your head smacks the pavement and the bus rolls over you. The eyes of a loved one, as a snow-white pillow covers her face and steals her last shallow breaths.

I opened my eyes and looked at June. Her eyes were open.

Offhul shiiit. She'd been talking about more than just those disgusting curds of cottage cheese. *Awful shit*, as good a phrase as any I could think of to characterize the months since her stroke—or, for that matter, the days and weeks ahead.

June was the strongest person I knew. If I told her everything, explained the hideous choices we were presented, she'd take the reins. Nursing home mannequin, daunting family burden, or mortal sin—what's it going to be? Through our deep connection or sheer force of will, I'd develop the power to read the answers in her eyes, or June would find a way to string the words together and give me one clean sentence, ten words, five even, a simple phrase to tell me what she wanted. Or maybe she already had. *Offhul shiiit.*

What if she had already done her best and there was no fight left? Then sharing the totality of her twisted nightmare might only serve to make things worse. She would understand the impossibly weighty baggage she had become, and live on, all the more tortured and trapped by her helplessness. Though it fucking should be, the world is never black and white.

I pulled the manifesto from my pocket and scoured it, searching for any measure of certainty. I looked at June, who looked at nothing, and I read the card again and again, looking for anything I could know for sure. A single place to stand where the ground wasn't shifting beneath my feet. But there's not a lot of solid ground out there. A few crystalline moments in four decades of worthlessness and muck don't mean shit, even if you laminate them.

I tilted my grandmother's face toward mine and stroked her cheek. What was left to say? What words might still have meaning? Love is mostly worthwhile, truth is usually better than lies, and family, like it or not, is as close as you get to having something outside yourself you can count on. There aren't many absolutes, but surely those few truths count for something.

"MORNING, JUNE." I mustered a grin on the off chance she was in there.

Blank stare.

"How was your nap?"

Blank stare.

"You look rested."

Her eyes were alert as they sometimes were now, and when I walked around the bed, her gaze followed me. She looked lucid and focused, as though she understood the gravity of her situation but, like a prisoner of war, was unable to speak the language of her captors to defend herself or beg for mercy.

"We need to talk." Finding the traditional conventions of conversation difficult to ignore, I paused and allowed time for the reply that wouldn't come. I tried to hold her hand, but she clenched a wad of crisp, white hospital sheet in her fist. I settled for resting my hand on top of hers.

"I want to be up front with you about everything that's going on..." Because total honesty was such a magnificent success the last time I tried it.

She stared ahead at the round, white hospital-issue clock that hung near a crucifix on the wall opposite her bed.

"Mom talked to the doctors, and they said you're doing well. You don't have to stay here anymore."

Though she didn't look at me, she gazed in my direction. The sudden realization that she could actually be listening unnerved me. "Mom would be pissed if she knew I was doing this without her. I'm going to grab a coffee and wait until she gets here."

"No," she snapped.

I jumped at the sound of her voice, nearly tumbling over the chair behind me. I'd seen the speech therapist work with June on a few one-syllable words, but it was more like dog training than learning language. Using words in conversation, if that's what had just happened, was new ground.

"Should I stay and talk?" She didn't answer. "Fine, let's wait for Mom."

"No," she said again. Her tone was halting, almost angry.

Patches of sweat grew on my forehead and under my arms. I checked my watch, as though looking at it could speed time and whisk my mother to the hospital. With the bedsheet still crumpled in her clenched fists, she stared directly into my eyes.

"June, I want to tell you everything, but I didn't think you'd understand."

Intense scrutiny showed in the old woman's hazel eyes. She remained silent, but she was listening and comprehending. "I need to know if you understand me."

Her eyes darted to the left.

I instinctively looked in the same direction. "What is it? Are you looking for something?"

This time her eyes darted to the right. Then, back to the left. Right, left, right.

"What are you looking for? Is something wrong?"

Sharp glance to the right.

"I'll get Ms. Broussard." Panic rose in my voice.

Another sharp glance to the right.

"Jesus, what have I started? I'm such a fucking idiot."

Her eyes rolled left, only this time the glance was accompanied by the subtlest pursing of her lips. It was brief, but I recognized the look. My grandmother, back from her stroke-induced coma, had managed a look of sarcasm.

"Are you agreeing? I'm a fucking idiot?"

Her eyes moved left.

I wanted to believe she was communicating, but I needed more proof.

"What about my mother? Is she an idiot too?"

Glance to the right this time.

"My father?"

Glance to the right.

"Aunt Doris? Is she an idiot?"

Rapid darting glance to the left, and a hard eye roll, straight up. Left meant "yes," right meant "no," like a geriatric Jeremiah Denton sending secret messages home on videotape.

I fought back tears. "I never thought we'd get you back. Do you understand?"

Her eyes moved to the left.

"I've missed you so much."

This time her eyes moved neither left, nor right, but filled to the brim with tears.

"Oh Christ, I didn't mean to upset you."

She looked to her left and a single teardrop escaped down her cheek.

"I have so much to tell you," I said. "Do you know what happened?"

Eyes to the left.

"The doctors...we never expected you to be conscious again. You've come a long way in the last few weeks, but we never thought you'd communicate again. Do you understand?" I asked, always a non-believer. She moved her eyes left.

"Knowing that you understand what I am saying changes things. It might make everything I was going to tell you irrelevant." She looked blank, like the cogs and wheels had stopped spinning. "June, are you still there?"

"Goh." She sounded as though she'd just finished a pitcher of margaritas.

I thought she wanted me to leave, but her face looked calm, relaxed. "Go on," she'd meant, and I did.

"You had a stroke on New Year's Day. You're at Sacred Heart now and you've been here for almost four months. The damage was severe, and we didn't think..." My throat tightened. I took a deep breath and slowly let it escape. "We had no idea what to expect. We thought we'd lost you, but we didn't and then it got worse. We kept you...but half-alive, like a fucking houseplant."

I stepped away from the bed, struggling to maintain my composure, steadying myself with the wall and wiping my eyes.

Her eyelids lowered and raised again. Her eyes drifted to the left.

"I'm sorry." I apologized for nothing in particular, and for everything in the world. "You don't need to be in a hospital any more, but we don't have a shitload of good options."

My one-sided rambling led me back to the place I started, the ugly dilemma. I didn't want to burden her with the depressing details, but June deserved to hear the truth, even if she lacked the synaptic capacity to fully understand it.

"You don't need twenty-four-hour nursing care," I said, "but taking care of you is going to take a lot..." I reached a dead end and started again down a parallel path. "It's going to be tough, and Mom and Dad don't know how long they can handle it. Handle you."

Maintaining the dignity of an adult with questionable mental capacity is a tightrope walk between clarity and condescension. Beads of moisture congregated on my hairline and rolled down my forehead as I contemplated how to tell her the better part of her future would reside within the narrow confines of a twin bed in a low-rent nursing home. I checked my watch and wondered where I might find a shot of Maker's or chilled Stoli at 8:30 in the morning.

In simple, straightforward terms, I explained that June would either go home with my parents, or be moved to a nursing home, which at this point seemed to be the best of the shit choices available.

She rolled her eyes hard.

"Mom and Dad are still sorting it out, though."

Her wide eyes and tight lips told me the stroke hadn't stolen her ability to sniff out a load of hot bullshit.

"We don't know what to do, but I thought you deserved to be told."

I sat on the bed next to her and stroked her arm. We didn't look at each other, but instead watched the clock across the room, its thin, black hands ticking away eternity with mind-numbing steadiness.

Desperate to change the subject, I gestured toward the window ledge and the Sesame Street chess set. "Did you see what Will bought you? And the picture he sent?"

Her face was calm, her hazel eyes wide and attentive. "Home," she said.

"Jesus," I replied. "That's three words today."

"Hoome," she repeated, dragging the vowel out this time.

"Yeah," I said, guessing. "Will went home a few weeks ago. He had to work." Her eyes rolled to the right this time. I was getting it wrong.

"Ho-oooh-m." She added syllables and slurred the word. Then it came again, sharper, like an exclamation, "Home."

"You want to go home?" I tried not to address her like an idiot, but it was like trying to determine if an indoor dog needs an outside potty break.

Eyes to the left.

"I know you want to go home, but it's not that easy. We're still figuring it out. You have to be patient." It sounded stern, which, all things considered, might not have been bad. There was little room for negotiation here.

She rolled her eyes to the right, leaving me confounded about whether I had misunderstood her meaning or, more likely, given an unacceptable reply.

She closed her eyes for a full minute and then opened them wide. "Kaahn home."

"Yes, I'm going home eventually. Once you're settled."

Eyes to the right. "Kaahn home. Kaahn home."

Her grip on the bedsheets tightened like a vise. I covered her hand with mine again, and kissed her forehead, offering the only comfort I could.

With a furrowed brow and a piercing stare, she strung three words together and said them twice. "Kaahn me home, Kaahn me home."

"June, you have to stay here a little longer while we sort things out. But we'll talk more when Mom gets here."

Her face pleaded. A pool of thoughts swelled behind her eyes, but there was no valve to release them. I stared into her large, blue-gray eyes, wishing I could understand and give her relief.

She struggled to form the next words, but they fell from her mouth with perfect clarity. "June home Tampa."

"What did you say?"

"June home Tampa," she said again.

"Your home is here, with Mom and Dad in Pensacola."

Her eyes rolled to the right. "June home Tampa."

"You want to visit Tampa?" I was stupefied.

She rolled her eyes to the right. No.

"You want to live with me and Will in Tampa?"

She paused, eyes on me, and then a grin and a gentle roll of her eyes—to the left.

I repeated the question three times, phrasing it differently each time to confirm her answer and make sure all of this wasn't wishful thinking or coincidence. It was not.

TWENTY-THREE

THE PLANE RIDE from Pensacola to Tampa was a one-hour jaunt on a small propeller plane with a handful of passengers and a single flight attendant. I'd booked a seat on an empty row, but wound up seated next to a towheaded boy who I guessed was ten or eleven years old. He wore earbuds and held a death grip on a Sony PSP. We sat in silence until the plane pushed away from the gate and the flight attendant instructed the kid to turn off his game.

"So much for Super Mario," I said. "You can turn it back on in a few minutes."

The kid ignored me.

"I guess electronics mess up the equipment, so they make you turn it off."

Still nothing.

He looked at me blankly. Deaf? Non-English speaking? A quiet flight, fine by me.

During takeoff, the solo flight attendant sat in plain view on a tiny fold-out jump seat directly opposite the front row of passengers. This particular moment on small commuter planes, when the singular flight attendant buckles herself in just like the rest of us, always unnerved me. I preferred to think that during these crucial pre-flight moments, the flight attendant was busily completing last-minute technical inspections and finalizing security processes, checking things off on an official FAA form attached to a clipboard she carried like a Bible. I preferred to think she was double-checking safety locks, confirming counts of life vests, and verifying oxygen supplies. The open view jump seat, where the flight attendant sat and thumbed through a James Patterson novel, robbed me of my fantasy.

The kid turned in his seat and tugged my sleeve. "You nervous or something, mister?"

"Nah, I'm good."

"If you're not nervous, how come you bite your fingernails so much?"

"Oh, I didn't realize I was." I curled my hands into fists, self-conscious about how my nervous habit had run roughshod over my ragged cuticles. "I'm not nervous, not about the flight anyway. Have you flown before?"

"Nah." He tucked the video game into the seat pocket in front of him. "So, how come you're biting all your fingernails off?"

"You're an inquisitive little fellow," I said, more to myself than to him.

"I don't know what that means," he answered.

"Never mind. I have a lot of grown up things on my mind." I faked a smile. "Are you heading home to Tampa or just going for a visit?"

"I don't know," he replied.

"I mean, do you live in Tampa or do you live in Pensacola?"

"I don't know," he answered again.

Maybe the kid was a little slow after all. "Are you going to see your mom and dad? Are they in Tampa?"

"I don't know where they are," he said, a lilt of innocence in his voice.

"So, why are you going to Tampa?"

"To see my grandma."

Finally, something to work with. "Well, that should be fun."

"I don't know. I stayed with her before, but that was back when I was little." Spoken like an older and wiser boy, someone whose age has finally crept into double digits.

"I see," I said, not seeing. "How long are you visiting your grandma?"

"I don't know. The last family only kept me a few months, like grandma did the first time. But she might let me stay longer this time. Maybe till I'm eighteen."

I eventually put together that the boy had been in foster care since his mother had been jailed, presumably for something lewd, if not lascivious. Grandma had assumed custody of the kid, but working full-time and caring for a young boy had proven to be too much for her so his stay was short-lived. She had since retired and was ready to try again.

"Sounds like you move around a lot."

He gave his head a thoughtful scratch. "Yeah." An awkward moment passed, though I doubted he noticed. "What about you?"

"What about me?"

"Why are you going to Tampa? Do your mom and dad live there?"

"No, they live here. I live in Tampa." Looking down and realizing we were airborne, I clarified. "Well, they don't live here, in the sky, but back in Pensacola."

The kid smiled and I noticed his teeth, yellowed, but straight as prison bars. Hygiene was obviously not a priority in foster care, but at least he had a few decent genes in the pool.

"Will you go to school in Tampa? I mean, you go to school, right?"

"Yeah."

"It must be hard, changing schools and leaving your friends behind." Now, I was probably depressing the kid. "Tampa has nice kids. You'll make new friends in no time."

He tilted his head and squinted, carefully weighing my sage words. "It's not that hard. I'm used to it."

Having finally put down the Patterson book, the flight attendant walked the aisle, taking drink orders and passing out snacks.

"Pretzels?" she asked.

"Diet Coke," I replied. "No pretzels." I never understood the choice of pretzels as an in-flight snack. In an environment lacking quick access to water, the last thing one might want to risk is a choking incident, and the pretzel, in my opinion, lends itself better than any other snack food to the possibility of an obstructed windpipe.

I glanced over the top of my soda at the kid. Legs swinging ninety to nothing, head rocking to an unheard internal rhythm, and eyes fixed out the window on the puffy clouds that littered the pale blue sky; an abandoned kid without a care in the world. He was a walking testimonial to the wisdom of keeping your expectations low, so that anything short of a brick to the head feels like a gift. He caught my stare, held it, and grinned at me.

"I love pretzels," he said.

Yes, pretzels, asphyxiating manna from heaven.

I closed my eyes and pretended to nap while I replayed the last days Will and I spent together to see if there had been an opening I'd missed, a key to his heart hidden in a light fixture or beneath a potted plant. I daydreamed about a tearful airport reunion. He stood just beyond the wall of security glass, wearing shorts and flip-flops, and holding a chauffeur's placard that read simply, *Be Mine.*

The rumble of the landing gear shook me back to the moment, and when I opened my eyes, the boy watched me from beneath his mop of uncombed blond hair.

"We're landing soon," I said. "You ready to start a new life with your grandma?"

"Sure." He was as removed and calm as outer space.

"Lots of people to meet and things to see. You'll do great."

"Yep."

"I have something for you." I presented him with two mini bags of pretzels I'd snagged from the snack cart.

"Thanks. Now I can give one to my grandma!"

"You sure can. She'll be glad to see you..." I hesitated, realizing we'd never had a proper introduction. "By the way, my name is Conor."

"Okay," he replied.

The small plane bumped onto the runway. "Well, what's your name?"

"August. Really Augusten, but everyone calls me August."

"It's been very nice talking to you, August," I said as we taxied to the gate.

The flight attendant told August she would escort him to meet his grandmother at the gate, as soon as other passengers cleared the jetway. I grabbed my laptop bag and stood in the aisle.

"Be good, August, and take care of that grandmother of yours."

He lifted one hand in a casual wave and clutched the mini bags of pretzels in the other. "You too."

MY STROKE-ADDLED grandmother wanted to live with us, but before I added that impossible variable to our equation, I needed to know for certain whether Will and I still added up to anything on our own. It didn't take long to deduce—we didn't.

He picked me up at the curb at Tampa International, and no bottle of red wine or bouquet of cut flowers awaited me in the front seat. There was no longing glance or witty innuendo. At home, I filled him in on general details about June's progress and told him about the lonely winter nights I'd spent at Bali avoiding my parents. He told me I drink too much and showed me pictures of an orchid exhibit he'd just finished at work. Conversation as scintillating as river mud.

I slept alone in the guest room, and before I awoke the next morning, he had already left for work. A note on the kitchen counter informed me that the coffee was pre-measured and ready for brewing, and that there were clean bath towels in the dryer. I'd anticipated awkward moments, but I hadn't expected to feel like a visitor in my own home.

A stack of mail Will hadn't yet forwarded to me sat in the middle of the kitchen table. I sifted through the pile, lacking the give-a-shit to open most of it, until I ran across an envelope with a Mangrove Press return address. I hadn't heard from the publisher in months. Since June's stroke, I had thought little about the sales of my first book, much less the outline of a second one. Mangrove hadn't forgotten. Sales of *Luck of the Irish* were sluggish, which I suspected was publisher-speak for non-existent, but they looked forward to reading the completed draft of my second book by the end of the summer, as noted, clearly, in my contract.

After breakfast and a shower, I paced inside the condo, treading the same path I walked when I took one of Marshall's "motivational" leadership calls from home. My indoor tranquility trail led me up and down the hallway, through the living room and around the sofa, and past the liquor cart in our dining area. On two consecutive laps, I paused at the cart and picked up a crystal decanter that was half-filled with brandy. Each time, I removed the sparkling stopper and smelled the contents of the container. On the third pass, I fished around in my pocket and found the laminated card whose midnight wisdom had first come to me in the dewy grass just a few yards away. I placed the card next to the decanter and resumed my neurotic stroll.

I was still wearing holes in the carpet when Will called and invited me to stop by Busch Gardens when his shift was over. Once upon a time, theme park beer-drinking and people-watching had been among our favorite pastimes, but that was long ago, before the English teacher, the ex, the Prozac, the puking, the firing, and the stroke. With less than twenty-four hours before my flight back to Pensacola, and having not yet broached the subject of taking on an invalid elderly roommate, I accepted his invitation. I'd initially planned to tell Will about June's request during a private dinner at home, but a public setting, even one surrounded by roller coasters and wild animals, somehow felt safer.

We met at the employee entrance where Will snuck me into the park for free. I suggested we grab beers and walk to a favorite bench on an out-of-the-way hillside. Positioned among lush tropical greenery and with a view overlooking the primate sanctuary, the setting made it easy to forget we were just a few blocks away from bustling strip centers of pawnshops, laundromats, and Mexican restaurants. The spot provided ample privacy for weeping and sufficient isolation for raised voices.

We sipped our beers and watched chimpanzees somersault across a grassy knoll in the distance. "I could watch monkeys all day," I said.

"Chimps are in the ape family," he replied. "They're not technically monkeys."

I pointed at his dirty khaki shorts and matching shirt. "I thought you planted bushes and flowers."

"You pick things up."

I drained my tall plastic beer cup and held it up to him. "You think you could 'pick up' a few more of these things?" He collected my empty and left to retrieve two more beers. While he was gone, I returned my attention to the primates who had settled down and were seated in pairs, inspecting each other's wiry body hair and removing bugs and sticks. Some animals were natural caretakers.

Will returned and handed me a sixteen-ounce Budweiser. "Sorry about the beer selection, but it is *Busch* Gardens."

"Will," I said, "I need to tell you something."

"Okay." He leaned back on the bench and swigged his beer. "Go for it."

"I told you June's communicating a little more, but I wasn't totally forthcoming." The gravity in my voice got his full attention. "You know how I said she's in no-man's-land—not well enough for rehab, but not sick enough for a hospital..."

"Yes."

"I told her too. I explained what's happening, but I didn't think she'd understand it."

"Keep going."

"If I had any idea she'd get it, I wouldn't have said what I did. It was supposed to be symbolic, you know? Out of respect."

"But she understood?"

"Yes, and it felt like I put a weight on her. A pile of cinder blocks." My voice trembled, and he placed his hand on my arm. "It's a huge fucking weight she has no way to bear."

"How do you know she understood?"

I explained the system of yes-no eye rolls.

Will listened, pausing to wave at a park employee who wheeled past us with a huge gray trash wagon. "That's unbelievable. Why didn't you tell me that before?"

"That's not the end of the story."

He pulled his hand from my arm, as though I'd just outed myself as a leper.

"She understands the situation, and she doesn't like her options."

"That's no surprise. None of us like the options." He sipped the beer.

"She's aware and thinking, and she came up with an idea of her own."

"Okay," he said, draining the last of his beer in a single gulp.

"She wants to live with us, Will."

"What?"

"In our condo. With us."

If there is such a thing as an audible silence, the next ten seconds yielded such a quiet.

"Jesus Christ." The empty cup in his hand fell to the grass. "I don't believe it."

"She said it, Will. I explained the nursing home thing, and she told me she wanted to live with us in Tampa."

"You misunderstood. Blinking leaves a shitload of room for interpretation."

"Believe me, I made sure."

"I love her, but I don't..."

"Don't panic." I did my best to reassure him. "I'm not asking you to make this happen."

"Have you talked to your mother?"

"She's scared shitless. She thinks we'd be way out of our league."

"She's right. And she doesn't even know *our team* split up."

"Will, I'm just telling you what June said."

"We don't even function as a couple. We sure as hell can't perform as a *team*. She'd get better support in Pensacola from your parents."

"That might be true," I said, "but it's not what she wants."

"What if one of us wants to move out?"

"No one is trapped. If you don't think it's working, I'll ship her back to Pensacola, and we'll fall back on the nursing home option."

"You can't put that on me. No way. I'm a fucking bystander here."

"It's already on you. If we don't take her, she'll end up in a home anyway."

He stood and paced around the bench as he unleashed a litany of logistical concerns. "We live in a condo, for fuck's sake. We have loud neighbors. We don't have medical training. I've never held a syringe. I've never even taken another person's temperature. We have jobs!"

"I'm on a leave of absence," I said, an unhelpful factoid that did little to slow him down.

"How much does a hospital bed cost? And how would we even get her here? Do we just throw her in the back seat with a Snickers bar and a book of Mad Libs and hit the interstate?"

"One step at a time."

"This isn't checking the neighbor's mail while they're vacationing in Key West. I need to think this through before I say anything else."

I walked to the edge of the primate habitat. At the bottom of the hill, only two chimps remained within view. They lay together in the ankle-high grass, the smaller of the two resting his head on the chest of the larger one.

TWENTY-FOUR

GETTING WILL TO agree to take on June was less difficult than I had feared. I swore on June's life I'd stay away from prescription drugs, which was a commitment I kept, and I vowed to quit drinking, which was more of a well-intentioned promise. But the semi-retirement of Henrietta Broussard was the serendipitous linchpin that sealed the deal.

After thirty years at Sacred Heart, Ms. Broussard was ready to leave hospital work. She wasn't finished taking care of the sick and dying, though, and she'd developed a fondness for June.

I was seated in a corner of June's room one morning, pecking away unproductively at the outline for my second book, when the nurse came in to check on my grandmother. She crossed the room and raised the blinds, careful not to disturb the photo of Will that leaned against the Big Bird king on the chess set in the window ledge.

"Good morning," she said to my grandmother. "Why you keepin' it so dark in here?" She asked the question as if it had been June's lazy choice to lounge in darkness.

"Hi, Ms. Broussard," I said.

"Morning, Conor," she replied, noticing me for the first time.

"I really appreciate how you talk to June."

"And how's that?"

"Like everything's normal and she's the most important thing on your agenda today."

"Everything *is* normal. As normal as it can be. And her care is the most important thing on my agenda today."

"I wonder if June knows how lucky she is to have you on her side."

"She's right here. Go on and ask her."

I smiled.

After she checked my grandmother's vital signs, she tidied up the room and then grabbed the television remote and flipped through the channels. She watched my grandmother's face intently, on the lookout for any subtle indicators that June preferred the chatty banter of *The View* to *Andy Griffith* reruns.

She finally settled on one of a half dozen *Law & Order* choices. "Conor, may I talk with you for a moment?"

I followed her into the sterile linoleum hallway and down the corridor to an empty lounge. She filled two foam cups with coffee and invited me to sit at a small round table.

"I spoke at length with your mother yesterday afternoon."

"Is something the matter?" I asked, suddenly a teenager who'd been called to the principal's office.

"I'm not one to beat around the bush," she said, "so I'll get to the point. Your mother told me you may be taking June to Tampa."

"True."

"And you're looking for some nursing assistance."

"Yeah. I can't handle her alone, even with help from Will, my...roommate." Though the descriptor was accurate, it rang hollow, just as it had the hundreds of times I'd used it in the past to euphemize our relationship to strangers.

"My grandkids are growing so fast, sproutin' up like wildflowers." Her voice was softer, sweeter. "I've been thinking about spending more time with them."

"In Tampa?"

"Right."

"Ms. Broussard, we really can't afford—"

"Conor, I'd like to continue caring for your grandmother. In Tampa. If you would consider me, that is."

"Are you fucking kidding me?"

She raised her eyebrows. "Is that a yes?"

"I'm sorry." I resisted the urge to high five her, running my anxious hands through my hair instead. "Yes. Absolutely, yes."

"There are just the details to work out then."

"I doubt we can pay you anything close to what you make here."

"It's not about the money," she said. "We'll work that out."

I heaved a sigh of relief. The ever-present crucifix pin she wore glowed in the fluorescent light of the nurses' lounge. "Ms. Broussard, you'd be working in our home. There's one other thing I need to be up front about."

She looked down at the Formica tabletop and twisted the plastic lid atop her coffee. "Conor, as you may know, I'm a Christian woman. As such, I have high standards for people."

I held my breath.

"You've been here every day all these months, holding your grandmother's hand, talking with her, reading to her. I can only hope the Lord would bless me with a grandson like you if I suffered a stroke."

"Sounds like I have you fooled."

"I don't think so. I know who you are and I like you just fine."

"When you get to know Will, you'll like him too. He's the better man."

"That's just what your mother told me." She smiled.

We finished our coffee, and despite my intense desire to embrace the old nurse, we shook hands.

She moved in with her son's family four weeks later. We transported June to Tampa shortly thereafter and the old nurse went to work.

IN HER FIRST few weeks at our house, June's condition continued to improve. She was lucid more often than not, sometimes stringing her thoughts together enough to carry on a conversation. This is not to say she was reading Tolstoy or lecturing on quantum mechanics, but if *Wheel of Fortune* was on, she could follow the action.

Ms. Broussard pursued an aggressive physical therapy regimen with June, which yielded mixed results. Though she could maintain an upright sitting position in her wheelchair, June lacked the mobility in her arms and legs to provide even the most rudimentary care for herself. She still relied on us to move her, feed her, and take care of her most private hygiene needs. Ms. Broussard took care of bathing her, but there were times when she was off-duty and delicate personal matters arose. Despite her vocal discomfort with the situation, June allowed Will and me to assist during these tenuous moments. I assured her wiping her ass was no treat for us either.

My elderly grandmother wasn't the only resurrection project underway around our house. Will populated our patio and the flowerbeds behind the condo with once sickly plants he had rescued from the mulch bins at work.

He arrived home one afternoon with a half-dead bromeliad and a withered croton in his arms. "Guess what I realized today?"

I glanced at the wilted greenery. "That nothing says I love you like flowers?"

"June turns eighty-five next week." He spoke as if he'd unraveled one of the great mysteries of science.

"That's how math works," I said. "Eighty-five usually follows eighty-four."

"We should have a birthday party."

The idea floated across my consciousness for a split second before I yelled, "Pull," internally and shot it from the sky. "She's not ready for that. Having people over could be hectic."

"I'm not talking about a lot of people. Just us and a few friends she already knows."

"Let me think about it," I said, having no intention of thinking about it.

"Me, you, Ms. Broussard, Ariel and David. That's only two people more than we have here every day."

"It'd be nice to see Ariel and David." I wasn't warming to the party idea, but I took his mention of Ariel as a positive sign that he might be moving beyond her inadvertent reveal of my botched rendezvous with the English teacher.

Ms. Broussard, who never weighed in on matters outside of June's health, called out from her post in the corner of the living room. "June's right here. Why don't you see what she thinks?"

Will stepped in front of June's wheelchair, partially blocking her view of Ellen DeGeneres. "What do you say? Want to have a couple of friends over for your birthday? Maybe get a cake?"

She stared blankly, a thin thread of drool stretching from her chin to the floral print blouse she wore.

"Nothing big," he said, "but it might be nice to have some company."

June looked past him at the television, captivated by Ellen's witty repartee with a smiling Zac Efron—or, more likely, by random specks of dust floating across her field of view in the late afternoon sunlight.

"I told you she wasn't ready for company. Can we drop it?"

"Sure," he said, then went to his room to e-mail an invitation to Ariel.

I RETURNED TO work at the bookstore like a celebrity, giving out cheek kisses and complimenting the team on the stellar appearance of the place as I strode down the center aisle toward the back room.

"Hi, Tom," I said, as I popped my head into the doorway of the tiny office. I held a sealed cardboard box, which I balanced on my knee.

"Conor." He spoke as though my name were a question. "Marshall said you were coming back today, but I didn't expect you this early."

"You look comfortable." He stuffed a half-eaten bagel into a Dunkin' Donuts bag and leaped from the desk. I squeaked past his hulking frame to my chair. "The store looks good. Marshall must be happy."

"He's pretty pleased with things."

"Thanks for holding it together."

"So, you're back? For good?" He forced a smile that failed to disguise his disappointment.

"Yeah. Can you give me a few minutes? Maybe finish your breakfast in the break room?"

"Sure." He grabbed his bagel and bucket of chocolate milk. "Close the door?"

"Please."

I dug around in the desk drawer until I found the new home he'd given my scissors and I unsealed the box. I unpacked some crackers and a box of microwave popcorn, and pulled out an extra pair of sneakers I liked to keep around for after-hours projects. I carefully unwrapped a framed photograph I'd taken of June and placed it on top of a four-drawer filing cabinet next to a droopy pothos plant. I snipped the tape that fastened bubble wrap around the last item in the box, a clichéd brown paper bag, then unlocked the filing drawer of my desk and stashed the bottle of Jameson behind the employee files.

For the next hour, I rifled through heaps of paper that spilled out of black stacking trays on my desk. In the middle of the pile, sandwiched between payroll reports and vendor invoices no one had bothered to file, I found a sheet of paper with the top right corner neatly cut out. The missing corner was laminated in my pocket, but seven business card-sized versions of my manifesto remained on the printed page.

I am older now, no longer a damaged child.
Everything is on the line, and I must deliver.

I will get my shit together and make amends.
I will stop taking pills and I will control my cock,
I will face my demons and stop sabotaging my life.

I pulled the laminated card from my pocket and matched it to the page like the missing piece of a jigsaw puzzle. I wondered if Tom had read my midnight river epiphany. Because I hadn't been summarily dismissed from my job, I guessed he hadn't.

Since the night I'd scurried up that slippery riverbank, muddy and drunk and afraid, Will and I had broken up, and June had become a slack-faced vegetative mess. I'd kept at least one of the vows I'd made, though. I'd gotten my shit together enough to take care of June and that was worth something. I shoved the plastic card in my pocket, crumpled the page, and tossed it in the trash can.

I spent the next few hours doing my best to pretend I was happy to be back. I read corporate memos and directives, chatted with staff members, and thanked everyone for their kind thoughts and words about June. I took Tom to lunch and made sure to give him another hearty reach-around for a job well done. Though I knew Ms. Broussard was taking impeccable care of June, I phoned home several times. The nurse patiently answered my questions each time. Yes, June had eaten. Yes, she had napped. Yes, she was watching *Ellen*. Parenthood was nerve-racking.

At the end of the day, I returned to my office to finish sorting the unfiled mess on my desk. I was a half inch deeper in the stack when I found a letter addressed, not to the bookstore, but to me. The postage date stamped on the front was seven weeks old. I glanced at the return address and closed the office door.

Dear Conor,

Tried to make contact several times, but have had great difficulty. Understand there have been personal challenges, but need to talk about the book(s).

Disappointing sales of Luck. *Hoped to talk through editorial process and outline of second book. Deadline fast approaching for first draft and have significant concerns. Please know that violation of terms may result in contract termination.*

Get in touch,

Sharon Barclay
President, Mangrove Press

Apparently, when literary matters reached a certain level of urgency, there was no time for complete sentences or pronouns. I closed my eyes and rubbed them hard, as if I might unsee the words. I wadded the letter into a tight ball and hurled it at the back of the door.

"Conor," the intercom chirped on my desk phone. "You there?"

A steady drumbeat pounded in my temples, but I composed myself enough to manage a syllable. "Yes."

"Call on line two for you," Tom said.

I considered asking him to take a message, but the new mother in me worried something was wrong with June. I picked up the call.

"This is Conor."

"Conor, it's Marshall."

Jesus fuck. "Hi, Marshall. What can I do for you?"

"How was your first day back?"

"Busy. Just trying to catch up."

"That's fine." He paused and exhaled loudly into the phone. "Listen, I won't bullshit you. We need to talk about something. In person."

Crashing cymbals now punctuated the drumming in my head.

"I've only been back one day. It can't be that bad."

"Can you meet me at the store tomorrow morning at 7:00?"

"Marshall, we have a party planned for my grandmother tonight, and I have friends coming from Orlando. I'm scheduled to work a mid tomorrow."

"You remember Aaron, the kid you termed around the holidays?" he asked.

I swallowed hard. "I remember. His firing was legit, Marshall. He bailed at Christmas."

"I don't care about that, but I heard some disturbing rumors about Thanksgiving."

"Jesus, Marshall. That was fucking months ago. What did you hear?"

"Look, it's probably nothing, but you're back and I'm required to conduct an investigation. Can you meet me at 7:00?"

A full percussion section banged away in my brain.

"I'll be here." I hung up the phone and glared at it.

I grabbed a handful of unsorted pages from the black plastic tray on my desk, and with barely a glance, I slapped invoices, memos, and general bullshit correspondence into sloppy piles. I snatched more pages and flung them haphazardly onto random stacks. The bin was nearly empty when I banged it hard with my fist and heard the snap of cheap plastic. The meaningless heaps overlapped on my desk. I swept them all to the floor. I tilted the tray over the trash can, dumped the last of the unfiled pages, and then tossed the broken bin in on top of them.

TWENTY-FIVE

CREPE PAPER STREAMERS hung in doorways, and shiny silver balloons bobbed around the ceiling. A string of pastel letters over the sliding glass doors spelled "Happy Birthday."

"This looks...festive," I said, loosening my tie.

"How was your first day back?" Will asked.

Across the room, June napped in her wheelchair and Ms. Broussard worked a crossword puzzle. "All we need is blaring TV and the lingering smell of death and we'll have our own little nursing home."

"Wow," he said. "Work suck that bad?"

"I'm just commenting on the low-end decor."

"With such pleasant imagery."

"It's the writer in me."

"It's the asshole in you."

I shrugged. "I'm sorry."

He walked to the bedroom, beckoning me to follow and closing the door behind me. "What is your fucking problem?"

"Nothing."

"Why would you say something so mean? What if June heard you?"

"She didn't, she's—"

"She could have. And Ms. Broussard heard it."

"I said I'm sorry. I meant it."

"You want to tell me what's going on?"

I glanced at the open walk-in closet, where the bedsheets I dragged to the sofa each night were piled in front of a three-shelf storage unit that housed extra diapers and medical supplies.

"Everything's fine." I snatched a T-shirt and pair of shorts from the dresser. Things were clearly not okay, but I had long since forfeited the privilege of confiding in Will. He would have listened, maybe even given me some reassuring perspective, but it was unfair to burden him more than I already had.

"You sure?" he asked.

"I'm good."

"Then stop acting like a child and get your shit together."

I'd never discussed my night in the river with Will, but he was practically reciting the laminated manifesto in my pocket, which he had no doubt seen on my nightstand.

"I'm working on it," I said. "I'm trying."

"Good. Try harder."

After I changed clothes, he sent me to the grocery store for extra sodas and chips we didn't need. I returned home with the superfluous snacks and a bonus half dozen bottles of red wine. Will gave me the side-eye, but maybe because it was a night intended for celebration, he spared me the lecture. He'd upgraded the party atmosphere while I was gone, adding a linen tablecloth, fresh cut flowers, and candles to the patio table. The decor was one rendition of *Funiculi Funicula* away from Italian restaurant, but it was better than low-budget nursing home community room.

Ms. Broussard and June disappeared into the bedroom for over an hour to dress and primp for the party. They returned to the living room, utterly transformed.

"That must have been one hell of a sponge bath," I said, already sipping my fourth glass of wine.

Will looked up from the playlist he was creating on his iPod. "Ms. Broussard, can I...?" The stunning shift in appearance of the two older women stopped him cold. "Would you like something to drink?"

Ms. Broussard, who usually wore a sensible low-maintenance curl, had pushed up and pinned her hair elegantly. Her tropical nursing scrubs had been replaced by a slimming knee-length black dress, and she'd swapped her white, thick-soled slip-ons for black glossy heels. Low heels, but heels nonetheless. I seldom thought of her as anything other than a nurse, and I wondered what else she might be hiding behind her sturdy professional veneer.

"Ms. Broussard, you look incredible." As I spoke the words, I saw that her overhaul was only half the spectacle. "My God." For an instant, I understood my grandmother's mute aphasic plight, as I could surface no other words in my brain.

She wore black pants and a smart striped Ann Taylor button-down, a favorite of mine and one of the few possessions we'd brought from her home. She wore shoes—real shoes not slippers. Ms. Broussard had combed June's shock of white hair in the same style she wore in a decade-old photograph that hung on the living room wall. A light touch of rouge gave my grandmother's face the color and depth that, until then, I hadn't realized it lacked. This version of June, thoughtfully reconstructed by Ms. Broussard, reminded me that my grandmother still existed inside the broken shell we'd cared for all these months.

Will pushed play on his iPod, and *Luck Be a Lady* streamed from the stereo speakers. He looked nothing like young Sinatra, but he was just as charming as he tilted his head, winked, and tipped an invisible hat to my grandmother.

"Happy birthday, June," I said. I gently lifted her hand over her head and held it there as I soft-shoed a slow circle around her wheelchair.

ARIEL AND DAVID stood on the doorstep, holding a dozen roses, a birthday card, and a bottle of wine. I invited them in and was surprised to see Harlan emerge from the shadows behind them.

"We celebratin', Mr. Conor?"

"We are," I said.

"I figured somethin' was up when I saw you carrying all that wine inside."

"It's my grandmother's birthday."

"That's what the smokin' hot redhead told me while she was waiting on you to answer the door."

"She's taken," I said. "By the smokin' hot guy who was holding her hand."

"Don't mean she can't window shop." He flexed his negligible biceps in the sleeveless Aerosmith T-shirt he wore. "She was checkin' out the guns."

"I'm sure she was, Harlan."

"Say, Mr. Conor...since the redhead brought another bottle of wine, I was thinkin' you might have one to spare?"

"They let kids drink wine in that swamp you come from?"

"Come on, man. Don't be a hater."

"You're sixteen, right?"

"Goin' on seventeen." He ran his hand through his matted mop of blond hair.

"Maybe next year, then."

"All right, I hear ya." He smiled and held out a clenched fist. "Hit it, Mr. Conor."

"Goodnight, Harlan." I fist-bumped the kid and stepped inside.

"Wait." He leaped off the porch and snapped two bright purple hibiscus flowers from a shrub. "Give these to Miss June for me. Tell her Harlan said happy birthday."

THE WHOLE POINT of having a drinking problem is to forget, to drop inside an enchanted bottle and hide from the nauseating throb of each day's humiliating kick in the crotch. Wine wasn't my favorite hiding place, but it allowed me to pace myself, and if I drank enough, the magic of forgetting still happened. By the end of dinner, the worrisome call from Marshall earlier in the day was a blur.

I'm not sure what peculiar expression the red wine euphoria left on my face, but my unusually satisfied demeanor showed. Will sat next to me on the arm of the sofa. "You okay?"

"Never better." And for the moment, it was true.

The conversation drifted effortlessly from tales of Ms. Broussard's grandchildren to the origins of the Sesame Street chess set, which Will had displayed on a table by the window.

"What a lovely...and interesting...piece." Ariel appeared unsure of whether the object was kitsch or art.

"Chesh," June said.

"I see." Ariel examined the game pieces. "Is this Conor's toy?"

"It's June's," Will said. "She promised to teach me to play. I gave it to her as a reminder."

"Chess, with a Big Bird king." Ariel chuckled.

"An uh Cookie Monshah queen," said June.

"A Cookie Monster queen!" Ariel picked up the game piece and gushed over it.

I'd never imagined these disparate continents in my world drifting together to form a unique family Pangea, but from my cheery vantage point inside the sturdy green glass of a Cabernet bottle, they did.

"Ms. Broussard—" Ariel said.

"Call me Henrietta."

"Henrietta, Conor told us how much help you've been to his family."

"Oh, these boys don't need me." She placed her hand on my grandmother's shoulder. "I only stick around because I like spending time with June."

"Don't we all," Ariel said, bringing a beaming half-smile to my grandmother's face.

WE MOVED THE party to the patio as the last ounces of daylight seeped beneath the horizon. Ms. Broussard read aloud the cards we'd given to June, and I lit eight skinny candles on her cake. What birthday wish does a once vibrant and now helpless eighty-five-year-old woman make? I didn't ask the question, but I wondered if the answer involved a private hospital room, a sturdy pillow, and a grandson with enough backbone to do the job.

I gathered the dirty dessert plates and coffee cups. Alone in the kitchen, I gulped wine from a bottle as I rinsed the dishes and peered out the open window over the sink. In the deep purple of a late summer evening, I saw it. I rubbed my eyes with the back of my soapy hands to erase the phantom, but I couldn't.

Fifty yards away, on the sloping edge of the Hillsborough River, a black mass crept along the bank. I assumed, at first, that a neighbor's dog or cat had wandered to the river's edge, but when it moved to a brighter spot along the muddy bank, I gauged its massive size. The precise shape eluded me, but when the animal plunged into the river to make an evening snack of an unsuspecting mallard or largemouth bass, I knew. The sound echoed through the open kitchen window: the slapping of a massive amphibious underbelly on the surface of the water, followed by the deadly silence of the creature scurrying unseen into the murky quiet below.

The shrill ring of the phone shattered the moment like a tray of dirty silverware crashing to the floor in a candlelit restaurant.

I snatched the handset. "Hello?"

"Hi, Conor, it's Uncle Martin." I chastised myself for not checking the caller ID.

"Hi, Uncle Martin," I sighed.

Uncle Martin didn't rattle me the way Aunt Doris did, but he wouldn't have called if she hadn't prompted him. He was a likable marionette, but I knew who pulled his strings. When he asked about my job and about June, I imagined Aunt Doris perched on the arm of his chair, holding up cue cards and kicking his shins when he deviated from the script.

"Conor, Aunt Doris and I understand June has an important birthday coming up."

"Actually," I said, "it's today."

"Right. We want to wish her a happy birthday."

"Unfortunately, this isn't a good time, Uncle Martin. We just finished dinner, and..." I paused, distracted by the sound of shuffling and muffled voices.

"Hello, Conor, it's Aunt Doris."

"Hi, Aunt Doris." I didn't mask my agitation. "I was explaining to Uncle Martin that we just finished dinner and we have guests. This is a bad time."

"Oh well, we only want to talk with June for a second. Your momma told us you all were having a little party, so we thought it'd be nice to call and wish her happy birthday."

"I appreciate that, and I'm sure June will too. I'll let her know you called."

"Listen, Conor..." She employed a maternal tone of authority she hadn't used with me in decades. "I want to talk with June for a moment, understand? I hear she's doing well, and since her *miraculous* recovery I've felt a certain kinship with her."

My face grew hot and several silent moments passed, unfilled by the response I would have made if words had been possible.

"I'm sure this won't make sense to you, but your grandmother and I have both been touched by the Holy Spirit. We share a bond of sorts."

The stroke could have engendered a religious epiphany for my grandmother, but in no distant corner of my mind could I imagine June and Doris sharing a spiritual connection.

"Like I said, it's not a good time." I paced the anxiety trail, around the sofa and liquor cart, down the hall, and back to the living room.

"Conor..." She lowered her voice to let me know the shit was about to get serious. "You understand you are only her caretaker. You aren't her keeper."

I was dumbstruck by her audacity, which gave her an opening to continue the assault.

"She doesn't belong to you, Conor. Certainly, there was a time when your relationship was *special,* but June has accepted Jesus into her heart. She's part of God's family now, and we're sisters in Christ."

If a how-to manual had been written on pushing my hot buttons, Aunt Doris was surely its author. My adrenalin surged to rage, and words, however poorly considered, came easily.

"Listen, goddammit, June is having a nice evening with me and Will and our friends." My voice grew loud and my steps were heavy now, more stomping than pacing. "We're having a good time, and no one wants to hear your Holy Spirit bullshit."

Dinner conversation came to a halt as Will, June, and our guests listened to my end of the conversation through the open sliding glass doors. I lowered my voice and continued. "You're not talking to her now. In fact, unless you and Jesus come to her in a dream, you're not talking to her ever."

"Conor," she said, "That 'bullshit' is my faith. Anyway, I'm sorry you're so bitter. I'll give you some time to calm down and contemplate your words, but rest assured, my concern for June, and for you, comes from a place of pure love."

"Good-bye." I took a moment to digest the horseshit sandwich. "And Aunt Doris, God bless."

My hands shook as I hung up the phone and returned to the party. Will gazed out at the dark river in the distance. Ariel winked at me and David sipped his coffee. Ms. Broussard sat rigid, staring at her hands, which were clasped in her lap.

"Wrong number?" I said. "I'll just finish up in the kitchen."

"Kaahn," my grandmother called out.

I stopped in my tracks, my back still turned to the patio. "Yes, June?"

"Fuck her."

Twenty-Six

WILL LEFT FOR work well before the sun came up, stopping by my makeshift sofa bed on his way out to shake me awake. Despite my wine intake the night before, I sprang to full consciousness. The thought of Marshall's pending interrogation already loomed front and center in my brain.

I straightened the sofa cushions and folded and stowed my sheets in the bedroom closet. Across the room, the numbers on Will's alarm clock glowed red. They read 5:22 a.m. I opened the medicine cabinet, gnawing at my fingernails as I rifled through old prescriptions. I prayed one of the labels might miraculously read Xanax, but none did. Giving up pill-popping was one of the promises I'd made to Will and actually kept. I remembered the half-frozen bottle of Stoli in the kitchen freezer, but drinking this close to the meeting with Marshall was risky. I glanced at the clock again: 5:23 a.m. I crawled into our bed, Will's bed, and I lay there searching for comfort in the still-warm silhouette of his body.

WHEN THERE'S NO physical evidence of wrongdoing, outright denial is the surest way to save your ass in a retail investigation. Dishonesty hadn't done much for me lately, though.

Marshall closed the office door and sat on the edge of my desk. "Tell me about Aaron."

"College kid, decent employee. Bailed on me for the last two weeks of Christmas so I fired him, which was probably a rash decision."

"Right," he said, "but I'm not asking you about that."

"Okay. What are you asking me then?"

"Tell me about Aaron last Thanksgiving."

"He was alone and I felt sorry for him, so I invited him over to my place for the holiday."

"And?"

"And he ate turkey and dressing with me and my friends."

"And you allowed him to consume alcohol at your home?"

"I did."

"And he's underage?"

"I suppose, but it was just a few beers. In retrospect, it was...questionable judgment."

"And you smoked marijuana with him?"

"No," I said.

"So, you deny this underage college kid smoked marijuana at your house that day?"

"Not with me, just with my friends."

The cross-examination continued for another ten minutes, before Marshall had me write and sign a statement attesting to the facts I'd admitted. He disappeared with his cell phone glued to his ear, no doubt sharing the sordid tale with an HR wonk who sat in a cubicle somewhere consulting a policy manual.

Tom and the regular morning crew arrived to open the store. I told them I'd come in early for a routine meeting with Marshall, and then I returned to my office and pondered the number of boxes I'd need to pack my belongings.

When Marshall returned an hour later, he pulled Tom aside and talked with him in the stock room outside my office. I couldn't hear the content of their conversation, but Tom's furrowed brow and solemn head nods led me to believe they were discussing my imminent termination.

Marshall entered my office alone and shut the door behind him. "Your honesty might just save your ass," he said. "I'm trying to talk them into letting me keep you."

"Seriously?" I hadn't expected a ladder-climber like Marshall to go to bat for me.

"You've been with us a long time. And I know you got your grandma now."

"I do. I have a lot going on and I can't afford to miss any more paychecks."

"I'm suspending you for the rest of the day," he said. "With pay."

"So, you're not firing me?"

"I don't know. I made the case for keeping you, but HR wants to sort through the details. We'll know for sure tomorrow."

"So what do I do now?"

"Go home. Meet me here tomorrow at 2:00 p.m."

"Let me talk to Tom."

"No need. I'll take care of it. Let me walk you out."

I'd escorted suspended employees out of the building before, but I'd never been on the guilty side of the perp walk. It felt like good-bye. As I passed the cash register, Tom caught my eye but didn't speak or wave. Dead man walking.

"He never struck me as the vengeful type," I said as we exited the front doors.

"Tom's just doing his job," Marshall replied.

"I meant Aaron."

"Oh. Don't know. I never talked to him. Tom showed me Aaron's Instagram page, though. Kids these days put all their personal business online."

HEADING HOME SO early seemed like a waste, since Ms. Broussard was still on-the-clock for a few hours. I needed time to let my situation soak in, an opportunity to contemplate where I'd fucked up this time and a chance to evaluate my severely limited options. I drove around to the back of the mall and parked in the faraway corner of the lot overlooking the airport runway. The last time I'd parked here was the night I had sex with Paul, the night I stomped on the neck of my already tenuous relationship with Will and broke it.

I opened the glove compartment and took out my emergency pint of Maker's Mark, which I'd apparently half drained during the fallout of some other crisis. I leaned back in the driver's seat, checked the rearview mirror like a teenager on the lookout for mall security, and swigged from the bottle.

Though I'd parked here plenty of times to drink and decompress, I'd never done it in daylight before. The bright morning sun glinting off the wings of airplanes gave the lives of those anonymous travelers an even greater air of glamor and possibility. As they jetted away on vacations to lush tropical places with their already tanned and beautiful lovers, I took another drink from the bottle and wiped a layer of dust from my dashboard.

I supposed Tom must have liked his time in charge of the store so much that he'd found a way to push me out permanently. The realization of his betrayal stung, but it also relieved me. At least it wasn't Aaron. My guilt over the impetuous firing would've been even worse if I knew the kid had carried the burden of a heavy grudge all these months.

I drained the last drops from the bottle of Maker's and slid my phone from my pocket.

I dialed his cell number. He picked up on the second ring.

"Aaron, it's Conor from the bookstore."

"Conor! Good to hear from ya."

"It's nice to hear from you too. Nice to talk to you, I mean."

"Dude, if you're calling to get me back, I'm sorry to say I'm not on the market."

"No," I said. "That's not why I'm calling."

"I got a sweet gig now doing graphic design work for this company downtown."

"Good for you. I'm happy for you."

"So yeah, not to be rude, but I'm kind of working right now. What's up, man?"

"Hey, about the whole thing last Christmas. I just wanted to say, I'm really sorry."

"Okay," he said. "All good." I pictured the exaggerated nod of his head.

"I was in a bad place, and I blew the whole thing out of proportion. It was my mistake."

"No worries," he assured me. "Water under the bridge."

"Thanks, Aaron."

"Heard you were gone for a while. You back in action at the store?"

"Actually," I said, "I think today is my last day."

"Oh, all right, dude. Something good lined up, I hope? You write another book?"

"Not yet. Still can't get anyone to buy the last one." He chuckled and his staccato stoner laugh made me smile. "Anyway, I won't keep you, Aaron."

"Oh hey, one other thing—how's your grandma?"

The generosity of his spirit left me momentarily speechless. "She's improving. Slow, but steady."

"Right on, Conor. Tell her I asked about her, okay?"

"I will."

"Dude, it's so awesome that your grandma smokes weed. Hit me up if her and your boyfriend want to spark up again some time."

"Sure thing." I hung up the phone and tucked the empty bottle under the seat.

I STOPPED AT the liquor store on the way home to replace the pint of Maker's and buy some wintergreen gum to mask any stale traces of bourbon. I hadn't decided if I would tell Ms. Broussard and June about the suspension, but either way, I didn't want my breath to inadvertently broadcast that bad news was afoot.

Ms. Broussard looked up from her needlepoint project. "I didn't expect you home so early."

"I haven't been...feeling so good."

"I shouldn't think so," she said. "After last night."

"It's not that."

"Mm-hmm."

June's wheelchair was parked in front of the sliding glass door. Her gaze was fixed on a flock of ducks that had gathered to shit all over the park bench behind our condo. "How about you, June? Little hungover?"

"I should be sho lucky," she said.

I kissed her forehead. "I'm going to lie down."

"If Will's not home, I'll wake you before I go," said Ms. Broussard. "Oh, you got a letter today. I signed for it."

An ink stamp on the front of the large white envelope read, *Return Receipt Requested*. No one sent certified mail with good news. I might not have recognized the long, twisty roots of the corporate logo emblazoned in the corner if I hadn't seen it the day before.

I'd just seen the first letter from Mangrove Press yesterday, although Sharon Barclay had sent it nearly two months ago. In the time between then and now, she'd received nothing from me. No pitch, no outline, no first draft. Not even a sorry excuse about a sick grandmother. There were check-in calls and e-mails in the last six months, but I hadn't responded. If they couldn't reach me, they couldn't shitcan me. Or so I thought.

I didn't blame Mangrove for dropping me any more than I blamed Will for tossing me aside. But even if you accept that fucked is the natural order of things, that doesn't make it any easier to take the punch.

TWENTY-SEVEN

I USUALLY STOWED the sheets from my sofa bed before Ms. Broussard let herself in, but since I didn't have to work until my afternoon meeting with Marshall, I'd fallen back to sleep after Will left. I was awakened by the twist of the nurse's key in the front door lock.

"Good morning," she said. "Sleeping in today?"

"I didn't get much rest last night."

She went to the kitchen to brew a pot of coffee. "Want a fresh cup?" she called out.

"Sure."

I raced to the bedroom to pull on a pair of jeans and a clean shirt. When I returned, she handed me a steaming cup of black coffee.

"Nothing in it, right?"

"That's fine." I sat on the sofa next to the stack of sheets she had neatly folded. "Thanks for the coffee. And for making my bed."

"You're welcome. Just don't get used to it." She sipped from her cup and flipped through the pages of the *Tampa Tribune* she brought with her each day.

"Ms. Broussard..."

"Yes?"

"Nothing." I held a hand to my mouth and chewed at my fingernails, spitting cuticle shreds onto the carpet.

"Doesn't look like nothing."

"I'm sorry about the thing with Aunt Doris the other night. Her timing is crap."

"All families fight, Conor."

"You don't know her though. She shoves her religion down my throat—"

"Actually, I do know her. I met her at the hospital, remember?"

"Right," I replied, fondly remembering the day Ms. Broussard had run interference with Doris and Pastor Lonnie. "Anyway, I'm sorry if I let Doris ruin the party."

"It's no big deal." She folded the newspaper and set it down. "Not for the rest of us."

"What's that supposed to mean?"

"There's no hidden meaning, Conor."

I set my coffee on the table between us. "So, what's the obvious meaning?"

"Some folks naturally focus on the bigger picture..."

"And I'm not one of those folks, right?" I picked up my mug and sipped my coffee like angry Jack Nicholson. "What exactly is this bigger picture I'm missing? Before you answer, let me be honest about one thing. I'm not sure a Jesus speech is going to help me at this point."

"Conor, I don't know what's on your mind this morning, but I suspect it's more than just your Aunt Doris. And have I ever preached to you?"

"You have not," I said.

"Not even once." She picked up the newspaper and opened it wide between us.

"There is something else. A ton of shit, actually. But I'm not ready to talk about it."

"Fine. I never preach and I never pry." She spoke slowly and calmly from behind the newsprint barricade.

"None of this is your fault." Sarcasm had never been more uncomfortable than when I aimed it at Henrietta Broussard.

She stood and collected both our empty mugs. "Life is complicated. But things work out, Conor. One way or another, they work out."

"Sounds like Will has been lecturing you on Buddhism."

She smiled. "We talk."

"I'm sorry," I said. "For being an asshole."

"I forgive you," she said. "For being an asshole."

I walked outside to sit in the fresh air, scowling as I passed the duck-shit-covered bench. At the river's edge, I sat in the damp grass, pulling my knees to my chest and bowing my head. Then I closed my eyes and I prayed that it would all work out. Let's be real, though, that kind of optimism fits me like O.J.'s glove.

AARON WAS A nice kid who didn't deserve to spend Thanksgiving alone in a dorm room, reading Twitter on his iPhone and eating cold, shitty pizza. I had honorable intentions when I invited him over, but supplying alcohol to a twenty-year-old was illegal, and letting a coworker smoke pot with my family was, at a minimum, questionable decision-making. Still, the incident was old news, and after months of caring for June and busting my ass to stick to my do-good manifesto, I hoped karma might finally be on my side.

I strode into the bookstore with all the self-respect of a disheveled sorority girl leaving a frat house at dawn. The looming loss of my job was a hearty kick in the balls I could ill afford, but what suffocated my dignity was the prospect of another self-inflicted wound, the realization of my fundamental ineptness as a human being. Failing when you don't care and haven't tried was one thing, but coming face to face with the undeniable recognition that your best isn't good enough, was another.

Marshall sat in my chair and gestured for me to sit across from him.

"Feels weird being on this side of the desk," I said.

"Feels worse over here."

"You said you were angling to keep me."

"I'm sorry, Conor."

"It was last Thanksgiving, for fuck's sake."

"I convinced them the Aaron thing was old news," he said. "I assured them he wasn't in the picture any more, and I talked them down to a Final Warning."

"So, why are you apologizing?"

"Because that was yesterday." He opened the desk drawer and removed the opened bottle of Irish whiskey I'd stashed behind the employee files. "I'm sorry, Conor."

THE PASTEL NEON glow of a restaurant sign was the only light left in the mostly empty parking lot. I'd snatched the bottle of Jameson from the desk, sat in my car, and emptied it. I'd walked across the mall parking lot to Ruby Tuesday's and ordered a double shot of Jameson, with a double shot of Jameson chaser. I'd finished both drinks and, after stumbling back to the car, patted myself on the back for having the forethought to restock the emergency Maker's pint in the glove box. Though I didn't remember anything else, judging from my gulf-front location and the sloppy splash of crab soup on my shirt, I'd apparently driven to Clearwater Beach and had dinner at Frenchy's Rockaway Grill.

I rolled down the car window, once I'd gotten my face unstuck from it, and inhaled deep. The cool salty air slowly filled my lungs, each merciful breath bringing me a little more back to life. I dug around my pockets for my phone but found only my car keys. I plugged them into the ignition and then took them out again. According to the dashboard clock, it was after midnight.

The grown-ups had gone home for the night, leaving me alone in the parking lot with the after-hours teenage skate crowd. I sat on the hood of the car, surveying the group to see if any of them looked more approachable than the rest. A shirtless kid in plaid board shorts and a backwards Yankees cap skated over before I could make the determination.

"Hey, dude," he said.

"Hey."

"Been sleeping it off?"

"Something like that."

"Been there, man." He pulled a cigarette from behind his ear and lit it. Judging from his pimpled face and slight stature, he couldn't have been more than fifteen. I doubted he'd been anywhere near where I'd been.

"Hey," I said. "You got a phone I could use for a minute?"

He laughed. "You got some important business to transact or something?"

"No, you little shit. I'm going to call your mommy and tell her you're smoking."

He laughed harder. "Fuck you, dude."

"Seriously, can I use your phone? It's kind of important."

"Seriously, can you buy us some beer? That shit is kind of important too."

Now it was my turn to laugh. I slid off the hood. Even in my hunched and debilitated state, I towered over the kid. "Never mind. I'm already in enough trouble."

My head pounded as I leaned into the car and rummaged around the seats and floorboards for the missing phone, which was probably resting on top of a urinal in a sports bar somewhere between Tampa and Clearwater. I didn't see the kid behind me.

"Dude," he said. "Chill. You can use my phone."

"Thank you." I took the phone and stepped a few feet away from the car.

"Don't run my battery down."

It was one in the morning, but Will answered on the first ring. "Are you okay?"

"I'm fine."

"Where are you?"

"I'm at Clearwater Beach."

"Do you need me to come get you?"

"Maybe," I said. "No. I'm good."

"You don't sound like you should be driving."

"I'm fine. I'm okay and I'm coming home."

"I'm coming to get you, Conor."

"You can't leave June alone."

"She won't be alone. Ms. Broussard is here."

I double-checked the time on the kid's phone. "What the hell is she still doing there? It's the middle of the night."

"We've been worried sick about you. I know you got fired. I called the bookstore this morning."

"You called the bookstore...this morning?"

"Yes. When you didn't come home last night—"

"Wait, wait, wait, goddamn it, wait." I turned to the skater, who stood by my car, waiting to get his phone back. I held the phone at arm's length. "What day is it?"

The kid looked over his shoulder at his snickering friends. "Dude, it's like, Saturday night."

I squatted and leaned my back against the car. My hand went to my face and rubbed the rough stubble of a two-day growth of beard. A lone bee buzzed frantically inside the hollow cavern of my empty head.

Will's tiny voice called out to me from the kid's phone.

I tried to speak.

"Conor, are you there? Say something. You're in Clearwater?"

My heart raced and my lips quivered.

"Whose phone is this, Conor? Are you okay?"

I collapsed to the ground, my face wet with tears, as the phone slipped from my hand and I uttered a single word. "Come."

TWENTY-EIGHT

WE ALL GET hurt by the same things in life—rejection, failure, and a slew of other regrettable shit that happens to us—but we each develop our own unique set of emotional scars, like fingerprints, only a fuckload more painful to acquire. Some of these scars heal over time, but others, the ones we get when our hearts are tender and we're too vulnerable to know better, those scars take a lifetime to salve and scab over, if they ever heal at all. Kid scars run deep.

My scars were like that, a fathomless maze of Marianas Trenches carved deep into my psyche before I even reached puberty. In one of those fathomless pits, an abandoned five-year-old drifts endlessly toward the bottom. Patrick lays dead in another, a taut twist of rope still carving lines in his neck. Old wounds aren't always visible from the outside, but they're there, festering inside and burning like a house fire.

For decades, I tried to douse those flames with shots of Jameson, but drinking brought me more problems than it solved. I learned my lesson too late, though. I doubt I could have picked up the pieces of my shattered life anyway, but it didn't matter. Soon enough, there would be no pieces left.

I LOADED JUNE'S wheelchair and a backpack of supplies in the trunk of the car, while Will and Ms. Broussard strapped June safely into the backseat. We drove across Tampa Bay to MacArthur Park, a quiet, tree-lined strip of Clearwater that ran along the bay and, incidentally, had nothing to do with any cakes left out in the rain.

June napped during the thirty-minute ride, but when we reached the bayfront park her eyes opened wide as she took in her surroundings. I filled my lungs with a deep breath of the salty air carried aloft by the warm gulf breeze. Majestic oak trees swayed around us. Seagulls cawed and dove in the distance. Tiny waves lapped at the seawall below us.

Ms. Broussard secured June in the wheelchair, and I tossed the backpack over my shoulder. An older couple on a park bench watched us cross the parking lot and start our trek down a long, winding sidewalk that ran adjacent to the seawall. I imagined we made an interesting foursome, like the cast of a twenty-first century *Wizard of Oz*, where even the gay, black, and disabled are allowed to undertake pilgrimages in search of answers.

Ms. Broussard helmed June's wheelchair. Will and I followed close behind.

"This was a good idea," I said, tilting my face toward the sun.

"It's certainly nice here," the nurse replied without looking back.

"I've always liked this place," I said. "Sunday barbecues and stuff like that. One of my friends proposed to his wife beneath a cluster of oak trees out here."

We walked in silence for a few minutes, before Ms. Broussard stopped and faced Will and me. She closed her eyes and inhaled. "So easy to forget, we are blessed indeed."

It had been less than a week since I celebrated my unceremonious shitcanning with a two-day bender that could have left me dead. I suppose that sort of thing does make it easy to forget how "blessed" we are.

I glanced at June's withered arms and useless legs, her crooked head, lolling to one side as the weakened muscles in her neck strained to do their job. A translucent string of spittle had dribbled onto her chin where it would cling until one of us tended to it. Her eyes were wide with the familiar look of perpetual surprise, or confusion, or maybe it was fear. If June was listening to our conversation, I wondered, did she feel blessed?

"This looks like as good a place as any," Will said, as we approached a bench in a sunny clearing a few yards from the seawall.

Ms. Broussard maneuvered June's chair into position so she looked out over the bay and then sat on the bench next to my grandmother. There was room for one more.

"Go ahead," Will said, gesturing for me to sit.

I plopped down next to the nurse. "Ms. Broussard, do you remember the heart-to-heart we had about focusing on the big picture?"

"Is that a conversation we've had only once?" she asked.

"I'm sure we've covered it a few times, but I meant last week. You said, 'things work out one way or another,' and that really struck a chord with me."

"I'm happy to hear it," she said.

"I've been thinking about it a lot. About everything, actually."

"Mm-hmm." She was doubtful but too polite to say so.

"Seriously, I started off the in the right direction this year, but I got sidetracked. I'm ready to try again."

She pursed her lips and looked thoughtfully at the ground as though a loved one was buried there beneath her feet. The sonic boom of silence was deafening.

"It's too late," Will said.

"I want to get rid of some baggage. Clean out the family stuff. The really old shit that's weighing me down."

Will kneeled in front of me. "It's too late."

"What the fuck are you talking about?" My gut tightened and my voice trembled. "Too late for what?"

He took my hands in his and kissed them. I felt the warmth of his tears on my skin. "Will..." My heartbeat quickened and pounded in my chest. "Please."

"It's not working. I'm so...sorry."

Every muscle in my body tensed and I ached from the inside out. My bones shuddered and snapped; my teeth cracked. The world shrank and darkness closed in, until only a tiny pinhole of light remained. A thousand miles away, Ms. Broussard sat still and upright, as strong as a pillar, her head held high as tears coursed down her cheeks, and just beyond her, my beloved June. Her head lolled to the side, but her eyes were wide and gazing into the distance, as though a songbird sang that only she could hear.

"It's okay," June said. "It's okay."

I SAT ALONE in darkness on the lanai, staring at the empty bottle of Grey Goose on the table in front of me. I'd taken the vodka outside hours before with the intent of carefully weighing my options, but as I'd quickly determined there were none, I just poured shot after shot and watched the moon play hide-and-seek behind the passing clouds. No one likes a quitter, not even me, but something about giving up now felt okay.

June was asleep when I pushed open the door to her room. Her head was tilted to one side, as it almost always was, and her arms were contracted and pulled tight across her chest. Her clenched fists looked tense and angry, as though they were the only expression of rage she could muster. I wanted nothing more than to comfort her through the connection of her hand in mine, but I didn't want to wake her. My fingers stroked the space just above her full head of wiry white hair, and the back of my hand moved down a parallel path inches from her face, before finally coming to rest on the pillow. I whispered a silent apology and kissed her forehead in the air between us.

It was hours after midnight, but a light still shone under Will's bedroom door. I pictured him inside, the glow of the bedside lamp we'd bought at Ikea barely illuminating him as he slept. *Leaves of Grass* lay open on the bed next to him. I placed my palm flat against the doorframe, as gentle as a lover, and rested my cheek on the cool wooden door.

IN THE CLEARING behind the condo, I pulled off my jeans and shirt. I lay down in the damp grass a few feet from where I'd collapsed in December, only this time not muddy and soaked by the river. For half an hour, maybe more, I searched the sky for answers, though in truth, I hadn't defined any worthwhile questions. I staggered to my feet and peered through the darkness at the river.

I took a step toward it but stopped to steady myself. Though my thoughts were as jumbled and turbulent as a harbor in a hurricane, I commanded my feet forward. I moved closer to the water, until I stood in the dewy grass just a few yards from the black river's edge. Tiny waves lapped at the soft, muddy bank, and I remembered the feel of its thick, cool ooze between my toes. Through the misty blur of my vodka-infused lenses, flecks of starlight flickered on the rippled surface of the water. It was close now.

As the water pooled around my bare ankles, my feet sank into the mud. The damp night air clung to my body, but the water washing over my feet was warm and comfortable, like an old pair of slippers. Two steps in, the water rose to my knees. There was no menacing shadow on the riverbank, no ominous wake on the water's surface. I waited for that telltale slap on the water, but there was only the baritone groan of lonely bullfrogs and the steady hum of cicadas.

I moved a step further into the river. The water felt cooler now as it ringed around my thighs. I craned my neck and looked into the still black night. Just as before, the sky offered nothing: no shooting star, no alien transport ship, no message from God blinked in twinkling starlight code. Across the river, as the faintest orange glow illuminated a distant horizon I couldn't see, a light came on in a nearby house. An alarm clock had sounded. A man had stretched and yawned and rubbed his tired eyes. Now he would shave and shower and go to work. Like people do.

I pried one foot from the muck, and then the other, this time with ease. I waded in deeper and the river bottom grew more firm. Small, sharp rocks pecked at the soles of my feet. I went deeper still, until I reached the slope where the bottom dropped off. The cool water circled my chest and lapped my chin. My heels skidded along the riverbed, as I searched in vain for solid ground. I stepped into nothingness and disappeared.

TWENTY-NINE

ALLIGATORS LIVE IN all sorts of freshwater bodies around the state of Florida—lakes, ponds, swamps, and of course, rivers. Full-grown alligators can grow to fourteen feet in length and weigh more than a thousand pounds. Gators are opportunistic eaters, making meals out of fish, turtles, or small mammals that happen to be in the wrong place at the wrong time. They don't chew as much as they rip and swallow. Gators are most active at dusk and dawn. In light of these wildlife fundamentals, I should have considered myself lucky when I woke up just after sunrise in a thicket of reeds, with my fingers and toes all accounted for and my limbs intact.

I lay nestled in the tall grass at the water's edge with part of my body still submerged. I opened my eyes and assessed my surroundings. Through the shadows of the filtered morning sun, I estimated the reeds around me to be three or four feet high. I had no idea how far I'd drifted. Sprawled in the deep grass, weary and wet, I heaved a deep sigh and buried my head in the crook of my arm, both grateful and disappointed to be alive.

I dozed or daydreamed in my grassy bed; I didn't know which, until a nearby pattering penetrated the haze and roused me. I lay still in my reedy hideaway and listened carefully to the steady trickle, which sounded man-made and wasn't cause for alarm until a warm splatter of pee hit the back of my neck.

"What the fuck!" I yelled as I sprang from the thicket.

"Jesus goddamn Christ!" Harlan stumbled backward, falling on his ass and launching a bamboo fishing pole into the air.

"Harlan, were you peeing on me?"

He stood and zipped his cut-off denim shorts. "I wasn't planning to, but how was I supposed to know you were sleeping in the grass?"

Filthy and disheveled, I stumbled up the bank, the drunken idiot from the Black Lagoon. "Where exactly are we?" I asked.

"At my fishin' spot," he said. "I'd guess about seventy-five yards from your back door." The kid inspected my matted hair and muddy boxer shorts, which, to my dismay, was the only article of clothing I was wearing. "You okay there, Mr. Conor?"

I shivered in the damp morning air. "Yeah, I'm fine."

"Put this on." He took off the black AC/DC hoodie he wore over a tattered and nearly identical black AC/DC T-shirt and handed it to me.

"Thanks." I pulled the hoodie over my head, grateful for both the warmth and cover it provided.

He retrieved his bamboo fishing pole and took a seat on a sizable oak tree stump a few feet away. He opened a grimy metal tackle box and took out a shiny silver package.

"Pop Tart?" he asked.

"What flavor?"

"Grape."

"You don't have Brown Sugar Cinnamon in there, do ya?"

"No offense, Mr. Conor, but that's like, the gayest flavor of Pop Tart there is."

I smiled. "I'll try grape."

He set the tackle box on the ground, making room for me on the wide smooth tree stump. We polished off the Pop Tarts and washed them down with a twelve-ounce can of Dr. Pepper.

"Breakfast of champions," I said.

"What's that?"

"Never mind. You're too young to remember."

"No, I'm not. Wheaties, right?"

"Wow. I'm impressed."

"My mom bought it for me once. One of my heroes was on the box."

"Michael Jordan?"

"Shaun White."

I laughed. "You do a lot of snowboarding up there in Starke?"

"I was a skater. It's kinda the same thing."

I nodded and swigged the Dr. Pepper. "Who drinks soda in cans anymore?"

"My mom likes cans. She recycles 'em."

"That's responsible," I said.

"She does it for the money. It's like one of her jobs."

I viewed my Pensacola upbringing as fairly rural, but Starke was a genuine backwater. If you weren't lucky enough to snag a job at Walmart or the state prison, your career options were limited and aluminum recycling was a bona fide source of income. I didn't mean to judge. I had just been fired from my job and my own life was disintegrating. In a weird way, I actually even envied Harlan's mom. When she recognized her world was shit, she had the strength to pack up everything and move to Tampa in search of something better. She had two jobs, and apparently did a lot of recycling on the side, to make sure her kid had a decent middle-class life. She worked her ass off to keep him fed, sheltered, and clothed in sleeveless rocker T-shirts. She was doing her best and it was paying off. Harlan was a good kid.

"You must've really tied one on last night, Mr. Conor."

"I did. Maybe even tied two on."

He slid off the tree stump, crinkled the silver Pop Tarts sleeve, and shoved it into the tackle box. "Sorry I didn't bring more to eat."

"It's okay. You probably didn't expect company."

"I sure didn't." Unable to suppress a smile, he added, "And you probably didn't expect to wake up with a kid peeing on ya."

We both laughed.

"Thanks for breakfast, Harlan."

He nodded and placed his foot casually on the stump. "You sure you're okay, Mr. Conor?"

I had no business sharing my complicated and self-inflicted woes with a sixteen-year-old cracker kid from Starke, but something about him unwound the tightly coiled springs inside me. He was confident and smooth, and his easiness disarmed me.

"Things haven't exactly been going my way."

"I hear ya," he said. "Shit happens."

I wanted to scream. *You have no idea the shit that can happen.* But I'd put a few things together about Harlan's childhood, and I suspected some tumultuous shit had indeed happened in his sixteen short years.

"I was fired from the bookstore."

"For what?"

"Long story."

"That sucks," he said, giving me the benefit of the doubt.

"And I lost my book deal."

"Awww, no way man. That *really* sucks."

"It does." I stared at the ground, pushing leaves and sticks around with my bare feet.

"Things'll get better though, right? They have to." He was no Freud, but I had to give the kid an "A" for effort.

"I don't know, Harlan." My river-damp hair was drying and the AC/DC hoodie was warm, but a chill ran through my body. I shivered and crossed my arms tight. "I don't know what happens next."

"You'll get another job, that's what. You got some nice ties and decent shoes. You just need to find a place to wear 'em."

Though I was shrouded in sorrow, I couldn't help but smile. "I don't care about the job."

"Then why do you look so sad?"

"Because the job's not the only thing I lost."

"Oh damn. Mr. Will was pissed when you got fired, huh?"

"It was more like disappointment."

"Did you have a fight?"

A lump swelled in my throat, suppressing my words and stifling my breath.

"People fight all the time," he said, "but they get over it." The kid wanted so badly to show me the blue sky beyond the dark clouds. His efforts were in vain, but the concern he showed moved me just the same.

I pushed myself up from the stump.

"They're leaving," I said.

"Who's leaving?"

"All of them."

"Goddamn, I'm sorry to hear that, Mr. Conor."

"Me too."

He nodded and kicked at the grass uncomfortably. I set the tackle box back on the stump and forced a smile to my face.

"Thanks for listening, Harlan."

"Anytime...Conor." As he walked to the river's edge, bamboo pole in hand, he glanced back at me. "Keep the hoodie as long as you need it."

EVEN IF YOU don't include the rented hospital bed and other medical equipment, the trappings of caring at home for an elderly stroke victim are voluminous. Before my parents arrived to pick up June, I packed and labeled our supply of swabs, antimicrobial gels, medical sponges, latex gloves, and other fun-time accessories. I called the supply company and coordinated the pickup of June's hospital bed once she was gone. My preparation for June's departure was thorough and immaculate, because I had no intention of being present for a prolonged good-bye. As soon as my parents pulled up to the front of our condo in a rented minivan, I kissed June, told her I loved her, and got the hell out of there.

Ms. Broussard retired and decided to stay in Tampa near her son and his family, so my parents had to hire a new home health nurse in Pensacola. According to Mom, she was no Henrietta Broussard, but she was competent, affordable, and friendly enough.

It didn't take long for Will to find a place to live. He'd been researching options for weeks, even before the catastrophe of my post-firing bender. I stayed away while he packed his things, some of which used to be our things, and as with June's departure, my need for a proper good-bye was dwarfed by my instinct for self-preservation. I was busy elsewhere the day he left.

I drained the last of my 401K, which wasn't substantial to start with, and used most of it to pay a few months ahead on the mortgage. If I was going to be a lonely, unemployed alcoholic, I'd at least do it with a roof over my head.

At first, I pretended I was free, an untamed stallion running wild and untethered on an open plain. No job to wake up for. No boyfriend wondering where I was. No crippled grandmother waiting to be spoon-fed. I drank late into the night with carefree strangers at bars all over town, sharing simulated laughter and forging counterfeit connections that felt genuine until the reality of last call set in. On occasions when I found myself in conversation with someone I genuinely liked; I kept them at arm's length. I was looking for drinking companions, not friends, and certainly not lovers. When one of my drinking pals inevitably showed a little curiosity about the details of my life, I deflected the questions. When that didn't work, I lied outright. I told amusing tales about my Buddhist gardener boyfriend and my crazy gambling grandmother. We all lived happily together with my grandmother's best friend in a sprawling McMansion in a posh South Tampa neighborhood. It was a fantasy life that was easy to lie about.

I was too ashamed to reach out to Ms. Broussard, and she never called me, though my mother heard from her each Sunday when she called to check on June. After my mother posed a few nursing questions to Ms. Broussard, she'd hold the phone up to June's ear so my grandmother and the nurse could have short "conversations."

Will called me every week or two, but I usually let the calls go to voice mail. He sent texts and e-mails on occasion, and I kept my replies brief and nondescript. The glue wasn't dry in the fragile joints that held together my make-believe new world. Introducing the reality of Will was a weight the structure couldn't bear.

Ariel invited me to visit her in Orlando, but I made up reasons not to go. A painter was doing pre-sale touch-up work on the condo. I was going to a local writer's workshop. I had a job interview. It would have been great to see her, but I was just so busy.

Even Aunt Doris attempted to draw me out. In her own way, she loved me, and I'm sure that after all that had happened, news of my gradual disappearance from the grid concerned her. I was sober when she called. Not completely sober, actually, but still home in the early evening, with only a few warm-up cocktails under my belt. I listened to her long, rambling message. Her voice was monotone and weary, like she'd been awake for days. Though her words were casual, the subtext was laced with worry and fear. Maybe, she'd seen the signs before, the putting on of a brave face, the pretending that in hindsight is so easy to detect, the slow and steady regression, the fatal backing away from life. Maybe she'd learned something from Patrick after all.

THIRTY

EVERYONE HAS BAGGAGE. Some of us have small overnight bags we can neatly stow beneath the seat in front of us. Some have heavier bags—nifty rollers with reinforced wheels that allow us to haul around our weightiest angst without herniating ourselves. Still others, people like Aunt Doris, have sturdy five-piece Samsonite sets with segregated storage spaces for tidy packing of all their miseries, regardless of shape or size. I stowed my tangled heap of shame and sorrow in a musty old steamer trunk with a hinged padlocked lid, the kind you seal your most valuable possessions in just before boarding the *Titanic*.

The galling thing is I had no right to carry as much baggage as I did. My tortures in growing up weren't so different, I imagined, from those of other boys who liked boys. Wondering why I wasn't enthused about the eighth-grade dance, despite the zeal shown by my unusually busty companion. Scheming to escape my first "real" relationship in high school without ever performing sexually beyond some minor groping. Growing up, I had some queer experiences, pun intended, and they left their marks, but I was never whipped with clothes hangers or locked in a dingy basement where I had to eat spiders to survive. I earned my scars the old-fashioned way, with a father who gave in to Jameson, a mother who gave me away, an aunt who gave herself to Jesus, and Patrick, who gave up on everything. That's the shit I carried, the shit I couldn't escape.

Baggage wasn't something I knew how to leave behind, but after June and Will left, God knows I tried. I spent summer days at beachside clubs and frequented the trendy pubs on Howard Avenue at night, but the luster of my newfound freedom from human obligation dimmed within weeks. Once I became a "regular" at a bar, the other alcoholic patrons expected me to maintain conversations and ask questions about their empty lives. Some of them had truly tragic stories and I tried to care, but I had little pity to spare. By the time the first credit card bill arrived with my accumulated bar tabs, what little artificial shine remained of my bliss was extinguished, and

I started drinking more at home in the evenings. It was cheaper and made for an easier transition between late morning and early afternoon cocktail hours. The only real downside to full-time residential alcoholism, the one serious drawback, was that I could no longer pretend my life was a party.

Late one afternoon, I was approaching too drunk to drive but had a desperate craving for a fresh bottle of Maker's. Harlan offered to drive me to Terrace Liquors in exchange for a forty-ounce Budweiser, and I accepted, under the condition that he promised to drink at home. Upon our return, I took the whiskey and a highball glass to the patio, along with a mostly unused leather journal I'd started keeping at my bedside. Harlan emerged from his back door with his fishing gear in one hand and a small paper bag in the other.

"Don't fall in," I said.

"This ain't amateur hour." He flashed a smile as he walked past.

When he reached the riverbank, he tossed his line in the water and waited patiently, occasionally taking a surreptitious sip from the paper bag at his feet.

As the setting sun crept behind the tree line, I opened the journal and a small plastic card fell out. It had been weeks since I'd seen the manifesto.

I am older now, no longer a damaged child.
Everything is on the line, and I must deliver.
I will get my shit together and make amends.
I will stop taking pills and I will control my cock,
I will face my demons and stop sabotaging my life.

I'd made an honest effort, and for a while, I had been a better man. I had stood and delivered, for June at least, and I'd cut out the prescription meds. I'd also apologized to Aaron, which was at least a step in the direction of making amends. Since the encounter with Paul, my cock had been practically dormant, a total non-factor. None of it had healed me, though. None of it had mattered. I'd lost everything anyway.

Harlan only "fished" for half an hour before packing up his gear and heading in my direction.

"You need any more trans-poh-tation?" he asked, adding extra Southern twang to each syllable of the last word.

"I'm good," I said. "You okay?"

"Never better." He nodded at the journal. "You 'bout to write another book?"

"Why? You wanna help?"

"I got one or two ideas. I ain't just another pretty face."

"No more beer for you." I smiled.

He laughed and rubbed his belly.

"G'night, Harlan."

"Keep it real, Mr. Conor."

I WAS AROUND Harlan's age when I first started writing. During those dark days before I was old enough to buy my own alcohol, writing was my catharsis, the opiate that helped me muddle through adolescence. I logged my struggle for self-acceptance like a journalist and poured out my angst like a poet. Writing kept me grounded as I searched, like young people do, to find my place in the world. It wasn't all pubescent trials and sexual confusion, though. One year, you can imagine which one, I wrote a lot about Patrick. I spoke of it to no one, but I shared it all in my journal. How he'd awakened something inside me I hadn't known was sleeping. How beautiful he was both inside and out. How alive he'd made me feel. I wrote about my breath, how I held it that night while we pretended to sleep, even as his leg casually brushed mine beneath the sheets and sparks of electricity popped. I wrote about the smooth, taut feel of his skin beneath my fingertips, how a shock of his sandy brown hair swept across his forehead, how my body was warmed from the inside out by his honest smile and his soft, sweet eyes. I wrote about passion and lust, how intertwined they were, how they felt so incredibly good and bad at the exact same moment. Patrick and I never mentioned that night. We never again ventured toward that warm and comforting place that Aunt Doris had poisoned with her words. But in the months after we learned that most beautiful and painful of lessons, I filled journals with my love for him, my love for Patrick, the tender boy who helped me understand.

Long before I wrote *Luck of the Irish*, that's how I wandered into prose, finding intimate and truthful themes at the bottom of my cerebral pond, after the muck had been siphoned. If there is one advantage to being a writer, and there may be only one, it's that the shittiest moments of your existence can become your life's best work.

I LIT CANDLES on the patio and sat hunched over the journal late into the night, emptying and refilling my glass, as the thick, messy slop of my emotions drained onto the pages. The rhythmic chirping of crickets was my only soundtrack as I slogged through a familiar bog of self-pity. If only pouring my sadness onto the page was a solution, a permanent fix. What an awesome fucking trick that would be. I could have broken free from the bitterness and had a regular life, with each day full of sacred and intimate moments, the kind healthy people string together into a happy existence. I could have saved the hours spent grieving and fearing and loathing, all that wasted time, filling the burdensome suitcases I hauled so faithfully from one human interaction to the next. If writing had ever changed anything, I would have hurled that baggage into the abyss and understood that half a life spent holding on is long enough.

By the time I drained the last drops of Maker's from the bottle, my barely legible scrawl had deteriorated to a series of loosely connected loops and slanted lines. I could no longer hold my head up. As the pale light of dawn crept across the lawn and my consciousness faded, I squinted into the darkness. Through the long-distance lens of twenty-five years, I saw him. We were there together on that single illuminating night, the night that began so filled with the promise of self-discovery, but ended in disaster. I've often wondered how my life would have been different, if only we'd locked the door.

When Patrick hung himself, thick veins of fear and anger were forever meshed into the flesh of my sadness. I was ruined by loss, by an accidental intrusion into a moment of innocence, by the supernova of self-loathing that sent a vulnerable boy into a dark garage on a cold December night with nothing to hold on to but his shame and a crisp knot of rope.

THIRTY-ONE

THERE WAS A banging, a hammering, the deafening thud of a hydraulic pile driver pounding steel rods into concrete. My head throbbed as though my brain had been forced into a new skull two sizes too small. I saw a faint, distant light, small and round like the end of a tunnel. I was vaguely aware of a stickiness on my cheek, which was pressed against the glass top of the patio table.

More banging and pounding.

My skin felt cool and moist, but the air smelled putrid. An ammonia stench wafted into my nostrils and permeated the cells of my lungs.

More banging.

A steady hum emerged from beneath the din, a distant boat on the river or a faraway bee. It buzzed softly at first, a whisper, and then drew nearer until it wasn't buzzing at all. It said my name, whispered at first and then spoken aloud. "Kaahn." It was slow and slurred, June's pronunciation but not her voice. My head was wrapped in thick cotton, but I heard it.

More banging.

The voice grew louder until it became a piercing yell. "Mr. Conor! Wake the fuck up."

"Fuck," I mumbled. I commanded my body to move, but it refused to cooperate. Through one opened eye, I saw Harlan standing outside the screened door.

"Open the fucking door, Mr. Conor."

I told my legs to lift me, my arms to stretch, my fingers to flip the lock. None obeyed.

"I don't know why you locked the fucking thing," he said.

I watched, helpless to participate in my rescue, as Harlan pulled a small knife from his pocket and flipped it open. He cut a small hole in the mesh, reached his hand through the screen, and unlocked the door.

"Fuck," I repeated with more clarity this time.

"Fucked up," he said. "As in, this shit is fucked up."

My eyes, which remained the only accommodating part of my body, followed Harlan into the kitchen, where he poured a glass of water and grabbed a roll of paper towels.

"Can you sit up?" he asked.

"No."

"You have to. You can't stay hunched over in a puddle of puke."

He stood behind me with his hands on my shoulders and pulled me back from the table. I slumped in the chair but managed to hold myself upright. He stepped back to survey the damage.

Harlan dabbed at my face with wet paper towels, gagging as he wiped vomit from my cheeks and forehead. "I don't mind saying this is some disgusting shit."

I opened both eyes wide and looked at him. "Water."

He held the glass to my mouth and tilted it slowly as I drank. I swished the cool water in my mouth and swallowed. Synapses sparked and fired in random corners of my brain like early morning lights in a high-rise.

"Stand," I said, willing the muscles in my legs to tighten and raise me. I was nearly on my feet before I fell backward and Harlan eased me into the chair.

"Whoa." He laughed. "We ain't ready for that just yet." He dashed into the house and returned with a bath towel. "Mr. Conor, I think you went and pissed yourself."

"Harlan..." I was awake now and starting to appreciate what I was putting him through.

"Wipe yourself off." He handed me the towel. "Then we'll get you inside."

I cleaned my face and swiped clumsily at the front of my shirt and soiled pants.

"I got an idea," Harlan said as he disappeared into the house again. This time he returned with a second towel and a blanket.

"You gonna make me sleep out here?" I asked.

"Nope." He tugged at the bottom of my shirt. "Lift your arms up over your head."

I lifted my arms. He pulled the vomit-stained shirt over my head and tossed it to a far corner of the patio.

"We can deal with that nasty shit later. You think you can stand up if I help you?"

"Probably."

He leaned down, put my arm over his shoulders, and hoisted me from the chair. The pulsing in my temples escalated, but I didn't complain.

"That wasn't so hard," he said, "but here's the tricky part. We gotta ditch those piss-soaked pants. You can lean on me if you have to, but I ain't looking."

Harlan turned away from me. I steadied myself with one hand on his shoulder, and with my free hand, I unbuttoned my jeans and pushed them to the ground. "Boxers too?"

He answered over his shoulder. "You pissed in 'em, didn't ya?"

I slid the boxers off and kicked the jeans and underwear in the direction of the pukey shirt.

"Good work, Mr. Conor. Now wipe yourself off with the clean towel I brought ya."

Trembling and nauseous, I wiped my naked body with the towel while Harlan stared out at the river.

"Okay," I said. "I'm done."

He draped the blanket over my shoulders and wrapped it tightly around my body. "Now we're gonna walk."

I pushed my rubbery legs forward one baby step at a time with Harlan bearing half my weight. I tugged the blanket tightly around me as we moved toward the bedroom to avoid inadvertently exposing myself. I'd traumatized the kid enough for one day. When we reached the bed, he'd already pulled the covers back. He eased me onto the sheets, lifted my feet, and swung them onto the bed.

"Be right back," he said as he sprinted from the room.

I tossed the modesty blanket to the floor and stretched out under the sheets, pulling them tight to my chin. Harlan returned with a fresh glass of ice water.

"You got some aspirin around here?"

"Medicine cabinet." I tilted my head to the nearby master bathroom.

He retrieved a dozen or so Ibuprofen, handing me three and setting the rest on the nightstand.

"Why not just bring the whole bottle?"

"Because you're still drunk, and I don't trust you with the whole bottle."

I popped the pills into my mouth and gulped the ice water.

"Better slow it down, Mr. Conor. Don't wanna start pukin' again."

"No," I said. "No, I do not."

"You got any bread?"

"Why? You feelin' like a sandwich?" I asked.

"Funny. I wasn't asking for me. You need something to soak up the alcohol."

"No bread. Not much of anything in the kitchen."

The gawky teenager pushed my feet aside and sat near the end of the bed. "I can go get you some Pop Tarts." A playful grin spread across the full expanse of his angular face.

I suppressed a laugh, which tightened my stomach and amped up the percussion concert in my head. "You're a real pro at this."

"I got plenty of practice with my dad before he left."

"He must have been a total fucking idiot. Walking away from a good kid like you."

He bowed his head and considered my words carefully before finally looking up and letting his wide smile return. "Who you callin' a kid?"

"Seriously," I said, "thank you, Harlan."

"Ain't no thing, Mr. Conor. Buy me a couple of forties and we'll call it even."

He refilled the glass of ice water and placed a plastic bathroom trash can next to my bed. As my eyes closed, I saw the silhouette of his skinny frame approach the window and tug the curtains tightly closed, sheltering me from the blinding shafts of nauseating daylight.

Just as the pounding in my head subsided, it was replaced by a muffled blast of digital tones. The series of muted beeps echoed randomly through the thick haze of my consciousness until they were interrupted by the faraway sound of a voice.

"This is Harlan."

I might have been dreaming, but the churning in my stomach reassured me I was not.

"Yeah," he said. "The neighbor kid. Who's this?"

I considered opening my eyes and dragging myself out of the half-stupor, but the thought was fleeting.

"Riiight," he said. "I definitely remember. So, how ya been, red?"

The last glowing embers faded in my brain and I drifted off, barely aware of the whispered smooth talk of the sixteen-year-old backwater Casanova who'd rescued me.

I STUMBLED FROM the bedroom in a T-shirt and a pair of clean boxers. The dim light of the settling dusk disoriented me, but it was the smell of frying bacon and the sound of NPR coming from the kitchen that had me truly perplexed.

I walked in unnoticed as Ariel pushed strips of sizzling bacon around a pan. "Welcome?" I said from the doorway. It was a sheepish question more than a greeting.

"Hey darling." She turned to hug me, a spatula in one hand and a sizable bottle of San Pellegrino in the other. Ariel looked generally unnatural in the setting of a kitchen, and the striped apron she'd pulled over her crisp, white blouse and swingy, floral-print skirt did little to dispel that impression.

"What time is it?" I asked, still struggling to get my bearings.

"Dinner time."

"What are you doing here?"

"Taking care of you."

"What?"

"I had a nice chat with your neighbor friend this morning. Harlan, I think it is?"

"When did you talk to Harlan?"

"After he pulled you out of a puddle of your own vomit and tucked you in bed." She smiled and returned her attention to the stovetop, pulling crisp slices of bacon from the pan and draping them on paper towels.

I rubbed my face and forehead hard with my fingertips. "It was nice of you to come. I had a few too many last night, but I'm feeling fine now."

"Really?" It was a one-word question, but she'd loaded it with implications.

"I'm okay," I said, backing away from the stove. "Not sure I'm ready for bacon, though."

"What, this?" She snagged a crunchy strip of bacon and bit it in half. "This is for me. I've been showing houses all day, and I didn't have time for lunch."

"So you're eating strips of bacon for dinner?"

"No, I'm making a BLT. Now, where do you keep the bread around here?"

THE HOSPITAL BED was picked up after June left, but I'd done nothing with the second bedroom. For the duration of her stay, Ariel took my bed and I returned to the familiar comfort of the living room sofa. It felt like home, the place I belonged.

She bounded through the front door the next morning with an armload of groceries. I pulled myself upright, groggy and still a little queasy.

"You're not going to fry more bacon, are you?"

"What's the matter?" she asked. "Still feeling seasick?"

I frowned. "I thought you came here to take care of me?"

"No bacon," she said. "Bagels and fruit and coffee. Lots of coffee."

While Ariel put away the groceries and made breakfast, I showered. The warm water trickled down my scalp and face, rinsing away the last remnants of the lingering toxic fog. I turned the temperature hotter and let the scalding water melt away the tension in each muscle and sinew of my arms and legs.

"You look alive again," she said, glancing up from a plate of fresh-cut pineapple.

"I feel human. Almost."

She set the fruit next to a plate of bagels on a tray she'd prepared. "It's nice out. Let's eat on the patio."

"Suits me," I said as she headed for the sliding glass door. "Wait! Let's eat inside."

I'd suddenly remembered my last night on the patio and imagined the grotesque scene I'd left behind.

"Calm your jets," she said. "I mopped up your mess."

I exhaled hard, letting loose a deep audible sigh. "If I believed in God, I'd say he sent you."

She paused in the doorway, breakfast tray in hand, and glanced at me over her shoulder. "By the way, your dirty drawers are in the washer."

MORE THAN TWENTY-FOUR hours had passed since Harlan's rescue at dawn, and I was gradually returning to normal, for whatever that was worth. I'd kept Ariel's breakfast down, and coffee notwithstanding, I'd rehydrated aggressively in hopes of restoring the plethora of fluids that had leaked, seeped, and shot out of my body.

Around mid-afternoon, we curled up on opposite ends of the sofa and rehashed the last two days over warm cups of Earl Grey.

"You know what we need to do?" I asked as though we were both lonely, unemployed alcoholics.

She raised her auburn eyebrows, which had been perfectly shaped to appear unshaped.

"We need to forget this bullshit. Let's bust open a bottle of champagne and celebrate...something."

"Oh, honey." She said it not as a term of affection, but as a commentary on my willful ignorance, as though she were about to proclaim there was no Santa and I was the last to know. "Honey, look at you. Have you looked in the mirror lately?"

I'd seen the dark, heavy circles beneath my eyes, the slump in my shoulders, the unkempt, disheveled mess I'd become. "I'm getting skinny," I said. "People love thin, don't they?"

"There aren't many fans of the binge-drinking diet."

"I need to chill on the drinking. I know that. I'm just working my way through everything."

"Right," she said with a laugh. "Working your way through everything in the liquor cabinet."

"Come on. I'm trying here."

"I'm sorry. I get what you mean. But why do you think you have to do it alone?"

"I'm not alone. You're here."

"I'm here on accident. I'm here because I called you at 7:00 in the morning hoping to catch you off guard, and your neighbor kid happened to answer the phone."

"Harlan's a special kid, isn't he?"

"He's a confident little fucker. I'll say that." She chuckled. "But Harlan's not the point."

"Right, the point is you're here."

"The point is I'm here because you're coming undone, and your life is a fucking mess."

My mug was empty, but I tipped it anyway and sipped at the air. "It's my mess. I made it by myself."

"That doesn't mean you have to clean it up by yourself. People care about you, Conor, but you have to pick up the phone every now and then."

"I'm sorry. Don't take it personal."

"You know me better than that. Anyway, Will said you weren't returning his calls either."

"You talked to Will?"

"He called. He was worried."

I peeked into her cup. "Ready for a refill? Something stronger, maybe?"

"I know how crushed you are. Will and June."

"And my job and my book deal." I turned the empty cup in my hands and watched a teardrop of tea circle the bottom of the mug.

"It's a lot," she said.

"It's everything."

"You can't drink it all away, Conor."

"I can try." I stared into the empty cup and swiveled it faster, as though enough centrifugal force could spin a single drop of tea into a double shot of Jameson.

She took my cup and set it on the table. I lifted my feet to the sofa, pulled my knees to my chest, and rested my head in her lap.

"Sometimes, you have to let go." Her soft voice was just above a whisper.

"I want to."

She stroked my hair. My body shuddered and I lay quietly weeping until I fell into a deep restful sleep.

TUFO'S WAS A mom-and-pop Italian bistro Ariel and I had loved for years. The restaurant held forty or fifty people at capacity, and since it wasn't far off the Busch Gardens' tourist path, the place was usually packed. I ordered takeout and returned home, laden with gnocchi, chicken parm, and Mama Sophia's homemade tiramisu, just as Ariel finished setting the table.

"Perfect timing." She plopped a liter of San Pellegrino in front of each place setting.

"Jesus Christ," I said. "How much of that stuff did you bring?"

"I thought you'd like it. It comes in a bottle."

"If this is your way of cutting me off for the rest of the weekend, I guess it'll do."

She filled two glasses with the sparkling water. "It is, and it will."

We passed the next two hours grazing on the Italian feast and talking about the things best friends talk about. The inevitability of change, the anguish of loss, the nearly irresistible temptation to let yourself be swept out to sea by all of it. I laid out my seismic fuck-ups, rehashed how each meaningful element of my life had withered, fallen apart, or just burst into flames. There was no room for bullshit with Ariel. She knew all of it. What I owed to June, what I'd lost with Will. She even knew about Patrick, how he'd hanged himself in Aunt Doris's garage. What she didn't know was how loved and alive he'd made me feel one hot Georgia night. She'd never know that. And she'd never understand the empty hours I spent wondering what his life might have been like, who he'd have loved, how he might have changed the world, if only I had beaten him to the punch, if only I had climbed on top of that five-gallon painter's bucket and stepped off into nothingness. But none of that mattered any more. Sometimes you had to let go.

WE PASSED A lazy and sober Sunday in our pajamas, snuggling on the sofa and reminiscing until we talked ourselves out. Perhaps by Ariel's design, we stuck to mostly happy memories, and by late afternoon, my stomach ached from laughter and the residual soreness of retching. We warmed up the Tufo's leftovers for dinner and decided to host our own classic movie marathon. Ariel chose *Some Like It Hot* and *Breakfast at Tiffany's,* movies we'd seen and loved, which we watched and loved again. I flirted with the idea of Hitchcock movies when it was my turn to pick, but Will had taken them all, which was just as well. I picked the first two *Planet of the Apes* movies instead, neither of which, unsurprisingly, Ariel had seen.

By the time Charlton Heston and his mute companion galloped through the surf near the end of the movie, it was closing in on midnight.

"Clever," Ariel said flatly as the couple reached the mostly buried remains of the Statue of Liberty.

"You didn't like it?"

"Doesn't matter. Shirtless back-in-the-day Charlton Heston was worth it."

"He was rocking the pecs," I said, as I gathered our dirty cups and plates from the coffee table. "Anyway, it's late. I'll let you off the hook on the next one."

"You sure?"

"It's telepathic mutant humans in an underground city."

"I'm sorry I'll miss that." She let out a deep throaty laugh, the kind you'd expect to come from a large black man with a cigar dangling from his lips.

"You have to work early tomorrow?"

"Who, me?" She shook her head. "You're not getting rid of me that easy."

"Seriously, I appreciate you being here. I obviously needed it. But I'm upright again."

"Maybe, but my work's not done here."

I gave her a puzzled look. "You gonna do some more laundry? Vacuum the floors?"

"Whatever it takes."

THIRTY-TWO

THE DON CESAR, a mammoth pink art deco hotel on St. Pete Beach, first opened its castle doors to the rich and famous in the twenties. Ariel and I never stayed there, but in the boyfriendless days of yesteryear, we often sat at the piano bar on Saturday afternoons and watched wealthy old ladies get knee-walking drunk.

"Why are we here?" I asked as we pulled up to the hotel entrance.

"Give your car keys to the handsome gentleman," she said, tilting her head toward the valet who'd opened my door.

We entered the hotel and nodded at a smiling desk clerk as we passed. The marble floors glowed beneath glimmering chandeliers that hung from impossibly high ceilings. Miniature palm trees were tastefully positioned in giant pots around the lobby, and stunning sprays of tropical flowers were centered on huge, glass-top tables. We cruised past lush, well-appointed sitting areas, where pristine white walls were adorned with giant paintings of sea-oat-crested sand dunes and ocean sunsets. I gawked like a ten-year-old farm boy on a visit to Manhattan.

"I'd forgotten how the other half live," I said.

"*Très chic.*" She rubbed her thumb against her fingertips. "Old money."

I stopped in the center of the corridor. "So, why are we here again?"

"To celebrate."

"We going to the piano bar?"

"Yes, Conor. We're celebrating a week of soul-searching sobriety by shooting tequila with rich, elderly widows."

"Harsh," I said.

"Get over it." She smiled and pulled me down the corridor. "We're having lunch."

THE MARITANA GRILLE was a classy, white-linen place that was billed as the "signature" restaurant at the resort, which was hospitality industry code for "most overpriced." The maître d' led us past saltwater aquariums full of neon fish and colorful corals that were strategically placed around the dining room to partition it into intimate spaces. When we reached our table, it was impeccably set with cobalt blue chargers, polished silver, and what appeared to be enough sparkly clean glasses for a party of eight.

"Two chairs and a dozen glasses," I said to Ariel.

"People get thirsty in expensive restaurants."

"I'm sure they have a fine selection of premium wines to offer."

She flicked her long, auburn curls with a wave of her hand and leaned across the table. "Don't even think about it."

After a savory seafood lunch that set Ariel back a hundred bucks, we strolled through the manicured hotel courtyard and past the pool toward the beach. At the end of the boardwalk, we rolled up our pant legs and slipped off our shoes and socks. We crossed fifty yards of sugary-soft sand and stood at the edge of the vast expanse of blue-green water.

Behind white-framed designer sunglasses, Ariel closed her eyes. She raised her arms high in the air and inhaled a deep breath of warm, salty air. "I like Orlando fine, but it's too damned far from the ocean."

"This is the gulf," I said. "The ocean's on the other side of Florida."

She gave me a sideways glance and kicked sand at my feet.

The air was hot and thick, and the warm gulf water washed over our feet and nipped at the rolled cuffs of our pants as we meandered down the beach. We walked a quarter mile or so, lost in our respective thoughts and quietly soaking in the afternoon sun. When we eventually reached an open stretch of beach, we climbed a nearby dune and sat at the top. I scanned the horizon and surveyed the shimmering gulf that spread out before me, as much my kingdom as anyone's.

My stomach trembled and tears welled in my eyes as I took Ariel's hand. "Thank you."

"Jeez, it was just lunch. Don't get all sentimental on me." She stared out at the gulf, and the wind whipped the ends of her flaming hair. As she pushed auburn strands behind her ears, I saw that her eyes glistened too.

"This was just what I needed," I said.

"It's amazing what a couple of chick flicks and a few days sober can do."

"I guess it is." I couldn't repay her kindness, but I could at least reassure her that her efforts hadn't been wasted. "I have a lot of shit to sort out, but I'll get there."

"You will." She cleared her throat. "And I don't want to nag..."

"But, you will?"

"Hey, I've earned at least one annoying nag."

I nodded and put my arm around her shoulder. "Go for it."

"You can't sort out jack shit if you're drunk."

"I hear you, but drinking comes so naturally."

"You come from a long line of alcoholics. That shit messes kids up."

"It does. But there's a lot of other kid shit I've never dealt with."

"You're older now," she said. "So deal with it."

They were nearly the exact words June had said to me, the same words I'd used to anchor the laminated manifesto that I hadn't seen, or even thought of, in weeks. Like so many failed strategies, my plan hadn't been wrong-headed, as much as it was poorly executed.

"I've mostly just been getting shitfaced the last few months, but lying in bed staring at the ceiling has given me time to think."

She lifted the Dolce & Gabbana sunglasses and pushed them back on her head, turning the expensive shades into an overpriced headband.

"I think I'm ready to move on from everything," I said.

"I'm no Dalai Lama, but that sounds like a start."

The sound of waves crashing on the beach grew louder, as the tide came in and the water edged closer. A few feet away, the delicate towers of a sand castle were slowly eroded and washed out to sea.

"I told you about the beach vacations we took when I was a kid, right?"

"Yeah. Your mom and dad rented a cottage."

"We got a house on Pensacola Beach for a week every summer. But it wasn't just my parents, it was grandparents, aunts and uncles—the whole fucking lot of McLeishes."

"Sounds like...fun?" She laughed, amused by the notion of so much family dysfunction under a single roof.

"It was."

"Really?"

"Really. When I think back, those were the best days of my childhood. I loved the gulf, even then. So did Patrick. We'd hit the water after breakfast and play outside all day until Mom or Aunt Doris dragged us inside."

Ariel noticed the sand castle at the water's edge, which had been reduced to a collection of random amorphous mounds.

"Uncle Henry took my dad and Uncle Martin mullet fishing every day, and by the end of the week, they had a big enough haul for a fish fry. We had homemade coleslaw and hush puppies, and a shitload of Jameson and beer. We always built a bonfire that last night."

"Irish campfire sing-alongs with all your drunk aunts and uncles?"

I laughed. "Sorry. You've heard the stories."

"I don't mind hearing them again. You seem happy when you talk about it."

A steady breeze blew in over the gulf, but it was no match for the pounding afternoon sun. Beads of sweat trickled down my back, and Ariel's cheeks had turned a rosy shade of pink.

"You're starting to roast," I said. "Ready to head back?"

"I'm okay," she replied. "Are you?"

I paused, recognizing she was asking about more than just my comfort. "I'm ready."

I BOUGHT A stack of blank books at Barnes & Noble, all of them the same, with Van Gogh's straw hat self-portrait on the cover. I scrawled and scribbled for two days, stuffing the journals with my mistakes and regrets. I sifted through my history and replayed my most vulnerable childhood moments: the afternoon my mother packed a small suitcase with my clothes and left me with Aunt Doris; the day she returned three years later to pick me up. I rehashed my adult failures and fuck-ups too. I wrote a love letter to Will, one I would never deliver, and I penned a sorrowful apology to June that she'd never read. I sketched images of Patrick, nude and grinning in bed beside me, then dangling from the garage ceiling, as cold and lonely as a burnt-out bulb.

I poured it all out on the page, and I did not drink.

When I reached the point where there was nothing left to say about the past, I wrote about the days to come. I fantasized about ambling into old age, a weathered smile on my face and Will's hand in mine, as we strolled carefree along a quiet, golden beach. Any future could flourish in that imaginary sunset, if I could find a way to bag up the hurt and betrayal I'd left along the shore like crushed empty beer cans and shards of broken glass.

Untangling four decades of clusterfuck wouldn't be simple. No single deed or series of actions would liberate me from the past, but I didn't need a panacea or grand plan, just a jumping-off point, a safe time and place to confront my demons.

I wondered if I wasn't so fucked up after all, if maybe this was what middle age was about for everyone. I'd always had a theory about aging—or, more specifically, about how we react to it. No one actually gives a rat's ass how old they are. We don't want to be witness to our own decay, but the inevitable physical falling apart isn't what really gets people down. What fucks us up as we get older, especially on our birthdays, when our physiological clocks tick loudest, is how unhappy we are in that moment. It's not the fear of what will happen in the future, it's the disappointment of what hasn't happened yet. That's how it was for me anyway. Each year, when that wretched fucking day rolled around, I believed, if only for a moment, there was still a chance I could turn the guy in the mirror into what I once thought he could be. If only I could do something different.

This time, I was ready to clean things up, to shovel out the bullshit once and for all. Where the ends were loose, I would tie them, and where they couldn't be tied, I would cut them off. I didn't expect to cast off a lifetime of baggage by spending a few vacation days with my family at the Gulf of Mexico, but if I was going to face my demons, forgive those who wronged me, and finally let go of everything, then returning to a peaceful place and a simpler time felt right. I found a five-bedroom gulf-front house for rent on Craigslist, and then I emptied my bank account and booked it.

I LAUNCHED A blitzkrieg on the disaster I'd made of my life, getting my personal shit together with a vengeance. I opened stacks of mail, paid the few bills I could afford to pay, and closed accounts. I washed mountains of laundry and watered half-dead plants. I replied to notes on Facebook and responded to phone messages from people who'd forgotten they'd called in the first place. I thanked them all for reaching out to me and assured them I was fine.

Picking up the physical pieces of my life wasn't so hard. Repairing the human relationships I'd damaged would be trickier. The beach house scheme, the notion of getting the most significant people in my life together in one place, was a stroke of genius, though. I would show them I was sober. I'd confess and ask forgiveness. I'd do what I needed to do to rectify the mistakes I'd made and find a sense of peace, and then I'd leave it all behind.

I had a strategy, and as ill-fated and irreversible as the end game might be, it was something to give a shit about.

I'D SHELTERED MY parents from the ugliest details of my collapse, but when I was forced to send June back to Pensacola, it was apparent I was in a pretty deep pile of shit. My mom had called a couple of times each week since then, but I had let most of the calls go to voice mail. Pure avoidance was the safest route an alcoholic could take with Sylvia McLeish, a woman who knew what a lying drunk sounded like.

With my new plan taking shape and a couple of weeks of sobriety under my belt, I called home. I could tell from the giddiness in my mother's voice that she knew I'd stopped drinking.

"It's been a month, Mom. Not a drop." I may have embellished by a week or two.

"I'm so glad to hear it. I knew you could do it."

"Let go, and let God, right?"

"Seriously?" she asked. The naive optimism in her voice nearly my broke my heart.

"I mean, it's however you understand God, you know?" My mother, of all people, would get an Alcoholics Anonymous reference.

"Step three." She was brimming with hope.

"Yeah," I said. "Anyway, I want to make amends. To everyone."

Her breath quickened. "Steps eight and nine. How are you going to do that?"

"I want to have a party for my fortieth birthday. I'll do it then."

"That's only a few weeks away, Conor. Are you sure that's not moving too fast?"

I assured her I was ready to admit my wrongs, and quickly moved her ahead to the notion of a beach house family reunion. I invited her and my father, and after pausing just long enough to wonder out loud how we'd manage June, she accepted.

I hadn't seen or talked to Uncle Henry much since around the time of June's stroke, but he'd always tried to make me feel like I mattered. His support made a difference in my life, and I wanted to be sure I told him so. When I called about the beach house, he promised to bring his "big red

Coleman full of beer." He clearly wasn't up to speed on recent events in my life, and I didn't have the heart to tell him he'd be mostly drinking alone.

It took a couple of days for me to gather the strength to make the next call, but if I planned to face my demons, Aunt Doris surely had to be included. I started the conversation with an apology.

"I'm sorry for the way I acted when you called on June's birthday."

"It's okay," she said. "Jesus tells us to turn the other cheek."

"It's not okay," I said, brushing past the Bible reference. "I acted like an ass, and you didn't deserve it." The sincerity of my regret as it rolled off my tongue surprised me.

"Well, thank you."

"So, did Mom talk to you about the beach house?"

"She did, a whole week with family. And the twelve steps and making amends on your birthday. How nice."

My mother had clearly latched on to the optimistic notion that I had started Alcoholics Anonymous. I didn't disabuse my aunt of the idea.

"Yeah," I said. "I thought the night of my fortieth would be as good a night as any. Anyway, it's short notice for a week's vacation, but what do you think?"

"Timing isn't an issue, but I do have a couple of questions."

I silently braced for the worst.

"Will your friend be coming to this shindig?"

I realized she and Uncle Martin didn't know Will and I had split, and I saw no reason to tell her now.

"Yes, Will's coming." I hadn't talked to him, but I wasn't prepared to explain the totality of the situation to her. "It's my fortieth birthday. Of course, he'll be there."

"I see," she said. "What kind of sleeping arrangements are you planning? You know I'm a little particular."

Particular? Was that what they called bigoted these days?

"The house has five bedrooms. We'll have enough beds. And plenty of privacy, if that's what you're concerned with." If privacy was her issue, it was less how she would ensure her own privacy and more how would she invade everyone else's.

"I see." She held her cards close to the vest. I imagined the wheels turning in her head as she calculated the ratio of couples to bedrooms, which was something I foolishly hadn't thought through.

I had no more talking points, and as the silence grew, the notion of the beach house reunion as somehow therapeutic began to feel ludicrous.

"Aunt Doris, if you and Uncle Martin can't make it, that's okay."

"Oh, we'll be there," she said. Just like that.

"You will?" I instinctively eyeballed the nearby liquor shelf, the contents of which, to Harlan's great despair, I'd poured down the drain.

"Uncle Martin and I wouldn't miss your fortieth birthday party, Conor."

"It's settled then." I struggled with what to say next.

"I can't wait to see you, Conor."

The hell of it was she meant it.

I WAS EARLY for lunch, so I sat in the driveway outside the impeccably restored South Tampa bungalow of Cedric Broussard. The A/C was cranked full blast in my ten-year-old Honda, but a thin layer of sweat still formed between my back and the driver's seat. Just as I screwed up the courage to get out of the car, Ms. Broussard stepped outside, onto the front porch.

"How long you going to stay out here?" she asked.

I shut the car door and stood next to the car.

"Well, come on in," she said. "Lunch isn't going to eat itself."

She ushered me through the living room decorated with handsome leather furniture and mission-style tables, a couple of which held antique wooden lamps with colorful glass shades.

I paused to admire the gloss of the lustrous wood floors. "I thought you said Cedric was in the Air Force."

"He is. Colonel Cedric Broussard."

"I guess the Air Force pays better than I thought."

"Cedric does okay." She laughed as she said it. "And so does his wife, the Honorable Sheila Broussard."

In the kitchen, a pot of gumbo simmered on the stove and a loaf of homemade bread cooled on the granite countertop.

"You didn't have to go to so much trouble," I said. "I wanted to take you out to lunch."

"And I wanted to have you over." She gestured to a small table in the kitchen nook. "Have a seat. We're going to eat right here in the kitchen."

"It smells incredible," I said as she ladled bowls full of Cajun-seasoned shrimp and okra. "I didn't know you were such a good cook."

"You haven't tasted it yet. Might want to reserve judgment."

"I'm the last one who should judge anything."

She smiled as she cut the bread and shingled the thick slices in a basket. "Let's eat."

I was a few spoonfuls into the gumbo before I realized the old nurse was offering a moment of silent prayer over her meal. "Sorry," I mumbled through a mouthful of bread.

"It's fine," she said. "You seem to be enjoying the meal."

"Delicious." I offered a groan of approval.

We ate the next few bites in silence and then she rested her spoon on the edge of her bowl and waited to catch my eye. "You look good, Conor. Healthy."

"Thanks. I've been...healthy...for a few weeks now." I substituted "healthy" for "sober" as I assumed she'd done.

"Well, I'm so very glad." She reached across the table and touched my hand, in a way that her commitment to professional decorum would not have allowed before.

"I have something to tell you," I said.

"Okay."

"Something to ask you, really. You're not working anywhere now, right?"

"I'm 100 percent retired."

"Ms. Broussard," I sputtered, "would you want to join me and my family..."

"At a beach house?"

I leaned back in the chair and smiled. "How did you know?"

"The last time I called to talk with June your mother told me you were renting a place for your birthday."

"It's kind of a family reunion, something we did when I was a kid."

"I have to say, other than your grandmother, I never got the impression you were that big on family."

I loved a lot of things about Henrietta Broussard, not the least of which was her brutal honesty, and I did my best to return it. "I want to make amends. I need to."

"Sounds like a good thing to do."

"I've hurt a lot people, and that's something I want to fix before..."

She sipped her iced tea and waited patiently, as the end of the sentence dangled in the space between us.

"Before it's too late, ya know?"

"Our business relationship had an unfortunate ending," she said, "but you don't need to make amends with me, Conor. I'm not one of the people you hurt."

"No," I said. "You're one of the people I owe."

"Horse sense. We're all even, young man." She traced her spoon around the bottom of the bowl, collecting enough gumbo for one last bite. "I appreciate the offer, I really do, but I'm retired. I don't need a vacation."

"Think of it as a favor, then."

She cleared the table and carried the dishes to the sink.

"June would really love to see you."

The nurse rubbed her forehead, and though she faced the sink, I knew she was grinning. "And I would love to see her."

"So?"

"So, what's the date?"

THIRTY-THREE

I SLOW-COOKED A pot roast and set the patio table with candles, a vase of fresh-cut flowers, and a Spanish red wine I knew Will liked. The smell of the simmering beef and onions wafted through the house and greeted him when he arrived. The set-up was outside the realm of my usual modus operandi, and he suspected something was up.

"You know, if you're feeling frisky, all you have to do is ask," he said.

"Please," I said, faking insult. "If I feel frisky, I just have to undo a button or two on my shirt."

"If this isn't foreplay, what's going on? Why the romantic setup?"

"Jeez. Do I have to have a reason to do something thoughtful?"

"Umm, usually?" he replied. "Are you about to break some bad news?"

"No. I didn't run into Paul today and decide to cheat on you again, if that's what you're asking." I felt surprisingly defensive over his implication that I was only romantic when I had an ulterior motive—probably because I had an ulterior motive.

"Calm down," he said. "I was kidding about the bad news." Then, to lighten the mood, he added, "But you didn't suck any dicks today, did you?"

"No." I smiled and added, "And it doesn't look like I'm going to either."

WILL SHOOK ME awake on the couch. "Wake up, lazy."

I rubbed my eyes and sat up, adjusting my boxers in a futile attempt to hide the bulge in my shorts. "Guess I better change those locks. You never know who might wander in."

He held a Starbucks cup in his outstretched hand. "Vanilla latte?"

"Thanks. I meant to have breakfast ready when you got here, but I fell back to sleep."

He pushed my feet aside and sat at the end of the sofa. "You know, I moved out. You can sleep in the bed now."

"Funny as ever," I said, swinging my feet to the floor.

He leaned down and looked into my eyes. "You alive in there?"

I sipped the latte. "Yeah. Weird dream."

"Better talk about it or you'll forget."

I considered telling him the dream was about him, about us, teasing and sweet talking each other, my subconscious reinventing the best of the good old days.

"I forgot already."

"Were you up all night?"

"I stopped drinking," I said matter-of-factly.

"That's not what I asked."

"It's what you meant." I sounded defensive and regretted it. "Let me throw on some pants and I'll make breakfast."

"No, it's okay. I have to stop by work anyway, so I'm kind of pressed for time."

"Working on a Saturday? Is there a floral emergency?"

"I transplanted a bed of gardenias yesterday. They need a little extra TLC."

I smiled. "I'm going to eat a bowl of Lucky Charms. You sure you won't join me?"

"Yellow moons? Green clovers? Purple hearts? It's tempting."

"The hearts are pink," I said.

"Pour me a bowl."

It was no great rekindling of our love, not even the flirty banter of my mid-morning dream, but the conversation was civil and a stable enough platform for the leap I had to make next.

He quickly finished his cereal and poured a second bowl. "I was hungrier than I realized."

"They're magically delicious," I said.

"So I've heard."

"I want to have a birthday party, Will. And I want you to come."

"Okay."

I mindlessly chased the last few marshmallows around my bowl. "I'm inviting my family too. I want to make amends."

He glanced up from his cereal bowl, a spoonful of toasted oats poised inches from his mouth. "Jesus, you really did stop drinking."

"I really did."

"Wow." The word was breathy, barely spoken. "Congratulations."

"Thanks." I smiled, earnest and proud. If I could have looked into my own eyes, I'd surely have seen a twinkle. "It feels good, getting all my shit in order."

"Ariel told me you guys had a good week, but I didn't expect this."

"She helped me dry out and get my head on straight." I paused, waiting for him to raise his gaze from the cereal bowl and look me in the eye. "I don't want to keep sleepwalking through life."

"That's good to hear," he said. "Really good." The moment was uncomfortable. Will was unprepared to find me sober, much less coherent and rational. We floated adrift in the awkwardness, each of us draining our Starbucks cup to fill the empty space where words might have been.

"I need more coffee," I said. "Should I make enough for two?"

"Yeah. The gardenias aren't going anywhere."

I brewed coffee and poured two fresh cups, adding half-and-half to one and setting it in front of him.

"If the service was always this good, I might have stayed." He flashed the near-smile that had first left me smitten a decade earlier.

"Funny. Sarcasm will get you everywhere."

The clumsy attempt at flirtation fell to the floor between us like a half-cooked omelet. "Keep it in your pants, mister. Tell me about this birthday party."

"I rented a beach house in Pensacola for a week."

He blew on his coffee and looked at me over the top of the steaming mug. "Haven't you had enough of Pensacola this year?"

"I don't know. It's not like I spent time anywhere outside of the ICU at Sacred Heart."

He nodded in agreement and raised one eyebrow, a trick I'd never mastered.

"Anyway, this year sucked," I said. "I'm leaving all of it behind."

"Who all is invited to this beach house birthday party?"

"Mom and Dad and June, Aunt Doris and Uncle Martin, Uncle Henry. Oh, and Ms. Broussard is coming."

"Okaaay." He said it as if I'd just announced I was getting a circumcision for my birthday. "Don't take this wrong, but are you sure this is the best way to stay sober?"

"You can't make amends with people without interacting with them."

"Yeah, but a whole week in one house with all of them?"

"It's efficient."

"What's the hurry?"

"Look, I'm turning forty. I need to make things right."

He shook his head, unconvinced. "Sounds a lot like a mid-life crisis."

"It's the end of a mid-life crisis." I needed Will to be there, but I was walking a tightrope. "I've been a little introspective," I conceded. "Thinking about how short life is and all that."

He looked past me for a moment, gazing out the sliding glass doors at the river in the distance. "Fine."

"Fine?"

"If everyone else is up for it, I'll go." The words were affirming, though he frowned into his coffee mug as he spoke them.

"What?" I asked.

"What, what?"

"What are you not saying?"

One thing I loved about Will was his commitment to honesty without brutality, the standard infidelity exception notwithstanding. He could be both mirror and magnifying glass, taking whatever shape was most beneficial to helping the other person see. Of course, both mirrors and magnifying glasses only work if you open your eyes.

"Are you sure you're ready for this?"

"Yes."

"Are you doing it for the right reasons?"

"What would be the wrong reasons?"

"Thinking you have something to prove to your family or yourself. I'm not sure."

"I don't need to prove anything. I need to make things right." Though I hadn't told him everything, I'd told him everything I could and none of it was a lie.

"Making things right sounds a little lofty and self-righteous..." Several seconds passed before he finished the thought. "But I know your intentions are good."

I smiled. "Well, now you're just sweet talking me again."

"What?"

"I miss you, Will. I really miss you."

THE DAY BEFORE I left for Pensacola, I ransacked the bathroom and linen closet, packing boxes with sheets and towels, toilet paper, and other provisions we'd need for the beach house. I was staging the boxes near the open front door when I glimpsed a figure hunched over and peeking at me through the screen.

"Jesus Christ. What are you doing?"

"I'm creepin' on ya." Harlan burst into a fit of laughter that was an endearing mix of redneck yee-haw and stoner staccato.

"You're pretty good at prowling," I said. "You should consider a career in stalking."

He leaned against the doorframe and spoke through the screen. "Awesome benefits, but I hear the pay is shitty."

I tried in vain to suppress a grin and shook my head in mock disapproval.

"What you working on, Mr. Conor?"

"Come on in. If you help me carry this shit to the car, I might forget a forty outside the back door."

"That's a grand plan." He smiled, but as he surveyed the stacks of boxes, his tone grew suddenly serious. "You ain't fixing to relocate, are you?"

"Why? Would you miss me?"

"Hell yes, I would."

"Awww," I said, nudging him with my elbow. "I didn't know you cared."

"Simmer down. I'm just worried about losing my liquor hook-up." He erupted into the cracker-stoner laugh again, this time giving me an accompanying punch in the arm. "Seriously though, you ain't moving away, are you?"

"I'm taking a trip."

He peeked into an open box filled with cleaning supplies and paper towels. "To some place really dirty?"

"I rented a beach house in Pensacola. You have to bring your own groceries and supplies."

He counted the cardboard boxes, silently moving his lips as he tallied the cartons. "Damn man, did you leave anything here?"

"Not much. I can't afford to buy stuff when I get there."

"I know, right. Still don't have a job?"

"Have to say I haven't really been looking too hard."

"Better get on it. Money don't grow on trees." He rocked and tilted random boxes, gauging their weight.

"Let's haul this stuff outside," I said.

He grabbed two boxes from the top of a stack and waited for me to open the screen door.

The midday air was warm and thick, and by the time we finished loading the car, we were sticky with sweat. I grabbed chilled pilsner glasses from the freezer, poured two cold Blue Moons, and then invited Harlan to join me at the patio table.

"I thought you quit drinking," he said.

"Special occasion."

"What's that?"

I raised my glass to toast. "Welcome to manhood."

"You ain't gonna try to get me drunk, are you?" He winked and lifted his shirt, showing off his pale, flat stomach.

I rolled my eyes and suppressed a grin. "You wish."

He laughed and sipped his beer, leaving a thin foam mustache on his upper lip. "Seriously, Mr. Conor, when you coming back?"

"I rented the beach house for a week."

"You going alone?"

"I invited my family and Ms. Broussard. Will's going too."

"Aww yeah. Gonna rework that love connection?"

"Something like that." I grabbed the base of the pilsner glass and traced small circles across the table top, sending slow amber swirls around the inside of the glass. I missed the feel of a frosty mug on my fingertips, the refreshing cold on my lips, but I knew I would stop when the glass was empty.

Harlan sat across from me, gazing out at the river, looking as thoughtful and content as the Marlboro man. "This is the life, Mr. Conor."

"That it is. How's school, Harlan?"

"What now?"

"You're at Hillsborough, right? How's it going?"

He raised a quizzical eyebrow. "You know it's summer?"

"In general, I mean. How do you like it?"

"I ain't a big fan of high school, to be honest with you."

"You're not thinking of dropping out or anything?"

"I'm leavin' in a year." He stared sullenly down at the tabletop.

"No." I leaned toward him. "You're not quitting. Absolutely not."

He rolled his eyes and kicked at my shin beneath the table. "I graduate next year, fool."

I sat back in the chair and stared him down. "You were fucking with me?"

"Yes, sir. I was fucking with you."

"Good thing." I smiled. "You don't want me to father-son lecture your ass."

"I wouldn't know if you did," he said. "Not like I heard one of those speeches before."

I took another sip of the ice-cold beer, savoring the orange, wheaty taste on my tongue. "Remember the last time we were on this patio?"

"Sure do. You were tore up good." He accentuated the last three words, clearly enjoying the memory of my condition more than I did.

"I've had better nights," I said. "But I appreciate what you did for me."

He waved off my gratitude, having had, perhaps, enough sincerity for one afternoon.

"Decent human beings aren't as plentiful as you'd think, Harlan. You're a damn good kid."

"I know." He let a long silence pass. "But I won't shit ya— it's kinda nice to hear it every now and then." He put the pilsner to his lips and tipped it, waiting patiently for the last drops of beer to run from the bottom of the glass.

THIRTY-FOUR

WILL AND I made the seven-hour drive north to the panhandle on the day before check-in at the beach house. That night we lay as stiff and straight as pencils on our respective halves of a queen-sized bed in a cheap Pensacola Beach motel. He read a Buddhist paperback about the virtues of hopelessness, and I wandered the wasteland of Friday night television. I surfed dozens of channels before settling on the early late-night local "News at 11:00," which now aired at 10:00.

"Jesus," he said, glancing at the television. Bands of yellow police tape circled the twisted chrome-and-steel remains of a mangled motorcycle.

"Guy hit a tree," I said.

"Drunk?"

"Maybe."

"Dead?"

"Apparently." I clicked off the television. "I'm sorry about the sleeping arrangements. I reserved a room with two double beds."

He shrugged. "It happens. But if you offer me a glass of wine and a light sleeping pill, I'm not taking it."

"You found me out. Date raping you is the thing I want most for my birthday."

"You didn't pack a Polaroid, did you?"

"Goddamn." I smiled and turned my head away in mock disgust. "I thought being a pervert was part of my charm, not yours."

"Just keep your big Muppet paws to yourself. I don't want to wake up with your hands in my boxers."

"You should be so lucky."

"And don't grind me in your sleep."

"I don't grind."

"Are you kidding? I've seen Starbucks baristas who grind less than you."

My mouth hung open until I managed a few disjointed syllables and the conversation dissolved in laughter.

"Anyway," he said. "I can do anything for one night."

"Yeah," I said. "About that..." He leaned up on his elbow and shot me a quizzical look, which told me he hadn't already done the math on the guests-to-bedrooms ratio at the beach house.

"You've gone to a lot of trouble to get me in bed for a few nights."

"Everyone deserves a last chance," I said, jerking the conversation in a suddenly serious direction.

He fluffed his pillows and sat up against the headboard. "What's that supposed to mean?"

"Doesn't mean anything. I was thinking about the guy on TV."

"The motorcycle accident guy?"

"Yeah." I rolled onto my side and faced him. "If it was an accident."

"You don't think it was an accident?"

"I have no idea."

"You think it was murder? A conspiracy between his wife, his insurance agent, and his bike mechanic?"

"Could've been lots of things," I said. "It was probably an accident...or maybe he just decided it was his time to go."

"Not that I've given it much thought, but I can think of better ways to take myself out than slamming a motorcycle into a tree."

"Me too." I rolled back onto my pillow and stared up at the popcorn ceiling like I was counting stars in a bright night sky. "What would you do if you could choose?"

"Choose how I die?" he asked.

"Or when."

He considered the question. "That's some morbid shit, Conor."

"Maybe, but it doesn't have to be."

AN UNDERCURRENT OF tension snuffed out our conversation, but before the silence became too awkward, my cell phone chirped from the nearby dresser-desk-TV stand. I swallowed hard at the sight of Aunt Doris's name on the caller ID.

"Hello, Conor."

"Hi," I replied as though my heart hadn't just catapulted into my throat. The notion that she might be calling to cancel both relieved and stressed me. I didn't relish the idea of confronting her at the beach house, asking her forgiveness and hoping she'd come far enough in life to ask for mine, but it was work I had to do.

"Did I wake you?" Without waiting for a reply, she added, "I hope not, but I figured you stay up late on Friday nights." She sometimes seemed to forget I was no longer in middle school and could now stay up late any time, even on school nights.

"We were awake. Just watching television."

"I don't want to keep you from whatever it is you're doing," she said as though I hadn't just told her. "Listen, Uncle Martin has to work all day tomorrow, and we're going to be late. We won't be at the beach house until tomorrow evening."

"Okay." I paused long enough for the other shoe to drop. "Is that all?"

"That's all," she said. "Did you expect more?"

"No, Aunt Doris. Sorry. I didn't expect anything else. See you tomorrow night."

"Okay dear, bye."

And that was it. I crawled across the bed to my pillow.

Will raised his eyebrows. "Everything okay?"

"Aunt Doris."

"I gathered. So, is everything okay?"

The call had been shorter and less dramatic than a local weather forecast. I replayed the conversation in my head looking for signs of hidden danger, but I found none.

"Yeah, everything's fine. Uncle Martin has to work tomorrow so they won't be at the beach until tomorrow night."

"How about that? Evil Aunt Doris called and you didn't lose your mind. Keep your expectations realistic and this little reunion might not be so awful after all."

"Your optimism is inspiring."

"I'm nothing if not supportive."

"Actually, you really have been supportive." I scooted to Will's side of the bed and rested my head on his shoulder. "Thank you."

"Easy," he warned me. "This is still a no grinding zone."

"Come on," I pleaded. "Just once, for old time's sake."

"Keep one foot on the floor, perv."

I flung myself back on a stack of pillows, folded my arms across my chest, and stuck my bottom lip out in an exaggerated pout.

He picked his book up and pretended to read. Without a glance, he said, "Don't waste your time. But behave yourself a few days, and maybe I'll give you a cuddle for your birthday."

Beneath the sheets, I inched my foot closer to his until my toes rested against his ankle. His foot didn't move, and I fell into a sound and satisfying sleep.

I AWOKE BEFORE sunrise. Will lay asleep next to me with his arm draped across my torso. The contact was likely incidental, an old habit dying hard, but the familiar presence of his touch paralyzed me. The warmth of his skin on mine, the whisper of his breath on my shoulder. Half an hour passed before I mustered the emotional will to move.

I drove to Starbucks and was standing outside with a few weary vacationers when a distressingly enthusiastic barista unlocked the doors. We queued up inside, and I couldn't help but notice the attractive mid-thirties guy who stood uncomfortably close in line behind me. With sandy-blond hair, a square jaw, and a model's smile—actually, a model's everything—he looked like Wall Street money, only with two-day stubble, flip-flops, and board shorts.

The stranger's hand grazed my butt, and as I instinctively turned to face him, he raised his arms above his head and stretched, causing the bottom of his T-shirt to ride up and reveal the lower portion of his ripped abdomen. He yawned and, when I finally moved my gaze away from his taut stomach and back to his face, he grinned.

"You coming or going?" he asked.

"I'm sorry?"

"It's Saturday at the beach. Everyone's checking in or checking out."

"Just got here last night," I said. "Have a long week ahead of me."

"I was heading back to Atlanta today, but maybe I should stick around." The outline of a growing erection showed in his shorts, and he made no effort to hide it.

Eight months had passed since Will and I had reunited for a single evening of what turned out to be regrettable New Year's Eve breakup sex, and for eight hours last night, I'd lain in bed just a few inches away from his untouchable body. No one could blame me for flirting a little, which is why I can't explain the next words that came from my mouth.

"Don't stick around on my account. There's nothing here for you."

A door opened across the cafe and an attractive blonde woman walked out of the bathroom. She wore white shorts and a yellow tank top that highlighted her deep natural tan. As she glanced in our direction, her lips parted, revealing a genuine and carefree smile. She stopped at a table to gather two beautiful children, a teenage boy with earbuds firmly entrenched, and a younger girl sporting a pink Disney princess backpack. They followed her toward the exit.

As she approached the door, she called out to the hot stranger in line behind me. "Hurry up, Tommy. The kids are starving and you promised pancakes."

"Shouldn't be long," said the Wall Street-beach hottie. The woman herded her kids outside, and he leaned closer to me and whispered in my ear. "Women."

If he was a late-blossoming closet queer, a pathetic middle-aged fraud who revealed his truest self only to desperate strangers in empty parking lots and highway rest areas, I pitied him. If he was a horny lech who got his rocks off by masturbating with the hand of fate just beyond eyeshot of his family, I pitied all of them.

It was my turn to approach the counter, but before I placed my order, I turned to him. "You have a beautiful family. Do you ever think about what you're doing?"

He smiled. "Go fuck yourself."

I bought lattes and chocolate chip scones and headed back to the motel.

WILL WAS AWAKE and showered, and we talked in hushed tones, as we devoured the sugary breakfast. I wanted to tell him about the stranger, how watching him was like seeing myself in a fun house mirror of sexual dysfunction. I wanted Will to understand how pathetic and ashamed I felt about chasing the stupid fucking English teacher and having sex with Paul. It wasn't a couple of fucked-up nights; it was a lifetime of fucking up. I wanted to tell him, once more, that I was sorry, and I wanted him to believe me.

I was out of the fun house now, and when I gazed in the mirror, I saw nothing but a hollow man hiding behind the sorry details of his life. A mother who chose her drunken husband over her five-year-old son. Substitute parents who loved the idea of him, but not the reality. The unfair theft of a radiant soul filled with possibility, stolen by a sturdy beam and a five-foot length of rope. I'd been alone, dimming and dying by degrees, for most of my forty years.

No one left me; they just didn't love me enough to stay close. The people I held dearest kept me at arm's-length, because not doing so was painful. I had hurt them. I'd learned my lessons, though. I knew I'd made mistakes, some of them colossal, but I was not rotten, not at my core. Maybe I was before, but not now. Like the walls of a canyon with a river running through it, I was a work-in-progress. I believed in love, and even though there was a pile of evidence to the contrary, I was committed. I didn't always keep my dick in my pants, but I was long-term loyal, an ally in the toughest times, which was only fair since I was usually to blame for them.

I was the bad penny, and I always fucking turned up. I pissed in my own Wheaties and shit in my own bed, and the people with whom I shared my life could only take that for so long.

Those were *my* truths, though, and Will shouldn't have to face them.

THIRTY-FIVE

WITHIN MINUTES OF leaving the motel, we pulled into the circular driveway of the gulf-side beach house. Like most residential structures on Pensacola Beach, the rental was rebuilt from the foundation up after Hurricane Ivan. The house was raised on stilts one story off the ground, which was ostensibly the elevation needed to keep the next storm surge from rushing through the living room and washing wall art and sofa cushions into the neighborhood. People who owned gulf-front beach houses understood the inevitability of hurricane strikes. The filthy rich, those who kept beach houses as summer homes, kept their valuables elsewhere. Everyone else stored their most precious belongings efficiently, so they could be collected in a hurry when it was time to get the hell out.

The house was exactly as described online. Five bedrooms, a spacious kitchen with a large island in the middle, and a family room with a wall of windows and sliding doors that led to a deck overlooking the Gulf of Mexico.

Will and I settled into one of the bedrooms, laying claim to dresser drawers and staking out our respective sides of a queen-sized bed. I was plugging my cell phone into a charger when the phone rang in my hand.

"Hi Daniel," I said to my cousin. "How are ya?"

"Not so good. I tried to call your mom this morning, but she didn't answer."

"Something wrong?" I asked.

"DJ's been home sick from school the last few days, so we took him to the walk-in clinic this morning. He has strep throat."

"Awww, you're kidding," I said as if a sick kid was a freakish natural anomaly.

"I wish I was. Anyway, I wanted to let you know we're not going to make it out there for the birthday party on Wednesday."

I pieced together that my mom had a secret celebration planned, and hadn't clued Daniel in on the surprise element. "That sucks."

"Yeah, I'm sorry we're going to miss it. You and me, and Patrick of course, we had some good times out there when we were kids. Swimming as soon as the sun came up."

"Some of my best memories," I said, unable to hide the melancholy in my voice.

"Mine too. Anyway, you'll have the rest of the clan there from what I hear."

"Mom and Dad and June should be here shortly. And your dad too. Uncle Martin and Aunt Doris are coming later tonight."

"Martin and Doris?" he asked, with no detectable sarcasm in his voice. "I just saw Uncle Martin this morning when I took DJ to the clinic. He was walking into Cordova Mall."

"That's weird." I remembered my aunt's call the night before. I didn't give a rat's ass when they showed up to the beach house, but why lie and say Uncle Martin had to work?

"If you think him hanging out at the mall is weird, check this—he went in through the Victoria's Secret parking lot entrance." He chuckled and lowered his voice. "I never thought of Aunt Doris as the sexy underwear type." He groaned as though someone had just passed by with a plate of cabbage and rotten eggs.

"Thanks for the image." I laughed uncomfortably as a vision of Aunt Doris in a frilly, red bustier and lacy panties sashayed through my consciousness. "Let's hope he nabbed a good parking space and was just cutting through."

"Listen, I gotta run, Conor. Have a great birthday. Let's try again next summer."

"Maybe," I said. "Take care, Daniel."

During those ancient summer weeks with my family, I felt a sense of belonging that evaded me for the rest of my childhood. This time around, though, the beach house was just a stage, a familiar venue where I could open myself up, lay my hurt out on the sandy white shore, and swim away forever.

WILL AND I unpacked boxes of linens and household supplies, and by the time we finished, it was close to lunchtime. He made a quick trip to Island Grocery for some cold cuts and bread, and while he was gone, I set a table for lunch on the raised deck that adjoined the living room and overlooked the beach. The store-brand paper towels and green melamine plates I found in the kitchen cabinet made inelegant but adequate place settings.

From the deck, I heard the faint chime of the doorbell. I opened the door, expecting to find Will with an armload of groceries, but instead found Ms. Broussard waiting on the porch. She held her medical bag in one hand and a backpack in the other. A small suitcase rested at her feet.

"Welcome," I said, bear hugging the nurse as though I hadn't just seen her a few weeks before.

"Thank you, Conor," she said, maintaining an air of formality. "I'm glad to be here."

"You look like you came ready to work." I nodded at the medical bag as I retrieved the suitcase and ushered her inside.

"I like to be prepared."

"Like a Boy Scout."

She pursed her lips and looked at me skeptically over the top of her glasses.

"Like a professional?" I asked.

"I talked with your mother. I told her I'd help out with June since I was here."

"That's kind of you, Ms. Broussard."

"I don't know about that," she said. "Since I stopped taking care of June and retired, there's a hole in my life."

"You miss being a nurse?"

"Heavens no. I miss June."

I gave her a quick tour of the house and showed her to the bedroom Will and I had picked out for her.

"Where will June be sleeping?" she asked.

"Just on the other side of this wall." I pointed in the direction of June's room.

"This will do fine, then."

"Ms. Broussard, I hope you're planning to relax a little. I invited you here as a friend of the family, not as a nurse."

"I love spending time with your grandmother, and taking care of her is no bother. Besides, I bet your mother could use a break."

It wasn't intended as a dig, but the comment played on my guilty conscience nonetheless. "I'm sure you're right" was all I could muster as it occurred to me that the nurse had likely kept better tabs on June's progress in recent months than I had.

"Lunch!" Will yelled from the living room.

"We've set up a lunch table on the deck," I said with more enthusiasm than necessary. "I hope you're hungry."

"You go ahead." She set her suitcase and medical bag on the bed. "I'll be along as soon as I get my things organized."

WILL AND I had assembled various combinations of breads, meats, and cheeses, producing an impressive array of sandwiches, which we halved and displayed on platters. We transferred plastic tubs of potato salad into a serving bowl, and Will arranged fresh-cut flowers he'd bought into a glass tea pitcher and placed them in the center of the table. It wasn't a William Sonoma catalog photo, but it would do.

Ms. Broussard emerged from her bedroom. Just as the three of us sat down to eat, the doorbell rang again. When I opened the front door, a creased and sun-weathered face peaked out from beneath a well-worn canvas safari hat.

"Uncle Henry!" I said, taking custody of a bulging paper grocery sack he'd brought. He entered the living room and his grin, sincere and gentle as it was, filled the room like an ocean breeze. "Conor, you been working at it?"

"Sure have," I lied. Before I published *Luck of the Irish*, Uncle Henry's customary writing inquiry had been intended to elicit a meaningful answer. Now, it was more tradition than motivation.

I handed Will the sack of groceries and went outside to help my uncle unload his myriad fishing gear from his truck. In the truck bed, I spotted a large red ice chest and two cases of beer. Uncle Henry had a longstanding fondness for Miller Genuine Draft, a beer preference that, in my estimation, represented the most significant lapse in judgment of his life.

"Sorry 'bout that," he said when he noticed me eyeballing the cooler. "I talked with your mom on the drive out here, and she told me you were taking a break. I'll leave the cooler in the truck."

"I'm on a drinking hiatus, but that doesn't mean you have to be. Bring the cooler inside."

"Nah, I'll live." He shook his head and rubbed his smallish beer gut. "Wouldn't hurt me to take a few days off."

"Uncle Henry, temptations are always there. I might as well get started resisting them."

"You sure?" he asked.

"I'm sure. Besides, Will still likes a cold beer."

"Well..." He smiled wide. "How about that."

We joined the group outside, and I nervously made unnecessary reintroductions. "Uncle Henry, you know Will, of course, and this is Henrietta Broussard. She was June's nurse at Sacred Heart and at our house in Tampa." I paused and added, "She's been a great friend to all of us."

"Ms. Broussard," Uncle Henry said as he offered his hand to the nurse. "I've heard all about you, but I don't think I've had the pleasure of your company. Henry Murphy." She took his outstretched hand, gave a subtle tilt to her head, and glanced up at him. She looked so smitten and demure, I expected her to stand, curtsy, and greet him in French. "*Enchanté, monsieur.*"

"Please," the nurse said, "call me Henrietta."

We made room for Uncle Henry at the table, and for the next half hour, we pecked at the sandwiches and potato salad. Uncle Henry entertained us with vivid recollections of the early days of the McLeish beach house tradition. Harmless tales from the era when my grandfather was at his sodden and colorful best. We filled the salty air around us with laughter, and for a while, I forgot the weighty unfinished business that had led me here.

I STARED AT the beads of moisture on the outside of Uncle Henry's beer, and though I had no love for MGD, I longed to hold one of the cold, wet bottles. The honk of a car horn in the driveway snapped me back to reality.

Even with Will and Uncle Henry pitching in, it took more than half an hour to unload my parent's car. My mother and I converted the largest bedroom in the house into a seaside progressive care suite for June. We unpacked her clothes and toiletries, and we organized bandages, gauze, salves, adult diapers, and the prescription meds she'd need for the week. On a table in the corner of the room, we set up the portable suction device that was used to clear mucus from my grandmother's throat and lungs, when she couldn't do so on her own.

"All done in here. Visit with your grandmother while I get your father and me unpacked." She exited the room, leaving me alone with June.

I leaned down and kissed her on the cheek. "They treating you okay?"

"Yep," she said.

I rolled her to the far side of the room and parked her wheelchair in front of the giant window that overlooked the pristine white sands and shimmering blue-green water of the gulf.

"What do you think?" I asked.

"Nice."

I squatted beside her and put my face close to hers. "I've missed you."

Eight months before that moment, June had suffered a severe and debilitating stroke, transforming her into something...less. There was no kinder way to describe the virtual disappearance of the person I loved most in the world, the near-complete sacrifice of her persona, as her identity was conquered by her own disobedient body. In the months since the stroke, her most fundamental needs, the building blocks of Maslow's pyramid, the base upon which everything else rested, had become someone else's responsibility. Every change of clothes, every brushing of the teeth, every spoonful of every meal. Each subtle movement of her body, the crossing of her legs or the folding of her arms, engineered from outside. This was the world I had come to know, until that moment, when June lifted her arm from the acrylic tray attached to the front of her wheelchair, and touched my face.

"Missed you too," she said.

The touch of her hand siphoned the air from my lungs. Before now, she could turn her head, move her eyes, and make facial expressions. She could squeeze my hand and wiggle her toes, but since the stroke, she had never been capable of this kind of autonomous movement. She never would be, or so I had thought.

The tips of her fingers stroked my cheek as I fought back tears. *Amazing.* I mouthed the word, but didn't say it out loud.

"Ahshide," she said

"What's that?" I asked, struggling to regain my composure.

"Ah-shide," she repeated, enunciating each syllable separately.

I knelt in front of her, tilting my head like an attentive puppy.

"Go ah-shide," she said once more, this time with an impatient tone that implied the word "dumbass" at the end of the sentence.

I was still grinning like an idiot when I wheeled my grandmother onto the deck and parked her next to Ms. Henrietta Broussard.

A WARM BREEZE blew across the deck as evening fell and we gathered to celebrate our first sunset of the week. Ms. Broussard and my grandmother, who had napped away the late afternoon, emerged from the house, and both appeared rested and refreshed. From our now familiar perch on the raised wooden deck, we opened two bottles of sparkling grape juice, a cautionary gift from my mother, and prepared to toast our first successful day together. I filled a spill-proof toddler cup for June, and red Solo cups for the rest of us, except for my father, who clutched a bottle of non-alcoholic beer. We arranged ourselves in a semi-circle near the weathered wooden deck railing, and I positioned June in the center of our arc, where she was flanked on either side by my mother and Ms. Broussard. Beyond the sugar-white sand dunes and thin clusters of sea oats, the coppery majesty of the vast Gulf of Mexico sprawled to the horizon.

I leaned on the rail and rested my hand next to Will's, close enough for my pinkie finger to rest against his. In the dusky light the touch was invisible, but just as a light bulb needs only one frail filament to shine bright, the contact was enough to connect us.

I wanted to toast the moment, so intimate and precious, but words eluded me. *To the unloading of half a life's baggage? To letting go...of everything?*

I lifted my Solo cup high. "To a week of peaceful sunsets," I said. "Just like this one."

"I'll drink to that," said Uncle Henry.

"Me too," said Will.

They each raised their cups and sipped, except for my father, who guzzled O'Doul's like a desert island castaway.

"Slow down, Eamon," my mother said. "It's not a race." We all chuckled over the predictable sentiment, except my father, who had long since grown used to ignoring such comments.

As I removed the foil wrapper from the top of the second bottle of imitation champagne, I spied Ms. Broussard out of the corner of my eye. She leaned across June's wheelchair, her patient and steady hand holding the hard, plastic straw from the sippy cup to my grandmother's lips. My grandmother's gaunt cheeks tightened as she sucked at the straw and slid her wrinkled hand across the table into the soft, fleshy palm of the nurse.

THIRTY-SIX

AUNT DORIS AND Uncle Martin arrived just after nine o'clock. Uncle Henry, who'd done good work all afternoon with the Miller Genuine Drafts, had gone to bed, and Ms. Broussard had put June to bed and retired to her own room. My father had settled in front of the television where he lay sprawled and unconscious on the sofa, leaving only me, Will, and my mother to greet our last guests.

My aunt and uncle herded a half dozen suitcases just inside the door and then proceeded with the customary exchange of half hugs and air kisses.

"Did you leave any clothes in your closet?" my mother remarked, surveying the skyline of luggage.

"You know Martin," Aunt Doris said. "He packs an outfit for every occasion."

Uncle Martin surveyed the bags and smirked. "Don't listen to her. These aren't all mine." He gave me a wink and added, "That little blue suitcase is hers."

Aunt Doris took both my hands in hers. Though we could measure our time apart in weeks, she looked me up and down like a son she hadn't seen in years, or one she'd thought she'd never see again. I half expected her to marvel about how much I'd grown over the summer, but instead, we indulged ourselves in lies about how great we all looked.

The noisy reunion woke my father, who bid a sleepy hello to his brother and sister-in-law and invited them into the living room.

"Conor," Uncle Martin said, leaning in a little, "we sure are proud of you. Those twelve steps really work if you stick with 'em."

"Aunt Doris told you." It was a foolish and irrelevant reply, but I was unprepared for such an immediate reference to my larger expressed purpose.

"Making amends, setting things right with people. That's powerful stuff." He patted my shoulder and winked.

"A birthday present to myself."

"Right. The big four-oh. We sure appreciate you includin' us in this shindig."

In Pensacola, the map reads Florida, but the accents often read lower Alabama.

"Glad you could make it, Uncle Martin. I thought it'd be nice to spend time together as a family. Like the old days, you know?"

"Speaking of family," said Aunt Doris in her own exaggerated twang, "where's everybody at?"

"In bed," my father said. "Henry and June aren't young like us."

"Who're you kidding?" my mother said. "You've been napping for an hour."

"Can I get you something to eat or drink?" Will asked Aunt Doris and Uncle Martin. "We have some sandwiches left in the fridge."

Aunt Doris sat rigid, poised on the edge of the sofa, cemented in place by the stick up her ass. "No, thank you, William," she said.

"Martin?" Will asked.

"We're fine," she answered again. In search of confirmation, Will made eye contact with my uncle, who scrunched his face and shook his head.

We nattered for a few minutes but soon wound our way to an awkward conversational dead end. My mother came to the rescue, initiating the most dependable senior citizen conversation starter known to mankind—a pessimistic pronouncement about the declining health of a "beloved" but distant relative. In this case, an elderly Texas uncle with a faulty gall bladder.

Uncle Alfie's internal organ failure opened avenues to other spirited topics of discussion, including updates about a second cousin's pancreas, a sister-in-law's angina, and the intense discomfort caused by the shingles. An endless supply of McLeish friends and family members suffered a wide variety of disorders, and as it grew later, I struggled to maintain interest in the diseases afflicting so many relatives I'd never met. Uncle Henry's big red Igloo called out to me, but I ignored its plea.

Though I was no closer to forgiveness, absolution, or whatever the hell I was seeking, I had them all under one roof and that was enough to declare the first day a success. Will and I made eye contact, wordlessly arranging a kitchen rendezvous to scheme on how to herd the cataract crew to bed.

A long, granite-topped island divided the living room from the kitchen.

We spoke in hushed tones as we wiped the counter and rinsed glasses, taking care not to appear conspiratorial. I overheard enough sound bites from across the room to conclude that the senior citizen dialogue had evolved from a review of known illnesses to a discussion of speculative diagnoses.

"You know," my father said, "Big Tommy can't see anything out of his left eye. And when we went to the ball game last week, he had to pee every twenty minutes."

"Diabetes," said Uncle Martin. "I guarantee it."

"Mm-hmmm." Aunt Doris provided a confirmatory second opinion.

Will and I snuck unnoticed through the living room and gathered the luggage Aunt Doris and Uncle Martin had brought. A double bed took up most of the floor space in their assigned bedroom, so we stowed the suitcases in the empty closet.

We returned to the living room, and as I was about to interrupt and announce the delivery of the luggage, a lull occurred in the conversation.

"We're all set for the night," I said. "Aunt Doris, we took care of your bags. I can show you and Uncle Martin to your room whenever you're ready."

"I'm ready to get some sleep," said my father as if we had rehearsed the script.

"Again?" asked my mother. "You just woke up." My father slept often and anywhere, and my mother took it as a personal affront as if his napping was an avoidance technique and not a sign of creeping old age.

Will and I accompanied my aunt and uncle to their bedroom. As they stood in the doorway, Aunt Doris leered at Uncle Martin, who shook his head in disapproval. She frowned and shot a dissatisfied glance back over the top of her thick, rimless glasses.

"Martin," she said to my uncle, "there's no harm in asking."

"It's not a big deal," he replied under his breath.

"Not to you," she said, literally turning up her nose. "But I'm the one who stands to lose sleep."

My stomach tightened and a swell of heat rose in my face. I desperately wanted to avoid confrontation, to keep the peace and end the day amicably. I looked at Will, expecting to see my own concern reflected in his face, but I saw only an eyebrow raised in curiosity.

"We're guests here, Doris." My uncle attempted to exert influence he didn't possess over my aunt.

"Quiet, Martin," she snapped. Looking at me, she forged ahead. "Conor, I wonder if I might inquire about the bedroom situation. I have concerns."

In my more pessimistic moments, I had visualized this conversation. On the phone, she'd asked if Will would be at the beach house, and I knew she wouldn't approve of our sharing a bed, but I had hoped she lacked the balls to bring it up. Part of me thought, if she had "concerns" over sleeping arrangements, she should have kept her ass at home. I was no longer a teenage boy in bed with her son. Will and I were consenting adults who had slept together nightly for the better part of a decade, and if the notion of two grown men sharing a bed offended her delicate Christian sensibilities, tough shit. But I needed her here. I needed to mend the fence we'd torn down so many years before.

I steeled myself, resisting the urge to stand up to her, to try to neutralize the fear and shame, the hurtful burden of her rejection I'd carried since childhood. It was too late for that. I was here to shed baggage, to take the final steps in letting go of the deep and abiding pain I had clung to since the sixth grade.

I took a gulp of air. My hands trembled and my voice quavered. "Aunt Doris..." I swallowed deep and started again. "Aunt Doris, I have to tell you..." I struggled to find words that could even begin to express the decades-old hurt and humiliation.

"Doris," Will said, his tone calm and even, "I'm wondering what specific concerns you have about the bedroom situation."

"Conor..." She addressed me despite the question posed by Will. "Uncle Martin and I discussed this on the way here. He says it's rude to bring it up, but I know that, as good hosts, you and William would want to know if there was anything you could do to make us more comfortable."

I stared at her, giving no visual clues to encourage or deter her. If she wanted to say something hideous and inappropriate, she would have to muster the courage to say it without provocation from me.

"What I'd like to know is if Martin and I might have a room with one of the bigger beds? I should have asked before now, but Martin has this restless leg thing." She uttered the last statement as if she had just admitted my uncle's heroin addiction.

"What?" I asked.

"It's awful. His legs spasm and thrash around, and I'm afraid if we sleep in anything smaller than a queen-sized bed..." She paused and frowned at her husband. "Well, he's just going to kick the living bejesus out of me all night long."

I exhaled with such force that Will's head swiveled in my direction. He grinned and to no one in particular said, "There's a queen-sized bed in our room. We can swap with you."

"If it's no bother," she said. She tugged at the front of Uncle Martin's shirt and smiled. "Looks like the good Lord is watching out for me."

Yes, that's it, instead of wrestling with weighty issues like Middle East peace and climate change, Jesus is focused on protecting your shins and ankles.

THE DAY WAS exhausting, not because of the things I did, but because of the things I hadn't done. Not drinking, not lashing out, not being honest with anyone about what this week was really about. You'd think after all those adolescent years of hiding who I was and, later, all the late nights I spent sneaking around, that dishonesty would come naturally to me. But I took no joy in lying. I never had.

Before bed, I peeked into June's room just as I'd done several times each night during her time in Tampa. I listened for signs of irregularity in her breathing, the awful gurgling and bubbling of mucus in her airway, but I heard only steady, albeit shallow, breaths. I whispered a quiet goodnight from the doorway and dragged my weary body into the bedroom Will and I had traded for our own. I fell back against the door as I closed it behind me.

"What a day."

Will wore makeshift pajamas—a pair of Busch Gardens lounge pants and a pale green Walden Pond T-shirt. He tossed back the covers and patted the mattress. "Get in."

I shed my clothes and, uncharacteristically, left them in a pile on the floor, before turning off the light and crawling into bed. Behind me, Will's warm body slid closer, narrowing the space between us until there was none. I closed my eyes as he slipped his arm across my body and his hand found mine.

We lay together, not speaking. He rubbed his hand back and forth through my short brown hair. "I forgot how soft your hair is."

The affection bewildered and excited me, but unwilling to do anything that might bring a premature end to the moment, I lay still and made no mention of his touch. "I might not be as ready as I thought I was."

"Ready for what?"

My eyes grew moist and I was grateful for the cover of darkness. "Ready for what I need to do."

"You're putting a lot of pressure on yourself, trying to put decades of pent-up shit behind you in a week."

"I'm confused, Will. I need to get past it, all of it."

"What's the rush?" he asked. "Take a step, maybe two—see how it goes. You have the rest of your life to deal with it."

"Right," I said.

"Maybe, it won't all work out the way you want. Life is like that sometimes." I liked when he spoke, how the air moving through his lungs and diaphragm changed the shape of his stomach and forced a space between our bodies and then how that space closed again when he was silent.

"I won't let her piss me off this week, humiliate me like she did when I was a kid."

"She'll be fine," he said. "Tonight was okay."

"She's only been here a couple of hours, and she kept her bullshit focused on Uncle Martin. She'll come after me, though. Trust me."

"Sounds like you want a showdown."

"I don't. I want to make amends with her, with all of them. I want to let it go."

He cleared his throat but said nothing.

"What?" I asked.

"Nothing." He stroked the top of my head once more. "Such soft hair."

THIRTY-SEVEN

AFTER LESS THAN twelve hours at the beach house, Uncle Martin and Aunt Doris drove back across the three-mile bridge into Pensacola to attend Sunday morning services at their church. Their absence went largely unnoticed as the rest of us enjoyed an uncomplicated morning of swimming, beachcombing, and reading in the sun.

Despite a generous slathering of sunscreen, Will and I were more than adequately bronzed by early afternoon. We returned to the house in search of shade and air conditioning. Ms. Broussard quietly worked a crossword puzzle in the living room while June napped in her wheelchair nearby. The Sesame Street chessboard Will had given my grandmother sat atop a worn leather ottoman between the two women.

After a cool shower and a change of clothes, Will and I joined my grandmother and Ms. Broussard in the living room. June was awake, and as soon as Will entered the room, she called his name and gestured toward the chess set.

"You ready?" she asked.

"Maybe," he said. "What's the table limit?"

"First lesson's on the house." She laughed softly out the side of her mouth that, despite her increasing mental dexterity, still sat crooked on her face.

"I read a beginner's book," Will said, "but I could use a refresher on how the different pieces are allowed to move."

"On second thought, go get your wallet." June cackled louder this time, raising her hand an inch or two and slapping it back to her lap.

My grandmother instructed Will on the fundamentals of chess, as best she could recall them. Will listened intently and asked occasional questions, sometimes for clarity, and other times to redirect my grandmother's wandering mind back to the task at hand. I stood behind June and rested my hand on her shoulder while they played a practice game. Will patiently moved both their game pieces. When her Oscar the

Grouch rook slid across the board and captured his Big Bird king, June hooted so loud Ms. Broussard let loose a surprisingly flamboyant, "Sweet Jesus!" I never asked if he'd let June win, but I had my suspicions.

WHEN AUNT DORIS and Uncle Martin returned from church, my father and Uncle Henry were putting hamburgers on the grill. In the kitchen, Will played an Aretha Franklin blues album on a countertop iPod docking station. While he and I washed lettuce and sliced tomatoes, we performed a clichéd and depressingly white version of the Motown-cooking scene from *The Big Chill*.

Aunt Doris changed out of her church clothes and settled in the living room, where she extolled the spectacular beauty of the summer day outside and raved about how blessed we all were to be alive. Her observations were thinly veiled references to the masterful glory of God, but it was better than hearing her regurgitate the specifics of Pastor Lonnie's Sunday sermon.

Uncle Martin, clad in khaki shorts and a light-blue Polo shirt, pillaged the fridge in search of a cold root beer, presumably the closest he was allowed get to the real thing.

"Howdy fellas," he said. He stepped between Will and me, squeezing our shoulders simultaneously. His hands, strong from decades of loading delivery trucks, lingered in a show of affection before he patted us both on the back. "What's happenin'?"

"Burgers," Will said. "After a lovely day at the Gulf of Mexico."

"I'll drink to that." I raised one of my father's O'Doul's.

"Me too." Uncle Martin winked and hoisted his root beer.

We clinked our bottles and took hefty swigs, laughing as we each swallowed and punctuated the toast with a loud "ahhhh."

I waited for Uncle Martin to punch me in the arm and leave for the safety of the backyard, where the older and straighter men tended the first round of burgers on the grill. Instead, with Aunt Doris momentarily occupied on something other than policing him, he moved to the other side of the kitchen island and took up residence on a black leather barstool.

"Fortieth birthday this week," he said. "You're getting old, Conor."

"I may be getting old," I said, "but I'll always be younger and sexier than you."

"Yes, you will, young man." He grinned with an air of concession. "You staying out of trouble down in Tampa?"

I hesitated, wondering if he'd been kept completely out of the loop on the collapse of my personal and professional worlds. "I'm doing my best."

"I know it's been a tough year, son. But I gotta tell you, Aunt Doris and I really respect what you boys did for your grandmother."

I wondered if he'd included Aunt Doris in his comment in the way that spouses sometimes communicate on behalf of the collective—*"we're so sorry for your loss"*—or if maybe they had actually spent time talking about what Will and I had sacrificed to care for June. Regardless, it was generous of him to focus on the singular positive of the last year while letting my plentiful failures go unmentioned.

"June means the world to me," I said. "To both of us." I realized I was the one now using couple-speak, despite my separation from Will. "I wish I could have kept it together for her."

Uncle Martin glanced across the living room at my grandmother. "Looks like someone's been taking pretty darn good care of her."

Will shingled tomato slices on a foam plate and affirmed the observation. "She's a special lady, Martin. And we treat her that way." *Looks like we're all fond of the royal "we."*

My uncle paused, taking a long draw from his root beer, turning the bottle up like a cowboy with a canteen on a dusty Old West trail. "Conor," he said, pointing the empty bottle at Will, "you're lucky to have this one."

So my uncle really hadn't been kept abreast of the self-imposed tragic turns of my life. "He's something else," I said.

He rose from the stool and walked to our side of the bar. As he popped the top off a second root beer, he glanced into the living room where Aunt Doris sat with her back to us. He gave me a long full embrace and whispered to me. "I've always been proud of ya."

NOT LONG AFTER Uncle Martin left for the manly comforts of the barbecue grill, Aunt Doris came into the kitchen. Like a vampire, she often appeared in a room more than entered it. The writer inside me usually liked to share such quirky observations out loud, but I knew Aunt Doris would despise it. Even a joking comparison to the fictional undead would align her too closely with the dark forces of evil.

Her post-church outfit consisted of knee-length pink shorts and a white tank top, over which she wore an unbuttoned stripy pastel blouse. Summery, but not revealing. Pink, but not loud. Comfortable, but not sloppy. A conservative ensemble that would have instilled pride in Pastor Lonnie.

Content to let Will slice and dice on his own, I cracked open another O'Doul's. "Can I get you something, Aunt Doris?"

"Can't I just come in to visit my favorite nephew?"

"Of course you can," I said. That was the trick with Aunt Doris. She could heap on thick layers of flattery and fawning with superlative sincerity and, in the next sentence, undermine all of it with a judgmental waggle of her tongue.

"Well, if I'm being honest..." She paused and looked over the top of her glasses. "I did come in here for one other reason."

My stomach tightened.

"I'd love to get one of those frosty root beers. I had a sip of Martin's and it was delicious." She found a comfortable space to lean on the counter as she waited for one of us to fulfill the request. I retrieved a root beer from the refrigerator and popped the top off.

"Need a glass?" I asked.

"No, thank you," she said. "There's nothing like a tasty root beer drunk right from an icy cold bottle."

"I think a perfectly chilled beer on a hot summer day is pretty damn close." I salivated at the thought of a cold Blue Moon.

"If you say so," she said, "but this is a *very* fine root beer."

I sat on the barstool next to her and contemplated the absurd merits of a chilled Blue Moon versus a cold bottle of A&W, resisting my normal urge to take my aunt to the mat over almost anything. I'd arranged this week to cast aside decades of anger and bitterness, to break my patterns and find resolution. I wouldn't fall into old habits.

"By the way," she said, "Pastor Lonnie asked about you this morning."

"Oh." I feigned surprise.

"I mentioned we were staying at a beach house for your birthday. Pastor Lonnie sends you his best."

"That's nice. I hope he said a couple of Hail Marys for me." I slid to the edge of my barstool, planting my feet on the floor. Will detected the subtle movement and, though he didn't insert himself into the conversation, he sidled toward the end of the bar in my direction.

"Conor, you know we don't worship Mary like Catholics do." She said it as though she was lecturing a first-grader on the inherent dangers of nose-picking.

"Right," I said. "All Jesus, all the time."

Will edged closer and gave my ankle a warning kick.

"Conor," she continued, "Pastor Lonnie has no ill will toward you. He knows how stressful it was in the hospital in those days before the miracle."

I laughed out loud at her characterization of June's improvements. "Are you kidding?" I felt the sharp sting of a second ankle kick. "June learning to slur a few two-syllable words is hardly loaves and fishes shit."

"Dammit, Conor," Will said, gesturing to the living room where June was within earshot.

"I don't understand why you're so hostile," Doris said. "I mention Pastor Lonnie and you turn everything ugly. It's just not necessary."

I slid back on the barstool and swigged the O'Doul's. Though not for the reasons she believed, she was right. This was unnecessary. Debating the merits of Pastor Long-dick was a distraction from my bigger purpose. "You're right," I said. "Sorry."

"Jesus said we should turn the other cheek," she replied. "I'm sorry too."

Will cleared his throat. "Almost finished here." By now, hamburger and hot dog buns, assorted condiments, and plates of lettuce and tomato had begun to crowd the kitchen counter. He washed his cutting board and grabbed two large onions from the fridge. He peeled one of the onions, and his eyes welled with tears as he made the first deep cuts.

Aunt Doris strode across the kitchen and stood next to him. "Well, darling, I just hate to see a grown man cry." She wiped a tear from his cheek with the back of her hand.

The silliness of the gesture startled Will. He stopped cutting the onion in mid-slice and then quickly recovered his poise. "I just get emotional about produce."

"You don't have to cry those onion tears," she said, sounding almost sympathetic. "Let me help ya," she added, nudging him out of the way.

"Sure thing." He wiped his hands on a paper towel and stepped aside.

"I'm gonna show you an old kitchen trick I learned from my momma." She took the cutting board to the opposite counter and ran the onions under cold water as she peeled them, then expertly cut them into burger-thin slices and shingled them on a plate. "There you go." She slid the plate onto the overcrowded bar.

"Thank you." I inadvertently emphasized the second word, making it sound more like a question than an expression of gratitude. Her kindness toward Will, whose presence she'd never once bothered to acknowledge on holiday phone calls, baffled me.

She rinsed her hands in the sink and, with a familiarity I didn't believe possible, she grabbed the dishtowel Will had draped over his shoulder to dry her hands. "I better get out there to check on those burgers," she said. She folded the towel, replaced it on Will's shoulder and then walked out.

AFTER A BREATHTAKING sunset and a leisurely dinner, Will and I cleaned the kitchen. My mother and Ms. Broussard settled June into bed. The rest of my family soon disappeared behind their respective bedroom doors.

Will, who was not an abstaining alcoholic, had consumed more than his share of wine with dinner. He was already asleep when I slid into bed next to him. I longed to encircle him in my arms, to put my head on his chest, hear his heartbeat, and feel the softness of his warm, smooth skin as I had the night before, but physical closeness was a choice he was allowed to make, not me.

I wanted to tell him how the volatile stew of my grief and emptiness had cooled and congealed. I wanted him to understand what I needed to accomplish now, how I had to cut ties and discard my excess baggage, how I could no longer carry the burdensome weight of the past. I wanted him to be proud of me, to know that I had established a creed and worked to follow it, to recognize how hard I had tried. Though I would soon leave everything behind, I wanted him to know it had never been my intent to give up—on us, on me, on life.

I closed my eyes and imagined the hotness of his breath on my neck as he whispered that everything would be okay, that things always worked out one way or another, for better or worse. I fell into a light, fitful sleep and my subconscious took charge, flooding my mind with random images. June, wearing shiny red trunks as she danced across the canvas in a boxing ring. Aunt Doris on her knees fellating Pastor Lonnie as he wiped Miller Genuine Draft tears from his onion-shaped eyes. A root beer rain falling from a deep brown sky. And, sometime before dawn, alligators.

THIRTY-EIGHT

AUNT DORIS HAD always worn the polyester pantsuit in her family, but over the next couple of days she needled and demeaned Uncle Martin even more than usual. She poked fun at his thinning hair, ridiculed the closet space his abundant clothing required, questioned the extended length of time he took to shave and shower. She was skilled at pointing out any perceived flaws, and Uncle Martin seldom stood in his own defense.

The charade felt like bait, but I refused to take it. She was genial enough with the rest of the family, and like them, I plastered on a cheerful mask and guiltily ignored her digs, leaving my uncle to fend for himself.

I joined my father and uncles on the deck outside as they sipped coffee in the warm morning sun. In the kitchen, Aunt Doris floated across the linoleum, cooking and assembling custom breakfasts. In between short orders, she hummed a tune, *Jimmy Crack Corn and I Couldn't Give Two Shits* or some other Old South ditty. She took modest nibbles off the plates of food as she served them. Aunt Doris never seemed to care much about acceptance into the McLeish clan, but her show of generosity felt like a subtle attempt at strengthening her place in the family.

Aunt Doris was delivering hot plates of bacon and eggs when Uncle Martin's cell phone chirped in his shirt pocket. He stepped inside to take the call and returned a few moments later with the news that one of his peers had been injured on the UPS loading dock. Uncle Martin was needed to cover the swing shift.

Aunt Doris, who had blown sunshine and bluebirds out her ass all morning, yanked off her apron and hurled it at an empty deck chair.

"Didn't they just call you in on Saturday? Does your idiot boss comprehend the meaning of the word vacation? Who knew a company as big as UPS had to shut down their trucks if Martin McLeish takes a week off?"

She allowed no time between accusatory questions for reply. Uncle Martin stood helpless as the rest of us stared at our plates and picked at our breakfast.

"I warned you time and again about these bloodsuckers, Martin. You never listen and you never learn. People will take advantage of your kindness if you don't stand up for yourself."

Amen to that one, sister.

AUNT DORIS ISOLATED herself in her bedroom for most of the afternoon. When she eventually emerged from her self-imposed exile, she was chipper and pleasant, as though Uncle Martin's absence had never been an issue. She and my mother prepared a spaghetti dinner, while Ms. Broussard, under the careful "supervision" of my grandmother, tossed a mixed green salad. Uncle Henry, who had now been clued in on the gory details behind my sobriety, had brought along two bottles of Cabernet, which he was reluctant to contribute to the dinner effort. I reassured him that drinking was *my* problem, not his, and to reaffirm the strength of my commitment to sobriety, I insisted on opening the first bottle myself.

By the end of the night, with some of us on the wagon and others abstaining for Jesus reasons, Will and Uncle Henry had taken on the work of downing both bottles on their own. Judging by the degree to which he relied on me to help him navigate the living room furniture, Will had done most of the heavy lifting.

Near midnight, a few minutes before the official start of my birthday, I shuffled him down the hallway and into our bedroom. I remembered his words from a few days before. Maybe a cuddle on my birthday, he'd said. Not sex. With my family so nearby, physical intimacy would require a level of precision and quiet I wasn't sure Will could deliver anyway. But on my last night on earth, I wanted nothing more than to feel his arms around me, to feel him loving me, even as we slept.

After I tucked him into bed, I took a habitual last peek at June. I opened her bedroom door, leaned inside, and listened for evidence of respiration. I recognized the disturbing and all-too-familiar sound of her measured but raspy breathing. I mouthed a silent *I love you* and pulled the door shut.

When I returned to our bedroom, I was surprised to find Will lying awake. I was even more astonished when I climbed under the covers and discovered he had shed the pajamas he'd worn to bed all week. He beamed a grin that landed somewhere between sheepish and come-hither. I was struck by how adorable he was and told him so. He pulled my T-shirt over my head, tossed it on the floor, and pushed me back onto the pillow.

"We can't," I said. "I want to, but we can't."

"I know," he said, a hint of intoxication in his voice. "It'll be nice just to be next to you."

He inched closer, resting his head upon my bare chest and then touching my face with his fingertips. He traced across my forehead and down the side of my face to my neck and shoulder. I wrapped my arm around his muscled back and pulled his body closer, as I stroked his soft, short hair. He slid his leg between my thighs, and we lay like a twisty croissant, no beginning to him and no ending to me, until we drifted off to sleep.

I forgot to switch off a table lamp that sat atop the dresser, but that's not what woke me a short while later. It might have been the click of the twisting doorknob or the subtle change in air pressure when the bedroom door opened. Or maybe I was stirred awake by that odd sixth sense warning you get, even while you're sleeping, that someone is watching you.

My eyelids fluttered open and focused on Uncle Martin's slumped and silent figure. He leaned against the frame of the open bedroom door, arms folded, his eyes fixed on Will and me. Though mostly covered by the bedspread, we were still locked together, as tangled and knotted as vines.

He said nothing, but in the twinkle of my uncle's eyes, I saw acceptance. He looked at me and, at the same time, looked through me to a faraway place and time. In the sad lines of his face, I saw longing, or envy.

"Hello," I said, groggy and unalarmed, as if his presence in the intimate space where I slept naked with Will was as regular as the mail.

"Hey there." He spoke softly, but the sound of an unexpected voice woke Will, who lifted his head from my naked chest and squinted at the shape in the doorway. Uncle Martin raised his hand and waved half-heartedly. "Mornin', Will."

"Umm...hi, Martin," Will said. "Is it morning?"

"No," my uncle replied. "It's just after one."

"Good, because if it's morning and I'm still this drunk, something is really wrong."

Uncle Martin chuckled. "I'm sorry 'bout barging in. I came up the back steps like you told me, and I guess I got the bedrooms mixed up."

"It's okay," I said. "It's fine."

He shifted in the doorway and waved again. "Well, goodnight then."

A wide grin crossed his face, as if his work here was done. He backed away and pulled the door shut as he disappeared into the dark hallway.

He had said the right words, all the things I would have imagined him saying if I had fabricated the scenario, but something wasn't right.

Will yawned and pushed one arm out in a long stretch. He returned his head to its place against my chest. "That was queer. And not in a good way."

"Yeah," I said, preoccupied with pinpointing what exactly had been amiss. I reflected on the conversation, brief though it was, and it hit me. There had been no frown of disapproval, no turning away in revulsion. He could have slammed the door as soon as he realized his blunder, but instead, he took up residence in the doorway and stared at us as we slept in each other's arms. My uncle was in no way embarrassed. His words weren't formal or emphatic, but casual, more acknowledgement than apology. He hadn't appeared self-conscious, as you might expect a dedicated soldier of Christ to be when confronted with such sin. He seemed...satisfied.

Will rolled back on his pillow and stared straight up, as if an explanation for my uncle's behavior might be encoded in the popcorn ceiling. "I'm serious. That was really strange. How long was he there?"

"I don't know. I woke up and he was just there, watching us."

"Did you smell him?" Will asked.

"That," I said, "would have been really queer."

"No, I mean did you smell beer on him? I think he'd been drinking. I can still smell it."

"I think you're smelling your own breath."

"We only drank wine. I lived with you long enough to know the difference between the smell of decent wine and cheap beer."

"I don't smell anything, but so what? He loads trucks with a bunch of guys at a warehouse. I'm sure there are plenty of good ol' boys at UPS who like a cold Bud after work."

"He doesn't drink," Will countered. "Jesus wouldn't approve, remember?" He clearly believed there was more at play than a mistaken room choice after a long day's work.

"It's the middle of the night in a strange, dark house."

"He's been here a couple of days already."

"What are you saying, Will?"

"I'm just wondering if Martin's problem picking the right room has more to do with him knocking back a few beers than anything else."

I considered the possibility of my uncle harboring a secret drinking habit. Living with Aunt Doris would be incentive enough to drive most people to drink, so if Uncle Martin hit the bottle from time to time, I couldn't blame him.

"I don't know," I said. "Maybe he likes to stop off after work and have a couple of beers. For all I know, he does tequila shots and smokes pot too."

Will rolled his eyes, silently pushing me back from the hyperbolic cliff's edge.

"Okay, probably not, but you've seen what he puts up with. She's on him nonstop. She treats him like a dog and he just takes it. That has to wear a man down."

He pushed himself away from me. "I didn't mean to get you worked up. I'm just saying maybe your uncle was a little tipsy and that's why he came into the wrong room."

"Maybe he was drinking." I exhaled at last. "But it wasn't a big deal to him, so it's not a big deal to me."

Will hesitated, reflecting on the encounter with Martin, or perhaps being careful to swing the mood of our conversation in the right direction. "No, it wasn't a big deal. It really wasn't." He reached his hand out to my chest and walked his fingers down to my belly button, adding, "But it could have been a big deal that traumatized all three of us."

"You're not wrong." I wanted to resist, but his playfulness caught me off guard. I had dreamed for months of holding him once more, telling him I loved him, reinventing what I'd destroyed. But it was too late for that now.

His hand, strong from decades of digging earth and tilling soil, rested on my stomach, and his breath tickled my neck. I had no idea if this was truth or just the Cabernet, but it no longer mattered.

"It's late," I said, "but it *is* my birthday."

He pointed to the lamp on the dresser across the room. "Be sure you turn that light off when you get up to lock the door."

THIRTY-NINE

TWENTY-FIVE YEARS BEFORE, in a muggy attic on a sticky south Georgia night, Patrick and I were discovered in an act deemed so despicable that it ultimately cost him his life. Alone and ashamed, a boy took the only way out he could see, leaving nothing behind but unanswered questions and wasted possibilities. Death as the interruption of life.

I don't know if Doris McLeish ever forgave herself for the death of her son, but since that summer night when she spied us together, she has never forgiven me. She withdrew the mother's love she gave me. She moved her heart to a distant place I could see, but no longer reach. If the truth had been less painful, we might have helped each other, but she withheld herself, pushed me aside, and hid in the robes of Jesus, taking with her the only part of my childhood where I felt I belonged.

It was time for forgiveness. For Aunt Doris, for my parents, for myself.

I have lived, loved, and lost. I am no longer a boy. I am a man. Aware and able. I will leave this world, not in desperation, but because I am finished, because I have done the things I needed to do. Death as the culmination of life.

I smiled at the satisfying serendipity of it all.

WHILE WILL SHOWERED and dressed, I bounded into the living room like an antelope. My family, all of whom lacked recent experience in post-coital euphoria, interpreted my energetic start to the day as eager anticipation about my birthday, which I suppose in a way it was.

The mullet fish fry was a long-standing northwest Florida tradition that McLeishes had adhered to for as many summers as I could remember. The deep-fried galas were seared into my childhood memories. I didn't balk at the idea of a fish fry as my birthday dinner, or for that matter, my last meal.

Based on calm waters and the morning's cloud cover, Uncle Henry guaranteed a sizable haul of fresh mullet and blue gulf crabs. My father and both uncles packed nets, buckets, and a cooler, and headed out for a day of fishing, while my mother and Aunt Doris made a lengthy list of grocery items they'd need for homemade coleslaw, hush puppies, and baked beans.

"I'll run out and pick this stuff up," Aunt Doris said.

"Really?" my mother replied. "You don't have to do that."

"Martin's going fishing. I might as well make myself useful."

My mother eyeballed the lengthy list of groceries. "This is a lot of stuff, Doris."

"I'll take our minivan," she said. "Plenty of room."

A COUPLE OF hours later, I heard the honk of a car horn as Aunt Doris pulled into the driveway. I recruited Will and walked outside to help with the groceries.

"Impressive haul," I said, peeking into the rear window of the minivan at the sea of plastic bags.

Aunt Doris offered a tight-lipped smile and walked past me. She popped the hatch and grabbed a couple of Publix bags, leaving the rest for Will and me. I picked up as many sacks as I could carry. As we trudged together up the dozen steps to the front door, arms laden with the grocery haul, I attempted to lighten her apparently dark mood.

"If they have to build beach houses this far off the ground, they oughta put in an elevator."

She didn't answer or even bother to crack a polite smile. Her anger, like Uncle Henry's outdoor deep fryer, bubbled hot just below the surface. I pushed on, saving my strength for the long night ahead and trying not to take her mood personally.

"They'll be home soon with an ice chest full of fish," I said, fumbling with a bag of groceries as I opened the front door. "Even if they had to stop at the dock and buy the fish off the boat." She followed me silently through the doorway, leaving my half-hearted attempt at engagement hanging on the porch, as sad and lifeless as an empty windsock.

I was sure she'd have more to say later, when I apologized for getting naked with her son and raining decades of shame and hurt on her. Later, when I asked for her forgiveness, she'd have plenty to say. In my fantasy version of the events to come, she'd embrace me and tell me she loved me. She'd say she freaked out that night and handled the whole thing wrong, that she was young and foolish, that the world then was different than it is now. Her words would help me understand the fear and ignorance, the bottomless darkness that drives a mother to torment her son to death. She'd say she was wrong to turn on me when I was a vulnerable boy. She'd acknowledge that she was partly responsible for the damaged fuckwit I became, and she'd tell me she was sorry.

That's how I hoped Aunt Doris, and my parents, for that matter, might process the torrent of honesty I planned to unleash on the night of my fortieth birthday. Though they might not see it until they looked back on the night, I wanted them to understand what led me to this place, to this end that wasn't so far from the beginning. I hoped they would believe, as I finally did, that it was all okay.

Aunt Doris plopped the groceries on the bar with a thud and surveyed the crowded counter space with a scowl.

"You want some help putting this stuff away?" Will asked.

"I'm sure…Conor…would appreciate a hand." Her tone was stiff and cold, her words measured.

"Happy to help." He sounded forcibly upbeat.

"I'm getting too old for this sort of thing," she said, addressing no one in particular. She left the kitchen, head low and eyes down, and walked to her bedroom where she slammed the door behind her.

Thoroughly confused, Will mouthed a soundless *what the fuck?*

I shrugged and mouthed an equally silent *no fucking idea.*

We spent the next half hour stowing fish fry ingredients and dinner party supplies, and speculating on the source of my aunt's sudden foulness. Though he hadn't said as much, I suspected Will believed I had something to do with the unforeseen shift in Aunt Doris's demeanor.

"It wasn't me. She was pissed when she got home."

"Maybe it's Martin," he said.

"She's always pissed at Martin." I stooped into the fridge and rearranged sodas and condiments to make room for more sodas and condiments. I looked up from the bottles of root beer I was stocking. "Maybe, she misses her boyfriend."

"Pastor Lonnie?"

"Yeah." I pulled my head out of the fridge to whisper. "Pastor Long-dick."

"Jesus, Conor." He shook his head and laughed.

Aunt Doris emerged an hour later as my father and uncles filleted their sizable catch on the cement patio behind the house. She had changed into a different pastel Walmart short set, and as she pranced into the kitchen to help with dinner, she hummed and sang unrecognizable ditties, most of which, I surmised from the capitalized "He" in the lyrics, were Jesus tunes.

When Aunt Doris turned away to rifle through the kitchen cabinets, Will caught my eye. He shrugged in disbelief at her radical mood swing.

I pinched my thumb and index finger together, bringing them to my lips and inhaling deeply from an imaginary joint. He rolled his eyes and mouthed a word to me. *Idiot.*

It was doubtful Aunt Doris had ever smoked pot, but I smiled at the image of her sneaking hits from her favorite pipe, or better yet, from a water bong emblazoned with a yellow cross on one side and the words "Jesus Saves" on the other.

IN THE LATE afternoon, Ms. Broussard wheeled my grandmother to the deck to soak in the last peaceful remnants of the day. I peered out the sliding glass door and watched the heavyset nurse position my grandmother next to the railing. She dragged a worn wooden Adirondack chair next to my grandmother and eased herself into it. In Tampa, the nurse had typically stood or seated herself behind my grandmother, preferring a more clinical and observational deportment than sitting nearby afforded. It was unusual, but pleasing, to see Henrietta Broussard relax.

It was precisely because of her professional and sometimes antiseptic approach that I was surprised to see Ms. Broussard not only sit next to June, but also hold her hand. And it wasn't the one-way comfort handholding you see with an out-of-her-wits elderly patient in an old folks' home. This was hand-on-hand-on-hand affection the kind you see between old ladies who pass Sunday afternoons on a park bench, the touch that says "best friends forever."

From my vantage point in the living room, I saw periodic nods and alternating turning of heads, the carrying on of conversation. I imagined the topics they might discuss, and worried that any movement on my part would somehow disrupt the serenity of the moment.

I watched for fifteen or twenty minutes, until the sun sat just above the glistening choppy waters of the Gulf of Mexico, and only after several silent minutes passed between them did I allow myself to wander outside. I slid the glass door open loudly to announce my arrival and carried a white plastic chair from the patio table to the rail where they sat.

As I approached, both women sat with their eyes closed. "How's the sunset working out? Everything going as planned?" Their eyes popped open as I slid my chair into the space next to June, opposite the old nurse.

"Hello young man," said Ms. Broussard. My grandmother offered her recently patented half-smirk smile.

"Did I catch you napping? Resting your eyes?"

"We were listening and smelling. The gulf." It was June who answered. Her voice was scratchy, and she spoke with a hint of the slur that had rendered her unintelligible months before, but the sound was like a favorite old song. Though I hoped there was no direct correlation, she'd made significant progress since leaving Tampa.

My grandmother and I took turns expressing appreciation for our surroundings—the salty ocean smell, the distant thunder of crashing waves and the cawing of circling sea birds, the warm summer breeze on our skin. We weren't speaking in haikus or sonnets. Slow was her only speed, and our dialogue was full of lengthy pauses. Still, the conversation was a fucking miracle.

As my grandmother and I spoke, Ms. Broussard grew quiet. She leaned closer to my grandmother, and their hands, which I had forgotten were intertwined, stayed cemented together.

I'd made my peace with Will. It was June's turn now.

"June," I said, "I need to tell you something. Two things, really."

She looked at me, mouth shut and eyes wide open, as if to say, *get on with it, boy.*

I rubbed my lips and chin as though I could coax the reluctant words out of my mouth. "First, I want to tell you how sorry I am."

"For what?" she asked.

"For everything. But mostly for failing you. For not being able to stay sober so I could take care of you."

She pursed her lips into a pouty frown.

"I let you down," I said.

Her weight shifted almost unnoticeably in the wheelchair, but she stayed silent.

"You needed me and I let you down."

She looked away, focusing her gaze on the horizon over the Gulf of Mexico. "You did your best," she said. "But don't worry. I never thought it would work out."

I should have known better than to expect anything but blatant honesty from my grandmother. Her words stung, and at the same time reassured me. June was back.

"Anyway, I hope you can forgive me."

"Of course I do."

I leaned forward to draw her gaze. "That's one thing. I also want to thank you."

"For what?" she asked, again.

"For teaching me what matters, and for being there for me."

"You're welcome." She was matter-of-fact, as though I'd thanked her for picking up my mail.

"I know I wasn't always easy to love."

"What?" she said louder, annoyed.

"I fucked up so much. Complicated things...for everyone."

"Nonsense."

"I'm serious. I wasted a lot of people's time, and most of my life."

"Ridiculous," she said. "How do you think I feel?"

"What do you mean?"

"I'm just a burden now...to everyone. Is my life worthless?"

"I'm just saying it's too fucking hard sometimes."

"Life hurts, Conor." She looked straight into my eyes. "But you just keep going."

She beamed a half-smile, as much as the frozen muscles of her face would allow, and drew in a breath of the cool evening air. Sitting quietly next to her, Henrietta Broussard closed her eyes and turned her head, hoping to hide her own satisfied grin and the single tear that slid down her cheek as quiet as the setting sun.

FORTY

SOON AFTER WE gorged ourselves on fried mullet and hush puppies, black clouds rumbled in across the Gulf of Mexico and forced us inside. My sated father and uncles sank into the living room furniture, so Will and I pulled extra chairs in from the dining room. We filled gaps around the sofa and formed an arc that faced the sliding glass doors. I parked June's wheelchair at one end of the semi-circle and seated myself next to her, hoping sheer proximity might lend any moral support I'd need. The seating arrangement allowed each of us a front row seat as we watched gray sheets of rain settle like an enormous tarp over the Gulf. I gazed out at the heaving swells that would soon be my watery grave and wondered, ironically, how difficult it would be to stay afloat.

I'd made amends with Will and June—as much as I needed to, anyway. Now came the trickier tasks of saying subtle good-byes to the rest of them, and finding a way to make peace with Aunt Doris. I hadn't thought through the rest of the evening as thoroughly as I could have, but it didn't matter. A warmth had been building inside me for days, a comfort with my decision. Aunt Doris couldn't change that. I would apologize to her, beg her forgiveness if that's what she wanted. I'd be sure she knew I never meant to be queer, and that I certainly never meant to be so with her son. I'd tell her I was sorry for who I was, for how I'd wrecked our lives, and for Patrick. I was most sorry for that.

AUNT DORIS STUCK with her Pollyanna demeanor throughout dinner, and as we settled into the living room, she offered us a "sweet treat" she and my mother had made. My father and uncles groaned with abdominal discomfort from having stuffed themselves already and then promptly asked about the available ice cream and cake options.

"None!" said Aunt Doris. "Sylvia and I whipped up a homemade banana puddin' for Conor's big night."

"And we made decaf," said my mother, a clear preemptive strike against further alcohol consumption.

As Mom and Aunt Doris delivered mismatched cups of coffee and plastic bowls filled to the brim with banana pudding, a gust blew through the screen of the sliding glass doors, sending napkins flying and toppling empty Solo cups. Will leaped from his seat and slid the door shut. As he turned to retake his seat, his eyes fixed on the wall across the living room. My mother handed a heaping bowl of pudding to Uncle Henry and then looked up and stared at the same wall. Neither of them spoke as they gawked at the shape, frozen in bewilderment as if they'd seen the face of a dead relative in a distant storm cloud. It could be, but it couldn't be. I turned to see what had mesmerized them, and then I fell under its spell. Dangling from a piece of decorative driftwood mounted on the wall was a pair of women's panties. Lacy, silky, lavender panties.

The sight of women's undergarments has never had much impact on me. On this night, though, in a rented beach house at a family reunion I had organized to say my good-byes, seeing a sexy piece of women's lingerie hanging on the wall flummoxed me. At first, when only the three of us had seen the panties, my instinct was to race across the room and snatch the underwear from the wall before the night was derailed. But I was paralyzed. I settled onto the sofa, my shock unnoticed by everyone except my mother and Will. Despite what my more presumptive relatives might assume, I didn't own any ladies' undergarments. Nor, to the best of my knowledge, did Will. Judging from the look of relative horror on my mother's face, it was safe to assume the panties didn't belong to her either. I'm no expert, but the underwear seemed neither the style nor size Ms. Broussard might choose to wear, and my paralyzed grandmother, who in her better days was likely quite a seductress, had no need for provocative undergarments now. That left only one possibility, and if these were indeed Aunt Doris's panties, I had no idea how to broach the subject.

"Whose purple panties are hanging on the driftwood?" my mother asked. She blurted out the question in the same tone she used when chastising my father for leaving his dirty briefs hanging on the bathroom doorknob.

They craned their necks in turn to see the underpants, as my mother's question floated over their heads, alarming and toxic, dangling as awkwardly as the panties themselves. Ms. Broussard rolled her eyes in apathetic disbelief and whispered a barely audible, "Oh my." My grandmother, who saw the purple panties clearly from her vantage point, smiled wide. If she had been capable of placing the panties on the driftwood, I would have read the look as guilt, but even with her newfound alertness and dexterity, she could not have hung the panties there.

Will and I, along with my parents and Uncle Henry, crossed the room to get a closer look at the offending undergarment. We maintained traditional gallery distance from the wall, leaning in and clasping our hands behind our backs as though we were scrutinizing the surrealist symbols in Dali's *Hallucinogenic Toreador*.

"What on earth...?" my father said, the proximity of women's panties to his face rendering him unable to finish the thought.

"It's pretty clear *what on earth*," my mother said. "The question is *why on earth*?"

Uncle Henry, assuming the role of docent at the purple panty museum, shared his artistic impressions with no one in particular. "Kind of pretty, really. Nice shade of purple. Would you call that violet?"

Will, who also appeared to be taking the incident none too seriously, offered his color interpretation. "Lilac, I think. It's a slightly lighter shade of violet."

Uncle Henry nodded in agreement. "Is that what they mean when they say bikini-style?"

"You know, Henry," Will said, "we grow a lot of flowers at Busch Gardens, and I'm familiar with various shades of purple. But identifying the color is where my panties expertise ends."

I was grateful for their attempts to keep the bizarre event from taking on too much gravity, but the panties had already changed the course of the evening. There was a staggering absence of commentary from Aunt Doris, and though the incident had nothing to do with me, I knew she would view it as my fault. Hoping to minimize the sordid distraction, I determined the first logical course of action was to remove the panties from the wall art.

"Let me take those panties down," I said for perhaps the first time in my life.

I returned armed with a pair of plastic salad tongs, but my mother already held the panties in her hand. "It's just underwear," she said. "And it's clean. Never worn, see?" She presented the dangling Victoria's Secret price tag as evidence and then tossed the panties at me.

"Thanks, Mom." I was dismayed to find that I was suddenly in charge of dispensation of the rescued undergarment. "Honestly, I have no idea how this...*lingerie* got here." I avoided the word panties with all my might. "At any rate, I don't have any use for them." I clasped the underwear in the salad tongs and held them at a safe distance.

A quiet moment passed as we studied each other's faces for clues, a roomful of Hitchcock characters surveying the scene of the crime. Uncle Henry, eager to cut the tension and move on to dessert, broke the silence. "How about that banana puddin'? It ain't going to eat itself."

FORTY-ONE

WE STARED AT our bowls, pushing and prodding spoonfuls of banana pudding as though a hidden message in the dessert might reveal who owned the panties my mother had plucked from the wall art. It was Aunt Doris who finally blinked.

She cleared her throat to draw our attention. "I hung the panties on the wood, but I have no idea who they belong to." She showed no emotion as she grabbed a handful of napkins from the kitchen and distributed them around the room.

"Well, that's...an interesting thing to do," my mother said.

Aunt Doris ignored the remark and then matter-of-factly recounted the details of her shopping expedition earlier in the day. The drive across the bridge to the mainland grocery store had been uneventful. The store was more crowded than she'd expected it to be on a weekday. The clerk who'd helped her load the sizable grocery purchase into the van had practically demanded a tip. Things had gone more or less as planned, until she began her drive back to the beach house. A stalled car on the bridge slowed traffic to a crawl, and once she made it to the island, she was trapped behind a long line of tourists at the toll bridge plaza. She grew increasingly frustrated behind the wheel of Uncle Martin's minivan. By the time Aunt Doris reached our small island neighborhood, her patience had worn thin. She coasted through several four-way stops on Maldonado Drive before Escambia County Sheriff's Deputy Austin Boles swung into action. With a short blast of his siren and a flash of his headlights, he'd pulled Aunt Doris over just a half mile shy of the beach house.

Good afternoon, ma'am. Yes, ma'am, it certainly is warm outside. Do you know why I've pulled you over? Oh, you have no earthly idea? You just drove through three consecutive intersections without once coming to a full, safe, and complete stop. Yes, ma'am, I know how easy it is easy to be distracted, but it's important to be attentive when you're behind the wheel.

In the eyes of the law, this exchange would start and end as nothing more than a routine traffic stop, which in this case, didn't even yield a citation. In the eyes of Aunt Doris, it was a minor safety oversight that would result in nothing more than slight embarrassment and a short delay in getting home. Routine, minor, slight—appropriate descriptors until the moment Sheriff Austin Boles uttered the phrase that would ultimately culminate in a pair of purple panties hanging on a piece of decorative driftwood in our rented beach house.

License and registration, please.

Aunt Doris remained calm as she narrated the events of the afternoon, sharing the details with no more emotional intensity than she might have used to explain the plot of the latest Sandra Bullock movie.

She placed a napkin on the end table next to Uncle Martin and stood uncomfortably close to his chair, looming over him like a schoolyard bully. When she resumed the story, she spoke directly to my uncle, who made no move to look up at her. Her voice, at conversational volume seconds before, grew high-pitched and angry.

License and registration, please.

"Imagine my embarrassment," she shrieked, "when I opened the glove box to fish out our registration, and a pair of purple slut panties sat right there on top." The veins in her neck grew thick and pulsed. "I was shocked, of course, but I stayed calm. I tried to work around them, tried to casually move them from side to side to find the paperwork, but the goddamn glove box was a mess." The unexpected shock of having spontaneously taken her beloved lord's name in vain slowed her momentarily, but it didn't stop her.

She glared at my uncle. "I had no choice, Martin. No choice but to take those panties out of the glove box and lay them right there on the passenger seat. That whore underwear, right out in the open for God and everybody to see."

Uncle Martin sat unmoving, staring blankly at the bowl of banana pudding balanced on his knee. He offered no acknowledgement or explanation. He hadn't uttered a sound since my mother first announced the presence of the underwear hanging from the driftwood. Since that moment, he must have known this was coming.

Intent on relaying the full impact of her horrific, albeit overly dramatized, interaction with Sheriff Austin Boles, Aunt Doris leaned down, her face inches from my uncle's. "Just imagine my embarrassment. Imagine it, Martin." She nearly spat his name.

Uncle Martin maintained his catatonia, stunned, or perhaps withdrawn for safety like a tortoise.

"Do you have any idea how ridiculous I looked holding that pair of panties? I have to tell you, I was mighty surprised to find them, and I'm damn sure that showed on my face." Then, almost as an afterthought, she added, "Imagine what that policeman thought of me. What these people think of me."

These people? I had fantasized that Aunt Doris and I would end the night wrapped in an honest and forgiving embrace, weeping together for all we'd lost. The notion seemed naive and foolish now. She would always count me among *these people*. I would always be...other.

"You made a fool of me, Martin." Tears filled the creases in her pale and sunken cheeks. "It's no wonder you've been so disinterested in our bedroom life for years. Some hussy's been taking care of you."

He made no attempt to deflect the relentless assault, simply absorbing the brutal blows, which he no doubt felt he deserved. As his wife collapsed in a heap on the couch, emptiness replaced the concern in his eyes. His cheeks sagged and his Munchian face reminded me of my grandmother's useless and palsied countenance in the days just after her stroke. His body, so stiff and resistant moments before, looked weak and battered. Like a bruised and beaten prizefighter, he'd withstood a hail of body blows until the last bell, only to lose the fight on points.

Uncle Martin had been careless, and the price for his sloppy behavior was the obliteration of his wife's narrow worldview. She had imploded in front of *these people*, annihilating a considerable chunk of her self-esteem along with her marriage. With every ounce of anger having gushed out, she sat next to me, lifeless and exhausted. For the first time in years, I felt nothing tense or rigid in the places where our bodies touched.

Aunt Doris dried her tears and blew her nose into a napkin. As she composed herself, I marveled at the boldness with which she had confronted him. Surely, Uncle Martin was guilty, but the plan for his punishment had been premeditated and executed to devastating perfection. She had sought to damage him in the most profound way possible, making a public spectacle of his mistake to ensure we all knew how much he had hurt her.

I made awful mistakes too, costly fuck-ups that had ruined my relationship with Will. But at least we sorted out our dirty laundry without hanging it on the line. Or on a piece of artsy driftwood.

Uncle Martin pulled himself up from the armchair, clambering to his feet with a Christ-on-Golgotha degree of difficulty. He stood in front of the sliding glass door and faced us. His chin was pressed to his chest and his eyes fixed on the carpet. He opened his mouth to speak, but no words came out.

"Uncle Martin..." I said, though I had no end to the sentence.

His voice was dry and hoarse when he finally spoke.

"I'm an awful man." He lifted his head to meet his wife's gaze. "I'm sorry, Doris."

Aunt Doris, taking her turn at numbness and catatonia, gave no indication that she heard the apology.

"I'm sorry to the rest of you, too," he said. "I've shamed myself, all of us, really."

I stiffened as he uttered the words. They could just as well have been mine. They should have been—that was, after all, the whole fucking point of this ridiculous week. Uncle Martin talked on, but I no longer heard him. I was lost, traipsing through the ruins of my own ambitious plans for the evening and wondering where the news of his carelessly wrecked marriage left me. The mood wasn't exactly right for reconciliation and forgiveness, and I wasn't sure I could disappear without at least a vain attempt to make things right.

Uncle Henry spoke up at last, uttering a loud reassuring "eh" and shrugging his shoulders. My father, who wanted to offer support but was wholly unequipped to do so, tried to normalize the situation. "Things happen," he said unhelpfully. The rest of us, including my mother, who had flung open the lid to Pandora's Box, kept quiet, knowing there was nothing comforting or worthwhile to be offered.

"It's best if I leave." Uncle Martin fished his keys out of his pocket and hurried across the room, but before he could end the nightmare, Aunt Doris called to him.

"Martin, who is she?"

"Don't do this," he pleaded.

"I haven't *done* anything. You're the one who's done something. I just want to know who you did it with."

"Not here, and not now." He barked the words in a deep, guttural tone I was sure she'd never heard from him.

"Who is she?" Her voice matched his in its steadiness and strength.

When he refused to answer, she spoke slowly and asked again, through clenched-teeth. "Who...is...she?"

The rosy pallor in his cheeks deepened with anger. "Believe me, Doris, you-don't-know-her." He spied Uncle Henry's red Igloo ice chest next to the bar. Without another word, he tossed open the lid, loaded his arms with beer, and raced out the door.

FORTY-TWO

AUNT DORIS QUIETLY exited the living room, presumably to gather her belongings and what little dignity she had left. My mother followed behind for moral support. I surveyed the semi-circle of those who remained and saw that my grandmother was now slumped in her chair, her eyes closed and a thin string of drool connecting her mouth to her blouse.

"She okay?" I asked Ms. Broussard.

"She's just tired. It's past our bed time." The nurse had endured more than enough McLeish family assholery for one night, and I couldn't blame her for using my unconscious grandmother to liberate herself from the situation. She closed her crossword puzzle book and stood up behind my grandmother's wheelchair. "I hope you'll excuse us."

"I'm sorry," I said.

"This type of environment is *not* good for your grandmother." She grabbed the wheelchair handles and backed my grandmother out of the room. "Hell, this ain't good for nobody."

I wasn't sure I was supposed to hear her closing comment, but I couldn't argue with it.

My father and Uncle Henry attended to their respective bowls of banana pudding.

"Creamy and delicious," Uncle Henry commented.

When their bowls were empty, Will collected them and carried them to the kitchen. He scraped his own untouched dessert into the trash, poured his decaf into the sink, and retrieved a cold beer for himself from Uncle Henry's cooler.

"Henry?" Will held up a second beer.

"Yes, sir," Uncle Henry said.

"Bring me one of those too," my father said.

"Not happening, Eamon." Uncle Henry was suddenly stern and serious. "We've had enough bullshit for one night."

"It was worth a try," my dad said. "Bring me one of those piss-tasting half-beers."

"They aren't even half-beers." I retrieved an O'Doul's for both my father and myself. "But, apparently, we can't behave ourselves if we drink anything stronger."

AN HOUR LATER, my mother emerged from the bedroom with Aunt Doris, who explained that she would stay the night and leave for home in the morning. Puffy-eyed and red-faced, my aunt positioned herself in front of our semi-circle of chairs, an arrangement that was beginning to feel like group therapy.

"I hope you all can forgive Martin's behavior," she said. She rambled on about the betrayal and embarrassment we must feel, projecting her emotions onto the rest of us whether we felt them or not. She expressed deep regret for the unseemly escalation of this "private matter," though she notably omitted any mention of her decision to highlight my uncle's transgression by draping women's lingerie from a piece of living room wall art.

"This is certainly not how any of us expected the night to go," my mother said.

"What else is new?" I asked. Despite my efforts at sounding rhetorical, my disappointment was clear.

"Oh, right," Aunt Doris added as a bitter afterthought. "I'm sorry we derailed your party and your little twelve-step thing. I'm sure you can make amends and whatnot tomorrow."

The notion of attempting to wipe the slate clean with her was ludicrous at this point. I felt stupid at having imagined an honest outpouring of hurt that would culminate in a tearful embrace as memories of Patrick flooded our shared consciousness. Still, I felt sorry for Aunt Doris. Pity is not a kindness, though, and her feeble apology chipped away at any real compassion I felt for her.

Aunt Doris carried on her pathetic soliloquy, martyring herself and backing the bus over Uncle Martin a few more times, while my father made periodic, somewhat subtle checks of his watch. Between sips of O'Doul's, he stole anxious looks at the front door, anticipating the reappearance of his brother, who had disappeared nearly two hours before with car keys in hand and an armload of beer. As she exhausted her venom, Aunt Doris deflated like a hot air balloon and collapsed into a chair at the dining room table. Unsure of how to offer any comfort, my mother did what mothers everywhere would do; she delivered a bowl of banana pudding and a cup of decaf to my aunt.

An eerie quiet settled over the room and the sound of Aunt Doris sipping coffee was magnified. Across the living room, my father removed his cell phone from his shirt pocket and gave me a not-so-furtive signal indicating he was stepping away to make a call. He went to the hallway bathroom. After a minute, he flushed the toilet but didn't come out. Eamon McLeish, master of espionage. I imagined him crouched in the bathtub with the beige seashell shower curtain pulled shut for added camouflage, and a towel draped over his head to muffle the sound of his surreptitious whispers to my uncle.

My visualization of the secret cell phone mission was interrupted by the faint sound of music. The volume was low, but there was the unmistakable twang of country music. Will and my mother heard it too. We exchanged confused glances as the music abruptly stopped. Within seconds, the music started again, and my mother and I searched the kitchen, attempting to discern changes in volume as we opened cabinets and drawers. Again, the music stopped.

"What in the devil?" my mother asked.

As suddenly as it had stopped, the music started once more. Same melody and, as far as I could tell, the same song. We wandered into the living room. As we approached the sliding glass doors, the woeful lament of the steel guitar grew louder.

"That's Carrie Underwood!" my mother shouted as if we were game show contestants.

"*Jesus Take the Wheel!*" Uncle Henry said, jumping in just before the buzzer.

"Martin!" Aunt Doris exclaimed.

What the fuck!

I slid open the glass door and, in the glow of the moonlight, saw Uncle Martin's silhouette slumped in an Adirondack chair at the far end of the deck. His cell phone blasted the Carrie Underwood ringtone and lit up in his shirt pocket, a drunken E.T. with a Nashville soundtrack. Before he had passed out, he had dragged the chair to a dark corner of the deck and faced it toward the house, allowing him to remain unseen while he peered inside and assessed the damage.

With my mother and Aunt Doris trailing, I approached and asked if he was okay. He tilted his head up though his eyes remain closed. He said my name and returned to his intoxicated slumber. The cell phone quieted, and a moment later, my father strolled onto the deck. *Nice work, James Bond, looks like you got your man.*

I wedged myself under one of Uncle Martin's arms and my father slid under the other. We lifted him to his feet and carried him across the deck and through the open sliding glass door. I wondered if the scene felt all too familiar for Will, who more than once had lugged me inside from our patio and tossed me on our sofa.

Uncle Martin slowly began the climb from stupor to cognizance, and as inebriated people do, he told us how much he loved us all and then waxed poetic about the majesty of the starry night sky. He had finished at least a half dozen beers in about ninety minutes, and while he was more practiced as a drinker than my family realized, he was far beyond his normal limits. The formation of coherent sentences was a hopeful sign, but his words were badly slurred and I expected his lucidity to be shallow and short-lived.

Aunt Doris hadn't spoken since we discovered her husband passed out on the patio furniture. She busied herself in the kitchen, brewing a full pot of regular coffee and then bringing a steaming hot mug to Uncle Martin, along with a damp kitchen towel for his forehead. For the next half hour, we pretended nothing had happened while my uncle regained his focus and his wife mopped his brow and refilled his coffee cup.

A series of contagious yawns broke out across the room and I checked my watch. It was after eleven o'clock. I hadn't had much time to reconsider my own plans for the night, though I had glanced out at the gulf enough times to see that the swells had calmed. I was thinking about how the cool summer rain had likely dropped the water temperature, when Aunt Doris finally broke her long silence.

"How are you feeling, Martin?" she asked, sounding sincere though not overly concerned.

He sat slumped, shoulders sagging, but his gaze was focused on her face, showing an alertness that had been missing an hour before. "I'm okay," he said. "Doing better, I think."

"Good," she said, "because we aren't done." The room was vacuum sealed, every molecule of air sucked out, as it became clear that she had only sobered him up to finish him off.

FORTY-THREE

SALTY TEARS TRICKLED down the rough terrain of Uncle Martin's stubbly face as he prepared to face his demons. The scant emotional will he had initially barricaded himself behind had been washed away by a half dozen bottles of beer and the sinking recognition of the consequences he faced. His frail, deflated form sank into the soft pastel-striped sofa. He was fragile, in no state to handle additional interrogation, but Aunt Doris had yet to hear the answers she needed, and, I supposed to some extent, the answers she deserved.

"I don't want to fight, Martin. We don't have to draw this out." Her calm and reasoned approach netted nothing from him, which lit a short, angry fuse in her. She raised her voice and announced her demands. "I need to know two things—what's her name and how long has this been going on." I was astounded by her ability go to from broken to blaming to rage and back, with blazing speed and effortless fluidity.

I had lost track of the damning evidence of my uncle's unfaithfulness until I saw the purple panties clutched in Aunt Doris's liver-spotted hand. She kneaded and wrung them between her fingers, as though she might squeeze them out of existence.

"You listen to me, Martin McLeish. I won't sit here and beg you to name your whore."

Like a tiger, she bounded from her seat and was on him in a few quick strides. She thrust the underwear in his face and rubbed them into his tear-stained cheeks. "Dry your eyes with these, you pathetic son-of-a-bitch."

He knocked her hand away, sending the panties flying across the room and onto the shade of a table lamp. He righted himself on the sofa and sat rigid and tall, as if he had spontaneously regenerated a spine. His lips disappeared as his face tightened, and his soft brown eyes grew wide.

"You want to know who my whore is, Doris?" He forced the words out through clenched teeth, as though his brain was battling his mouth to suppress the words. "You have to know." His voice trembled. "And it has to be right here, right now?"

Just as the gulf tides ebb, leaving behind a trail of broken shells and stranded starfish, the glint of indignation in his eyes receded and left behind only sadness. The tension in his face softened, replaced by sorrow. His last stand had failed and surrender was his only option.

"There is no Jezebel. I'm the whore." He crumbled into a defeated, heaving mass.

"I don't even know what that means," Aunt Doris said as though she were addressing a petulant child with whom she had finally gained the upper hand.

My uncle's unimaginable fuck-up had been the cause of this shit-storm, but I could no longer sit back and watch as she leeched the last drops of his self-respect.

"Uncle Martin, don't do this now." I placed my hand on his shoulder and squeezed; an inadequate gesture, but under the circumstances, it was all I had. "Aunt Doris, these are private things between the two of you, and no matter how much you want to flog Uncle Martin publicly, you can't keep doing it. Not here."

"No," Uncle Martin said with a sniffle. "It's okay." He patted my hand, which remained on his shoulder. "I need to get this off my chest."

"At least let us give you some privacy," I said.

He stared at the carpet and shook his head. After a minute, he stiffened and looked at each of us, meeting the befuddled gaze of Aunt Doris last. "There is no other woman." He took a deep breath and dragged his shirt sleeve across his wet face to mop the stream of tears and snot. "Henry, you were right." He tilted his head toward the purple panties that were still draped across the lampshade. "Those are bikini-style. And Will, you were wrong. The color is lavender, not lilac."

Aunt Doris sat quiet and slack-jawed. Her husband met her gaze. "Doris, you were wrong too. There's no one else. Only me and a secret I've carried a long time."

And then he came out to us. Sort of. Uncle Martin had no active or even latent homosexual tendencies. In fact, he assured us he had always been interested only in women. Women, and their clothes. As a child, he recalled, he adored Sundays, partly because this was the day his mother and sisters broke out their finest dresses and shoes to attend church, but equally so, because this was laundry day in the McLeish household, the day each week when young Martin volunteered to help his mother with the burdensome work of folding and putting away the family's clothes. And as he grew, so too did his love of women's clothing. In adolescence, he explained, he began to indulge his secret fetish for dressing in women's garments. As a part of this compulsion, he developed a particular fondness for wearing lingerie.

In his twenties and thirties, Uncle Martin tried several times to suppress his love of women's apparel, but to no avail. Through furtive purchases and the occasional pilferage, acts of which he was doubly ashamed, he would amass an impressive assortment of dresses, slacks, blouses, and lingerie. Guilt and shame would eventually overrun him, though, and he would purge the entire collection. After a few months, his unstoppable urges would return, and he would buy and steal again, perpetuating the endless cycle of secretly acquiring and discarding.

As he matured, he learned to accept his delight in the feel of velvety fabrics against his skin. With the advent of the Internet, he met other men, some of them married and some devoutly Christian like him, who shared his love of women's clothing, and he befriended them. These men gave him support, a depth of understanding that only kindred and similarly tortured souls can provide. Compassion and friendship, he assured us, was all he shared with them. Of course, he met his share of perverted sexual fetishists along the way, but he weeded through them and cast them aside. Now, in his sixties, he sometimes enjoyed the company of a small, trustworthy group of respectable cross-dressing friends, and yes, they got together from time to time to enjoy a beer and model their newest acquisitions, but there was never anything sexual. Ever.

We listened to my uncle's story with rapt attention as though he were explaining how aliens had kidnapped and probed him. He eventually worked his way to our current situation, to a recent shopping excursion to Victoria's Secret, to last Saturday morning when he had spied an irresistible pair of lavender bikini-style panties on a window mannequin. He told us how, on that same day he'd been called in to work, he had left the mall and driven to the UPS warehouse, where he had thrown the Victoria's Secret bag and its accompanying cash-paid receipt into a large green dumpster, just after he stuffed the purple panties in the minivan glove box for safe and secret keeping.

For a while, Aunt Doris listened without interruption, but if Uncle Martin's cross-dressing revelation had paralyzed her, the effect was short-lived. By the end of his story, her normal ghostly pallor had been replaced with a shade of red so deep it approached purple, a color Victoria's Secret might call Scarlett or Ruby Wine. Her wrinkled hands trembled.

"After all these years of marriage..." She wound up but then lost her way. Her mouth hung open as she gasped for words and phrases.

Determined to force-feed my uncle her special shit sandwich, a recipe comprised of anger and blame served between hefty slices of Christian guilt, she gathered herself. "All these years I worked to make our home some place special, buying nice things for us, keeping house and doing your dirty dishes, all the holidays we spent with your godforsaken family..." Her voice quieted before returning in its full, screeching glory. "What about our sacred vows, Martin? Is this your idea of love, honor, and cherish?"

"No. I don't do the things I do—"

"Good Lord Jesus Christ in heaven. What about all the Sundays we spent worshipping together? And the marriage counseling? Was it all for show?"

"Of course not," he said, gaining strength as her meltdown escalated.

"Our marriage was a joke to you."

"This isn't about us, Doris. It's about me."

"No wonder you never wanted children!" she shouted. "And you choose *now* to announce you're some kind of pervert? You tell me here, in the company of these...homosexuals!"

He inhaled deeply, filling his lungs to capacity and holding the air inside until a burst of breath exploded. "Actually, Doris, you decided that *here* is the place and *now* is the time." He had built a head of steam, and her attack on Will and me was the valve she twisted to release it. "You say what you want about me but leave them out of it."

He glanced at me, offering a silent apology for the last thirty years of his wife's behavior before he continued. "These boys are just two people in love, Doris. Are you too goddamn blind to see that? This isn't Satan's work. It's just love. Plain and simple love."

She took a step back, blindsided by his attack, which wasn't over yet.

"For what it's worth, you should pay attention to what they have. You might learn a thing or two." Earlier in the week I was glad my aunt and uncle still thought Will and I were a couple, but hearing his words now saddened me. Will and I clearly still looked so naturally right together.

Judging from the authoritative smackdown he delivered, outing himself had empowered my uncle. *Welcome to the world outside the closet, Uncle*

Martin. Granted, as a heterosexual cross-dresser, he and I didn't share the same closet, but we were only one or two doors apart.

Being chastised by her husband was foreign terrain to Aunt Doris, and the harshness of his words must have stung. She felt for the sofa behind her and lowered herself onto it. Seeing her mute and helpless in the face of his condemnation was a role reversal I hadn't expected. For the second time that night, I felt sorry for her.

Uncle Martin stared at his drained and withered wife. Equally unfamiliar in the territory, he seemed to recognize that his newfound zest for the truth had crossed the line into meanness. "What I am saying, Doris, is regardless of how you feel about me and my...lifestyle, or whatever the hell people call it, you ought to at least see that what Conor and Will have is love."

She pursed her lips, looking at me but addressing him. "Do you honestly think I haven't spent years trying to figure out how to accept that?" She attempted a smile, the strained, dissatisfied look of the Oscar favorite who didn't win.

I made a half-hearted effort to return the favor.

"Every day," she said, "every single day since Patrick...passed...I've thought about it, read about it, prayed over it. And I just don't understand it. I loved that boy with all my heart, but I believe what he and Conor did is an abomination before God."

The seemingly out-of-the-blue mention of my long-dead cousin left my parents and Uncle Henry thoroughly confused, which is how it would stay.

Aunt Doris wiped tears from her eyes as she straightened her blouse and stood to leave. "I will say this for these two, though..." She paused and looked at my uncle. "At least they have the balls not to lie about who they are."

FORTY-FOUR

I ANTICIPATED A drywall-loosening door slam when Aunt Doris retreated to the shame-filled privacy of her bedroom, but her exit was the least dramatic act of the evening. Her parting shot at Uncle Martin, delivered with a sniper's accuracy, had taken the last of her ammunition.

He sat shell-shocked on the sofa while the elder members of my family, unsettled by the cadence of the night's events, grappled with their conflicted emotions in the way McLeishes had been taught for generations—total avoidance. After a few comments about the lateness of the hour, they stood one by one, stretched and yawned with exaggeration, and excused themselves to their respective bedrooms. My father, in a show of unconditional solidarity and support, offered Uncle Martin an awkward handshake. "That banana pudding was something else," he said. Interacting with a newly outed heterosexual cross-dresser, who also happened to be his sixty-three-year-old brother, simply wasn't in his wheelhouse.

The living room cleared out and Will and I were left alone with Uncle Martin. I headed to the refrigerator to grab a Blue Moon, but poured myself the last O'Doul's instead. I offered beers to Will and Uncle Martin, but both declined.

"Drinking has gotten me in enough trouble," said Uncle Martin.

Will shook his head. "Those beers didn't make you who you are. They just made it a little easier for you to talk about it."

"All the same," my uncle replied. He spoke in a quiet whisper as if the real damage hadn't already been done. "None of this would have happened if I hadn't gone off and gotten looped. I should have left the house *without* the beers and gone home. I would've figured out something a helluva lot smarter than blurting out the truth in front of God and everybody."

"Uncle Martin, there was nothing you said tonight that God didn't already know."

I sat on the sofa next to Will, whose eyes remained focused and bright as he leaned toward my uncle. "Martin, tonight you revealed things that hurt Doris and made you feel ashamed. But you also did one of the bravest things any of us ever has to do—you told the truth about yourself. If you needed a boost from a few beers to make it happen, so be it."

My uncle closed his eyes and rubbed the side of his neck. "I appreciate what you're saying, but I made a mess of things and I don't know how to clean it up. I've kept this secret my whole life, and today I got careless. I let one pair of panties and a handful of beers ruin me. I don't expect you to understand, but I love Doris. She's...rough around the edges...but she's full of good intentions. It kills me that I hurt her."

"Uncle Martin," I said, "she's sat in judgment of me for twenty-five years. She did the same thing to Patrick." Will kicked my foot. "It's fucking karma," I added, undeterred.

"Let's not talk about Patrick," my uncle said.

"Was that your approach twenty-five years ago?" The question came out of nowhere, a quick, pointed stab. I wanted to regret asking it, but I didn't. If this week was about tying up loose ends, this one had to be addressed.

"That's not fair, son. You don't know everything about us."

"I know how well everything turned out."

"Aunt Doris ain't a perfect person and neither am I. I made big goddamn mistakes and none of them haunt me more than that one."

My uncle's face was gaunt, lined with pain, but the words rose in anger from the burning rage inside me. "Why didn't you do something!"

The world blurred and turned gray around me, until only the sight of my uncle's worn and ashen face remained. Noise and sound disappeared. The crash of the surf and the faraway hum of a television in my parent's bedroom, something Will said—all of it faded into a single, high-pitched tone. My heart pounded and my temples throbbed. I stopped breathing. *Is this what it will be like?*

His eyes were wet and his hands shook.

"Why didn't you do something?"

"I couldn't," he said.

"Did you even try to save him?" My voice was lower, calmer, as if the mere act of accusation somehow lowered the swell of heat inside me.

"I didn't know how."

"Well, it was your fucking job to figure it out."

"I'm so sorry."

Will rested his hand on my back, and the power of his touch pulled me slowly back from the edge. I had arranged this charade to find absolution and to be delivered from the past, not to relive it.

"We've all fucked up, Uncle Martin. And we've all paid for it." I was somber and sincere. I remembered the wistful look on my uncle's face the night before, when he peeked in on Will and me piled together like newborn puppies in a cardboard box. He had seen a vibrant picture of love, but he didn't know that love was a lie, an echo in an empty room.

We all pay for our mistakes.

"The idea of losing her now..." Uncle Martin's body went limp and he sank deep into the upholstered chair. In his moment of coming out, he had been emboldened by the remarkable power of truth. I remembered the deep sense of satisfaction, the inspired joy I once felt, when I read about some gay kid who learned to accept himself, who opened himself up to a fuller life than he ever believed possible. But Uncle Martin was not a boy; he was not some just-sprung-from-the-closet queer finally coming to the electrifying realization that his life really could get better. Uncle Martin was a grown man with an adult life he had constructed in the only way he could imagine it. He had segregated the disparate elements of his happiness, stashed them in different rooms in different buildings on different streets: a home, a church, a rented five-by-ten storage space, different dimensions that were allowed to coexist so long as they remained blissfully ignorant of each other. He had a career, friends, a relationship with the God he believed in, and a wife he cared about. He had everything to lose. Still, there's immeasurable value in being true to yourself, even if your defining moment comes late in life, and at great cost, even if your life is the final price you pay for your honesty.

"Uncle Martin, I know how fucked up this is for you." Noble sentiments seldom translate into gracious words. "You must be panicked about people finding out, what they'll say, but I have to believe you did the right thing."

There are excruciatingly raw moments in life when there is little anyone can say that is helpful. I put my hand on my uncle's arm, finding myself in the unusual role of comforter. "What I am saying is Will and I..." The sincerity of the sentiment hit me hard, and I choked up as I finished the thought. "We're proud of you."

"Thank you." He attempted to sound cheerful but failed miserably. "You boys have done enough. Get to bed, and I'm going to head out." He stood to leave.

"We have this comfy sofa," Will said. "And I'm sure we can find some sheets."

"I'm not sure Doris will be ready to see me in the morning, and honestly, I'm not sure I'm ready to see her—or anyone else."

Will raced to the hall closet and returned with a set of pale orange sheets and a floral print bedspread. "We have everything you need right here."

"I'll tell you what," Uncle Martin said, "I'm not in the best shape for a long drive, but I won't stay inside." He took the bedspread from Will and headed for the moonlit deck. He glanced over his shoulder as he slid the glass door open. "A little more time staring up at the stars might do me good."

THE HOUSE WAS quiet. I sat alone at the kitchen island as filtered moonlight illuminated the legal pad in front of me. I tapped the pen on the haunting blank page. There was so much I could say, but none of it seemed to matter. I had wandered pathetic and drunk into those midnight river swims, but this time I was sober, alert, and aware. I had planned this week, this moment, and though the train had rocketed off the rails earlier in the evening, I was ready to see it through. Still, no words came. I chuckled at the irony of a so-called writer struggling to pen a suicide note, at how the absence of profundity was somehow fitting, that I'd wracked my brain and couldn't come up with a single juicy morsel worth sharing.

I scribbled a single word on the page—*surrender*. It was an idea whose beauty they could all relate to. They had surrendered—to Jesus, to Jameson, to the featherlight touch of satin on skin. The letting go, the giving in, the sweet, soothing relief that comes with surrender was something they'd understand, something to help them make sense of the choice I had made.

I scratched the word out with a disgusted vengeance and started again. Life was two steps forward and one step back, unless, as June had once said, it was one step forward and two steps back. I had barely finished scrawling the sentiment when I balled up the paper and tossed it into the kitchen trash.

Before I began a third time, I spied Uncle Henry's red Igloo cooler out of the corner of my eye. I opened the lid and fished out a chilled Miller Genuine Draft from the icy pool. I popped the top and tilted the beer to my lips, swallowing a cold, refreshing mouthful. I wrote a single sentence and poured the rest of the beer down the drain.

I could never stop sinking.
—Love Conor

A THICK PILLOW of gray clouds shrouded the moon, but in the dim light that escaped the silvery edges, I saw the dark, rolling waters of the gulf. The air was heavy and the surf was calm. The modest midnight swells barely curled and broke before sacrificing themselves on the shore.

I walked through the sugary sand to the water's edge, where I stood as still and solid as a statue. I closed my eyes and drank in long, slow breaths of salty ocean air. My heartbeat disappeared and my mind grew as calm and quiet as the night sky. I waded into the surf, and in the warm water that lapped at my ankles, I felt the last vestiges of the sinking sun that had dipped below the horizon hours before. I stepped out of my shorts and stripped off my shirt. As I turned to toss my clothes onto the beach, the faint glow of distant house lights twinkled through the weary prism of my tears.

I eased in and swam through the blackness toward the invisible horizon, never looking back to see my life fade in the distance. I took no notice of the expanse of ocean that grew between me and everything that ever mattered. In truth, the people I loved the most had slipped from my grasp long ago. They had floated near me for years, letting my current bring them closer and then push them further away, but eventually, they lurched out of my life to save themselves. They were innocent bystanders treading water. I was a drowning man, desperate and clawing.

I don't know how long I swam before I stopped to take in my surroundings. The moon and stars shone brighter now, glimmering on the peaks of the gentle waves that lifted and lowered me. I had no idea how many feet separated me from the sandy bottom below, nor did I know how deep it needed to be.

I floated on the glassy surface, bobbing in the comforting endlessness of the rolling sea, and staring up at the night sky, where the cold glimmer of a few ancient stars penetrated the streaky clouds that remained. Starlight, a cruel fucking trick of nature. Imagine making an infinite journey across an eternal cosmos, only to find out upon reaching your destiny—you're already dead.

I offered little resistance and drifted where the tide took me. Still, my arms grew tired and a slow ache spread from my shoulders to the rest of my body. Random images fluttered through my consciousness, darting in and out, disappearing like the tiny silver fish in the murky depths below. Uncle Martin, wide awake on the deck, hoping for absolution or begging for relief, marveling at the same dead stars that hovered above me now, only he believed they might still hold answers. Aunt Doris kneeling beside her bed, praying to God for solace and understanding. Will tossing and turning, fitful and alone, his arm coming to rest on the cold pillow where my head should be. June, slowly dying.

I flapped my arms and kicked my feet beneath the water, thrusting my shoulders high. I craned my neck and saw darkness in every direction. Everything and nothing, not so different. The cool water lapped at my chin and filled my ears. I gulped one last breath, lifting me higher in the water so my head bobbed just above the surface. Will's voice floated on the breeze, whispering June's name, calling out to me, as I exhaled and let the sea swallow me.

I forced bursts of breath out of my lungs, sending my body on a slow, swirling descent to the bottom of the sea. I extended my arms and legs, gliding and twirling through the depths like a dancer. I floated free, letting the water embrace and envelop me, its velvety softness caressing every inch of my flesh. I sank into the noiseless calm, the vacuum of space, the lonesome safety of my mother's womb, where I was unaware and unburdened. In the open arms of the sea, I was warm, alive, and unafraid, just as I had come into the world, before I'd made such a fucking mess of it all. When my feet nestled into the soft, spongy bottom I looked to the surface, and, as the Gulf of Mexico filled my mouth and throat and lungs, the black, watery sky disappeared.

FORTY-FIVE

BAYVIEW MEMORIAL WAS the eternal home to two previous generations of Jameson-soaked McLeish corpses, but the place was hardly old by graveyard standards. The cemetery was located on a winding stretch of two-lane road, unimaginatively named Scenic Highway, which ran along steep bluffs that overlooked the crystal blue waters of Escambia Bay. Clusters of mammoth oak trees draped with long strands of gray-green moss lined the road, and in the short stretches between them, the wide-open highway afforded spectacular views. I want to be cremated in a giant Burning Man funeral pyre so I won't need a permanent in-ground resting place, but if I had to be buried, Bayview was as good a place as any for my bones to rot.

Years ago, my parents bought four plots at Bayview, two of which will keep them together once they're dead, and a couple of extras to use in the event of unforeseen family tragedies. Like June.

I tried to convince my mother that, like me, June would prefer cremation, but she feared one day walking through the pearly gates and being greeted by an angelic but chargrilled version of my grandmother. I reminded her how ungodly that would be, but she refused to budge and insisted on holding June's interment at Bayview. I fared better with my request to forego a religious ceremony, particularly one officiated by a Catholic priest as my father would have had it. My grandmother was a free spirit, a woman who couldn't be pigeonholed into a religious sect, or any other societal circle for that matter. Convincing my mother to accept Ms. Broussard's suggestion that her pastor, the Right Reverend Arthur Franklin, lead a brief non-denominational ceremony was easier than I had anticipated. Coming from anyone else, I would have rejected outright the recommendation of a Southern Baptist preacher presiding over June's funeral service, but Ms. Broussard understood what June would want as well as anyone. Ms. Broussard had grown to love my grandmother, and I trusted she and her pastor would respect June's beliefs, or the lack thereof, even when she was no longer around to express them.

THERE WAS NO funeral home wake filled with weepy mourners, nor a winding cross-town procession reminding bystanders to appreciate the finite nature of life. The entire ceremony, short and simple as June would have wanted it, was conducted at Bayview with only a small gathering in attendance at the graveside. When Will and I arrived fifteen minutes before the scheduled start time, a shiny black hearse was already parked a few yards away from the intimate crowd huddled around June's grave. A pristine silver-gray coffin, my grandmother's tiny home for the rest of eternity, hovered above the rectangular hole in the ground that would soon swallow it whole. The casket was adorned with a breathtaking spray of pure white lilies draped neatly from end to end.

With no surviving family on my mother's side, the throng of funeral guests consisted mostly of my father's family and close friends of my parents, many of whom barely knew June. I saw the unfamiliar faces of a few old men, who I determined were long-time friends of my father. The elderly do that; they attend each other's family funerals, regardless of whether they knew the deceased, in order to pay respects or reminisce, or maybe just to pump up the attendance numbers. Anyway, funerals need old people. No one appreciates a celebration of life like the nearly dead.

Nearest to the casket at the top of the circle of people, three black visages stood out in the assembly of pale Irish faces. Minister Franklin stood tall and straight. He wore an immaculate black suit, coordinated with a perfectly pressed black pinstriped shirt and a deep purple tie. With his Bible in hand, he greeted approaching guests with an appropriately tight-lipped smile and nod. Ms. Broussard and her son Cedric had positioned themselves arm-in-arm next to the minister. The old nurse, though puffy-eyed and slumped, looked elegant, clad in a knee-length black dress, and sporting a black satin hat with a short lace veil across the front.

Uncle Henry was flanked by his son Daniel. That my uncle did not typically attend formal occasions was apparent, as the dark blue blazer he wore failed to match his pants or his current stature. I was certain the necktie he wore was the same one he had worn to his wife's funeral more than twenty years before, quite possibly the last time he'd worn a tie at all.

As Will and I waded through the gathering of mourners, my wandering glance froze on the opposite side of the circle, where I spied the unmistakable sight of Ariel's fire-red hair. Beneath her impeccably piled flaming tresses, she wore a fitted charcoal gray jacket that buttoned to the neck, and a matching skirt that fell just below her knees. Her gray suede heels, though not ideal for long cemetery walks, boasted a tiny silver decorative buckle. David stood next to her, dressed in a dark suit, a white Oxford shirt, and pencil thin black tie. The pair looked like they just walked out of a sixties era law office.

WHILE I WAS swimming in vain to the bottom of the Gulf, June suffered a second massive stroke. From the moment Will dragged me out of the sea and told me the news, the world was a blur, muddled and distorted as though I still saw it from under water. I'd given no clear thought to the eulogy my mother had asked me to give, deciding instead to let my heart do the talking. Will had said that's what June would want and I knew he was right.

At one o'clock, the Reverend Franklin approached my parents and offered his condolences. They traded casual comments about the splendor of the spray of lilies and then decided to delay the ceremony a few minutes to allow for stragglers who might still be finding their way across the cemetery. With a sunny forecast, there was no need for the telltale forest green tent that sometimes accompanied graveside services, but the absence of such a cover made it more difficult for guests to eyeball the funeral from across the expansive grounds.

As we waited, my anxiety over the eulogy mounted.

"I'm nervous as fuck," I said to Will. "This would be so much easier if I were the one in the casket."

"You think?" He patted my chest reassuringly, recoiling when he felt the flask in my inside coat pocket. "Is that what I think it is?"

"I've only had a couple of sips," I said, telling the truth. "I'm still quitting, just not today."

He put his arm around me, pulling me close and squeezing my shoulder.

"Did you know Ariel and David were coming?" I whispered, hoping idle gossip might facilitate a change in subject.

"Yes. Did you see who's standing next to them?"

I had been so distracted by Ariel and David's fetching attire that I hadn't noticed Aunt Doris and Uncle Martin standing next to them. Judging by the drape of my uncle's arm around my aunt's shoulders, the pair was in attendance together.

"I figured they'd be here," I said. "Although, I didn't think they'd show up together."

"They look chummy," Will whispered.

"Just keeping up appearances," I speculated. "He didn't stand that close to her, even before his panties nuked their marriage." As if on cue, my uncle leaned in and planted a soft kiss on Aunt Doris's cheek.

Will nudged me. "If that's keeping up appearances, they're selling it hard."

"Un-fucking-believable." I had unintentionally used my outside voice, drawing a stare from my nearby parents.

"Calm down," Will said. "It was just a peck."

"Not the kiss. The pocket square."

Will looked casually around the gathering before zeroing in on my uncle.

"Does it look familiar?" I asked. "That shiny lilac—no, lavender fabric?"

Our eyes locked on the bright shock of purple, folded and stuffed, or maybe even sewn, into the breast pocket of my uncle's suit. I followed the lapel of the sports coat up to his face, but my uncle's gaze was directed toward the Right Reverend Franklin, who was about to begin the proceedings.

I glanced at Will's face, expecting to find his unhinged jaw hanging down to his chest, when I felt someone was leering at me. I surveyed the crowd beyond the swath of lilies atop June's coffin until my eyes met the soft gaze of Aunt Doris. She raised the corners of her mouth, morphing her flat, somber face into what I recognized as a grimace of consolation. With the subtlest of winks, she turned to my uncle, brushed off the lapels of his jacket, and straightened the shiny purple pocket square.

THE REVEREND FRANKLIN began my grandmother's funeral ceremony with a short segment from a nineteenth century hymn.

When peace, like a river, attendeth my way,
When sorrows like sea billows roll;
Whatever my lot, Thou has taught me to say,
It is well, it is well, with my soul.

He delivered an inspired oration, quoting Dickinson and Thoreau, and working in Bible verses he'd thoughtfully selected to invoke reverie, without clichéd mentions of "welcoming angels" or "pearly gates." He referenced my grandmother's strength before the stroke and her courage afterwards. He chuckled about her eccentricities as if he knew her. Ms. Broussard had prepared the pastor well for the ceremony, and the payoff was an effortless walk along the tightrope between spiritual and religious, and a graceful tiptoeing of the fine line between mourning and celebration. The reverend's elocution was so engaging that I was caught by surprise when he called on me to add a few final words about June. With nothing prepared, for the first time in my life I stepped forward and let go.

"A FEW DAYS ago, at this beach house we rented, I sat outside with June and Ms. Broussard and watched a sunset. At the time, I didn't know how special that night would be." I paused to swallow the lump that had formed in my throat and gave a purposeful nod to Will.

"You all know how...opinionated or feisty or whatever...you know how June was before her stroke. And how devastated and destroyed she was afterward. A shell of her old self. Well, I wish you could have seen her that night at the beach. Jesus, she was awake and alive, just as ornery and honest as ever."

I focused my gaze safely downward, looking at manicured grass and shiny shoes, and the deep, rectangular hole in the ground beneath June's coffin.

"Just when we got used to that empty shell, she came back to us. Moving and talking and even smiling a little. Toward the end, she made a strong comeback, you know?"

I summoned the strength to look up and saw Ms. Broussard, smiling broadly. I took another gulp of air to gather myself, but then made the mistake of looking at my mother as she wiped her tear-stained face and mopped faint black streaks of eyeliner with my father's handkerchief.

"Ms. Broussard told me a few months back that none of us knows when the Lord is going to call us. I don't know about all that..." I squinted and squeezed my eyes shut.

"My grandmother didn't suffer fools; she was more inclined to avoid them. As you can imagine, in our family that means she spent plenty of time alone." Heads nodded and laughter rippled through the crowd.

"I'm grateful for everything I learned from June. When I was a boy, she taught me to respect those who were different. As I grew into a man, she taught me to respect myself. Even in the last year, June was still teaching me."

I fidgeted and kicked at the ground as I struggled to organize the swirl of emotions and words inside my head. I raised my head and saw the faces of family and friends and strangers.

"I don't know how it is for everybody else, but I've spent most of my life looking for security, trying to feel stable. And you know what the fuck of it is..."

Oops. I mouthed the word *sorry* to my mother.

"The crazy thing is I thought I was actually getting closer to finding it earlier this year. I thought I found one small patch of solid ground to stand on, but then I fucked up. I fucked up something awful, and everything shifted, again. And now, June's gone, and I'm still learning. There is no solid ground, not even the ground they bury you in."

Eyes were drying and I had run out of things to say.

"I was somehow hoping June's funeral could be a celebration, a joyful remembrance of the best of times. But most of you know me well enough to know that's not my strong suit. Anyway, those good memories will come flooding back when we least expect them, and I'm sure we'll all be laughing then."

I inhaled deeply, savoring the taste of the faintly salty air carried by a westerly breeze from nearby Escambia Bay.

"If June were here now, she'd say something like, '*Jesus Christ, Conor. Wrap this thing up. It's a eulogy not a novel.*' As usual, she'd be right."

Reverend Franklin stepped forward as though we'd rehearsed the transition. He thanked those in attendance, and then, to my surprise, he closed the ceremony with this.

You are a child of the universe,
no less than the trees and the stars;
you have a right to be here.
And whether or not it is clear to you,

no doubt the universe is unfolding as it should.

Therefore be at peace with God,
whatever you conceive Him to be,
and whatever your labors and aspirations,
in the noisy confusion of life keep peace with your soul.
With all its sham, drudgery, and broken dreams,
it is still a beautiful world.

The depth and strength of his voice rang each word in the poem like a bell, and for a moment, I believed him. Despite its sham, drudgery, and broken dreams, it was a beautiful world after all.

FORTY-SIX

A FEW MOURNERS lingered at the graveside. My gaze narrowed to a select few. My mother's tears had run through her makeup, leaving faint tracks on her cheeks as shallow and dry as a riverbed. She looked old and sweet and frail, not like a woman who once pawned her own kid. My father, with his hand looped firm and supportive around my mother's waist, hardly looked like a selfish drunk who'd nearly killed his family in a house fire. June's fierce independence and go-fuck-yourself attitude, which were once so readily on display, were trapped inside the sealed silver coffin, as invisible as the hole in Uncle Henry's heart.

My eyes fell eventually on Aunt Doris. She was a woman in recovery, advancing through the stages of her own personal grief. She'd been force-fed the same devastating medicine she'd given to Patrick. To my surprise, it was Uncle Martin who administered it, leaving me holding the worthless handful of bitter pills I had once hoped to make her swallow.

As we stood close, leaning on each other for support, even Will and I weren't what we appeared to be, unless you thought we looked like two people who had fallen out of love.

Nothing was ever what it seemed, not for long anyway, and events are no more predictable than people. I had lugged the emotional baggage of my childhood to a rented beach house in hopes of leaving it there forever, but my uncle's desire to clothe himself in women's underwear robbed me of the chance. It's strange, the way things turn.

Still, things have changed since that December night when I first begged the universe to drag me under water and deliver my cold and lonely death. I can't say I repaired even a single loose end, but all of it became a little less poisonous to me, which is worth something. I am older now, no longer a damaged child. A better man than I was a year ago, but still broken.

AFTER A FEW minutes of requisite mingling and sharing of sympathies, my parents rushed home to heat the ham and assorted casseroles we'd arranged for the post-funeral partygoers. Will and I stayed on to hug and kiss the few remaining stone-faced friends who had yet to offer their condolences. Ms. Broussard had drifted into the background, but as the crowd thinned, she made her way forward. I commended the nurse for her perfect preparation of the pastor, and then we held each other for a long moment. I savored the embrace and hoped it wouldn't be our last.

As the last car pulled away down the dusty cemetery road, I leaned on Will and stared up at the powder blue sky.

"Thanks for being so sweet," I said. "You don't have to keep up the charade."

"Too bad. We were just getting good at pretending we still belong together."

"We could fake it a while longer." I reached out to him.

He interlocked his fingers with mine. "For old time's sake."

"Let's walk across the highway to the bluffs," I said.

"Are we going to jump?"

"Nah. I'm not in the mood."

We approached the silvery coffin one last time, and Will reached into his pocket and fished out a small yellow object. He nestled the Big Bird king among the pure white lilies and squeezed my hand.

ACKNOWLEDGEMENTS

Being a writer is like all the other jobs I've ever had, except, of course, for the long stretches of utter isolation, the endless toiling over unimaginable minutiae, and the fact that you work for free for the first ten or fifteen years. Oh, and there's the soul-crushing self-doubt. What I mean to say is that writing a novel isn't the kind of thing most of us can do on our own.

I'm grateful to Raevyn McCann at NineStar Press for helping me launch my fiction writing career, and to my editor, Elizabeth Coldwell, for believing in this novel and working with me to make the book better (and Merriam-Webster compliant!).

I also want to thank the many people who read early drafts of the manuscript and shared their perspectives and expertise. I'm grateful to Connie Brown for the insights she shared with me (very) early in the process, and I can't thank enough my friend and mentor, Jeff Galipeaux, for his incredibly valuable story guidance. I'm a better writer today because of the detailed (and entertaining) feedback I received from Joan Reginaldo. Shout out to my friends in both the Black Hats and Seaside Writing groups, as well. This novel would not exist as it does, or maybe at all, if not for the encouragement and support of Kyle Sheridan—multiple manuscript edits, countless weekend mornings thinking out loud together, and meatball sandwiches every Friday night—all the while, expecting nothing in return. Thank you, Kyle.

I'm grateful to the many friends I've had over the years who have listened to me ramble about writing, and who encouraged or distracted me, as required at the moment. Thank you, Kevin Mosher, Jolynda Sandon, Lex Poppens, Jane Regenstreif, Jen Huss, Beth Peery, and Doug Gonterman. Thanks also to Hope Tadema and to Dr. Carrie Forrest for your caring and flexibility. I'm grateful to the Starbucks crew at Laurel and Arroyo (San Carlos, CA) for letting me stay all afternoon and evening until it was time to put the chairs up, and to my gigantic extended work families at both Borders and Barnes & Noble, thank you—we had one helluva ride.

To my partner, Paul Gagne—who has kept me in brandy, Apple Jacks, and Dr. Scholl's foot spray for the last decade, and who has never once complained about my artistic insecurity, my mood swings, or the hours I spent in the writing room. I know his introversion led him to secretly relish those quiet moments, but he always made me feel like I was missed when I emerged. I love you, Paul.

I'm eternally grateful to my family for their support throughout this process. To my parents, Woody and Diane McKown—who have always let me grow as I needed to and who have loved me without condition since the beginning. To my sister, Jennifer Lyons—who has laughed, loved, and cried with me along the way, and to her family, Richard Lyons, Brandon Vidal, and Meghan Lyons—who have always given me a reason to smile. I'm grateful to my extended family, as well, for their support and for believing I'd get this thing finished, eventually.

Lastly, I'd like to thank my grandmother, Gwendolyn June Humble, who died at the age of fifty-four on September 7, 1983. She was fearless, wise, and ahead of her time. I did my best to listen.

ABOUT THE AUTHOR

Jeff McKown writes fiction. In his work, he is especially fond of exploring tragic flaws, unfortunate circumstances, and the small moments that matter. In life, he obsesses over tennis, politics, and whiskey, not necessarily in that order. He endeavors to be a better Buddhist — which hasn't always worked out that well. He lives near Monterey, CA with his partner Paul and their best friend, Kyle. *Solid Ground* is his first novel.

Facebook: https://www.facebook.com/jeff.mckown.7
Twitter: https://twitter.com/waythingsturn
Blog: http://thewaythingsturn.blogspot.com/
E-mail: jeffmckown1@gmail.com

CPSIA information can be obtained
at www.ICGtesting.com
Printed in the USA
LVOW12s1408100717

540839LV00001B/42/P